The
WAKE
of the
WIND

J. CALIFORNIA
COOPER

DOUBLEDAY

NEW YORK LONDON TORONTO SYDNEY AUCKLAND

PUBLISHED BY DOUBLEDAY
a division of Bantam Doubleday Dell Publishing Group, Inc.
1540 Broadway, New York, New York 10036

DOUBLEDAY and the portrayal of an anchor
with a dolphin are trademarks of Doubleday,
a division of Bantam Doubleday Dell
Publishing Group, Inc.

This is a work of fiction. Names, characters, places, and incidents are used fictitiously. Any resemblance to actual persons, living or dead, events, or locales is entirely coincidental.

Library of Congress Cataloging-in-Publication Data
Cooper, J. California.
The Wake of the Wind / by J. California Cooper. — 1st ed.
p.   cm.
1. Afro-Americans—Texas—Fiction. I. Title.
PS3553.05874W35   1998
813'.54—dc21   98-21594
CIP

ISBN 0-385-48704-5

Copyright © 1998 by J. California Cooper

All Rights Reserved

Printed in the United States of America

October 1998

First Edition

1   3   5   7   9   10   8   6   4   2

Dedication

Joseph C. and Maxine "Mimi" Cooper, my parents
Paris A. Williams, my chile

OTHER IMPORTANT PEOPLE

Every Black, Brown, Yellow, Red, or White person in life who tried to help any slave, particularly the African-American slave. AND those who have tried to help the Poor of all colors because it is true: The root of all evil is money.

There are so many names I have discovered during my research I cannot write them all down, but they are in my heart. I will name a few: Quakers of the Underground Railroad. Abolitionists who stood to gain nothing but God or death. And Adam Clayton Powell, Martin Luther King, Ronald Dellum, Beverly Smith of "Our Voices," the United Negro College Fund, Mary McLeod Bethune, all African-American Colleges, Booker T. Washington, Malcolm X, Lyndon B. Johnson, Maxine Walters, John F. Kennedy, SNCC, SCLC, CORE, the NAACP, NAG, CMFC, the Black Panthers, Stokeley Carmichael, Eleanor Roosevelt, Paul Robeson, Franklin D. Roosevelt, Septima Clark, Thurgood Marshall, Bayard Rustin, Jon Carew, Richard Rodgers, W. E. B. Du Bois, Marcus Garvey, Alice Walker, Angela Davis, Jesse Jackson. And others, others, others.

ESPECIALLY

ALL THE SLAVES WHO HAD TO LIVE THROUGH THIS AMERICAN BLOODY HISTORY AND OTHER BLOODY HISTORIES OF THE WORLD. THEY ARE THE REASON "WE" ARE HERE TODAY. I WILL NEVER BE ASHAMED OF MY ANCESTORS. IF YOU ARE . . . YOU ARE A FOOL.

Acknowledgments

My special thanks to my editor, Peternelle van Arsdale, for her patience and direction which helped me so much. To Siobhan Adcock, her assistant, for a fine job done. To the extremely competent, professional, and considerate Pauline James and Gerry Triano. I am in debt, always, to Martha Levin, one of the finest people I have ever known.

Respect and gratitude for Sharon Elise of Encinitas, Patricia Quintal Gifford, and Terri McFadden of Altedena. I love you all.

I truly thank Paul Goodnight, Artist Extraordinaire, for allowing his art to be used as my cover. I am so pleased.

I thank Rhonda Dixon, Attorney, Los Angeles, for being patient with me. She always knew the answer to whatever I asked.

I really just thank everybody. Especially my readers for liking my work. I really, really, really hope you like this book. The deepest part of my heart is in it.

Author's Note

Around the time of the Civil War there was a saying, "Gone with the wind." To me, it meant for them a way of life was gone; some of the South's most important ways of life. It was meant that way by slaveowners, landowners, businessmen. It was not always said by slaves, in the same context. To them, it was good that it was gone. But . . . the wind had left its wake behind. We were in it.

Let me speak of the wind.

Some of us take the wind we breathe from, lightly, for granted. But one must take the wind seriously. We, our ancestors, had to live in its wake, survive. Typhoons, cyclones, the hurricanes, the monsoons, disruptive, destructive, powerful, deadly wind. Powerful. Makes ocean waves hundreds of feet high, builds sand dunes a thousand feet high. And leaves, always, a wake in its path.

The path of the wind often shapes obstructions that makes passage difficult. Makes a mockery of all our attempts to defend ourselves. It even carries, pushes, fires. The wind can carry away everything in its path. Destroying almost all . . . or all. We cannot predict its behavior.

Even a gentle wind can leave tracks.

Winds help to create lightning. Lightning strikes, burns, kills in the wake.

In any storm you have to keep your eyes on the sky, the trees, the land, your living, your family, your treasures, and any flying debris.

That was how our African-American ancestors had to live, to survive. I tried to write of that survival, and the intelligence required to have any hope for a future.

For those who are ashamed of their history, we have a history to be proud of, long before slavery raised its ugly head. We did not begin when the white man came into our lives.

Mankind has a bloody history of its inhumanity to men of all colors . . . even their own. There are many, many cruel people, always have been, of all colors of men. There are only "many" good people of all colors of men. That is why, ultimately, your culture is not in your color . . . It is in the God you serve.

I name this book what it is about; some of the struggle, in *The Wake of the Wind.*

—J. California Cooper

PROLOGUE

I am Africa. I am a place. I am a state of mind.

Hundreds of years ago my children lived free. We had our skirmishes, within my shores; even small wars that did not disturb my great and sprawling land. We were not perfect. But . . . we never left our shores to seek to destroy and rob any other culture or people; to steal the fruit of their land or minds and leave the land and people ravaged. Nor did we seek to steal any people's love of themselves. Nor tell other peoples they were ignorant savages and inferior while we were superior, as the whitish ones said to us. They lied so much and long they began to believe it themselves. They cried "GOD" with their mouths while holding a knife in one hand and a gun in the other; slicing and firing at a vibrant life. When the strange whitish peoples came they brought with them their diseases, diseases grown from filth and spread with alacrity. They also brought with them other diseases including endless greed, envy and hate; our nations changed. Yes, they, the savages, called us savages. But, now, look . . . the true savages are they, the strange whitish ones. They kill for land, women or gold, spreading their savageness to all others, even among themselves. And . . . they have now influenced others. Anathema!

They spoke of their civilizations. Civilized is not what most of them are or do. They ridiculed our raiment. Because they wear European clothes; what have clothes to do with the character of the soul? We of Africa dressed for our country, our seasons. The beauty of it; free to be naked in the sun; to be surrounded with the abundance of lush green growth and magnificently beautiful animals the whitish ones have mostly all killed. One does not need a suit or dress to be civilized. Our civilization was inside our minds and hearts, not just on our backs, as was theirs. We dressed to suit our needs and freedoms.

They are proud of their concrete streets and steel buildings, but are they happy owning them? No. They are only hard places to form more hard plans.

The point of life, I believe, is happiness, satisfaction. Are they, the whitish ones, happy? Satisfied? Why do they want others to be as dissatisfied as they? Why did they not leave the world alone? As God had made it. It was a better place, a more beautiful place. Whole nations are completely gone . . . with the whitish ones "care" and religious "love."

They, the whitish ones, have built a world they no longer wish to live in. Now . . . they reach out to space. But, if there is life in space . . . and if that life is wise . . . they will not let the whitish ones invade space. After all, they had the earth and see what they have done with it. Also, they took my children, the people of Africa. They have desecrated the earth, and are enraged because they have not extinguished my children; my African people have survived.

I have made note of one other thing. One must not be the worst of what the enemy is. Among the whitish ones . . . there are those who do have a heart. Who are souls that can contain love, not just fear. These are the good who are dispersed, here and there, throughout the land. But . . . I say to you, my people, you do not need sticks and guns, they do not often help. You need brains . . .

and love . . . which you have in abundance as your motherland has, still, an abundance . . . of everything.

The Teller

I cannot tell you exactly just who I am . . . right now. But I want to tell somebody this story of my made-up life with the people who helped me to build it. People who came to be my family. I cannot read. I cannot write. Someone else will write the story. But I'm tellin the tale. Cause I have the memories.

I go a long way back and tells a great many things and I hopes to bring it all up to you. I cannot tell you how I know all these things cept to say many memories go a long, long way back, back into the past. When life and pain and time has pressed down on you so heavy and so deep in your memory . . . it lasts, and you pass it on. Some of these memories was passed on to me and some . . . I lived.

See . . . the past has power. That power BURNS memories into a heart, into a mind, so much that they leave scars there. It's the only way you can touch people you have never seen, would love and do love, can never touch again . . . or ever. Your ancestors. This power of the past makes me pass it on. Now . . . I'm passin it on to you. Now and then, mayhap you will think of it and . . . pass it on again. And again.

ONE

Now and Then

Once upon a certain year, 1764 or so, over 200 years ago, someone in the world requested a number of African longhorn steer and the African men who knew these cattle and could breed and raise them on a foreign soil; the southern states of America.

Later, along a river in Africa where slavecatchers did not usually seek their prey, and where tribes did not sell their people to slavecatchers (a lie made bigger from a kernel of the truth), these cattle and men were sought for. There were two quiet and content villages at least forty miles apart in this area. These two villages did not socialize much, they were working people and only seldom married others from the different tribes. Even so, some of them were related. Some of the cattle herders knew only in passing the herders from the other village. But Suwaibu and Kola knew each other and when they passed each other in the nights, would stop and talk awhile, exchanging knowledge and small gossip. They liked each other; were friends. Kola wanted Suwaibu to meet and love his younger sister; to marry and become part of his family, to exchange knowledge with him. Suwaibu had sneaked one night to peek at the sister; she was beautiful, he liked her and planned to speak to his father and mother.

These villages did not know their young and able people were in danger at that time and so there were no precautions taken along the river against the heartless thieves of life and men.

Suwaibu, sixteen years old, from the upper river, was herding his father's cattle because he loved the beauty of the land and loved being out on it living under the stars and the sun. His father was a merchant and traveled many places even as far East as Egypt and as far North as Timbuktu, to the University of Sankore. Suwaibu, the eldest son, traveled with him sometimes and loved most the Northern lands where the University of Sankore was. His father was a supplier of paper, salt and books to the university and knew some of the learned people there. Suwaibu could read, write and certainly count, as his father could. Because Suwaibu had begged him, his father was making arrangements for Suwaibu to attend the University at some future time when he could spare his son for a while.

Kola, twenty years old and from the middle river, was married with two children. His father was a keeper of livestock, content with his lot in life; he had an excellent wife and a family of many children, plenty to eat and the whole world, it seemed, to roam in at will.

Soon thereafter, these young men, and other cattlemen from both villages, happened to be out at the same time, late one night, to prepare for a cattle drive along the river, were taken by the thieves, along with their livestock. When these stolen men were thrown into the hold of the ship, mixed amongst each other, no one could explain what had happened and even living so close to each other the dialects were not the same and most of them did not always understand each other.

Suwaibu and Kola were shackled together. They were crowded in the hold face to back over the thousands of miles. Smelling the breath and the body odors of the other, lying in their combined urine and waste. Blood and pus from their wounds mixed as it oozed from their bodies. Some of them who could not understand the language of their brother spoke to each other with their eyes and the tone of their moans when conscious. But what was there to say except of terror and pain, fear and loss, which all those in the hold understood from all the others in the hold. You know of these cruel, unwanted voyages, what more to add?

Finally arriving in a town in the Southern United States, they were taken from the ship to holding cells in a rough-hewn building. There were not too many other buildings in this town, but there was this one new, solid, sturdy and strong building where human beings were stocked. Human beings for sale. To become slaves.

Hosed down and scrubbed (Suwaibu losing much of his skin), they were fed at troughs like animals and prodded into cells with dirty, vermin-filled straw on the floors. Some captives had died on the ships, some died at the trough, some died in the cells. Oh! they had died all along the way! Suwaibu and Kola, among others, did not die; they survived to be taken, at last, to the auction block. Suwaibu and Kola were bought, with the remaining cattle that had survived, by different plantation masters. After breathing each other's breath and mixing blood daily for months, they were separated. They were never to see each other again. Suwaibu was taken to Texas; Kola was taken to Mississippi.

They both grieved for their old homes of family and warmth, love and a future. They looked, often, toward what they thought was the direction of their old homes and Gods over long and miserable months as days grew into a blur of time. Their work was long, hard and heavy. In time and finally, in lonely desperation, Kola was forced to take a woman (a wife?) and begin his life, for true, in America. He fathered children that reminded him of his children back in Africa. In his lifetime in America he had three wives (?) and all his children sold away from him. His grief, daily, became too huge and heavy to bear and so he died after fifteen years. He was about thirty-five years old. An old, old young man. His children all sold or dead, he was leaving no one behind him to grieve for him (which men of all nations try to have), only a master who cursed him for dying and said not a good word about Kola or the beautiful cattle roaming his fields that Kola had raised for him. Not even the master's money could buy more slaves that knew how to raise the cattle as Kola had.

The master raged, "These black devils cost too much to just die and leave you! I blive they only do it for meanness, the good-for-nothin black bastards!"

Another female slave had died the day after Kola died. She died giving birth in the sugarcane fields where she should not have been sent to work. She might have survived it anyway and given birth, but the overseer did not believe the child was coming yet and she was whipped, unmercifully in the heat of the afternoon sun for "trying to get out of work," he said. She and the child gave up the ghost, gladly. Kola was thrown in a pit with her and the baby, back to face, and covered with dirt. So Kola was buried in this new country the same way he was brought to it. Back to face, though now, with someone he did not know; a crying, desolate stranger whose dying blood and child still clung to her and now, with him. All uncared for, unwashed, just thrown away.

These kinds of whipping deaths happened so often, the whippers would have been called serial killers or psychopaths, by an honest people, had the words been in use.

Yes, Kola died . . . but he had had children and his blood was still living in this new world of pain. His blood still rushing, striving, pulsing on toward some future.

Suwaibu was living his pitiful life as a slave and he chose to live it alone. For many years he did not want a wife or woman or children, to lose to the vast unknown space beyond his vision. Sold . . . or killed. Many years he dreamed of and longed for his home and family in Africa. Thought of the future he had had before him, the university, his father's commerce. His reading, writing and speaking in four different languages he had learned working with his father did him no good here; they did not recognize there was no "th" sound in his language. They called him ignorant and savage in this country where his Master could not even speak his one language well. He grew to hate his cruel and ignorant masters.

He was not allowed to remain alone, however. Though he was very religious and wanted to maintain his honor to his God, Suwaibu had to be forced on pain of death to father several children. He worked all the days of his life, dying a truly beaten, bent old man, full of hate and rage. He had been beaten many times when they sold his children and even the wife he had grown to care for. He had raged and grieved. They said that was only the savage part of him. "Animals!" they said. From the day he was taken from his home, Africa, he was not happy One day, One hour, for all the days of his life. Not One. Not even when his children were born was he happy, because he knew they were born to be slaves.

When Suwaibu was about fifty years old, grayhaired and almost sightless, for his tears had washed away his sight and the tears of his body, called sweat, had drained his soul. He died, sitting in front of a tired, dilapidated, old shack. Looking, still looking, yearning, toward his old, true home.

When Suwaibu's master was informed of his death by a man Suwaibu had trained to tend the special cattle, the master leaned back in his chair, removed his cigar and spat a piece of tobacco to the side, saying "Well, we can stop wastin that there food he was eatin and doin no work with."

The slave cattleman, who, with most other slaves, respected Suwaibu, said, "We done pared him for buryin, Massr. We knows where to put em. Can we'uns put im away now? Dis here heat . . . gonna make his'n body . . ."

The master spat again and said, "Naw, not now. We got to get them fields in fore the rain sets in." The slave answered, "I can do it, this ebenin. We'uns can dig his grave affa supper, in da dark." The master frowned, "Ya'all ain't tired, huh? If I want you to work, you'd be tired."

The slave bent his head, begging. "He was a fren to all o us."

The master turned back to his glass of bourbon. "Well, get it done quick, cause I don't want no tired niggers lazyin round my cattle tomarra. Now, get on away from me and wastin all my time talkin bout a dead nigga."

"Yessuh Massr." The slave backed down the short steps. "Yessuh."

And Suwaibu was buried in a hastily stolen (they made us steal so much), ragged horse blanket with the tears of his fellow brothers and sisters falling down into his grave. They would miss him. He had shared his food with them, his wood for warmth in the freezing winters. They would miss him.

Though by pain of death, reluctantly, Suwaibu had fathered children. He had seen some beaten, a few die, some sold, but living, because he had taught them the secrets of the Longhorn cattle and they became valuable. Those living children carried his blood out all over the Southern lands of America. His blood was rushing on into the unknown future through the veins of his black children, and their children.

AND THEN, AGAIN

Forty years after the death of Suwaibu, about 1830, Suwaibu's blood still rushing toward the future, one of his descendants, a great, great, great-grandchild, was born. The child was named Mordecai by another of those religious, yet cruel, masters.

Years later in another place, around 1840, the rushing and descending blood of Kola made an advent in the form of one of his great, great, great-granddaughters. She was born in Louisiana, supposedly a child of the white master and his private concubine-slave, her mother. The baby was named Life by a dramatic housemaid, close friend of the mother. "Ah, she has come from such a life; what life will her birth bring to her. We must pray she will not be a slave, nor a fool. That she will find a way to live. Lifee."

Another gift was given to Lifee when she was older, by the close friend of her mother, the old mulatto slave housemaid. It was a small, exquisite enameled box. In it were two daguerreotypes. One of her mother and a stolen one of her true father, an African man. Also in it was the towel used to catch her when she was born with the initial "I" embroidered upon it and a delicate handkerchief in the shape of a heart. It was all she had that she truly treasured. It was all of her heritage.

Lifee had been born to a mulatto mistress and an African man, so she was hastily given away by her mother who knew she was in danger from her master, since he expected his white child. He thought she suffered grief because their child had died, but she suffered because she had to give her child away to one of the women who worked for her, a faithful old Negro woman, Lala. Lala had been freed because she was too old, and less beautiful now, to serve her white lover who wanted a younger woman. He freed her and sat her on the streets with nothing. She had found her sister, also free now, and they lived together, raising the child, in clean squalor.

When Lifee was three years old, the faithful old Lala died and her sister could not afford to keep Lifee. She told Lifee's true mother who then convinced her white master to buy Lifee for his daughter as a gift. It was all the mother could do for her child.

These two people, Mordecai and Lifee, were born hundreds of miles apart physically. Their lives were lived thousands of miles apart mentally because she had learned in a classroom sitting beside her young mistress and he had never held a book in his hands. But they were traveling on the broad, broad map of life and though they seemed to be going on different paths, they were slaves, heading in the same direction leading to one road. In the irony and beauty of life, after one hundred years, the bloods of Kola and Suwaibu were about to meet again through their descendants, Mordecai and Lifee. You never know, exactly, who is carrying your blood. It is now, a lifelong, endless search for relatives. Somebody. Often fruitless for many.

TWO

And Then, Again . . .

On a very, hot night in the fall of 1865, the earth exuding the heat of the day, the air so hot and dry you could feel it searing through your lungs as you breathed. Mordecai was standing in the deeper darkness beside a tree near the slave quarters, watching the other slaves bring luke-warm meals from their sweltering cabins to eat outside in the clearing.

He only half listened to the sounds of life around him. The mosquitos zinging through the air seeking their evening meal of tears, sweat and blood. The sounds of busy little earth bugs, crickets and spiders rushing hither and yon, seeking water and perhaps nourishment for the night, while birds flew home to nests, settling in, but keeping a wary eye out for a crumb dropped from a slave's lap, for a last minute meal, or a poacher. Snakes, even worms seeking water, moisture. Field mice and other rodents seeking a dead anything to stave off hunger. Mordecai could hear the cows lowing in the distance; horses restlessly stirring in their stalls, still hungry even after they had eaten what was given them. They worked hard in this heat, also. The mules standing with their sad, lowered eyes, still hungry and angry because they worked even harder, their sores, constant from a bridle, rubbed and scratched, leaking blood and pus all the days long. Chickens clucking as they made for their roosts, a few late roosters crowing the end of the day. Mor heard and didn't hear.

Mordecai, called Mor for short, watched the other slaves with dull, uninterested eyes as he chewed slowly on a straw. He had friends among the slaves, but they knew he was a man who liked to be alone, who did not talk much unless it was about work to be done. He did not like attachments.

No wife had brought his meal because he wanted no wife. His one wife had been sold five years ago with his two children. Master hadn't needed the money, just made a good deal. No. No more wife, no more children did Mor want. He had seen too many men sold away from their wives and children. Families broken and lost. Children gone. Gone. Forever. He had never gotten over losing his wife, his children that way. Even lost a brother, Job. He had grown up a bit with Job, til he was fourteen or so, then Job was sold. He had decided, "No more, no more."

He, also, knew the pain of seeing those you dearly loved, beaten and bloody. A son had died when the master's lust for blood blinded him to killing his own piece of property. So, now, Mor kept to himself and looked at no woman to be his own love; because slaves do know love, always have known love. Slaves are human and real. Slaves knew loss. They knew thousands of years of love. Now, long years of savagery and hate. They were passionately human.

Mordecai's owner, Master Floyd, had been away for a week or so. He had been gone to do "bizness," he said. He was due back any-time now. The master did not take Mor on trips too far from the plantation because "I trust em, but I see in that nigga's eyes, when he gets a good chanct he will run, this here war and all upset'lin em. He a good worker, a good boy. I keep em right round here. One of the bes I got and I aims to keep him!"

As more and more talk of abolition and the sound of war moved deeper into the South, even with the North winning, many of the

Negroes couldn't wait for the freedom they had long craved deep in their hearts and so they struck out on their own. Who knew, finally, who would win the war anyway? When the South told it, they were winning. Some slaves ran not even knowing which way the North was or what place was free. They could not read any signs except the stars. The whites had made it a law not to teach any Negro, free or not, to read and write. You wonder, what could they have been so afraid of since they said the black man was not intelligent, was more like an animal than a human? Why the fear of a happy, singing, animal child, no matter how old? But the running Africans preferred to face the unknown than remain with the known, so they stole away into the nights, seeking their freedom to be the humans they were born.

Mor thought of running, but didn't. He waited to see what would happen, as many others did. He wanted to help the North fight. but didn't know which way they were and didn't want to be forced to help the South fight, should he run into them first.

It was a time of waiting. Waiting, though silent, was in the very air. It was a time of waiting and patience. Waiting . . . waiting. He did not feel old, but he knew he was not young. He did not feel time. He lived in an endless, timeless place where there was nothing but work and waiting in tired solitude, frustration and endless, endless loneliness.

Mor was tall, 5'10" or so, with well-developed muscles, strong arms and large, sturdy feet. His face was handsome and hard, yet a very kind face, sunburned and deeply lined from frowning at the sun and the pain in his life. It had an earthy bluntness and he himself had a healthy masculinity that even being a slave did not take away. His body bent a bit, though he was only in his early thirties, but you knew the strength of a whole man was there. He was deeply browned, from birth and years in the sun. His voice was low, patient and kind and full of years of controlling the rage he felt. Now he waited and chewed on the straw, thinking of his freedom, in the dark, where no one can see him thinking. What was this freedom? How, what, would, could, he do with it? We had to learn to do our thinking that way.

The wagon was still some distance from the plantation. Master Floyd was tired and not feeling too well because of his usual festivities with his friends he had met on the trip. Some of the men like himself, who believed the South would win, took advantage of the traveling Southern plantation owners who were selling their slaves cheap because the North was winning and they were trying to cut their losses. Floyd bought all the good, sound slaves he found on his business trips. Floyd KNEW the South would win though he struck not a blow for his side. "God is on our side!" He said as he laughed and took advantage of the "fools." Cheating them even at the already low prices, he went lower still. He was proud of himself. He was even proud of this gift he was bringing home to Morella, he told himself. This girl could crochet, knit, weave, could just do all kinds of things around a place. Morella would save some money on all those things she was always wanting to order from New York, but instead had to order from New Orleans or Charleston.

As the wagon moved slowly toward his home he was thinking about his "bizness." He was excited about the new woman he had bought at the auction for several other reasons. "I was sho lucky, hot-dammit!" Someone had brought the woman to the auction at the last minute. A slender, richly dressed woman in a hurry to rid her house of this "brown-skinned, good-lookin nigga bitch" had wanted her sold "in a hurry, as soon as possible." Before her husband found out the girl was gone, no doubt. She hadn't sent her maid to do it because she wanted to be sure the job got done. Also, she felt something sensual and thrilling in the slave-filled atmosphere. The woman had taken a loss on the deal, so much in a hurry was she. "Good!" Floyd smiled to himself, thinking, "I'm sick of them ugly, wore-out niggras the old man bought on my place. This one will be mine!" He frowned briefly. "I'll find a way to keep Morella happy so she won't be tryin to get rid of her. What's the nigga's name? Lady? That won't do. Well, we'll just have to change it to . . . to . . . Hell, I'll think of somethin!"

Floyd Petty was not the original owner of the plantation. His wife's father, Clifton Wilton, had been. Morella Mamie Wilton had been an unhappy, willful young woman who worried her father to find her a husband in the East, New York or even Chicago, and even let her live there! She knew money could move mountains and he could do it if only he would. Her father loved her and thought she was the most beautiful young lady in the entire South. He wanted to keep her with him on his land.

Morella Mamie was not the most beautiful. But when she was happy she was pretty with the fresh bloom of youth and health. She had been a medium-sized woman, slim before her marriage, but now plump, which would have been alright, but she let herself go after her marriage because she was unhappy. Her red hair she had always been so proud of was no longer "flaming," but dull with lack of interest and care. Her skin flushed red easily from the least excitement, waves of color moving over her face and neck. Her features were small and ladylike, but with her unhappiness, she ate more and often. And time and annoyance at Floyd, cows, horses and chickens and the like, her face was becoming pursy and peevish. Her breasts were more than ample, her legs and arms rather large, but smooth. Her eyes could have been pretty, but she kept them narrowed with suspicion, so now, they looked beady. She was confused and angry because she was supposed to be on a pedestal, as her father said, but no one remembered that except her. Mr. Wilton didn't want to hear of his only child moving away from him and the South, so, five years ago, to keep his Morella with him, he had summoned his best overseer, Floyd Petty, and married them off.

Father Wilton had found, upon closer living with Floyd, that Floyd was rather dumb with a gift for repeating what he heard and thereby sounding like he had some sense, but the sense was only slighter deeper than his mouth. Realizing his mistake, Wilton told only his daughter where he kept his secret cache of gold. Then, three years ago, before the old man could do anything to correct his mistake in marrying her to Floyd, besides telling her where his own secret cache of gold was, he died and Morella was stuck with her ignorant husband.

Floyd held most of the purse strings. Not all. Morella had been putting back money, gold, silver and her few jewels for years. Even her father hadn't known Morella was "stealing" from herself. Morella hadn't been entirely dumb. She had sought to take care of herself even before her father told her about his gold. Still, Morella grew to hate her dead father more everyday, whom she knew had loved her. "He didn't do right by me. It would seem Floyd was his child!"

Morella Mamie loved Floyd only when she was very lonely. The rest of the time she hated him with such a passion he would have been alarmed and shocked. He thought she believed all his lies.

Floyd weighed about 250 pounds. It was almost all stomach, but he was tall. His face and skin always looked red because he liked his bourbon throughout the day. His hair was black and he wore a handlebar mustache, waxed. He was vain of his mustache. He combed water through his hair and smoothed his mustache all through the day. His small hands trembled all the time. For such a large man, his features were small; a knobby chin, narrow, pointed nose, thin, bloodless lips, close black eyes and already evidence of hanging jowls to come. He would have died had anyone ever known how frightened he was of Morella. Even she didn't know. He really didn't believe he deserved all the wealth he had, and certainly, not his wife. She was too good for the likes of him. "But, she is mine and she belongs to me and everthin with her!" he would say outloud to himself on his trips away on business and sometimes in the barn.

But, now Floyd was thinking of the new negra woman he had riding in back of the wagon. "She is mine and she belongs to me, too!" He smiled and looked back to satisfy himself that she was still there and saw her bowed head. He shouted to her, "Lady! We gettin close to yo new home. My plantation!"

Lifee raised her head slowly. Her eyes touched him and slid off to look at the countryside. In her heart she was crying, "I am alone . . . I am so damned alone." The surrounding land looked ugly to her and seemed to be the color of death. Even the cries of birds seemed to be a lament. There was no sun any longer. There was no sound except the crying of the birds and the sad sound of the wheels turning, turning, turning. Wheels turning, taking her where? To what? Lifee's shawl flapped around her head as the cold wind blew around her. The days were hot, but the nights were cold here in this new place. She tried to huddle farther down into the wooded plank that made a seat for her across the wagon, but there was no shelter from the cold wind. Her hands, face, arms and entire body were cold, perhaps from fear as well as the wind. She had been given a worn old coat, the good one she had been allowed to make for herself had been taken from her. Even the gloves she had knit for herself had been taken. Her feet were cold and had been still so long they were numb. In her misery, wishing for better things, she thought of her youth.

Lifee had been given to her first mistress as a gift. The family had been wealthy Louisianans, her mistress's father (the same who loved her mother) the only university professor in the family. He had built a fine, huge library in his home. Lifee read almost all of the books over the years. The young mistress had been kind to Lifee, treating her more as a friend than a slave, or . . . at least as a slave-friend. Lifee was treasured and was treated kindly all her early life because she worked hard. Lifee had learned to read, write, sew and even play the piano a little, right beside her young mistress.

As they grew older, Lifee had been taught other things her mistress was not interested in; to knit, crochet, weave and to sew expertly. Things her mistress did not need to know because she could pay for them to be done and she had Lifee. All the fashionable ladies envied the mistress of Lifee and she sought to learn more to become even more treasured; to be kept, not sold.

When the young mistress began to travel and divide her time

between the North and South, she had taken Lifee so she could be taught millinery and pattern-making, so she could make all the things in the European magazines the mistress wanted. She had even been taken on a few trips to Europe with her mistress. Lifee had learned well, she was an accomplished couturiere after several years. She had never thought to run away while in Europe or the North because her life was so good. "Run for what?" she asked the colored people of the North when they offered to help her to freedom. "I'm happy in my home." She always returned to her young mistress.

During her youth Lifee had a Negro friend, Anne Mae. Anne Mae had blue eyes and golden hair atop a lovely, shapely body. Anne Mae planned, always, her escape from slavery. She planned to marry a white man. "He will never know what I am and I am more beautiful than any of these white chits I see around here."

Lifee laughed lightly, "He will know cause you have a mistress and your mother is brown."

Anne Mae laughed with her, "He will never meet them. I am making a plan. Something will come along. My color will take me where my dear mamam did not." Lifee did not always laugh at Anne Mae because she knew what the fierce seriousness in her eyes meant.

Then Lifee's young mistress fell in love and, in time, became engaged to a man of the East Coast. She looked upon Lifee with new eyes and saw the beauty there, the graceful, full and feminine body. She saw Lifee through the eyes of her betrothed, and suddenly Lifee did not seem so dear to her any longer. She decided she did not need Lifee any longer. She even began to hate her friend because of Lifee's brown beauty, but could never admit it. "She is ugly, she is too ugly to attend me any longer!" Instead of giving her to some kind friend among those who had envied her her servant, she put her out to be sold in the violent Deep South. All Lifee took with her was her mother's box wrapped in a bundle of clothes.

The young mistress moved to New York and never looked back

. . . nor gave a moment's thought to Lifee again for many years except when she looked upon a brown beauty. Then she would have the brown beauty removed from her presence, wherever it was, if possible.

The wives and daughters of Lifee's new masters did not like Lifee even as skilled as Lifee was, because Lifee was a pretty woman and made a lie of their words, as many black, brown and yellow beauties did, that negras were ugly and were animals. And their men? Their men could not seem to keep their eyes (nor hands, when possible) off of Lifee. She had been taken with force repeatedly and, once, became pregnant (which proved further to the white ladies that negras were sluts). At first sight of the whitish baby, the mistress struck Lifee with the handle of a riding crop; it left a light scar on the satiny skin at the corner of her eyebrow for life. The male baby was taken from her and sold because of the resemblance to the father. Lifee was sold cheaply in two days, weak, hardly able to walk, but glad to go while at the same time terrified of where she would end up and where her baby was. Ahhh, what Black women have suffered without the least honest cause and no consideration.

Lifee had large, slightly slanted dark eyes. Soft, full lips, a short, pretty nose that flared delicately wide at the nostril. She was slender, around five feet seven inches with smooth, clear skin the color and texture of golden brown satin, with full, medium-sized breasts, curvaceous hips made for love, plump, rounded buttocks. Yet her weight was about 125 pounds. No, the white women did not like her, they paled even more beside her warm aura. These women were never protective of their black sister, they sold her as fast as they could maneuver it. From Louisiana to Alabama, then to Mississippi, now to Texas.

And now . . . she was on her way to yet another new home. Another new prison and . . . what? She moved her eyes slowly to the man sitting beside the driver; her new master. She hated him already. He had sat back beside her the first day of the drive home. She had pulled her threadbare dress and slip between her legs, pulled her thin, torn coat and shawl tight around her, but his hands had crept over and under and around the weak armor of protection. He had finally slapped her and all but had his complete way. The only things that stopped him were the fear of passing wagons that might have white people in them and the new knowledge that she would fight him. The presence of the other new slaves had not bothered him at all, of course. "Negras are not real human and they ain got no morals like white folks anyway," he thought.

He looked back at the new slaves now, only a few, but they were sound. He laughed to himself at the fools that thought the South would lose. Their loss was his gain. He would hold out until the tide would turn and the South would regain whatever little ground they had lost. "They got to win! This is the South! God is on our side!"

It was getting darker. Floyd pulled his own coat closer around his neck, "Hurry on, now, Wilt. Let's get on home!" Wilt, the driver, answered, "Yes, suh!" and tried to rush the tired horses along. They went no faster, but Master Floyd was satisfied because his black slave was trying to do his, the master's, will.

Finally, the wagon rolled clattering on the last piece of road to the plantation. The horses snorting and even rushing a little, knowing rest and food was near. Mor saw his master's wagon first, as it rounded the bend in the road. He started out to meet it, knowing he would be called anyway. When he was close to the wagon he saw through the darkness, a bowed-headed woman. The male slaves were walking beside the wagon. Mor took the straw from his mouth that had dried from hate, spat and waited for the wagon to get close enough so he could go help unload it and see the new nigras his master had bought back.

As Life raised her head and watched the plantation of her new life unfold around her, her craving for freedom ran through her mind, flooded her very soul. "Why didn't I leave when I could?

Why did I trust anyone when they owned me? I will never be able to buy myself. I will never be able to find my child they have taken." She sobbed silently within her throat which caused her more pain. No one heard the sobs of fear, pain and desolation coming from Lifee. "I will kill myself." Her mind whirled in anguish. "I might as well be dead. But, oh, God, oh, God . . . I want to live. I want to live. I want MY life. I want MY child back. I want my LIFE. If I die, will heaven be better than this? Or will white folks be there, too? I have read Your Bible, God. I know You are not white. I know you do not hate African people. The greatest poem in the world is in Your Bible, the Song of Solomon, and it is about the love and beauty of a black woman." Lifee cried in silence, grateful for the darkness that mercifully settled around her. "I hate life. I do not know one slave over ten or twelve years old who has their father or mother, sister or brother with them. I want to die, but I'm not ready to die, even though I can't believe there is any reason to live."

None of Lifee's last three masters knew Lifee could read, count or write. Lifee had told none others who had bought her since her second mistress had had her beaten to make her promise not to teach another slave and isolated her from the other slaves to ensure it. No newspapers were ever left around her at that time. Now . . . with no one knowing her secret she read quickly whatever she came across. Lifee knew of the abolitionists and the rumble of war. She thought the war was ending and the South was losing. Every day she listened for the sounds of cannon. Alternately striving to live and wishing to die.

See . . . it was a time of waiting for all slaves. A time of patience, longing . . . waiting. Dismal longing and wretched waiting.

Mor was at the wagon before Mr. Grimes, the overseer, because Mr. Grimes was in one of the slave-women's cabins trying to rape a young slave, Ethylene, who kept trying to find ways to avoid being alone with him. "Jes one more tetch before old Floyd gets back!" Grimes thought. He knew Master Floyd did not like any other white man workin on his land to bed the nigra wenches. Floyd hated white nigras. And he hated anyone to bed anyone he may have planned out for himself. When Grimes heard the commotion of the returning master, Mor was already at the wagon. Grimes slapped the crying girl-woman he had pinned to the floor and rushed to button his pants. "I don't know why yo keeps on cryin evertime! Yo knows it's gonna happin! Ya betta keep yoah mouf shut!" He finished fastening and rushed out the crooked cabin door which was hanging on broken hinges and twine. There was money on this plantation, yet no-one but the old man who had died had had sense enough to spend it on the most important property they had!

Grimes rushed to the side of the Big House where the wagon had finally stopped. "Evenin, Mr. Floyd! How was the trip? Oh, now, I see we is got some more darkies." Master Floyd did not answer, just pointed to some large bags of seed and a few new tools and wrapped packages. "Jes have em put these things in the shed. Those packages right there go in the house. Mor?!"

Mor looked briefly at the packages and started toward them, then looked back at the woman he had been staring at. The shawl had slipped from her head as she looked up at the large house with the broad veranda. Mor could see that her hair was short (because the white ladies she had worked for had not liked to see it long with braids hanging down her back, nor unbraided with kinky waves wrapped around her pretty oval face with all that smooth skin). He noticed her eyes were sad, but clear and bright with thought, while her movements were tired and slow. He could see she was lovely . . . and clean. It didn't matter. His heart hardened and he looked quickly away.

Massa Floyd was looking at the new woman, he pointed at her, "That's La—that's Edessa." He smiled because he knew Mor sel-

dom, if ever, fooled with women. He was angered at first because
Mor did not pay more attention to Edessa. He always felt good
having things that nigras wanted and could not have because they
were not as good as he was. "She goin to live in the Big House. A
seamstress for the mistress. She's right smart with her hands, knits
and embroidees, too!" Massa Floyd almost licked his lips as he
looked at Edessa-Lifee because he meant to have her. He wanted
her in the house away from all other men, white or black.

He thought he could fool his wife into thinking the woman was
all for her own use. "Hers in the day, mine in the night." Massa
Floyd smiled to himself again. Mor smiled to himself as he gathered
packages for the house, thinking, "If'n I can tell what he wants that
'Edessa' for, the mistress sho gonna know!"

Massa Floyd turned to Edessa-Lifee, "Get up and get out!" He
hoped his wife could hear him talkin mean to "Edessa."

Lifee began to move slowly, heavily, out of the wagon as she looked
over to the Big House and the surrounding yard. She could see the
slave quarters, the children, dirty and grimy from the day's work,
gaping at the wagon and her and the new slaves. The thin lean dogs
sniffing around, the fat cat sitting on the veranda. She knew what
was in store. Lifee was twenty-four years old and had seen so many
things she could now read the future from what she saw in the
present.

She thought of her beauty and hated the little beauty she had,
sometimes, because it caused men to see her. Then, again, sometimes she was glad of it, because perhaps it had made it possible for
a man to allow her to be taught reading and higher learning in
skills. A dead smile set about her lips as she thought "White women
do not like pretty Negro women. They aren't supposed to be human. They say to each other, with a smirk, 'She must have white
blood in her! Nigras ain't pretty!' "

The blood Lifee did have in her veins was some of Kola's blood. She was Kola's great, great, great, great-grandchild through her mother. His blood had rushed thus far, striving to survive.

As Mor emptied the wagon and Lifee sought to get out, the bloods of Kola and Suwaibu were close together again, after a hundred years. Of course, neither Mor nor Lifee knew that their ancestors had been stolen in almost the same place, the same night, taken in the same ship, separated from their ancestors of thousands of years. Separated from mother, father, sisters and brothers, plans and dreams; their whole lives.

Lifee had had one child taken from her and sold by the white father's wife. She was lucky there were not more because Negro women lost their children all the time. Conceived and gave birth to them only to lose, by the white man's plan, with never a thought of love and what it means to new life and old life. But love and more children were far from her mind, so Lifee barely looked at the black man near her own age who was helping to unload the wagon . . . Mor.

Lifee placed her bundle of clothes under her arms and carried small tools of her trade, knitting needles, sewing needles, small things she had time to grab in the other hand, the slowly walked toward the neatly aproned, middle-aged, tired-looking woman who had stepped out to the porch, frowning . . . Abbysinia, the cook. Abbysinia generally ran things on the house-servant level. A hand on one hip, a stirring spoon in the other, she squinted her eyes to see who this new woman was coming in the Big House.

Massa Floyd looked at Abbysinia, saying, "Take her on in, feed her and give her somemot place to sleep til yo mistress decides where she wants her." Abbysinia in turn called out over her shoulder, "Luzy? Come help this new biddy get set!" Then turned to Lifee asking, "Ya hungry?" Then looking at Lifee's clothes she said, "Ya needs some water to wash up in!" Luzy came rushing lazily, her usual slow way, to the two of them, "Whachu wan me to do wit her?" Luzy turned to Lifee, asked "Whachu wants?" Lifee looked around the hot, good-smelling kitchen, the old and new of things; looked down into Luzy's ten-year-old eyes then up to Abbysinia's wary, tired eyes and said, "Peace." She heaved a deep sigh, hefted her bundles in her arms, looked beyond the kitchen and said, "Jes gimme that!" Lifee set her things down, "Give me my peace and my mama." Neither Abbysinia nor Luzy wondered at these words, they understood them completely. Abbysinia turned to her stove, said, "If'n we could, whatchu would gi us back?" The answer came, "The same." And that is how they met, these two women and the child.

Lifee, settled in a corner of the kitchen, thinking in the mixed-up patois of good English she had learned from books and the poor English learned from listening to uneducated whites and blacks, "I longs to be free. I wants to seek my mother, see is she still alive. I want to find my child, see if he still alive." These thoughts and others filled her mind until she fell asleep; tears on her homemade pillow, a rage in her heart and a need for her own life filling her body.

THREE

In just under a week Mistress Floyd satisfied her suspicions that "the nigga gal who sleeps in the sewing room is trying to get my husband." She spoke to her visiting friend, Roberta. (She couldn't say her husband was after the nigga girl.) "That girl has learned like a white woman to embroider and crochet and she even knits better'n my own niggras! Her hands just fly." Her mouth twisted in a sneer. "My husband, Floyd, is always bringin me material for new pieces now . . . and he spends too much time provin to me what a fine gift he has brought to 'me.' I see her eyes. She is probly lustin after Floyd. She has to go!"

Her friend, Roberta, knew nobody was lusting after Floyd, but she smiled and nodded at her friend.

The following days, with wrinkled brow, Massa Floyd looked as if his thoughts were far away as he made his rounds on his plantation, hearing his wife's voice. "That negra got to go!"

"Mistress Floyd's demands! Hell, I say!" He did not want to sell Lifee, now called Edessa. "She purdy as a picture. I will have her fo my own. Hotdammit! I'm the man here!"

One particular day as Massa Floyd led his horse to the stable, Mor came to take the reins from him. Floyd's eyes followed Mor around as a new thought circled in his mind. "Mor don't seem to like women. He keeps to hisself. And that shack'a his'n is set part from all the othern. Mor done built that shack up from the ground for hisself, with the ole man's permission cause he a hard worker. He a ugly one, as all them Africans men is. Nobody, no woman would ever want him." Massa Floyd smiled as his thought came into clear sight.

He spoke to Mor, "Why ain't ya not taken yo one of these here wenches as a wife, Mordecai?"

Mor placed a blanket over the horse as he turned his face toward Massa Floyd.

"Naw suh, Massa Floyd, Ah don want none."

"Why? Mor, ya ain't one of them men-lovin men, are ya?"

"Naw suh, Ah don want nothin and nobody."

Floyd's mind clicked. "You need a wife." Mor was quiet as he rubbed the horse's neck, thinking, "Lawd, what this white man got for me to do now?"

Massa Floyd smiled, then looked stern. "You are goin to have a wife. Only one room in that shack of your'n, ain't it?"

"Yessuh."

"Well, ya build you another room onto that shack of yourn. I already got yo wife for ya." He thought of Lifee and forgot Mor immediately as he quickly left the stables.

Floyd strode into the Big House and up to the sewing room where Lifee was working, which room Morella hastened to right behind him. He smiled at his wife, said, "Darlin, I thought you was in here. I got some good news! Edessa will be movin out! She's gonna jump over the broom and move on out to the shacks with her new husband, Mordecai!"

Mistress Floyd looked up at him with suspicion. Lifee's heart leapt into her throat as she snapped her head around to look at Massa Floyd, her alarm and fear breathing from every pore of her body. She dropped the thread she was holding and, as quickly, decided to hide her feelings from these white folks who controlled her life. She bent to retrieve the needle and thread, when she raised her head up, her face was calm. Only the large, fear-filled doe eyes were unable to control themselves, but she kept them cast down while she thought, "I will run away from here!"

In the following weeks Mor gathered what he needed, with a heavy heart, and began work on the shack, to build a room for his "wife." He cleared a place at the rear of his cabin, away from the sight of the Big House as he was instructed. He measured, sawed, cut and hammered til the room was built. For some reason he made it as fine a room as he knew how. He built in cabinets and drawers using the finest lumber he could afford to steal from the stock. When Massa Floyd saw it, he cursed at the cost.

Mor bent his head, "I makes a mistake, Massa. I take it down and use the othern wood."

But Massa Floyd was impatient to get his hands on Lifee and Miz Morella was becoming more angry and cantankerous and urging him to sell Edessa. She had screamed at him, "I don't care bout Mor, nor marryin, nor her fine work or not!" So he told Mor, "Leave it up, for now. You c'n fix it later. You jes get ready to jump ovah that there broom. This week!"

Massa Floyd hung around the new room while Mor worked at finishing touches. Finally he spoke to Mor, "Now . . . Mor . . . you gonna marry her, that Edessa, but you ain't gonna sleep with her none. That ain yo job. An I'ma tell you, nigga, you get to sleep out here and pretend she yo wife, but she ain't. No, she ain't. You sleep in that other room, the old one . . . and she gon sleep in this one here. Alone. Alone. You heah me, nigga?"

"Yessuh. Done said I ain't wantin no wife no way."

"Well, now, don't you be forgettin that. Cause I will whip yoah ass til it sings halliyah and I will sell yoah ass, I don't care how good you work nor how long you bin heah. And my wife, Mistress

Morella, ain't never gonna know I come out here. You see to it that don't nobody else evah know either! I will sell them, too! And not with they chilren either!"

"Yessuh."

"She be movin out heah tonight."

"Yessuh."

"I be out here . . . sometime." He thought of how stupid and like children Negroes were, so he added, "You be a good boy and everthin work out alright and I . . . You got everthin ya need, but I will gie you a reward . . . or somethin."

"Yessuh, Massa Floyd." As he nodded his head, Mordecai thought of those faintest of sounds of thunder he heard at night when silence reigned over the farm land. He did not think it was thunder, real thunder, as they were told. "It's'a jest'a diffrun soun to it." He kept his thoughts to himself, as usual.

Mor did not want to get married, but he had no choice. Also, he had watched Life several times when she went to the slaves' outhouse. Always, she held her head down, looking at the ground as she walked, gliding it seemed. When she was finished she usually slowly walked some ways beyond the outhouse away from the Big House, among the many trees, breathing in the freest air she could reach. When she thought she was truly alone, she raised her head up to the sky in prayer and lifted her arms to the heavens. Lifee thought no one was watching her, that they were used to her now, but when Mor happened to be in from the cattle pastures doing some job close to the Big House and saw her, he would stop whatever he was doing and move to see her better. He would follow a bit as she moved farther out. He had seen her lean against one of the old oak trees or a great, tall pine and bend her head, sinking to the ground. He saw her body shake with her sobs. He was never close enough to hear her, but his heart was moved at the sight of her pain and a bond of feelings was born. He had seen so much pain among the slaves over the years and felt for all of them, that it did not occur to him that what he felt for Lifee might be the beginning of love. She was pretty, all over. But she was the massr's woman and what was beauty compared to life? His life?!

Then he would look down at his hands: gnarled, dry, calloused from all his hard work; at his clothes, half clean and ragged because they were only given two shirts and two pairs of pants a year for summer or winter; then his feet, callouses, bunions, corns because of the hard, tough leathers or rubber given to the slaves to make their shoes with, one pair once a year. His shoes were worn out now, gone. But the year wasn't up, so he wrapped rags and paper around his feet. As he looked at himself his eyes were dry, but inside his body moaned in sadness. He felt he would be ugly and unbearable to a woman and he was not even really old yet. As a slave though, he was old; even he knew that.

Lifee had become close with Abbysinia and Luzy. Often she tried to console Luzy after the many whippings Miz Morella gave her for any small infraction. Lifee was closest to Abbysinia. Abbysinia had an inner strength Lifee admired and plenty good sense. She a white, mariney-red color, but never seemed proud of it. She knew how to do many kinds of things, in the kitchen and out of it. Abby, as she was called, didn't talk much but she looked like she knew a great deal she could talk about and nobody really messed with her, not even the mistress.

Lifee felt a warmth for three of the other female slaves that came from the shacks to the house to work. Mona, a housemaid, dark-skinned, middle-aged with a temper, but much love in her body to share; love left over from her gone children and husbands. Sippi, also a housemaid, around thirty-two years old, dark mahogany-colored, quiet with bright, flashing eyes and a kind, but jealous heart. She, too, had been taken from her children. A girl, now dead, and a boy of eleven years or so, sold. She knew how to keep from having any more children to lose. Polly, a kitchen helper, golden-honey colored, was thoughtful, lazy, but hardworking when she did work. She seemed to know all there was to know about herbs and medicines and she was only twenty-five or so. They didn't talk much except for Polly, but they looked out for each other as most slaves did. Ethylene would come to the house to visit when she could. She liked Lifee a lot, because sometimes Lifee was a protection from the overseer, Mr. Grimes. He wasn't scared of Lifee, but he knew she worked in the Big House and would have the Massa's ear.

All of these women ranged in looks from attractive to pretty and could do wonders with the headkerchiefs they made and wore. But they tried not to be attractive, not to bring attention to themselves. They had no other way to protect themselves from unwanted sex and advances and they would be whipped if they didn't submit.

They were all friendly to Lifee because she was in their pain and there was no real reason for jealousy of her. Lifee still avoided any real contact with anyone, even though she made gifts for them. Little things that were pretty. An apron, kitchen gloves for hot utensils, things that did not attract attention. She worked steadily and was usually quiet unless spoken to or was with Abby.

Ethylene, giggling and girlish, had pointed Mor out to Lifee when they heard of the marriage. Sippi had been a little jealous because she had flirted often with Mor and he had paid her no mind. But she knew he had not chosen Lifee himself, so she was only bothered a little.

Lifee had seen Mor several times now. She watched him stealthily, because she had been warned by Massa Floyd what the circumstances were to be in her life. He had told her, one day near the wedding time, "You are sposed to sew, knit and crochet for my wife, the mistress, in the day. In the evenins you wait for me. Don't be afeared of Mor neither, cause he ain't gonna touch ya . . . nor look at ya too hard. Now, you gonna haf to cook and wash for Mor in case Miz Morella is watchin, but you each gonna sleep in yoah own rooms . . . for yo saf'ty."

Massa Floyd fiddled with some papers in his hands thinking, "I don have to splain to negras, but . . ." His infatuation overtook him, he continued, "That is why I didn't move you into his room and put Mor to build a new room for ya by the fire. Now you don't have to see him at night none. He has his own new door, jest like your'n. I don't give nigras no door inside a shack! But you got one. Use it . . . keep it closed!" He tried to scare her even while he could hardly wait to get her in his arms.

Lifee had thought at the time, "How foolish to think I would even think of opening my door to that old, worn-out man. Mr. Mor, indeed."

The day the new room was finished, Lifee was moved quickly from the Big House. Morella rolled her eyes at her husband and watched him even more carefully all that day. The wedding was set for that evening after the slaves finished their work.

The other field slaves gathered early as they could after the day's work to see Mordecai get himself a wife and they all wanted a better look at "Edessa." Their feelings were divided. One, they knew she was a slave, so they could like her; two, she was good-looking and was getting Mor and would have a new room. A dirt floor, but a new room nonetheless. So a little envy was in order.

Lifee was not dressed in even a fancy slave dress, which only meant a row of ruffles, for her wedding. Her face showed her heart, which was as sad and plaintive as her dress. She was a despondent, unhappy bride, with eyes cast down, no smile upon her face. She had never talked to Mor, but of the two evils she rathered to be away from the mistress's rage and jealousy and the master's leering face and quick hands.

In the two weeks prior to the marriage, Lifee had used much of the yarn and material Master Floyd had bought, to make Morella a pretty rose-colored knit shawl with green satin border and leaves she patterned, and a white dress with pink and green embroidered roses, a dress that was better fitted and prettier then any Morella had had before. But still . . . Morella's anger was directed at Lifee

in mean little ways. So though Lifee would have to be working in
the main house all day, she was glad to be leaving and free of
Morella at least for the nights.

Now that his touch was imminent, Lifee thought of Master
Floyd on her way to her marriage to Mor. He had not tried anything beyond groping covertly in the halls as they passed each other.
"Oh, dear God, help me." She turned her face away from the
thought of Master Floyd.

She turned her face, without thinking, to Mor. "Oh, please God,
help me." She sighed sadly and faced her future. "Well . . . I can
at least talk to him. Lord, I hope he is clean . . . and has his teeth.
Let him be gentle, Lord, let him be kind." Lifee thought of Master
Floyd again. "Please, Lord, if it has to be, let him not want all those
strange perverted things white men know of."

Master Floyd gave her the last-minute threat. "If my laws tween
you and Mor is eveh broken, I will take ya back where I got ya and
GIVE you, GIVE you away to the worstest poor white trash I can
find!" She was, finally, resigned.

All her things had been moved to her new room. The spinning
wheel was set there, also, so she could then spin at night when her
house chores were over.

Now she moved toward the marriage place. A little slave-girl,
Meda, smiled up at Lifee and opened the screen door to the kitch-
ens at the back of the main house. Lifee gently brushed the child's
head with her hand as she stepped out in the clean, print wedding
dress she had prepared. With another deep sigh, she began the
descent down to the yard, where the crowd was gathered and Mor
stood by the broom, staring at his bare feet. He felt ugly. It was
clear, he was not a happy groom.

From the window where she sat smirking, Morella could see the
only one who looked happy was Floyd. She wondered what he was
planning.

Mor wore his usual work clothes. Clean, because he had washed
them himself. Pressed, because he took several hours doing them

over and over trying to press the holes together. He had bathed from a small tin basin and washed his teeth and his hair in fresh water. He had even shaved his beard, with some pain, using an old razor of the massa. He thought it would make him appear younger even though he was not really old yet.

He would not answer any knock at his shack because he wanted to be alone with his thoughts and to listen for the slight sound of thunder that was getting just a little louder every other day or so. (Massa Floyd said, "They might be fightin bout a hundred miles or so on up the road, but the South is winnin, I betcha!") Massa didn't know much about geography and didn't know just how far he was from the North. The plantation was about seven miles from the main roads and any daily news. The Southern soldiers, hungry and hurt, hadn't started running away from the war front past his place in the daytime yet, so he didn't get news in that way either.

Mor did not, did not, want to marry, but as he waited with his calloused hands folded before him, for no reason he knew . . . a quiet joy crept through his body as Lifee came toward him. And, even beside that joy . . . was a sadness and fear. He did not like to be this close to any white man's business. Pain and death, too often, dwelled there. Mor kept his head down because he dare not look at Lifee as if in pleasure or anticipation. Massa Floyd had stared at his shaved face a long time.

Massa Floyd was standing just to the side of the white man who was to handle the broom and say the few words of marriage. This was the man's regular job. He performed this broom marriage, also, for poor white people who could not afford a regular preacher. Massa Floyd dared not look at Lifee either, because he knew Morella was looking at him through that window with eyes narrowed. He knew she was looking for the trick.

The banjo player began strumming as Lifee reached the last step and began her walk toward Mor. She, also, began to cry . . . not for marrying Mor . . . simply from life. But, she did not stop walking. When she stood next to Mor and he took her hand (not until Massa Floyd leaned over and told him to), her hand was cold and moist. Mor looked in her face without thinking and saw her eyes were blinded with tears. He felt her spine tremble, in truth, her body was cold, her heart was freezing.

Just before they jumped over the broom, Mor realized this woman was afraid deep to her heart and . . . was a slave . . . a person ruled . . . against her will. Just like he was. And . . . that she didn't want Massa Floyd! Just like he didn't want to be close to any white man's business!

A little deeper part of Mor's heart went out to Lifee. He squeezed her cold, numb hand. She looked up, into his eyes. Their eyes introduced them. She saw compassion and pity in his glance. He said softly, quickly, "Don be fraid." Her spine began to relax a bit in that instant. She wanted to look deeper into his eyes, his heart, but she felt herself pulled into the jump and then they were over the broom and when next she looked into Mor's eyes, he was her husband. She was his wife.

Because Massa Floyd had to act as though he welcomed the marriage between Mor and Lifee, there was fried chicken, no biscuits, but spoon bread, then some ice cream and a small cask of cheap whisky the slaves made for the master. There was some dancing, some laughing and some teasing. The bride and groom sat apart from each other to eat their meal. They did not laugh at the marriage jokes.

In an hour or so Massa Floyd had them end the little celebration and clean up the yard. Mor and Lifee were followed and playfully pushed into their shack. After the door was closed, the fun stopped. Everyone dawdled slowly along the paths back to their shacks, the desperation to hold and wring every drop of joy from whatever came close to them; to make it real, to be normal, was gone in a puff and the truth returned to the front of their minds again. The wedding dinner was better than what they would normally have had. But, they thought, "We done ate a piece of chicken, a dollop of ice milk on us tongue, we done laughed, but we still all time the same slaves. Back to work, negra!"

Inside the slave-shack, Lifee's "Good night" was punctuated by the sound of her door closing and Mor's door was heard a few seconds later. This cabin had doors!

Later that night Massr Floyd told Mistress Floyd that he heard the wild night animals movin roun the chicken yard, twice and the barn, once. Each time he explained to Morella "I betta go check" and grabbed his gun, headed outside. He knew Morella was looking through the dark outside her window trying to see him so he went directly to the yard and barn, the long way around. He stopped each time to lean and press his head against Mor's shack, waiting for a sound, a half hour at a time. He was afraid Morella might have got somewhere so to see him go in the shack, so he didn't go in. He heard nothing, no sound of lovemaking or even talking. But, if he could have heard Mor thinking and Lifee crying, he would really have heard something!

A week passed and Miz Morella seemed to relax. Massa drank heavily and made love to her two times that week. More than in the last three weeks. He was thinking of what was waiting for him.

One day, after Lifee was settled in Mor's shack, Massa Floyd had been especially busy popping up near Lifee, groping, pulling, patting her. That evening, frustrated to the point of having a nervous breakdown Lifee went to the shack, sat on her bed and cried in fear and anger. "I'm going to leave here! I'm going to run! Don't care if they kill me. Hope they kill me, then this all be over!"

Giving it no more thought or plan, Lifee rolled her box up in her old coat and when Mor was asleep, she ran.

Peeping had become habit for Morella. Watching the cabin from her window she saw Lifee come out of the cabin, look around, then suddenly walking fast a few yards, breaking into a run toward the road. She called to Floyd and smiling, said, "Yoah slave is running away."

Needless to say, they caught her. But Massa Floyd did not want to whip Lifee, the flesh he coveted. So after some thought he decided to whip Mor for not watching her, letting her get away. He had him tied to a post and gathered the other slaves so they could see and fear for themselves, though they never caused him problems anyway; they were waiting, waiting.

In his frustrated hankering after Lifee, he whipped Mor until the blood flowed from his back and buttocks. Mor dropped to the ground when he was untied, moaning from the pain. After Floyd left the scene, the other slaves carried Mor into his shack and lay him on his pallet as Lifee sat, tied to a board of the shack crying for herself and this man who had been so kind to her and for whom she had caused this horrible, bloody beating.

Mor could not work and so lay upon his pallet for several days, cared for by other slaves when they could come to him. Abby was the most help, making poultices for his body and feeding him stolen meat broth for his strength. After seeing how shamed and contrite Lifee was, Massa untied her and she took the job of caring for Mor. She bathed his body and rubbed oil into his stripped wounds. Gave him healing teas. Rubbed his whole body with healing herbs.

Mor lay there many days in deep pain for two reasons; the whipping had been brutal and he had not deserved it. His one recurring thought was "I knowed the white man's bisness was gonna cause me no-good." Yet, though he did not want to, he derived joy from the ministrations of Lifee. In time he healed, but where he had not hated Massa Floyd before, he did now. He still seldom changed words with Lifee. But she continued to be concerned for his care.

In a few more days, though not completely well, he stopped her from caring for him. He returned, stiffly, to work. But something had happened between Lifee and Mor in their joint pain. They became strong, silent friends. Added to her pain was her guilt, though neither of them was at fault.

Lifee worked all day in the main house, cutting, sewing, quilting, mending. She helped Abbysinia in the kitchen sometimes just to be able to have time to talk. Too, Lifee was looking for newspapers or any kind of news; there were none. "Miz Morella gits somp'n roun heah bout oncet or twict a mont, I reckin." Abby knew that Lifee could read by now. "Jes hold on. Im'a let you know wen it get heah."

Lifee helped Mona and Sippi in the rest of the house. Polly didn't want any help because she did not want anybody to find a reason to get her back out in the fields again by telling tales on her. She didn't want no master making her pregnant again. Enough of her babies had been sold. So she worked hard to be valued for her work.

Lifee also worked with the young girl, Meda, cleaning slave utensils and troughs outside. She finally made Abby an apron with lots of pockets of different shapes and sizes, with one deep pocket on the inside of it. She knew Abby had no children of her own left, but Abby secretly took food out to those that had children still. Lifee made her real pot holders and another padded glove for her right hand that wouldn't slip when she reached for hot pots and pans from the oven in the fireplace.

Lifee made Polly the same kind of apron in a different color, red with a headrag to match. She made Meda a patchwork dress that Meda cried over and loved immediately. Miz Morella noticed and asked, "You must not have enough to do, using up all my material and thread for the nigras. Things they don't need. You are here for ME!"

"They just scraps, mam. I sew on them when I go to my shack."

Miz Morella tightened her lips, "You mean you ain't tired when you go home?" She just couldn't bring herself to like this pretty negra woman.

"Yes, mam, I am tired . . . but—"

"I can start makin Christmas presents, if you got all that time."

"Yes, mam."

Miz Morella looked at Lifee thoughtfully, "Wheah you say you been livin? How come you speak so goo . . . like white people? Wheah have you been in yoah life?"

"Well, mam, mostly I've been in Louisiana, but I traveled some to New York and Philadelphia with my mistress and we . . ."

Morella snapped to attention. "You mean you have been to New York? City?"

"Yes, mam. That is where I learned about patterns and . . ."

"New YORK! That is wheah I want to go!" She grabbed Lifee's shoulders. "Tell me, tell me, sit right down heah and TELL me all about it as bes you can!"

Lifee wanted Miz Morella to be more relaxed around her, though she didn't expect her to like her and she did not trust white women any longer for herself, she needed to be close to someone who could get outside news and perhaps, that way, Lifee, herself, could get the news.

Lifee began that day to weave a thin web around Morella with her tales of the CITY and its beautiful clothes, people and places. She told her the truth, as she knew it, with just a little of the exaggeration necessary to make this woman want to hear more. Lifee had been only a slave-friend-maid, but she had traveled with a very engaging and social mistress, even to Paris. She had learned a lot. She didn't have to make things up about the men either. Many of them had sought the company of her rich mistress.

In a short time Lifee showed Morella how to order the right magazines from Paris or New Orleans, since New York was not allowed for commerce in this wartime. From these she shared beauty secrets, prepared and shaped Morella's hair. The make-up and perfumes ordered from New Orleans could send Morella into near swoons. When they could not secretly order the elegant and expensive frocks that Morella wanted, Lifee tore ruffles and bows from the country gowns Morella already had and remade them more fashionably. They talked hours, endlessly, about the men and places of the romantic and fabulous East Coast of America and Europe.

Morella carried these magazines proudly everywhere she went to visit her friends dressed in her finery, wearing her new and delightful scents. Her friends began to envy her, for once. She grew to appreciate and trust Lifee. She even called her by "Lifee" when she learned her true name. Master Floyd was almost glad of the change, but he resented Lifee never being at hand in the shack when he was free to go there. Lifee stayed as much as possible near Morella.

FOUR

Lifee tried to relax in the shack with Mor. She couldn't. She knew he was coming in. Sometime. She avoided Mor. She would watch him in secret when he first came in. The shack was small and dark at nights except for an oil-rag lamp. But he always washed before he went to get his food from the slave kitchen and offered to get some for her. She always refused and was in her room when he returned with his food.

He never tried to touch her. Never bothered her. Didn't try to talk once she closed her door. She was grateful to him for the way he was, so she began to have fresh, warm water there for him. She went to the slave-kitchen, bringing his food to their shack, keeping his food warm over hot coals outside by the shack door.

He was always, always tired. Tired and dirty and frowning. The first day he found the water, he knocked on her door and asked, "Is you gonna use this here water or is you already used it? I cn throw it out fo ya if . . ."

She answered as she pulled the door open. "That is for you, Mor. I thought . . . I thought I could help you some, you so tired when you get home . . . here. That's your food out there by the step. I tried to keep it warm for you."

Mor was speechless. He turned to look out the front door and heard her door close. He spoke for her to hear, "Thankee kindly."

Now, Mordecai was a man. A solid man. He hadn't let anybody do anything for him since his wife and most didn't think to do it anyway. Tears formed in his eyes which he wiped angrily away, thinking, "She a nice woman. She a kind woman." It was the closest he had come to feeling like a normal living man coming home since his wife was sold.

Two days later there was a small metal box left outside the shack door, made to hold hot coals with a shelf that could be lifted out. When Lifee came home and saw it, she wondered if he was trying to give her a job keeping his meals warm and heating his water. When he came home, she came out of her room to ask, but he spoke first. "I made at there so ya can heat yo water and keep yo vittles warm."

Lifee had been frowning, but now she looked at him quietly a moment, then said, "Thank you." And you know, his food and water for bathing was always warm when he came home, if possible. Mor began to bring a bucket of cool spring water to keep in the shack. It was fresh every evening.

Mor and Lifee got along. But they still never talked. Their doors were always closed.

Lifee came to the plantation in 1865 around October. It was now 1866 and many slaves had been freed in all the states, Texas among the last to let them go. Massa Floyd, in spite of the thunder of gunfire always somewhere in the background and of all he heard of the South losing the war, held on to his false dreams that the South would still come back and win. He spent his time thinking of Lifee and his not having what he bought her for.

Time passed slowly for Massa Floyd, but his desires grew hourly. "She mine! And it's been at least eight, nine months since that woman come here, but that hot-damn Morella jest always round her!" All his friends and neighbors were leaving for safety, but still he kept on going day to day as if no change was coming.

A day finally came when Miz Morella went to visit her friend, Roberta. She didn't tell Floyd how long she would be gone so he had to hurry. She had no sooner turned a curve in the road when Floyd had Lifee go to her shack for something and then he was there before she knew what was happening. He had waited so long and was so excited for the body of Lifee that he thought she had been longing for him, too. He came hurrying into the shack at this midday. Most all slaves were off working, but Abby took the time to watch where he was going and saw him go into Lifee's shack.

Lifee's door was open and she thought Mor was coming in, she turned, smiling. When she saw the massa the smile froze and turned to a grimace as she gave a soft moan of dread. She stepped back, but knew there was no sense in fighting. She was not weak, she was sensible. This man held her life in his hands and she meant to live. She knew, now, freedom was everywhere else and was near in Texas. Nearer every day. She would be able to walk away . . . soon. So just before Massa touched her, she sent her mind away where she could think of the freedom day and the road away from the plantation, hate and slavery. To life.

She did not help him as he snatched her clothing loose, tearing it enough to free the part he wanted. It didn't take long. When he was finished, panting, he spoke, "I done waited so long. It was just like I thought it would be. Don't worry cause things gettin to be alright with the mistress. She's a'likin ya. You a smart girl. Won't be long, I'll be out to see ya more." Then he was gone. He would have been back that night, but he expected Morella any minute.

When Massa Floyd left the shack, her home, Lifee took her torn and soiled clothes off and bathed herself, getting fresh water several times. She changed the one sheet she had on the bed so the used side was away from where she slept. She was too emotionally exhausted to wash it then. Tomorrow.

Lifee lay down on her stomach on the fresh side of the bed and cradled her head in her arms. She did not cry. There is a desolation beyond tears. Instead, she hated. However washed, her body felt slimy and filthy to her. She lay like that for several hours.

She was still there when Mor came home. He rushed home, slowly now, trying not to appear eager. Looking for her as he opened the door to the poor, little two-room shack. Her door was open again. He almost smiled as he reached for his water, wanting to wash up before he ate or talked to her.

When Lifee heard him come in, she raised her head. She had been lying there feeling alone and a bit frightened at her life and what Massa Floyd's coming in the shack daily would mean to her life. She had no protection from Massa Floyd except her own mind and Morella. She had finally cried at what appeared to be her endless desolate despair. "Alone. Alone. Alone. Nobody. Nobody cares. Alone."

She heard Mor washing up, she heard him throw the first water out. When he threw the second water out and came back in the shack, she slowly got up.

Lifee needed to be near someone who cared for her. She slowly walked out to him wearing only her long slip. He turned to her as he was reaching for his warming plate and he stopped in mid-move. His eyes full of her in her near nakedness, his mouth slowly dropping open in alarm. Then he looked into her eyes, so full of tears. Her pained face so full of questions and . . . a need . . . not of sex, but of love . . . any kind of love. Just let it be kind, real, be human, her eyes seemed to plead, wordlessly.

He moaned softly, "Ohhhhhh," for her. As he stood up, plate forgotten, again he moaned softly, "Ohhhhhh." He leaned his head to the side, "Din I do the bes I could, din't I?"

Without thinking, she raised an arm and placed her hand on her own forehead. Softly, she spoke, "Mor?"

He started to reach, but pulled his hands back from her. He moaned, "Ahhhhh" and murmured softly, "What cn I do now? I was happy . . . a lil bit. I feeled so good. You is . . ." Then his face changed, filled with anger, yet he still spoke softly, "I cn kill em."

Lifee stepped closer to Mor. "No, no, Mor. There are millions of THEM. We have to live. Freedom come, at last. We have to survive THEM."

Mor raised his calloused hands so slowly, so slowly. Finally, as he had dreamed of but wouldn't allow himself to think of, he was touching her. He was smoothing her, soothing her, gently, unhurried, in the dusky, sad, poor, little, suddenly rich, two-room shack. Then he was holding her. When she felt no lust in his touch, she slowly placed her arms around his neck and lay her head on the strong muscles of his shoulders. She cried quietly, not so much from sadness, but from a sort of relief. There was somebody. Here was somebody who cared. His eyes filled with moist sorrow while at the same time his heart filled with a gentle joy that he was holding the woman he didn't even admit to himself he loved.

After a few moments of his rocking her in his arms, he said in a low voice, "Go and lay down, I fix ya a cup o hot water and git ya som milk fo it." He gradually led her to her room, lay her down and placed the covers over her and started away. She reached out and grabbed his arm.

"Don't let go of me, please. Hold me, just hold me." Lifee had never said these words to anyone in her life. She had loved no one but her child after her first young mistress who had betrayed her. Her mother she had never known except for an image in her treasured box. A mother whom she loved, even though she did not know if she had ever held her. There had been none other in her lonely, long dreary life since the first betrayal. "Hold me," she said again. Mor was speechless again. His breath stopped, hesitated. Then he slowly and gently lay down beside her and held her even as he feared for his life. The love he felt, the need he saw, was stronger than the fear.

In a quiet time, when the quiet night had covered the little shack completely and he thought she was asleep, he moved to get up. She spoke, "Everything we get seems to be only for a day . . . a short minute."

He spoke, "It gonna be betta wen freedom come. And ya cn trust me. Trust me. I cares fo you. I blive freedom is truly comin. I'll take care of ya."

She murmured in a shaded voice, "Then . . . hold me. Hold me."

He spoke in a low voice, "If freedom come . . ."

She interrupted, shaking her head, "If freedom don't come . . . hold me."

Mor gradually loosened her arms, got up and removed his clothes. He lay back down and gently . . . gently taking her into his arms, breathed, "Ahhhhhh."

"Come closer to me," she said in his ear.

He did. When she pulled him on top of her, their eyes were open, looking into the other's, thinking, realizing what they were doing.

He caressed her hip. "You my wife . . . layin here wit me."

"You are my husband; call me by my real name, Lifee."

He whispered, with wonder, "Lifee, Lifee."

She opened like a flower to the sun and rain and he moved, never-endingly in. He prolonged it, savored it. He said one thing, softly, many times, "Feel so luve. You feel so good."

Deeper and deeper he went. They sucked in their breath, together, at the same time. She moaned and he held her tighter, saying, "I'm sho gon luve ya, all my life what I got lef."

She held him, marveling at her feelings in this act she had always hated so much. "I'm gonna need you all my life."

In time when it was over and they lay spent, but not apart, Mor spoke first. "Ahhh, my Lifee. My wife."

She answered, "Mor, Mor." Then she looked up at him and laughed a little laugh. "I mean Mordecai, Mordecai, cause I don't need no more . . . now." Then she folded herself down into his arms and slept. In a magic while his good sense returned and he got his clothes and went into his room. Got up again, got his plate and sat in his floorbed, smiling. Happy and afraid. But satisfied. Love.

Miz Morella returned the next morning and Massa Floyd was in the worst way because he could have gone back out to see Edessa had he known Morella wouldn't be coming round that bend all night!

Miz Morella brought news from her friend's house. Roberta's husband, George (whom Floyd did not like "cause he too citified") had just returned from Jackson, Mississippi, on a business trip and had reported the South was lost, had done lost almost a year ago, really.

Morella rushed in, hysterical and grasping an excuse to leave, saying, "Somebody name of Sherwood or Sherwin is burnin everything in his sight! That ain't that far from here! People are leaving, going anywhere but South! I'm leaving! I'm goin North, myself. You can't stop me!"

She stopped screaming at Floyd to turn and holler for her maids. "Mona! Polly! Come help me pack! Lifee!" Morella's voice echoed throughout the house as she ran up the stairs to her rooms. Floyd was right behind her. "You must be crazy! You can't blive everthin ya hear, woman!" He turned to go back down the stairs. "I'm gonna go see George myself! Don't you move til I get back! You are my wife and you ain't leavin! And stop scarin the negras."

Morella bent over the banister to scream at him, "These nigras ain't scared! They're happy!" She turned back to her maids, "Don't you leave me til I'm packed, you hear me! You all ain't free here yet! There's men out there with guns! Where is Lifee?!"

Morella was thinking of how to get her gold her daddy had hidden, how to get it out safely without Floyd knowing about it, when Lifee appeared. "Lifee, you got to go with me! To New York! Help me pack."

Morella was packing furiously when Lifee said, "Miz Morella, you don't need to take all this stuff. You can BUY better things where you are goin! Just take what you need for this trip."

Morella stopped moving. Thoughtfully, she spoke under her breath, "Yes. I will be free, too!" She thought of the plantation she had always thought she hated and realized she didn't hate it, it was her father's and now, it was hers. "My papa's papers, in his desk. My land! It's my land! I'll come back someday. Maybe."

She ran to what had been her father's office, now Floyd's storage room. She knew what drawers the important papers were in. They were locked! She didn't have time to find the key. She turned to Lifee. "Go get me a ax." When it was brought she chopped the drawers open and grabbed a box. "These are ALL important. Pack em all! Put em in my room, Mona." She turned to Lifee, "Lifee, get two spades, then come to the cold cellar."

Morella was thinking as she moved things around, searching, "I hear them yankers gonna take everthing we got to eat round here, so we better get this food out of here! Them yankers steal everthing! George said the paper money ain't worth nothin noway, so I'll leave that for em." She spoke aloud, "Where is Lifee? I don't trust nobody but Lifee, and not her all the way."

She took Lifee to the place in the cellar way back behind all the shelves of bottles and jars. "We have to dig this up, Lifee. You help me and we can both be goin to New York."

Lifee grabbed a shovel, but shook her head as she started to dig. "Miz Morella, you know you white and you rich. I'm not and I am poor. You don't need nothing but a maid and if I am free, I want to be FREE to pick my own life. You just go on ahead and get to live your life. We may meet again, cause I am going to try to keep living myself. You'll be alright. You got money, you'll be alright!"

Morella smiled as at a child and said, "But . . . how you gonna take care yourself without us white folks? What can you do? How will you make all these decisions in yoah life?"

It was Lifee's turn to laugh, but she didn't. She just said, "Miz Morella, white folks ain't been taking care of us. We have been taking care of white folks. Better ask what you all will do when we are gone and slavery is no more."

Morella laughed aloud as though it was a joke, and said, "Oh, I heard them men talkin at Roberta's house. When all them Northerns and that Sherwood is gone home, ya'll be right back where you are now!" Then she started digging in all seriousness. They finally made a thud with the shovels then worked with their hands to pull the heavy casket out of the earth that had been harboring it for years. Morella and Lifee dragged the chest out and over to Lifee's shack and put it under Lifee's bed. "Til the morning when I leave!" Morella said. "You go back and pat that ground down so Floyd won't know nothin happened in here. I got to go pack!"

Lifee went back to pack the earth down, but checked just a little with her shovel to see if anything was left. She heard a small ting and knelt to dig it out. It was a much smaller box, but it was heavy. Lifee didn't open it but a little, and something glittered. More gold and silver coins, some big, some little. She sat back on the ground. "It ain't mine, but must I give it to her?" After a moment, "Hell, no! It probably belongs to all the slaves who made this money. And I have worked hard and even changed her life." She got up and started patting the earth down. "They have took allll our lives. They took our children. They took our mothers. What do we owe them? They owe us! And I'm keeping this as mine. For a start." She finished patting the ground down, threw the shovel over by the door, closed it and went to her shack. Thinking, "We better build us a wagon, cause we leaving here!"

FIVE

Floyd had returned soon after the gold was safely hidden in
Lifee's room. Morella looked at Lifee with renewed suspi-
cion. Her mind was quick. She trusted Lifee and, yet, she didn't.
"My daddy say you don never know what a negra is thinkin!" Massa
Floyd was a little upset and thrown off his usual confidence in the
South, but he had not changed his mind. He found Morella.

"Morella, we jes can't jump up and run off. This is all our property. We got to stay to pertect it. They ain't burnin up everthing,
long as you cooperate. Yoah daddy trusted me!"

First she looked at Floyd like he was a stranger. Then Morella
smiled wryly, "I trust you, too, Floyd. You just stay here and
'pertect' things. I'm goin on to somewhere safe. I'm just not good at
pertecting things. I'm jest a lady. Daddy always said that and you
always say that. So . . . I'm leavin! Roberta and George are leaving day after tomorra, if not tomorra. I'm ready." She looked at him
with steel in her gaze. "And I'm leavin with them."

Floyd was trying to get mad, but he was afraid of her and he
understood her. "You cain't leave . . . Well, maybe you better. I'll
get some money ready for ya."

"Bless you, Floyd." She smiled at his back as he left. He hollered over his shoulder to her, "What else did George say to you to scare you so? He didn't scare me!" He didn't wait for an answer. He mumbled as he went to get the money for Morella, "I don't blive he knows what he's talkin bout. We . . . the South can't be losin! Not for long, anyhows."

She heard him and hollered back, "I believe him, Floyd."

Early the next morning when Morella went to get her chest of money from Life's room to pack in the coach taking her to Roberta's, the seal had not been broken, so she gave Life the small pouch Floyd had given to her. It wasn't much because he didn't want her to go too far. "There's no room for you in the carriage with Roberta and George. Well, the truth is that Roberta won't ride in a coach that far with a free nigra. Take this money pouch and hide it. If you get set free, come to New York and look for me." She smiled conspiratorially, "You will surely find me in the most expensive places." She was leaving when she turned back and said, "Don't let them damn yankers catch you. They do the most gawd-awful things to women, no matter what color you are! Can you magin that?! Treatin white women just like nigras! Northern men have no manners at all!" Then she was gone.

Of course, all the slaves knew what was happening, but most didn't know what to do. Some left when Massa Floyd or an overseer was out of sight. Mor did not leave.

He said, "Them pat-trollers out there and they hav fun jes killin nigras. I'ma wait til gen'l somebody tell me I cn go."

Miz Morella had gone. Mona, Sippi and Polly stayed, still washing, cleaning and hiding food away from whoever would come to take it, then running around getting things they felt they wanted to take with them when they left. Abby was hiding food only for Meda and Luzy and maybe Life. She was packing cooking utensils, pots, pans, salt and such. She had walked out to the barnyards, took a wheelbarrow and had her eye on a mule to haul her things. "I done worked here long nough for this." But Mor told her not to worry, he was making them a large cart with wheels they could pull. She held a joy in her old overworked heart. She spoke the word over and over. "Freedom, Freedom. Freedom. That word taste so fine to me. Freedom. Freedom. FREEDOM." Alternately, she felt fear. "These here white folks lie so much, reckon this all a lie?" Then the joy would come back. "Freedom. Freedom. Lawd, cn you magine? Oh, Jesus! Thank you Lawd!"

Soon, all the slaves were leaving, most had no plan, didn't know how to make one, didn't know what all their needs would be just yet. Well, they had never been allowed to plan their own life before. They were catching on quickly though. They knew they could now move their feet in any direction they wanted! FREEDOM!

Everyone had been running in different ways getting their selves together. Some were leaving together as couples, but many were alone. Abby had Luzy and Meda. Sippi was going to try to find her children. Mona didn't know what to do and she felt too old to start a new life. Freedom confused her, but she kept moving forward, toward the Freedom. Polly was making plans, but didn't know what was available to her. She was raring to find out though. Ethylene had just disappeared, nobody knew where she was. Everybody doing something. But beneath it all, many were afraid. No, no, they would never want to be a slave again. But Freedom was so new. They had never lived it. And the white men who had already hated them, hated them more now.

Mor was excited, but doing serious thinking about the future. He was not going to play with Freedom. He and Lifee had talked deep into the nights. They decided they were going to be together. Lifee thought of her education, his education. Her work and possibilities. His work and his possibilities. The difference. The future. Mor felt inadequate to Lifee. But, love is an equalizer. And Lifee loved Mor.

Mor went to say good-by to Massa Floyd, who was running

around trying to keep up with the work and the animals, trying to talk some of his slaves into remaining with him.

When he saw Mor, Floyd asked him, "Why ya goin, Mor. Boy, I been good to ya. You can stay on here and work. I'll even pay ya. Good as anybody. I need ya now, boy!"

Mor answered, "I got ta go now and see what Freedom is."

Floyd slapped his thigh, "You be free here as anyplace. I need ya, boy! I been good to ya! Ain't Ah?"

"Yo tried to make old marster whop me, hard, and you whipped me, bad."

"Ya did somethin wrong for it to be done. And he dint do it noway. You stay here, boy. Ya know more bout what goes on than these damn overseers."

Mor started to walk away, saying, "You pays em. Anyway, I got to go."

Floyd reached out to grab Mor's shoulder. "I tol you, boy, I need ya. Now . . . ya stay on here. I been betta to ya than most nigras."

Mor turned around to face Floyd. "Ya fucked my wife."

Floyd frowned, "I what? Yo wife? That nigra marriage?"

Mor turned away to leave. "That a marriage. Yo fucked my wife."

Floyd said in a strange voice loud enough for Mor to hear, "She goin with you? Edessa goin with you?"

Mor stopped one more time. "We leavin. And her name Lifee. Not Edessa. My wife, Lifee, goin wit me, her husban."

Then he was gone to meet Lifee and life.

She was waiting for him near the road with the wagon cart on wheels. A few of her house things, sheets and quilts from the Big House, the sewing machine, her precious small "box" of treasure, a larger box of tools that Mor worked his various trades with, some strapped to the sides. Her money was hidden in the clothes she had on. They wanted to get to the road at the same time and jump from the plantation to Freedom together.

He came, usual slow step, but, still, rushing, in his way, toward her. Feeling good about what he had been able to say to Massa Floyd. He corrected himself, "Jes plain ole Floyd. Ain no marster no more."

He smiled to himself, grabbed the wagon handle and they started to the road. Some other ex-slaves were smiling, packing, teasing and talking smart to each other. Some were just crying. A few were drinking. All were happy.

Many set off down the Freedom Road to find somebody from their family. Tired as they were, there was a spring to their steps.

Lifee had gotten some shoes of Massa Floyd's for Mor, but he just wrapped them up and put them in the wagon. Then he wrapped his big, wide feet in his usual rags and papers for walking. He had an old jacket with one button buttoned. His pants were old and thin in spots, but clean. He carried a good solid stick in one hand even as he pushed the wagon. (You could pull it or push it.) He would have been a worn-out-looking old man had Lifee not been with him. But she was. There was hope in his face. She was his wife. Maybe they had a future. Somewhere.

Now they were ready to jump the road to Freedom.

Mor and Lifee got to the place at the road to jump, where the plantation road met the state road. They were ready. They turned to smile at each other, bent to jump . . . and heard "Hold up, ya'll, wait!"

They straightened and turned to see Abby coming with Luzy and Meda pulling the cart Mor had made them. When they reached Mor and Lifee, they were out of breath. Meda spoke first, but they all joined in. "We'uns ain't got no place to go. Wheah ya'll goin?"

"Us . . . we don't know yet," Mor answered.

Abby said, "Well, you the ony fambly we know. Cn we go wit chu?"

Lifee said, "Sure." She looked at Mor and smiled. He turned back to the three and tried to say "sure," but said, "Sho."

Lifee was almost shouting, "Let's all leap to Freedom Road at the same time! Hold hands now! Here we go! One, two, three, go!" And they did, laughing together at the joy of Freedom.

Up the road a bit they heard someone else hollering and looked back to see Mona puffing toward them. "Cn I go wit ya'll?"

Everybody turned to Mor, who said, after looking at Lifee, "Sho. This here road blongs to everbody today!"

It wasn't long before they heard some more hollering, they looked back and saw Polly gaining on them. "Cn I go wit ya? Sippi goin to try'n fin her chilren. I think mines is on out this here way."

Lifee held out an arm to welcome Polly, saying, "We all gonna work somethin out together. We got plenty soul for the Lord, for work and for trying. You might say we got oversoul. One thing I know, we sure are gonna be strivers."

In this way, Suwaibu's and Kola's blood of Africa was rushing on toward the future, together, again. Alive, pulsing, strong, striving blood.

The straggly group drew together. Becoming serious between the laughter and tears. Mouths full of singing praise to the Lord. They were on the Freedom Road, together. Mor reckoned a little what might lie ahead.

He knew rich white folks hadn't liked black folks around except for work and poor white folks didn't like black folk because it gave them somebody they could look down upon and they needed that cause some of em was mighty low. Most all poor white folk would hate to give up that lie of their superior place and have the negra free as they were, cause that would seem to make them equal. Freedom was really the only thing they had that had made them superior. "They gon sho fight that! They done alredy lied on Gawd, now jes what they gonna think bout to make it be alright to kill us'ns or take our womens. That might be diffrun in de North. May be we'uns head that way." Life looked at him as he slowly shook his head at his thoughts. He turned to her, saying, "It gon be some hard, hard time ahead, I blive." She answered, "We can make it." She smiled. "We FREE."

The road looked long and rocky. But the future was out there. A free future. They all thought they could see it. But they couldn't see it all. There were some great, big, rocky, muddy roads ahead. But for now, Freedom, alone, would do.

It was around July, 1866. Texas had been late freeing slaves. Some, many, were still enslaved. Afraid to leave their masters.

The road from the plantation and the old slave shacks that had been their home had little more traffic than usual. But, as the travelers progressed to the main road, more and more people appeared. White men riding horses hard and fast; soldiers, some alone, some in groups, all looking disgusted, dejected. Many wearing bandages, using crutches. Looking over their shoulders with concern. The plantations along the way already looked empty and uncared for, sad.

Groups of freed slaves were happy, merry or seemed confused about where they were going, what they were going to do, but the question did not weigh too heavily on their minds. They had worked all their lives, so that was what they would keep doing, only now, the work would be for themselves; the money would be theirs, the land they worked would be theirs, the beatings would be ended. Oh! Freedom. Freedom.

Many, many were hastening to find sold mothers, fathers, children, wives, husbands. Almost all of them had a goal.

For Mor and Life the first goal was to get far away from where they had been. Their minds full of thoughts of the future gave each face a serious look. As he walked pulling the homemade wagon, Mor thought, "This here Life a educated woman. She ain't gon stay with me. I loves her, but I ain't gon count on her. She got plenty things she can do. I got plenty things, too, but I don't even not know where I'm goin and if I can go. Well, I will do the bes I

can. I ain't lackin in none of the things these white folk need and
they the onliest ones got some money to pay."

Mor had not thought out that the slaves were the only ones who
had been holding the economy up. The free labor that got the work
done, that grew king cotton that allowed even poor white folk to
have decent clothing on their backs. He did not know many, many
white people could not afford the wool or linen materials the
wealthy could afford. The poor, uneducated white people with
near-naked children, sometimes, most times, had only one outfit all
their adult lives, made from flour sacks or burlap, given to the next
in line when someone died, buried almost naked. The wealthy
white man kept ALL down. And that these same people, poor
white people, would worry that all the new colored labor would take
what few jobs they had unless they owned their own farm. The
cotton mills were in Europe or the North. Of course, many of those
poor people never worked anyway, not even when they owned a
little land. Some did work hard on their own land and prospered or
at least took care of their needs. But, now, even though there was
the cotton gin, cotton would cost more because the labor was no
longer free.

Lifee, staring straight ahead at the long road, yet noticing everything around her because her eyes were greedy for freedom, was
thinking, "This is a good man. He will work hard. He doesn't have
an education, but maybe I got enough for two because I care for
him. I'll teach him. I could maybe find someone else more suitable
to me, but what does that mean? He is suitable to me in every other
way, I think." She turned her face to him and smiled; he didn't see
her, he was looking down the road. "I have not told him about the
money I have yet. He would worry and maybe bring attention to us.
And death."

Farther down the road, her thoughts continued, "Maybe I could
go back to Louisiana. But I don't know my mother, there is no one
there for me. All I have is a box of my history. I want somewhere
else, somewhere new, now. I want to live near an ocean. Different

food. More kinds of jobs, better seasons. I want to be near the East. The Carolinas, Virginia. We gonna have to walk cross all those states. My Lord, my Lord."

Abby was pulling her cart with the help of Meda and Luzy and she was thinking as she looked down the long, long road. "Lord, I'm already old and tired. But I's free . . . at last. Nev'r thought it would come, Lord, nev'r did. No sir. These white folks usual get their way . . . or somebody gonna die, sho. But, I's free. And I got these two little chillin and I's gonna try to raise em. Somebody gonna need a housekeeper or a cook or both. I wants me a house with my own selfs kitchen with my own pots and pans and flour and sugar. I'm gon get that, Lord help me, I will. I just gotta live long nuff to do it. I will do it, please Lord."

It was early in the morning in early July, but the heat was already up and the sun glaringly promised a hot day. All the greenery, trees and thickets along the road were full of leaves, singing birds and humming insects. Many dry weeds and the hard, dry earth beckoned to the two already tired young girls to come sit, but they knew that ground was rough and sticky, full of burrs and maybe snakes. It was too early anyway, too soon to have to rest yet.

Both Luzy and Meda, twelve and fourteen years old, were excited and happy. They knew, even at their age, this was not a game. That freedom was very important; they had been slaves every day of their lives. But what it immediately meant was they were not in a hot kitchen today. They were free! walking on the road, free with Abby, whom they knew was no kin to them nor they to each other. But she was still the closest thing to a mother they had ever known AND they were going somewhere. They had started calling her Ma Abby long ago and now it had shortened to Mabby.

Of a sudden Meda almost screamed to Abby, "Mabby! Where is our trav'lin notes?"

Abby smiled, "Massa don need to make us no more note, chile."

"Why?"

Abby smiled larger, "We's free!"

A little farther down the road, "We's hungry, Mabby."

Now, Abby frowned, "We ain't but just left that house. We ain't stoppin til us get some distance from there, less'n them white folks change they mind." And there was silence and hurried steps for a while.

Then, "How long fore we stoppin to eat, Mabby?"

Abby sighed, "Reach in that there bag on the side top and get one of them biscuits! That's gon have to hold ya til we all stops to eat!"

"Yes'm."

The plantation had been about ten miles from a small town called Longview in Texas. As the small group neared the town, there were more soldiers and many freed slaves wandering around, laughing, searching for food they hadn't thought of in their haste to get away. The Confederate soldiers were rushing through the town on their way to their homes, hoping they were still there. But Texas hadn't been hard hit and the Yankee soldiers were glad it was all over, though they were a bit boisterous because they had won. They didn't know what to do with all the slaves milling around them looking for food or jobs. Some soldiers had thoughts of money to be made, but there was very little Yankee money, and Confederate money was no longer any good. Gold was the thing now, gold and silver, and everybody knew the slaves had none of that. The government Freedman Bureau arrangements were trying to work, but the greedy always came with them.

Mor's group walked closer together as they stared at all the situations of freedom. Life spoke first, "Mor, let's keep walking on to Louisiana. It's the next state and we got to go through it. It ain't far, bout fifty miles or sixty. We might could get thirty miles in today."

Abby spoke up, "These chillen ain't gon be able to haul no thirty miles pullin this wagon and hungry, too."

Mona and Polly, whose eyes were as big around as saucers, were holding their bundles tightly and trying to see everything and everybody in the little town at once. Mona spoke, "I blive I'm gonna get off here cause my people mighta come through here. I got to see if anybody know bout em." Polly decided to join her. "I blive I'm gonna go my ownsef. See can I get a word on somebody of mine. Thirty miles don't seem like what I wanna do fore I know nobody is round here." So everybody hugged and said their farewells and Mor's party, smaller by two, continued on the road to Louisiana.

Mor, looking at his ragged wrapped feet, thought, "These feets ain't gon make no thirty miles nohow." He said, "I don want to be near no town when we puts down tonight, and eats. Theys drinkin goin on and peoples is too hungry for everthing."

Lifee agreed, "That's right. We only have a little food and no money to speak of and we look poor enough to pass through, but I don't want to go to sleep without our things being well hidden."

Mor asked, "You think these here nigras would steal what little we got? They see me, I'm a man here with ya."

Lifee answered, "They hungry . . . and most all don't have no money."

Abby agreed. "This little food I got won't feed no mess of people."

Mor decided, "We keep goin, then, til we finds a good place to get off the road and hide in."

Lifee laughed lightly, "A safe place. Plenty snakes in these woods."

But Mor stayed serious. "We take care as we can."

Now, the little group of people kept walking out of the town and down the road that was full of ditches and ruts from wagon wheels and horses. The road was dry though, so the little wagon carts just bumped along nicely. The overhanging trees gave a little shade now and again and the future was still in front of them.

They had not noticed, but Ethylene was following at a good distance behind them ever since Longview. She had left the plantation very early to escape any last-minute grabbing the overseer might be planning to do. She stayed close to Mor and Lifee because she didn't have a family and she had chosen them. Besides, she felt

Abby, Luzy and Meda were her family already. She was getting hungry and she had packed a good little lunch with some boiled eggs. Her thirst was the most worrisome, but she dare not stop longer than a minute because she didn't want her chosen family to disappear.

The little group trudged down the long road, passing a few small farmhouses, evoking little interest from those who were now used to former slaves walking freely down the road.

Wiping his forehead, Mor asked, laughing, "What ya gon put in them there pots, Abby?" She laughed back, "You gon catch us a squirrel or two . . . I hopes." And Mor, stomach growling, answered, "We sho gon try."

On they went down that long Freedom Road. All the hot day long. Stopping briefly to eat a biscuit or two, mostly for the children. Freedom was so new, no one really wanted to stop. They wanted to get far away from the last place they had been slaves, their feet just kept moving on and on. As the sun slowly slid down the sky to sunset, Luzy and Meda tried to ride the carts, but the carts were too full and they couldn't ride long before they slipped off or made something else fall off. The grown-ups were too tired anyway to pull two big girls old enough to walk, tired or not.

Lifee told the girls, "You girls walkin on Freedom Road for the first time. Hold up a few miles more, then you have a hot meal and maybe a bath if a stream is nearby . . . then a good sleep." The girls were tired, but still excited, so they gave a tired grin and kept walking with these people who were their family.

It was getting dark when they reached close to Shreveport, near the border of Louisiana. They waited while Mor went into the woods to look for a stream or any kind of water. He found a small brook and took them in where they could not be seen from the road. There were no houses around so they thought they were safe for the night. He took off and came back with a wild rabbit which the girls did not want to kill. Abby told them, "Don't look then," and went off a ways and came back and cooked that rabbit over the small fire Mor had made. They washed everything up and put it away that night, then covered the carts with large branches a little way from their camp. Then everybody washed up in the creek and went stone out to sleep. It had been a long, long road on a long, hot, hot day.

The next morning before daybreak, Mor was up and had water heating on the fire. He had checked their belongings, which were safe, and woke them up to fix and eat a bite and get on the road. The dewy foliage smelled fresh and looked wildly beautiful. Still on the lookout for snakes, they made their way to the road. Mor could tell a few wagons had passed that way, but the road was clear. As morning broke, you could tell it was going to be another hot day.

They walked steady except for short trips into the woods to relieve themselves. Abby was tired and the girls were soon getting irritated and starting to drag their feet. They had almost reached Shreveport when the day was gone, and darkness found Mor seeking another place of refuge for his family. He was gone almost an hour, and when he returned he said, "I done made us a place and there's a creek by it. Jest follow me." And they did, breathing sighs of relief.

Because clouds were gathering overhead, Mor had arranged four strong tree limbs into a covered thatched roof for them to sleep under if it rained, and now he built a fire and set traps for the evening meal. They would save any scraps to have in the morning with cornmeal ash bread and hominy grits, with a little syrup.

Abby told the girls, "Make sure ya eat every bite cause we ain't got doodly to waste. All we'uns don't eat tonight, we eat in the mornin." Everyone nodded eagerly. They were starved.

As she chewed her food, Lifee said, "One thing we can't afford to get and that is get sick. So eat. I'm glad you're eating plenty."

Abby, also thinking, said, "When we's walkin and you see some maybe forgot cabbage or some greens in the fields, pick em, cause we can boil em at nights to eat with this here corn pone."

Mor, nodding his head, said, "Anythin ya see that's good eatin,

let me know, cause these fields could be somebody watching. They
know some hungry soldiers and slaves is passin by here and they got
guns. I don't want none of ya'll hurt nor killed . . . and some of
these white folks poor as we is . . . almos."

At last they lay down to sleep. Listening, in the warm, quiet
night, to the birds and other small creatures preparing themselves to
sleep or hunt for the night. Gradually they each closed their eyes
and all slept soundly from the long labor of walking. The moon
slowly crossed over these poor and ragged bodies, pressed close
together, not only for warmth, but for the need to have someone
who cared, near. Molding themselves into a family.

Before the sun came tipping up over the earth, Mor was up, as
usual, pacing the woods to see what was around there. He checked
his traps, skinned the rabbit and one squirrel, cleaned them and put
them on to cook, then woke the others up. They ate, cleaned and
packed up the little they had unpacked and hit out for the road
again. Hot water with a drop of molasses for tea, a cold piece of the
corn bread and a hot piece of meat and they were off again.

Mor spoke to them all, but mostly to Lifee. "Three day and we
ain't no more than to Shreveport, Lousana!"

Lifee smiled at him, said, "Well, we got this far and we still
living, so . . ."

"Wheah we goin anyhow?" Abby asked as she pushed forward,
frowning.

Lifee put her hand on Abby's shoulder and said, "Trying to find a
home, is all."

So the little group kept walking on steady and quietly through
the back side of the town. Soon they came to a river they didn't
know the name of that ran by Shreveport. There were people standing along the docks. The white people of the town and country gave
Mor's group fearful looks of hatred. They were poor and didn't have
anything else to do but stand around and talk about hard times and
"Gawd damned negras!" Most times they let the ex-slaves pass on
through because they were not sure how far away the Yankees were.

It was very clear, however, that ex-slaves were not wanted here in this small place of poor whites.

Mor and the others did not pause long by the river. He asked a colored man with a boat for safe crossing and was given it in exchange for some cornmeal. The man wanted more, but Lifee had seen to it they looked as poor as they were supposed to be. When the man asked for more, Lifee told him, "You see we got these chilren here starvin . . . and a old mother walkin with no food in her belly."

The man looked at Meda and Luzy, spit in the river and said, "Them gals ought to be marryin off and be wit they own husband." He had an eye for Meda.

Mor stepped in front of the women, said, "We just wants ya to help us cross this here river. We's gon plan our own life, please suh."

As the bedraggled group began to get into the boat, the slim brown girl, Ethylene, ran toward them, hollering, "Lifee! Mor! If ya'll gon get on that boat, I'ma lose ya'll. I can't walk that river. And I an't got nowhere to go!"

"Ethylene!" Lifee breathed. Abby reached out for the girl, saying, "Ethylene, chile! Wheah you comin from?" At the same time Lifee asked, "Where you come from? Did we pass you?"

Breathless, Ethylene hugged Abby. "No'm, I been followin behind ya. I wasn't gon stay back there on that plantation! I'm tired of bein chase and grabbed. I ain got no chillen and I don know my mama and daddy since I was a baby chile. So I follow you and Abby. I trusts ya'll. And Mor. I AIN GOT nowhere to GO!" She had begun to holler in her desperation. "I'LL WORK!"

The boatman spoke up as he looked Ethylene over. "Well, ya'll got to come on now, cause yo not payin nothin like it is." He nodded at Ethylene. "That one cost ya a little more now."

They all looked at him because he was a Negro man, but he didn't seem to want to help them. He kept talking as Ethylene got in when Mor beckoned. The boatman pointed at her, "That there one sure is big nough to marry. Get in, girl! I got to get this here boat cross this here river!" They all got in, all asking questions at once.

Ethylene explained. "I been sleepin close up to where you been sleepin. It was sho scary. I knowed snakes was out there!"

Of course Abby asked, "What you been eatin, chile?"

"Been takin. Fruits and seeds and berries. I's hungry now."

They laughed, but not much, because they knew what she had gone through. She looked tired and worn, young as she was. The boatman liked what he saw, though he knew it wouldn't do him any good. Mor was a man's man and this looked like his family.

The boatman had his own family to worry about, so he took the two cups of cornmeal and hid it so the poor whites on the other side would not take it from him when they looked to see what he was paid for the crossing. "Tell em you din't gie me nothin!" he told Mor in a low voice. He didn't have to explain anything because Mor knew what he meant.

The little group got off the boat keeping their heads down to avoid eye contact because white men didn't like that, walked hastily by the white men standing around. One of the white men asked, "Ya'll ain't not stoping here, is ya? Cus they ain't nothin for ya'll here."

Mor answered as he walked, "Naw suh. We's goin on lookin for our fambly if we can find em." After they had gone a little way, Mor stopped. "We's in Lousana now. What way we goin, to get where ya wants to go?"

The moist heat made the air thick and sticky. Lifee wiped her brow before she answered. "I blive it's a day or two to Monroe, then I think we'll be in Mississippi. We got to go straight across there, cause to go North is Arkansas and I don't know nothing about it."

Mor started walking again. "I does. I done heard some mighty mean things bout Arkansee. Say they the po'est, meanist people in the land."

Lifee, following him, said, "Well, let's face Mississippi. It's poor and mean, too, but maybe long as we just passing through." Meda, close behind her, asked, "When's we gonna get pass all these here mean white folks, Aunt Lifee?"

Lifee laughed softly, "You might not ever get pass them, chile. They everywhere."

Luzy, usually quiet, spoke, "Not up North."

Lifee answered with a sigh, "Even up North. Everywhere."

Abby, who now used a walking stick Mor cut and carved for her, said, "We wastin breath. Let's us get on up this here road. I wants to unpack, eat and set down a month!"

So the straggly little group continued their journey. It was starting to rain even in the sunshine, but the clouds were fast covering the sky. Some of them were dark clouds, menacing. It looked like a storm brewing.

They knew they were in Louisiana, but they didn't know anything about this part of the state. It was backcountry. They covered themselves as best they could from the sudden wind. Mor tried to lead them as far forward as possible along the road as his eyes desperately searched for a likely place to wait out the rain.

Lifee, the only one who knew anything about Louisiana, hollered through the wind, "It won't last long, you all, these Louisiana storms pass over quick."

Mor was looking for high ground under trees, to protect them and their belongings. His walk picked up speed. Raindrops were falling randomly, not started good yet.

A great rumble of thunder rolled angrily across the whole sky with a silver bolt of lightning punctuating the end of the rumble. In a moment there was another deep rumble, then another. Then a bolt of lightning shot across the whole sky, brightening the day that had become darkened. The great shaft of silver brightly lighted the waving trees, and Mor decided to take his chances on the next likely looking place. His rag shoes were coming apart, dragging in the muddied road. He stopped, reaching back for Abby's cart, pressing her forward. "Go on, ya'll. Ya knows what to look for! I's tot'in these here things fo ya! Go on!" But, still, even pulling two carts he managed to stay in front, desperately seeking shelter.

Then, around the curve in the road, there was a bit of high ground under a nest of trees. Mor pointed and directed and walked all at the same time. He pulled the two carts over the bumpy course. The weeds and thickets, now wet, slowing his and everybody's progress, cutting at their bare feet and ankles. The girls wanted to stop under the first trees, but Mor waved them on, hollering, "We got to get back from the road! We too close! Keep on, keep on goin!"

A little farther on he reached a place he was satisfied with, and a good thing it was, because then the clouds let loose and all wet hell came down. Mor had carried his four lean-to posts with him for sleeping nights, and now he hurried and hammered them down into the ground. Abby, Ethylene and Life were tearing branches from the trees for the shelter top. Then Mor was placing the carts in a drier place for their protection. Then they were all huddled under the shed of branches. They were wet, but they were in a dry place. First the trees sheltered them, then their awning of branches covered their shared warmth.

Mor had brought the oven he had built for Life. He rambled til he found it, it wasn't far because they hadn't brought that much except tools. He made a fire in it. "Cause we got to eat! Mayhap we be here all the day if'n it stay dark and all night if the rain keep up!"

"Can't set no traps. Won't have no meat."

"Tha's okay. It been like that befo."

"Watch out for snakes!" The young girls jumped and hollered out at these words.

"Oh, Lord! Yes!" And somehow, everybody laughed as they fanned the smoke from the fire away.

As the little fire burned and the caught rainwater boiled, the cornmeal fried and the fat drops of rain fell harder. The sky resounded with another long, clapping flash of lightning, and the deep rumbling of thunder was almost frightening there beneath the trees. Abby worried a bit about the flour and cornmeal remaining in the cart. Mor worried about lightning striking the trees, but the warmth of the little group that was his family made his mind turn to other thoughts. He was thinking, "Yessir, I got a fambly now, but I ain't worrin bout nobody sellin em off way from me. So you jes go on, ole cloud and sky, make all the roar ya wants, we can live right on." They lost time all that day, but the rain stopped sometime during the night and they were up the next morning before the sun and were on their way.

The earth was sparkling beautiful as they passed over the road. The rain had opened everything up and the sun came out shining brilliantly on the branches of dripping leaves and the birds that swooped through the air. It was a good day except for the little muddy gulches they had to walk through pulling the carts, but Mor was strong and they made it with no mishaps.

They went through some little villages people called towns, but there were so many travelers looking just like them, nobody noticed or cared if they did notice. From other traveling freed slaves they learned that those among them who should worry were young black men because they were being kidnapped and stolen by white men to be taken to work as prisoners on some farms. Already. Especially where there were no Yankee soldiers nearby to enforce the new laws. White men found it hard to let the "worthless" darkies go. White men needed their worthlessness too much.

That night, after they had found their place to sleep, Mor immediately set out his traps, and while he fished in a nearby stream, an hour or so, the traps had caught several small animals. They all helped in the skinning and cleaning of the small animals and the scraping of fish, then Abby and Ethylene put the meat in the stream to keep it cooled until they cooked it to preserve it while they traveled. They tried to eat it fast during the days, before it could sour and turn poisoned on them.

Abby fussed over her homemade oven, the food smelling good all through the woods. They hoped it didn't attract the wrong things, like people. "I damned should'a brought me more salt. Could'a cured this here meat enough to last a little longer."

Mor, always working, was also taking strips from oak trees and others special to him for making baskets. Baskets for holding anything and baskets for catching fish. He had found he could sell these cheaply in the little villages they passed through. He could also make brooms and many other things, to make some money to support his family along the way. Lifee was proud of him. Meda and Luzy asked to be taught to make these things as well, and their lessons helped to while away the evening hours til sleep, and it helped to make a living.

The days were very hot, and since it was July, the nights were almost just as hot. It made everyone a bit cranky. Abby fussed all the time as she stirred her pots, about all the things she hadn't brought. Lifee told her, "Well, Abby, you brought everything you could and the pots and pans, spices, cornmeal and even some flour."

"It's almos gon."

"We gon get some more," Mor said quietly.

Lifee added, "We're going to get some more of everything you need." And Abby would smile, shake her head and wipe the perspiration from her face. But she was not unhappy.

As they crossed Louisiana, almost into Mississippi, there seemed to be more devastation of the land. Many plantations were decaying from neglect, some had been partially burned, some were burned to the ground. Houses that belonged to the not-so-wealthy whites were dilapidated and rotting away because their soldier-father or son was gone. Those who still lived in them wore soiled and ragged clothes. They looked starved. They followed travelers with hungry eyes. Those who had always been poor anyway just sank deeper into the pit of poverty. But, still, they remembered. They, now, had no one beneath them over whom to feel legally superior. They had nothing to use for their superiority except for their color, and they

clung to that fable with twisted, curving, dirty-fingernailed hands.
The tobacco- and liquor-filled mouths of many bitter old men
spewing lies and filth about the "nigras."

The wealthy had fled, the poor were scrounging to survive. Hate
and blame were plainly written on their faces. They blamed the
freed slaves for their misery. The poor had been poor and dejected
before the slaves were freed, but it seemed they didn't want to carry
the blame for that themselves. If they blamed the freed slaves, it
relieved them of responsibility for their own lack of ability to do
better. It gave many of them a reason to hate and kill, rape and
torture.

The Yankee soldiers were becoming more common now, and
they kept the ex-slaves safe as they could, but they had no real taste
for this business and were tired and wanted to go home to their own
states and families. Even the air in Mississippi seemed to carry the
taste of dejection, misery and hate. Tension, and fear, were in every
breath taken by all the freed slaves.

On the last night before crossing into Mississippi, they came
upon a high slope of land beside the beautiful, flowing river. Its
shores were crowded with people, most white and some black. Most
all were poor, but some were carpetbaggers, gamblers and prosti-
tutes, all white. They didn't have colored whores or whorehouses at
all in the South . . . then. Most Negro women had had enough of
sex and babies and men they did not want, from slavery. If a Negro
woman sold herself, she was starving . . . or couldn't get away.

Mor's little group looked so bedraggled and poor, they were
hardly given a glance. Lifee had wrapped herself, Abby and Ethylene in rags, even though their regular clothes were hardly better.
She kept in her mind the gold and silver she had on her body. "I
must not attract even Negro attention." The girls were wrapped in
rags, too, and Lifee was looking for some boys' clothes for them
because their bodies were entering puberty and it showed that place
between a woman and a child which is so appealing to some men.

The young girls were tired and hungry and wanted to stop, but

Mor urged his family on. He knew it was not a safe place to be, much less to sleep . . . or show a piece of food. There were fights breaking out among those who were drinking, and that included almost all of these shouting, staggering, tobacco-spitting people. The soldiers were none too patient with the white brawlers or the colored few around the edges of the gambling circles, running errands for their current chosen mas'r. "We freed ya! Galdammit! Go!" the soldiers said to the black lackeys who grinned and replied, "Us's got to eat, boss!"

There was no sheriff there, just Yankee soldiers. The sheriff was off with the deposed plantation owners, planning a way to get the slaves and the fields together again. They breathed heavy over words like "Equal!! My lilywhite ass! Them hotdammed northuns are plumb crazy!! But this here war ain't ovah! It's mor'n one way to skin a blackass coon!"

Mor and his new family had been on the hot, sometimes muddy dirt roads several weeks now. Sometimes in the same day, they were smoldering hot one minute and then soaking wet from the sudden storms the next minute. The heat of the sun was not abating yet. It was a wonder, thank the Lord, they had all not gotten sick from sunstroke or walking pneumonia.

The food Abby and Life had hoarded and rationed was almost gone. Mor had kept them going with the little money he made from his baskets and the crude brooms he made during the nights or on a rain-filled afternoon. The young girls were tiring quicker and were more often hungry and irritable.

Around that time Life began to look for her monthly period which she realized now had not come for at least six weeks. Mor and Life had not tried to make love since the trip began. Respect for the older women and fear the young girls would see and know, kept them from doing what they wanted to do. They touched in passing, hugged quickly before sleep and looked up often to catch the other looking at them "that way," but they chose to wait. They had seen, and never liked, the way the white Master had indulged himself sometimes with no care to the others around, like they were invisible. They respected each other. They would wait until they were truly alone.

Lifee was not upset as she realized she was pregnant, just sorry she was on the hard road and not even hardly at the end of the journey. She wanted a child, just didn't want it on the road. She looked across her mind to North Carolina, thinking, "It's a long way. Two babies walking and one on the way. Know where we going, don't know what's there for us. Can't spend no money, or even take it out, bringing attention to us. Robbers or just plain poor white folks who think taking from a colored man ain't stealing. And now, even poor, hungry Negroes are stealing from other poor Negroes." Aloud, she said, "Mor? You think we should keep on as long as we're able?"

Mor answered in his low voice, "We sho ain't not gon stay here. And we ain't nowhere yet noway. Let's us find us some Negro people and ask em what's round here. I would like to keep goin on. Heard some bad things bout Missip-pi. What you think, Mz Abby?"

Meda, Luzy and Ethylene, exhausted, were sprawled out over the grassy little clearing. Abby slowly chewed on a blade of grass for a moment, then said with a tired sigh, "What's the nex state gonna be, Lifee?"

Lifee laughed softly, said, "Alabama."

Mor laughed a little in return, "Oh, Lawd, I's heard some things bout Bama, too."

Still laughing, though it was laughter mixed with apprehension, Lifee said, "Not going to be no good places for Negroes for a couple thousand miles, maybe not then either . . . but some are better than others. Let's do like you said, Mor. Walk til we find us somebody to give us the way of the land."

So they commence to walk across Mississippi!

SIX

Time was passing, seasons beginning to change. The foliage and trees were turning to the glorious golden-red and brown colors of autumn. The land was beautiful, as Louisiana had been in the height of summer colors. They continued to choose the lesser used back roads because the main roads were full of wagons and people, including many ex-slaves, hungrier and poorer than even they were. They were still full of the joy of freedom even though they did not know where they were going to sleep in the night. Many still walking and seeking kin. A few had found some one or two of their kin. These people were the happiest. Others, pitifully frowning, still looking, with little hope.

In foraging for food and places to camp, they came across the dead sometimes. Killed by robbers or just wretched white hatred. Night riders. For these whites had almost always been even poorer in Mississippi than other states and had resented the slave that happened to be fed, sometimes, and clothed, sometimes, but was now free, as whites were. No more their tangible evidence of Negro inferiority.

Here, also, were often carcasses of cattle swollen and dead by the side of the road. Thin, rib-showing dogs ran in packs, searching for something, anything, to eat. It was a scavenged land. Buildings burned, stores boarded up, closed. Only a few taverns were open with stragglers sitting on benches in front, glaring at the world.

One night, exhausted, just over the border of Mississippi, they came across a dead man near a stream. His pockets had been turned out and his already ragged shirt ripped open, pants pulled down and his testicles slashed off. The little group shuddered as they looked at the poor dead man. They knew he had done nothing but be black. His packed hankerchief, tied to a stick, lay ripped apart not far from his body. A half-eaten can of beans had rolled, or been thrown, near the small burned feet. You don't stop to eat near anywhere you have raped, killed or robbed. He had been innocent. But some people like blood, love somebody else's pain, they love to kill.

After a few more moments of stunned silence, Mor said he would dig a grave for the man and began searching for his shovel in the cart. While he looked, Lifee bent down to remove the man's clothes. She said, "He will have to be buried naked." Abby bent to help her. Luzy and Meda stared at them in horror. Ethylene asked, "Why? Let that man be!"

Lifee answered as she worked. "We gonna move farther up this way about a mile and wash them over in this stream, then I'll sew up this here shirt and in the morning they'll be dry, and you"—she looked at Ethylene—"are going to wear them. You are too young and pretty a woman and you are going to draw attention we don't want. Mor and I talked about you last night, and we had already planned to try to get you some men's clothes since I am not able to make them right now."

Mor spoke as he dug the shovel in the ground. "Now, this here man is dead and he not gon need nothin no more. If he goin to the Lawd, the Lawd care bout his inside heart. If he gon to the debil, the debil don care nothin bout nothin of hisn nohow."

Bustling around, Abby looked at the girls, "Let's get to washin these here clothes! All o' us!"

Mor stopped them, saying, "No, we wait til we gets up stream a mile or two and gets set for the night. There be plenty nough light. Don want to spend too much time here. They might come back."

The next morning when the little group started out there were two men, an older woman and a middle-aged woman and two children trying to look younger. They planned it. For safety.

They walked the whole day and were just above Jackson, heading East to Alabama. When they reached Alabama the land, the people and even the weather seemed even more ravaged by the war. It was a dry, arid land. Even the air was dry. There were fewer wagons and no carriages on the roads, but they didn't expect to see many anyway because they took the small, less-traveled roads in order to avoid as much people traffic trouble as possible, as usual.

The local people were surly and angry, as well they should be, because Alabama had caught a lot of the war and had lost many of its native sons as soldiers, and some civilians. Families were moving to get away from the Southern blood soaked into the Alabama ground. Maybe blood of their own children, family and friends. And if the whites had nothing, the blacks had even less and there was no work. All the very wealthy had gone back to where they mostly stayed anyway, East and West and even Europe.

Everyone was tired, tired to their bones. But to cover more ground, Mor and his family group started walking earlier in the darkness of morning and walked later into the night. They ate what fruits or vegetables they could find along the roads and in fields that had already been picked. They wanted to avoid making a fire in the nights to avoid attracting unwanted attention. Nights were still warm enough in late summer not to need one. It still took almost four weeks to cross Alabama. They didn't even know when they got to the Georgia state line.

They found a place near a creek to set camp for the night. Mor made a fire and Abby set her little three-leg pot over the fire, filled it with water from the brook, which was clean and clear though you could hear the frogs croaking in it. They had four white potatoes between them. Mor went with his fish basket and his fish stick (a board prepared with long nails to slap into the water for fish) to try to catch some meat. He set his traps for any small animal he might catch, but he had no bait. "May I gets a little piece a that potato, Mz Abby, mam?"

Abby shook her head in despair. "Well, I guess ya got to try, but if you don catch nothin, we still got enough for everbody to have a piece of tater in a bowl of water soup. Salt's all gone, but I got some hot peppers here. I can scrape this bag for a mighty small corn cake. But, Lawd, Lawd, we down to the bottom."

Lifee thought of her gold and silver hidden in her clothes. "I am going to have to think of something. I cannot let my family starve. And this baby in my belly is bout twelve weeks now, trying to grow. This is the end of September and we made love just before July, I think. Then we left the plantation. Lord, it doesn't seem like it been almost three months getting cross three states." She mused a moment on the last, long time ago they had made love, smiling to herself. "We got to get to someplace of our own pretty soon. This baby won't even know he got a father!" Then her stomach growled and brought her back to her problems. "Lord, this water soup is not enough for none of us. And not enough people have money to pay for baskets and brooms. Oh, Lord, I can't be so dumb I can't think of a way to get something to eat for us and I have gold and silver, too. Sometimes, I wish we could eat it."

Lifee turned to see Ethylene and Abby piddling over the little bits of food. Ethylene spoke softly, "I be willin to give my share up for the younguns."

Abby answered her kindly, "You is nice to think so, but we don't need no sick people round here. We all be just as hungry tomorra again. You starvin extry for one day don't help nobody."

They all heard twigs breaking and turned to look for Mor returning, but it wasn't Mor. A fierce-looking man walked toward Abby, and behind him, as though it were a shadow, was a shorter figure.

"Oh, my God, you scared me!" Lifee spoke first.

The man spoke gruffly, "What chu'all got here? A bunch of womens and one little man!" He looked at Ethylene. "Ya bett not move, suh, I gots me a gun! What in that there pot there?"

No one answered him. The shadow behind him said nothing. The man saw their fear and walked to the pot. Said, "Gie me some of that."

Abby answered him, "It ain't done yet, sir. We just set it on . . . and we got chilren here we got to feed."

The man laughed a hungry, tired laugh. "I'm gon eat first and last. I ain et in two days." He turned to his shadow-like friend. "Come on, get yo some, lessen I eats it all!"

They were all surprised to hear a woman's voice from the other stranger. "I ain't gon steal these poor people food! That a ole lady there and these is two chillun." Her voice rose with anger, "This ain what you promise me when ya took me from my house. Ya ain said you was no robber!"

The man's voice raised, also. "Damn yo! Ain ya hungry?"

The woman answered, raising her voice more. "Sho, I's hungry! Didt ya eat my last bean two days ago? But I ain stealin from old colored folks and chillun! And I blives that woman is havin another baby!"

The man turned back to the pot. "Don ya pay no mind to her clapper mouth. I got me a gun and I's gonna use it, too! Iffn ya don gie me that there food!"

Suddenly the strange little woman ran, screaming as she jumped on the stranger-man's back, flailing her arms at his head until he was down to his knees, shouting, "Get off me! Ya crazy!"

Ethylene had run behind the man, ducking the blows as she felt for a gun in his pocket. "He ain't got no gun!"

Relieved, Lifee ran to stop the little woman beating his brains out. He was crying from anger and hunger. The woman stood back puffing hard and rolling her eyes at the man.

In the midst of all the furor Abby took a little cracked bowl from somewhere and put a piece of potato and some soup in it and gave it to the man. "Here. Ya'll take this, we share with ya. And ya'll go. Don't come back, please. We ain got nothin. Ya can see we poor as you cept for this pot of potato and water."

The man reached for the bowl, the woman took it away from him. "Don't give him yo last food! I see he a stealer and a stealer is always gonna find somethin to eat. Yo chillun needs this." She poured it back in the pot.

Abby stood up straight, "Lissen here, young woman, this my pot. I won't let God see me leave no man hungry if I got vittils to eat. Now! Hand this to that there man." It was one less slice of potato and the woman handed him the bowl.

Lifee said, "Take it with you. Go. Please."

The woman put her hand on her hip. Said, "I ain goin with him. We sposen to get married, but I ain marrying up with nobody is no stealer! I'ma stay right chere tonight and tomorry I'll go my way to my own house."

Then Ethylene said to the man, "Then go on. Go! She ain goin with ya! And gimme your belt fore ya go!"

The woman, glad to do something to defy the man she had been engaged to, went to him and loosened his belt. He didn't say a word. "Ya wants this belt? Take it, it blong to ya now!"

The man, through with the soup, left, saying, "I's sorry. I din want to robber ya'll, but I's hungry."

Lifee hollered after him, "Why take from us who have nothing? There's somebody out there with something, but I bet they're white and they got a gun. Just go." Then he was gone and he left with the bowl.

The woman drew closer, saying "My name Mema."

They all said, "Howdy, Mz Mema." Because they all liked her, their voices were welcoming. Lifee added, "Sit on down with us and tell us about Alabama, please."

Mema, smiling, answered, "I don know much on it, but I tell ya what I knows. Sides, ya just bout out'a Bama. I tell you what I knows bout Bama and Georgia." And she did.

Mema had been a slave for most of her life and had been on her own since freedom came. She was lively, very intelligent without knowing it, with a sense of humor to match. "I don know my lifetime age, nor my birth date, nor my mother, nor my father, nor any sisters and brothers I got, nor where I come from to Al'bama. I just don know nothin! I has lost two chilluns to slavery. Ain never really been married in no way. I loves love and aims to find some." Mema had a good and generous heart. She was not the type to hide her sorrow and pain inside herself. "I loves chillun." She broke off a blade of grass thoughtfully, then proudly said, "I name m'self." She tore more grass from the earth. "I can sho nuff cook. I know my letters, but I can't read yet. I's lookin for my chillun, but I don know whichsomever ways to go. So I'ma look for a fambly on my way." Somehow the small group knew she could be trusted and in that moment, Mema had a family. She would become one of Lifee's best friends.

"I lose my first lil baby when they need me to feed the mistress baby. Was a sickly, lil sweet girl baby. Then she say she don want her baby to feed after no black negra baby mouth, so they taken my baby away and I cry so . . . They sell him, they say, so I can't see him and be upset, lose my milk, they say." The words were drawn out long, like a song, and you could hear the tears in her voice. Mema sniffed her nose for the dribble from it, then wiped it with the back of her hand. She continued in a low voice, "I want to kill they baby, but I cou'nt, cause she so sweet and she so little." She took a deep breath and her voice rose again, "So my milk came back down and I nurses her and she grow up fine." Her voice softly fell again and the tears almost come back and her nose begins to run again; she does not wipe it away this time, she forgot to feel it. "But . . . my baby gone."

The little group knew about all these things, had seen all these same things, over and over, but they were spellbound by Mema. It was like she was handing them her heart and they were all leaning over it examining the pain all the grown ones knew so well, whether it be baby, mother, father or husband.

Mema continued talking as if in a trance. Her voice was as if it was in wonder at her own life. She spoke as she looked at the top of the trees waving over them. "The nex baby I borned, the mistress have one again, too, and she gon do the same thing to my new baby, but this time I damn don care if'n they kill me, I wasn gon feed no baby but my littl baby girl. But . . . they dint kill me. She tole em cut my milk titties off, so they got one off, befo the mas'r stop her. Said she cut his money away. But she sol my baby anyhow, say to teach me a lesson. So I had two chillun and two titties, so I lost two chillun and one tittie. So . . . now . . . I got one tittie to feed with and nothin to feed."

Mema came out of her trancelike self, took another deep breath and said, "I's still lookin for my chillun, walkin up and down these here state lands. Ain found em yet, still lookin yet." Mema stood up and walked to the fire where the pot of food was. She pulled some shelled peanuts out of one pocket and a small bag of cornmeal from the other. "Here ya'll, add this in yo pot, cause I's stayin for supper."

Abby reached for the bag, smiling, "Let's us just keep this for the mornin cause we got to plan for tomorra. Let's us see what Mor comes back with."

Mema looked surprised. "Who Mor?"

The voice surprised them all. "I's Mor," he said as he stepped into the circle of light. "Who you?"

"I's Mema and I just found yo fambly tonight." She turned to the others. "But, yo know, ya'll, ya shouldn't not be out here in the woods open like this. It's snakes a-plenty out here! Big ones, little one and plenty poison ones, on the ground and in these here tree branches, too!"

All the women stood up, looking alarmed. Mor said, "We just got chere. We don know nothin bout this country here. We got to stay by some water."

Mema laughed, "Got water snakes, too! Where ya'll goin to?"

Lifee was looking the ground over, "We looking for a home."

Mema laughed lightly, "Ain us all?"

No one answered. Abby took the skinned rabbits from Mor, pointed to Ethylene and said, "Wash these here and cut em up for to cook faster and let's put em in this here pot. It's boiling good."

Mema sat back down and, slowly, the others did, too, as Abby and Ethylene carried on over the pot and the rabbits. Mema talked as they worked.

"Well, I knows round here pretty good and I got a place I stay in. It's a nice little piece up the road. When yous ready you can go there to sleep. I done cleaned it out of snakes and most the bugs, but the bugs come right back in if'n yo stays way too long."

Mor settling in, asked, "What bout jobs, work?"

Mema shook her head, "Ain no work here now. Most been plant and done been picked. Cept maybe all the cotton. Maybe some late plantin for winter. But, this a cotton state. We's call the Black Belt. Ya'll deep down south here. Where ya'll come from?"

Everyone answered, "Texas."

"Whoo-whee, that's a long way, ain it? And ya'll walkin!" Mema leaned over to taste the soup. "Oh, that's sho hot! Put a lil more salt in that, honey. Here." She reached into her pocket again and handed Abby an onion. "Put that in there, cause I's hungry, chile."

Mor was moving around putting his things away. "Well, I reckon we don need to sleep out here tonight. I wus worryin bout the snakes and I dint know what else out here."

Ethylene yawned and stretched, "Lord, I's tired. Another step an I—"

But Mor interrupted, "Tired and safe is bettern tired and sick or dead. We got to do somethin bout these chilren. We is walkin a long way now, a long time. They is tired. We all needs a bathin. We needs some time to be still and get ready for the nex part of this here trip."

Abby added, "That's right, chile. You chilren can go a lil bit more can't ya?" Everybody answered with ohhhhs and ahhhhs and "We gon eat first?"

Mor answered them, "Yea, we gon eat first. Fire hot, rabbits clean and cookin, won't be long. Let's pack everthin so's we can hit out after we wash dishes." Everyone began to move around putting their things together and complaining about the move, but they were secretly glad to be getting away from the snakes.

Mor spoke to Lifee, "Mayhap I can find some work round here. We needs the money. We low on everthin. Deep winter be here almos now. We can't walk these chilren through no snow. And yo neither."

After Mema had spoken of Lifee being pregnant, Lifee had told them all she thought she was. Now Mor asked, "How yo and my lil baby doin?"

Lifee smiled wearily, "Tired, but I feel fine. You are right. Abby could use some rest, too. You, too. I'll talk to Mema, see what's around here."

Mor rubbed her stomach gently, "I finds me somethin to do round here."

Lifee leaned into his hand, her body wanting him even though she was tired. She smiled, "I know you will, Mor."

Mema sidled over to Abby, saying, "Let me hep ya, honey. Uhhh, this sho smell good, chile! Should'a had some mo salt in my pocket, but I was so cited bout gettin married, I plumb forget bout it and left it home."

⌒〜

After they had all eaten and checked the little campsite to see what they were leaving behind, they hit the long, dusty road and walked over the state line and about a mile into Georgia.

Mema walked briskly, leading them to her shack as though it was a castle. Georgia's land was lushly green even though it was late fall. Tall trees blowing in the wind. There were the oranges, reds and golds among the leaves and foliage, but there were so many different hues of green spread throughout, it could only be described as gorgeous. Mema said, "It pretty up in there, but what you don't see is all them spiders and snakes crawling round on that ground."

As they passed a small, burbling creek, they could only hear it in the darkness. About a mile up a ways, Mema pointed, "Turn up in that there pathway. I's moved up from the Black Belt. Goin North a lil bit at a time, honey! Keep on going, up that there walkway, chile."

Meda and Luzy asked, now and again, "Is we there yet? Is we almos there?" No one laughed because they understood it was dark in these unfamiliar woods, and it was scary not knowing where you were stepping.

They all had the thought "warm home" in their minds. But, home to them, except Lifee and Abby, was a shack of one or two drafty rooms sitting on the plain ground, outside privy, smoky fireplace, crude wooden shutters and doors, no glass windows, just holes, no boards inside, chinks in the walls, cornshucks, chicken feathers or maybe, now and then, a cotton-filled mattress on the dirt floor. So they weren't thinking of anything grand when they thought "home." When they finally trudged into Mema's shack they were neither surprised nor dismayed that it was just like all the other shacks everyone but Lifee had known as home.

Mema went straight to the fireplace to make a fire because it was cold in the little shack. "They got a bigger house back a ways, and I don take that. These here people been gone these two years pas, but if they come back here, I don want em to move me out too soon, so I took over this shack only."

Mor took over the firemaking as Abby and Lifee went about pulling out their bedmakings. Abby, looking around the room, said, "This here fine for now. We gonna look for our own." Lifee thought to herself, "Who said we were going to stay round here? Maybe just enough time for them to rest awhile is all I can see."

Mema bustling around, clearing here, moving something there, said, "I can show you round here. Ya'll got to be careful though, cause they's restin mens for prison-jail labor camps. Ya don need to do nothin bad neither, they makes things up on ya! And they don pay ya nothin." She bent to help Mor, "I done cut more wood outside what will hold us for tonight, but we gon have to cut some more in the mornin."

Abby sat on the floor, "Prison? Camp? Work? Lawd, theys tryin to keep slavery."

They were laying out the small room and taking places to sleep. They put the children close to the fireplace. Meda and Luzy were already half asleep on top of their blankets. Abby didn't bother with their nightly baths, because she didn't know the water situation in this new place and it was cold and dark outside the little glowing shack.

When Mor went out so the ladies could get undressed, Mema waited for Ethylene to go out, but when Ethylene started to undress, Mema said, "Wait a minute there, ya man! You cannot undress yoself in here like that! We . . ." The laughter stopped her. They had forgotten she did not know Ethylene was a woman because of the men's clothes and Ethylene being so quiet.

Lifee said as she laughed, "That ain't no young man, that's a young woman. We put her like that to keep her from being raped or stolen."

Mema finally laughed, saying, "Laaaawd! And I's justa tryin to walk cute front of him. I needs a husband! I's tired of bein alone and strugglin by myself."

"Well, we got to get you another one."

Finally, the people lay drowsily back, inside of four walls, such as they were, for the first time in what seemed like years.

Lifee liked Mema. But she didn't know whether to trust her or not. She had placed her own pallet close to Mema so they could talk quietly as the others slept. Mema was wide awake from all the excitement of company in her little, usually lonely shack. She smiled in the dark. "Maybe I has a fambly for today after all."

Lifee whispered, "Is this, Georgia, your original home?"

Mema whispered back, "My riginal home?"

Lifee smiled, "Were you born here, in Georgia?"

Mema laughed lightly, "I wish I could talk like you do. I's gon hear ya very much and pretty soon, I's gonna talk like you do. Naw, I was born somewher I don know. I been sold bout three, two, five times. I can't count, but I's this many fingers." She held up three fingers. "I been in Bama, Missippi, Kentucky. I likes Kentucky the most, but I lost my two chillun in Missippi. I blive they in Georgia, so . . . now I am here. I been here bout six months, this many." She held up three fingers. "I ain't find em yet. But they don't know me no way. They was litty, bitty babies. If I'd know they was goin to get em and sell, I'da killed my babies, or I'da run. But they daddy, was one on each one, and they couldn't help me. We all cried, but I the onliest one who fought, cause they'da killed a negra man."

Lifee moved closer, asking, "How do you live?"

Mema thought a minute, "Like you. I eat, I sleep. It's so many of these here empty house and shacks, ya can pick which en ever you wants. And I makes friends. Like you."

"Aren't you scared?"

"O what? I done been a slave . . . and lived. What's badder than that?"

"Being dead."

Mema took a moment to answer, "I blive in God in heaven. I don lie, ceptin to white folks and, God knows, you have to do that! I don steal, cept from the Lord's earth and He put that food in the ground and on them trees. I don cheat nobody. I jes leave em along and gets my own."

And Lifee began to trust Mema more; she already liked her quite a bit. She whispered, "I'm going to have a baby."

Mema breathed a sigh of pleasure. "Ohhhhhh."

Lifee continued. "Bout four months now. Gonna show pretty soon. Need some clothes."

"I see what I can do."

Lifee's voice rose a little, "I have a sewing machine."

Mema sighed in pleasure again, "Oh, Lawd."

"But we need a house."

"It's plenny of them."

"One of my own, our own, Mor and me."

"Well, if you don want to live in none of these here shacks round here, that gon take money. See, they cheap, but there ain no money round here."

"How cheap? What they got for jobs round here?"

Mema laughed a wry little laugh, "These white folks need everthin you can do, but then they cheat ya so bad, don nobody stay with em workin."

"We could work by the day. Mor could."

"If'n they let ya."

"If they don't let you, don't work but one day."

Mema nodded her head in the dark. "They find some way to fix it so ya don get no work and no house. No kind, not even them fallen-down ones."

Lifee was quiet a moment, finally she said, "So it's best to buy your own."

Mema nodded her head again, "Or be with somebody who can look out for ya. I's got a lady I wash for sometime. She a lone woman and she scared. A white lady, but she kind'a sickly and her husband didn come back from the war and she tryin to carry on, but she really want to go home to her fambly in North Caroline. She just ain got no money nough to go."

Lifee raised her head a little, "What kind of land is it?"

"Good land, look like to me. It ain been use for bout five years. Done built up."

Lifee lay her head back down. "I'd like ta talk to her."

Now it was Mema's turn to raise her head, "What yo gon do? Take my job?"

Lifee laughed a little, "No. I'm gonna try see can I work a plan to have a place to keep my family together in exchange for helping her work her land."

Mema started to answer, "That gon be . . ."

Lifee kept talking, "Then, if she want to go to North Carolina, she can go."

"But, she ain got no money."

Lifee smiled a little, "Well, maybe she will sell some land."

"She sho need the money, but who got some?"

Lifee hesitated, then said, "I have saved a little. Don't nobody know it."

Mema really raised her head and her whisper was almost shrill, "Yo got money? Union money?"

"Not much."

"Reckon it might not take much."

Lifee pressed her hand to Mema's shoulder. "I don't want to talk about it with anybody else til I talk to the white woman and I don't want you to tell her what I want to talk about."

Mema grunted, "Humph! She ain my true fren. But you almos is." It was quiet for a moment, then Mema continued in a lower whisper, "I sho hope ya ain gon try to farm none . . . cause the peoples here, white peoples, gon sho find a way to take all ya got. They done took everbody's everthin. Money to mules, gone. They lend yo seed and then ya looks up and the ground ain even yourn and in a year or two, ya deep in dept to boot!"

It was quiet for another little while, then Lifee said thoughtfully, "Nooo, I think I got a plan to work on that. We got plenty hands to work two fields, for our food and even cotton for our clothes. Abby and I both know how to weave and I think Ethylene does, too, and it's time the young ladies learned how."

Mema raised her head to ask, "You calls them chillun 'young ladies'? Ain that nice? Ain nobody ever all me a lady in my whole life! What else more you gonna do, Mz Lady?"

"We'll get a cow for milk and a few hogs and chickens, they'll grow. I don't want to depend on nobody."

Mema, dubious, "Well . . . mayhap you can make it, but ya gon have to pend on em for somethin."

Lifee, still thoughtfully, "I'll keep it low. We'll keep it low. You don't really have no home either."

"This my home, but, I ain got no home . . . naw. Never did have none in slavery neither. Could sell you anytime."

"Well, if we get a home, you have a home with us."

Mema, again, turned to Lifee in the dark. "Ya talk like some of them what been to school. It's purty. I can say some letters. I can read some letters, too. But I ain can put em suckers together."

Now Lifee spoke with pleasure. "I want to teach everybody."

"Ya can read?"

"And write."

With wonder in her voice, Mema asked, "An write? Ohhh, chile, yes, I hep you. Let's us get up and go on over there right now!"

Lifee laughed softly, "We both need to sleep. We'll go when I get my thoughts clear. I want to see the place first. See if it's right for what I'm thinking of." The last thought before Lifee slipped deeply into sleep was "Well, looks like we may be here for a while, til this baby comes, maybe. But, only for a while, cause I'm headin for the coast of North Carolina. I mean, WE'RE heading on for the coast of North Carolina."

SEVEN

The next morning all were up early, even Meda and Luzy. They wanted to see their surroundings and explore the empty Big House. Abby and Ethylene were patting and fluffing the beddings, Mema was preparing a breakfast of cornmeal mush, corn bread and syrup, and she had gone somewhere and even had a bucket of milk for the young girls.

"By this here evenin, I be done found somethin good for supper and Mor done set out his traps. These here woods is just full of critters running round hankering to be caught," Mema said as she stirred her pots. She turned to Life. "When yo due, chile?"

Life looked around at Ethylene and Abby because she hadn't discussed it with them yet, then said, "I'm three months now. I believe July, August and now September. It's due in March, I blive." She smiled and placed her hand on her almost flat stomach.

Mema laughed happily, said, "Well, I blive ya gonna change my luck. I'ma get round here and do a lil bit more work and get me a pretty good ole dress from somewheres; you knows them riches people left clothes in these ole houses sometime. I's gone make myself pretty and mayhap I find me a husband and a chile and make a fambly. Like ya'll done done. Yes, Lawd, I needs a fambly. I know I can least have one more baby, please Lord."

She opened the crooked window shutter and looked out of the hole in the wall that passed for a window. "Ya'll know it look like rain! Look at them black clouds up there! Well, that's alright, it ain gon snow for a mont or so yet. We can hold out jes fine."

Later, after they had eaten and slaked their hunger, the young girls were gone exploring again, Abby was beating out the blankets for the first time in many weeks and Ethylene, still dressed as a man, was helping her. Water was boiling in a pot over an outdoor fire for the washing. Mor was off setting traps. Lifee and Mema were in the shack alone.

Lifee spoke, "I got this one gold twenty-dollar coin and I need to change it for smaller money. But if I show it to the wrong person it's gonna be taken away from me, I swear, and I can't afford to lose it cause I got too many people to feed."

Mema nodded her head, "Ain nothin but federate money round here cept for one ole white man and he won't even pay it out for workers on his land. His son dint come back from the war yet. He got coins and such." She continued wiping the cracked bowls and dishes as she thought.

"There is one ole crazy white woman, she nice though. She from round here. Her husband marries her then when the war come, he too old to go, but he go anyhow. He go to war and she all alone. Her chillun died long time ago from the dipthrya and he still ain come back. I tell her he be back soon cause I's scared she lose her mind. She don know how to do with that land she got and can't get nobody to come work it nohow. And she ain got nothin what don need some mendin, house, clothes and everthin. I's gon ask her can you make a home there in change for yo and Mor doin some work. She oughter say yes, cause she sho ain got no friends left here to help her. If'n she don say yes, I got me another lady I works for sometime when she got money. Ah, she a young woman, but her husban ain come back neither and she want to go back to her home in Noth Car'lina. Name a' Mz Emmalee. She got bout seven slave shacks what is empty."

Lifee could only wait for Mema to decide who and where.

Mema put the last bowl away. "She kinda crazy like, be talkin to herself and all, like somebody in the house with her. I don hang round aft I get my chores done, if I do some. But I ain really fraid of her. She jes scared herself and don know what to do with all that land her husband got, is all! I don know is she got any money, but she could get that white man, Massa Wallace to change some for her."

"But she might keep it," Lifee said.

"Now, listen, I don know but I blive she got some he buried round there, her husband."

"Well, maybe I better go around there with you. I can sew. Got my sewing machine and all."

Mema was excited with her joy. "Lord, chile! Ya told me that last night. Yo own sewin machine!!"

"Yes," Lifee smiled, "and I am going to make you a dress, too, someday."

"Well, let's us get on way from here then! I go get some fresh water in to be heatin on this fire and then I's ready!"

While Mema was outdoors, Lifee removed one of the coins from the hem of one of her worn dresses. She washed in the last of the water in a pail. Mor came in from a search of the already rifled Big House. He had found a larger tub and more utensils and a few plates with fewer broken pieces. He had set his traps again with a little bait this time and had brought one of his fish traps in from last night.

Mema looked in the fish trap, said, "Ohhh, you done found my crawfish! I got some rice round here somewheres" (she knew where it was) "I put some on now so to cook good and slow with Abby watchin. I find us a tomato or two. Wish us had some flour for hot biscuits! I still got me some onions. Keeps em. I plants em!"

Lifee watched Mema as she bustled around the room. "You have to wash up, Mema, don't you? Before you go to fix food to put in our mouths? We can't afford to get sick now and you been round that diptheria. How long ago did those boys die from that?"

Mema put her hands on her hips and turned to Life, "Lookee here, you welcome here, Miz Mam, but don't not tell me what to do with my washin up! I's a grown woman . . . now . . . Ain no slave no more to tell what to do. I's the one helpin you!!"

Life was only slightly embarrassed. "Well, then, I know that. And I know you're helping us, but don't cook enough for us, we will cook our own, please, if you lend us some . . ."

Just then Abby came in the door, "I'm already washed up. I'll cook for all of us. I'm even already used to it. I don't want my girls or nobody else to get sick now."

Mema dropped the pot of rice and water with a clang on the woodstove. "Fine wit me! I hates to cook anyway! I hates all work right now! I is free!" She did a little dance around the room while Abby took the food over. But soon Mema took a clean rag and some homemade lye soap and washed her face and hands, wiped her legs and feet off, then she took the rag outside and dropped it in the boiling wash pot.

Later that morning Mema led Life to the house of Mz Emmalee. The land sat on the main road with the house set far back from the entrance to the land. The house had been burned on one corner because of a Yankee Lieutenant being overzealous until Mz Emmalee had pleaded with him with tears in her eyes because she had nowhere to go except home to Carolina and no money to get even there. His heart softened and he had the fire put out for the pitiful woman.

She still had the carriage, which had been a special wedding gift from her husband, a heady persuasion for marriage and leaving North Carolina. She still had the work wagon, but the horses, mule, the cows and all the hogs and chickens were gone. Spoils of war and hungry neighbors.

Emmalee was almost glad the livestock was gone. With no man and no money to hire any help, it was just too much work for a delicate woman. The fields seen from the road were filled with dried, stiff stalks of corn, long dead and dried, broken boles of cotton dotting the huge fields in the distance. All these fields had been sitting in this state of ruin for three or four years.

The house was not a fine house. Just a good wooden house made larger with the second story, the same floor plan as the first story. It was square and the builder had tried to make columns in the front, but they were now rotting with the help of carpenter ants. The porch slanted slightly to one side and you had to walk a bit uphill to the front door. Mema puffed her ample single breast out and walked to the door, saying, "I's free now. I goes in this way."

They waited a few moments for an answer, then Lifee said, "Maybe she isn't here right now." But Mema knocked again, said, "Oh, she here, chile. She just lookin out one of these here windows lookin at yo cause she know me, but she don't know you. She always take a long time. She a scared little thing." Mema peeked through the window. "I can go head and take ya by old Mz Tippydoe house though. She the old one I tole you talk to herself sometime. Oh! Oh! Here she come now."

The door opened and Mz Emmalee, with a frown on her face said, "Mornin, ya'll. What you here so early for, Mema? I ain got much work for you. I was waitin til I got enough to make it worth both our whiles."

"Oh, I want yo to meet Lifee here. Her husband and fambly is kinda new round here and they is lookin for work."

Mz Emmalee raised her eyebrows, "How come you to bring em here? You know I ain got the means to hire no family to be no help! And why you always come to my front door? I sure wish you to use the back door."

Mema waved her hand in the air and laughed, "Mz Emmalee, I knows you ain lookin for to pay everbody, but mayhap ya'll can work a plan and then ya both be helped." She reached out for Lifee and pulled her into the house as Mz Emmalee stepped back, frowning again.

Mema continued, "See, they needs a shack or two and you got you some of em out there in back. Then if they gets to stay here they be doin work to help. They ain lazy nigras, Mz Emmalee, they sho ain. They been cleanin up over to my shack even. Then, if ya see yo improvin round here, ya can pay em a little somethin do ya have it . . . sometime. They still be needin it."

Mz Emmalee didn't sit down or offer them to sit down in her parlor. She shook her head at Mema's words as Mema continued. "Sho is bad ya ain got no money and these damn Yankee done took yo horse and cow and all them hogs and chickens, cause if you could get more of em, her and her husban and they fambly could make this here place run, sure."

Now Mz Emmalee sat down, saying, "I'm not thinkin of this place. I'm thinkin of my old home."

Mema didn't hesitate a moment, "Oh, I know, mam, but ain no sense in lettin a good thing go bad, is it? Well, what ya think?" Then she looked at Lifee and asked, "What do you say for yo'self?"

Lifee stepped forward. "That everything Mema said is true. That we can make this a better place and clean it up and grow some food. I can make you what you need to get home and . . ."

There was a long minute or two of silence. Even Mema did not speak. Then Emmalee spoke, "When can you come and start? When do you want to move in them shacks?"

Lifee started to sit, then changed her mind. "Well, Mz Emmalee, we can come right now. I'll get everybody so we can clean up the shacks first." She was thinking other things to say to Emmalee, but they could wait until they had proved their value to her. "Then I'll be in to you to see what else you want me to do to help you in here.

This ain't no plantin weather, but Mor, that's my husband, can do what he can to get the land ready."

Mz Emmalee agreed, thinking that the land was just lying there and the shacks were just sitting there anyway. Maybe she could find some way to make enough money to get home with them there to help her. With all the free negras running round looking for work, all she had talked to wanted money. Here were negras wanting to work just to live there. "Well!" she thought. "They are so dumb sometime!"

After they looked over the shacks and around the yard a little, Mema and Lifee walked back to Mema's shack. They were both thinking. Lifee making plans, Mema trying to help.

"Ya still didn get yo money change yet."

Lifee answered, "But I think we have a home for a while and we can get off that road in this cold weather. The youngens are really tired, and I know Abby is, too. She is not as young as the rest of us."

They were walking fast because of the cooling weather and the cold hard ground. Lifee looked around at the deserted land they passed. She said, "Must be some food somewhere in all these dead ole fields. Some root food or fruit trees with something hanging on em. Mor going to see to the meat."

Mema's mind was running fast as a minute, but on another subject. She turned to Lifee, "I's gonna move, too. I's gonna move with ya'll. I don need to hide from her from doin all that work I can't do now, cause ya'll be there."

When they reached the shack and told the good news to Abby, Ethylene, Meda and Luzy, Mor was out hunting. He had fixed a few cracks in the house to keep the wind out and hung the door straight so it would close tighter. Mema frowned, "It's gettin fix and we movin."

They were all packed when he returned with a few skinned rabbits and another load of crawfish. Lifee hugged him, said, "We got a new home. A shack of our own on another plantation right on the main road." Mor eased his things down, putting his arm around Lifee, said, "I shoulda been the one done that."

Lifee hugged him again, saying, "No, no. You did right! You feeding us. We need food to keep going. You always do your part."

Abby and Mema echoed Lifee, "Sho do! You does yo part!" Abby added, "You the backbone of this here fam'ly."

Abby took the meat and started washing it to prepare. "Whilst ya'll finish packin, I'll cook these here, cause we don know what's at the other shack. We can eat whatever left tonight aft we gets our new shack done."

After the meal, which was hurried because everyone wanted to see what the new home would look like, they all checked again for their belongings. Mema, the last to leave, backed out of her little shack. "Bye, shack. I might be comin back to ya. Can't never tell!"

Packed, carted, full and getting sluggish tired, they struggled to arrive at the new shack about two miles up the road. There were few passersby and they made it by late afternoon. Few spoke that afternoon, as each was full of their own thoughts.

Abby broke the silence first, "Is we now gonna be makin this our home for sho?"

Mor answered, knowing everyone's thoughts, "Mayhap not, but we needs to be settled in befo snow time."

Mema always had a few words to put in. "Oh whee! I gots me a fambly! Come on ya'll! Let's us go faster!"

There were seven shacks, a smokehouse, a shed and a barn in back of the main house. Lifee had looked earlier and knew which shack she wanted for herself and Mor. They were going to be alone at last. Her body looked forward with all its unused passion. She was tired, true, but she had been thinking of such a time many times on the road in the last three months. She wondered at herself that she should feel that way, because sex was not something she had ever welcomed in her life.

Lifee wondered how she could feel the love she did for Mor. He was not educated, but she didn't ever expect to run into a colored man in the South who had had her education and travel experience. And Mor liked to learn, was interested in most everything. He wanted to learn to read and had already started with a letter here and there learned on the road with the others learning also. And best of all, he loved her and the baby growing inside her. He was a home for her. And when she remembered the way he made love to her, she blushed and smiled to herself. "Never felt like that in my life. It's love does that. It must be love." She rushed to try to clean out her shack and at least get the bed clean and made. It looked like more rain was coming. "Lawd, Lawd! Rain coming, too!" she whispered to herself.

Abby took one of the shacks to clean for herself, Luzy and Meda. Tired as they were, you could hear them singing thanks to the Lord as they washed walls and swept the dirt floors. Abby set her towels and pots out. Luzy and Meda aired the straw mattress after tearing it open, cleaning bugs out. Abby told them, "Wishin I had time to wash the cover. I will tomorra. It's too late today now."

Mema just swept into a shack, said, "I takes this un," and went to cleaning it up and setting her little personal things out.

Ethylene, quietly as usual, looked through what was left and finally selected one. "I's gonna be alone. Good! This'un mine, ya'll!"

They could feel the eyes on them from the windows of the main house, but that didn't bother them. They were used to being watched by white folks.

Mor filled the cracks and chinks in the ceilings with hard clay mud mixed with dried grass. Cleaned out the chimneys and made fires so they could try to keep warm as they worked and certainly as they slept. He patched up all the largest holes in the walls he could in all the cabins they were to use. The sky was darkening. "Gon get it better in time," he thought to himself. He smiled everytime he thought about being alone with Lifee. Together. "Nobody to see or hear!" And his hammer rang out louder.

Mema stood watching them after she swept her shack, then she went back in to wash things as they were doing, muttering all the time, "All this here work for nothin but to sleep in! Eh!" But, soon, she was singing in her low, throaty, deep voice. She would stop every once in a while to go look out at the others to be sure they were still there. "I gots me a fambly! A free fambly!"

It was dark when everyone was finished for the day. They were famished and Abby had all the remaining baked rabbit laid out on clean oilcloth and it was soon gone. Mor had caught seven squirrels and cleaned them. Abby smiled up at him as she took them from his hands. Mema said to them, "Now, ya'll let me clean em things, cause you, Abby, always cookin and, Mor, ya always catchin em. I got to do some work round here for my supper!"

They had all been smelling the good aroma of food and now discovered Mema had been cooking pinto beans all afternoon. Had squirrel meat in it, onion, salt and pepper and some wild mustard. It smelled good! They all wondered where she had gotten everything, but Lifee suggested that they would never know all the little places Mema got her supplies. "Just count our blessings and eat what she brings to us." They agreed.

Another small storm blew up that night, but they were all full and warmer. Abby, Meda and Luzy had their shack, Ethylene had her shack, Mor and Lifee had their shack, Mema had her shack. In the night Mema knocked on Ethylene's door with her bedroll and came in saying, "Ain no sense in we's bein here alone right now. Plenty time for that. We in another life now and ya got friens." They talked a very little as they looked into the fire. Ethylene hadn't wanted company, but after a while, she felt better somehow. She went to sleep to the safe snores of Mema.

Abby and her girls were snuggled together on the floor near the fireplace, snoring in each other's face until Meda got up and lay at the foot of the bed away from Abby snoring and their breathing in her face. She thought of going to Ethylene's shack, but loved Abby too much to leave her. Finally she went to sleep.

The next day Mor was up early checking for old tools in the barn and the shed. He found some hoes, shovels and even one plow along with some buckets and other implements of farm labor. They were all lined up when the others came out.

As the little group looked over the things, Mor told them, "Ain no need of tryin to clean up the land. Snow is bout to fall. But we can look around and see can we find anythin we can use for seed when the time come. I's . . . I'm gon set my traps now." After he set his traps he went to the main house to see what he could do there.

Mema was in the main house talking with Emmalee about all the things that they were going to do. Now Mor told Emmalee, "Make out a list for some them things ya need done round here and I see can I get em done, Mz Emmalee."

Emmalee was startled. With big, wide eyes, she asked Mor, "You can read?"

Mor laughed lightly, "No'm, but ya tell me what's on it and we will mark it off. And I wants to thankee for helpin my fambly."

"Oh. I surely wondered." Emmalee turned to the window. "I see ya'll got the cabins cleaned up."

Mor looked toward the window. "Had to get them shacks ready, we's in need."

Emmalee turned back to Mor. "Where ya'll from? What's yoah name?"

"Name Mordecai, called Mor. We from Texas."

Emmalee just stared at him, "Ya'll a long way from Texas, ain ya?"

"Well, mam, my wife, she a-headin East. But we's got younguns and they needs to be off the road in the cold of the winter."

Emmalee looked out the window again, said, "Ya'll can't clean up the land nor plant in the winter. I don't see what good ya'll gon do me for stayin in all them cabins of mine."

Mor didn't smile because he heard her words and their message. "Well, we be findin somethin to do to make a provement whilst we here."

Emmalee looked around the room as if she was exasperated. "Mmmmm. Well, I'll make a list, but ya'll look around and do what you see needs to be done outdoors and I will thank you not to steal things."

She started to close the door, but Mor spoke, "No'm, we not stealin from nobody. When we walks away, yo can look over the load we carry. It be the same load we come with. Sides, look like all could be stolen already gone."

Emmalee bristled, "The Yankees done that. They have ruined the whole world now. Everythin was better befo they came."

Knowing that was not true for the slaves, Mor turned to go, "Yes'm. Well, mam, I gets on to my work." The door slammed behind him.

Mor moved slowly down the stairs, returning to his "family," who were still bustling around the shacks, bathing and preparing food. Later they would go out around the land. Mor sizing the land up, stooping to hold a handful and let it sift through his fingers, trying to decide what to plant. He was really a livestock man, not a seed farmer, but he knew generally what to do because he had learned a little of everything needed to be self-sufficient in the country. All of America was mostly country. The others just looked at all the land, thinking of all the work they would have to do when spring came.

Mor spent the afternoon cleaning and sharpening the old tools. Cleaning the barn and shed out so no one would be surprised by a snake or other small critter trying to find a home for the winter. Then he tackled the smokehouse. "We's gon smoke some of these here rabbits and squirrels roun here and get us a different taste."

Mema went off and came back with a sack full of peanuts, more onions and more pinto beans in her pockets. Lifee laughed with pleasure, but said, "Now, listen here, Mema. Where you getting these things? We need to pay for some of this cause we don't want you gettin in any trouble."

"Oh, chile, I got friens! Ya'll ain met nobody roun here yet. It's some people go to my church. Everybody got a little somethin. White folks cheat em out the fair price for what they plants, so sometime it be best to eat em yo own self. They gives me some, I takes some."

Lifee shook her head, "No, no, you can't do that, Mema. They are poor people, just like us. Ain't got as much as we have, maybe. Don't steal from them."

Mema looked down at the floor sadly. "Ya always fussin at me and I hope after slavery, nobody fuss at me agin."

"I'm not fussing with you, Mema. Don't you believe what I'm telling you is right?"

Mema shook her head now, "Mayhap it be right, but I know it fore I took them things. I pay em back in some nother way. We all poor, that's how I came to take em. I's got a fambly to watch out fo."

Lifee put her arm around Mema and said, "We can't steal cause we want God on our side. We need His respect. Now, where is this church you'all got? We're going to go this Sunday! And another thing, we got to start having some school around here. I got to get hold of some paper and make us some books. We are ALL going to learn to read and write and count." Then she looked at them very seriously and said, "But one thing is very important. Very important. No white person must ever know I can read and write and that you are learning to read and write. Most of them cannot read and write and white folks take it into their head to hate you cause they are jealous of you and they will kill you. And every one of you know that's true. So ALL our business stays in our house and minds. Don't even tell colored people cause they have white friends sometimes. Your power lies in your hands and how much you keep that power to yourself."

Everyone was very excited about the school and about going to church. School and reading and writing and being able to figure was the dream of every slave of every age. It was no longer against the law for them to learn these things, it was just that many white people did not know how to read and write and they resented the negras knowing.

The day finished off with all of them clean and full and knowing a little more about the place they lived on. It was still a little strange to Ethylene, Luzy and Meda that there was no white person telling them what to do and when. Freedom was becoming a little clearer to them. They had always been ridiculed about their thoughts, but now they depended on their own minds without ridicule and they were doing very well.

When all was quiet and all were in their shacks, Mz Emmalee looked from her cold window out at the shacks. The warm orange light of lamps glowed through the cracks and slits of the shack boards and it seemed good to her, grudgingly. Like company. Her own stomach was full of Abby's food that warmed her body. Lifee had come in today, so Emmalee's bed was clean and made. She slept in the same gown that she had had time to wash, but didn't. In her heart she felt good, in her mind she felt safer now. "They done all that work, they must gonna stay."

But as she looked at the shacks, she didn't feel so grateful because she planned to exploit her new helpers. "They owe me now. And that's my land, now, they restin on tonight. I got to make em stay least one year to set a crop so I will have money to get home to my mama and family." She was alone and she felt like crying. "Oh! If only Jason had told me where he hid any money. If he had any to hide. I know he did! He must'a! He did own them slaves til he got into bankruptcy after that war came!" She looked sternly through the window again. "But, if they stay here! . . . they will work! And I will get home. I'd sell this thing if somebody had the money to buy it. I hate this farm!" Her voice lowered, "Plantation! This ain't no plantation. It's a farm! He lied to me. Fifty acres ain't no plantation. Just like my neighbors, that liar and his mama. They lyin, too! Want me to marry Rufus and Jason might not even be dead, just late gettin back. That ole liar Rufus with one leg. Humph! I'll get back to North Carolina and I'll have more than a one-leg, lazy man with another poor 'plantation' for a husband!"

There was no lamp lighted in the shack of Mor and Lifee, just the light of the fireplace burning low. They lay on their backs on the fresh clean mattress. Their stomachs full, their bodies clean and warm. Lifee's head was turned to Mor, looking at him in the dim firelight, thinking, always thinking. She pictured what he would be when she really cleaned him up, shaved him right, made him smart, nice clothes. Bought him decent shoes and socks. Taught him to speak better, to read, to write. "I will then be able to love him even more for that. But his lovin, his good, full, sincere lovin makes up for all that now. And his goodness, his kindness. He is my man."

This was the second night they had been alone and made love. Lifee raised up on her elbow and looked down at him. He turned to her, smiling, rubbing her back. "What you thinkin on?" he asked softly.

She answered softly, "I'm thinking of all that time we were on the road, out in the open, surrounded by everybody and we didn't make love. You didn't seem to mind at all. You didn't care if you held me in your arms or not."

He simply smiled wider and said, "I minded. I was all the time ready. I jes din let ya know. And you was always seem like ya din't mind. So . . ."

She lay back down, closer to him. "I did mind, but I didn't let you know cause everybody was there." He pulled her closer and asked, "Why you thinkin bout that?"

She smiled and raised her knees up in remembered pleasure. "Because . . . you have made love to me two days in a row and each time it was like you really wanted to."

He placed his hand on her knees and rubbed her slowly all the way up to her breast, where his hand lingered lovingly. Said, "Only twicst?"

She turned her body slightly to him and said in a faltering, breathless voice, "Well, we only been here two days."

He rolled gently onto her and just lay there lightly, holding her. Said, "The way I loves ya, we can make us a week outta tonight. If'n ya don mind."

She didn't mind.

After the loving, lying beside him, Lifee reached for his hand, he met hers halfway. They laughed softly. He leaned over her, stroking her hair, her shoulders, looking down at her. He didn't seem to move on top of her, but, all of a sudden, so gently, he was. They whispered.

Mor rubbed his lips across her forehead, "I just wants to lay here for a little bit."

"I just want you to."

He kissed her lips, "We done come a long way."

"Yes . . . we have."

He raised his head to see her eyes, "I's happy to be with you."

"I'm very happy to be with you."

"I knowed you was gonna hear that soon as I say it. I AM happy to be with you."

They were quiet a moment.

Then Lifee said, "I'm happy to be having your baby."

His voice raised. "My baby! Lawd, my baby, our baby. Can't nobody take em and sell em. He our'n."

She spoke in wonder, "And it only took that one time to make our baby. Ain't life something?!"

It was a wonder to Mor, also. "Life sho is somethin! My baby. And it be free."

Lifee smoothed his face with her hand, tenderly. "No-one can take it."

He pressed closer to her in his happiness and she felt the hardness of his body. He said, "No one can sell it."

Lifee laughed softly, "It is OURS, alone."

But Mor was very serious, "We be truly free."

Lifee moved slightly beneath Mor. He looked down at her and said, "Oh, sweet woman. And you is mine."

Lifee laughed softly and tenderly again, "We all ARE yours. Me and the baby." Then she felt his movement pressing her knees apart. "What you doin, Mor? Trying to make a week?"

Mor pressed his face into her neck and whispered, "I be tender gentle. Eeeeasy. Won't hurt my baby or my woman."

They didn't know when his body entered hers, but all at once it was there. And they lingered, gently, at their lovemaking. Making love.

Much later, when they lay back falling asleep, but still talking a bit, Lifee said drowsily, "We need us a name for our child."

"Let's make one now." Mor yawned and smiled.

"What you thinking?" Lifee put her hand on him.

"I wants our name to mean somethin. Somethin real good for us's."

"Yes. Grand? King? Peace?" Lifee asked.

"They's good."

"Love? Or Good?"

"I likes Love, me."

"Mr. with Mrs. Love. It sounds good to me. But, you know what, Mor?"

Another yawn, "What?"

"You and everybody are so glad to be free, why don't we make it Freeman, huh?"

Mor really woke up. "That's right! Lifee! I likes that! I am Mr. Freeman! And you are Mrs. Freeman."

And so . . .

In the Southern states illiteracy among whites was the highest in the country. Not only the poor masses, but very many of the planters and plantation owners who had been given land grants to cultivate never learned to read and write. They worked hard and worked slaves hard after they could afford them. Many of the now wealthy kept no books in their homes except the Bible. Hence they did not want the slaves to learn to read and write. If they, the whites, were going to be superior, it had to stay that way. They had temperament but no intellectual training. As their money grew, their children were sent away to school and good colleges and universities.

Because of the jealousy and suspicion the school might arouse, Lifee had to be very careful about the little school she wanted to start among her little group. She had to sneak to buy the paper and the pencils.

The Freedman's Bureau which was placed in the South was there to help the newly freed persons. One, Mr. Winston, who was from the North, also had a general store. He could read and write, but did not know all his customers who could do the same. When Lifee traded at the store for Mz Emmalee, she would purchase big paper tablets "for Mz Emmalee, please." Then, later in her cabin, she would make a dozen pages each for each lesson of the ABCs. The school was started and they all kept very quiet about it as they learned.

Everyone was learning. Mema was beside herself, she was so excited. When she was singing now, she was singing the alphabet, softly, inside her shack. Abby would have been the slowest because she was always working, but having Meda and Luzy in the shack with her and them repeating letters and numbers all the day long when they were in their shack, she learned quicker. Ethylene was ahead of everybody because she had a plan for herself and she dreamed of reading.

Lifee had to be careful with Mor. She couldn't let herself correct him all the time. She did not want him to feel dumb. He wasn't. He learned, he just had so many chores to do, he didn't get to practice as much as the others. But he paid attention and never missed a class, no matter what. He didn't get all the rules about English, but his speech became better and he was proud.

Mz Emmalee often watched them from her windows. One morning as she looked out at all the people in the shacks moving about doing their duties in the light snow that had fallen during the night, she frowned, "Damn this snow. No real work can be done outside." She did not have a "list" yet. She could not write well and did not want the slaves, "them," she corrected herself, to know. That she could write at all was because she had come from a larger town in North Carolina and they did have some schooling for some children whose families could pay for it. Her mother had scrimped as much as she could to spend on Emmalee so she could learn as much as she could.

The knock on the door startled her. Emmalee was pleased they were ready to do her housework so early. She opened the door, but it was not Mema nor Lifee. It was Rufus Bingly, her closest neighbor. She looked past him in his long-tail coat and saw his cold, old, hungry, tired horse stamping his hoofs, slowly, in the snow.

Rufus had lost a leg in the war. He had traveled, seen new places, met new men from these Southern states of America. He had often been hungry growing up at home, but in the war he had truly experienced hunger and pain with his sweat. He had plodded through rivers seeking to catch fish, over hills and forests scavenging for wild vegetables and fruit. Even raped a few women. Learning new things to think about and things to say. He was full of love for his Southern land, and full of hate for the black slave he blamed for ruining it. Blamed for taking away a way of life the average Southern white person had been lied to about so that they thought they had had a wonderful life. Most had never had any slaves. Lied to that they were, indeed, superior, when in fact they were very poor and had less than some slaves.

Rufus had seen dead bodies and blood covering the ground of the South he loved. And by the end of the war, he had left a part of his own body somewhere in this wonderful American land.

His father owned his land from a grant, but did not work too hard on it, just did what he had to do to keep it. He made liquor to sell to keep his family with the bare necessities. Though Rufus had been hungry and poor before, he had been, he thought, of the freest, intelligent and superior, the happiest people in these states, if not, even, perhaps, the world.

Now his father was dead. Rufus was therefore expected to support both his mother and his sister, who hadn't married before the war had interfered with her courtships. Now she was five years older and many eligible bachelors were dead. He had to be the breadwinner now. They depended on him. He wanted to marry Mz Emmalee. She had land, and now she had slaves out back working for her. "Together," he thought, "we can get respectable again."

Rufus was melancholy today. Watching, feeling the winter come, his leg that was not there ached. The winds whipped around the log cabin he and his family lived in. All inside were hungry. He wanted to get away from them today. Everyday. Because, you see, Rufus was lazy and he didn't like looking at what needed to be done.

Oh, he could get around, walk with a crutch, do things for his mother and sister they could not always do. But not too much. Just enough to feed them awhile, or clothe them awhile. Just like the rest of his neighbors and friends. Then he would rest under the shade trees with a plug of tobacco or a jug of white lightning. He was an angry, angry man and full of hate and it was directed at the Yankees and the Negroes. The Yankee was not so close around anymore. But the Negro was.

The cold winds, the cold fallen snow and the almost empty cupboard had brought Rufus out to propose to Emmalee again, and he had seen the negras working in back of her house. His pitiless and pitiful heart had warmed at the sight of slave shacks full again.

Rufus slapped his shoulders to keep the warmth and smiled as he entered Emmalee's house. Startled, she had stepped back, for she did not like to let him in. She was a single woman even as she was a married woman. She was alone, but her husband might not be dead. "And Rufus poor, too!" she had often thought.

Rufus smiled happily as he asked, "What you got there? Some negras! They gonna work for you? Ohhhh, you told me you was with no money!" He blew on his hands and looked around for the fireplace and a table where a plate of breakfast might be sitting out. It was not. He moved into the room.

Emmalee frowned and said, "Come into the kitchen, Rufus, it's the warmest place. What are ya doing out so early on this cold mornin? Is yoah mama alright?"

"She fine, just fine. Little hungry. Things ain't been goin so well, this weather and all." He looked around the kitchen at the stove. Emmalee had some squirrel smothered in gravy on her woodburning cookstove. She saw his look.

"That is for my supper. Mor, he is the Negro man, hunts for their meat. Keeps some food comin in."

"Somebody been hunting? Ya got grown men out there, Mz Emmalee? Is they gonna stay? Til spring?"

"Well, I reckon they have to, weather and all is bad for travel."

"They gon be here to lay in a crop? Lord, lend em to me, us, after they get yo crop in."

"My Lord, Rufus, they ain't mine. Slavery abolished and I don't want them Yankees comin back out here."

"Them Yankee doings is mostly in the big city or them towns what got everythin. They ain't much out here." Rufus dipped his fingers in a pot on the stove and Emmalee slammed the lid on the pot. "Oops!" He smiled as he chewed on the little morsel he got.

"That is my supper!"

"When they gonna get you some more? Make him hunt for a

heap of squirrels, or a coon or a possum. He might even catch a wild hog if them Yankees ain't got em all."

Mz Emmalee folded her arms across her breast. "Why don't you get out there and see what you can catch?!"

Rufus reached down to his leg and patted it. "Well, see, Mz Emmalee, a man needs two legs to catch them critters and I ain got but one. Even if I had two good dogs, could I afford em, I could do better. But one leg and . . ."

Mz Emmalee waved her arm toward a chair. "Well, sit down, then! Only for a minute, cause I got to get busy preparin a list of work for em."

As Rufus takes a seat, he asks, "Ohhh, I sure wish you send em over to help me . . . us. Mammy sure would be appreciatin that."

Mz Emmalee calms herself down and tells him, "I can't send em nowhere til I get this place workin again. What did ya want, to make ya ride over here in the snow and all?"

Rufus scratched his ear as he pondered how to say this seriously. "Well . . . I just came to talk to you again . . . cause . . . I love you, Mz Emmalee, and I wants to marry up with you and get your life straight and this farm straight and workin."

Emmalee took a deep breath and answered, "I can't marry ya. I'm already married . . . anyway. But, if I was not married anyway, I wouldn't marry ya til I saw your farm straight and a'workin, then . . . I'd give it a thought."

Rufus shook his head sadly, "You hard on a man, Mz Emmalee. Ain't you lonely none?"

Emmalee closed her eyes, said, "None."

Rufus stood with a little stumble as he held on to the table, "Well . . . I am. I done lost a leg, but I'm still a full man. Red-blooded, strong and white. I needs a wife, but I only love you."

Emmalee almost wailed softly, "Oh, Rufus." She looked around for something to give him. She took a paper and scraped the last of the squirrel and a piece of corn bread into it and handed it to him. "Give this to your mama, Ms Bingly. Tell her I said eat it with

God's blessin. Now . . . ya got to go cause it ain't fittin for a single woman to be in here with a single man."

Emmalee rushed him, as fast as she could decently, to the door. He was fingering the bag of food. She ushered him out so fast he barely had a chance to say good-by. He hollered through the closed door, "I'll look out for ya, Mz Emmalee. I'll oversee these negras for ya."

Emmalee hollered back through the door, "Yes, thankee, Mr. Rufus."

Then he somehow got up on his horse, fixed his crutch behind him and trotted down the driveway to the road. Mz Emmalee looked through the window at the forlorn man, already digging in the bag of food. "Poor Ms Bingly and poor Rufus. I just got to get away from roun here!"

Christmas came and passed. It was a bleak Christmas season. It was very cold weather, but it was warm in the shacks and Emmalee's house was clean and repaired as much as possible with no money to buy material. Mz Emmalee had no money except for a few Yankee dollars she kept hidden.

Mor chopped firewood for all, which was quite a job. He hunted every day wearing an old woolen coat that had been Emmalee's husband's for warmth, and torn rubber boots to protect his feet. They searched the land and forests for miles around for critters, wild greens and roots. They survived and kept Mz Emmalee alive.

Lifee had taken on the main house care because it kept her inside and warm in her condition. She mended curtains and aprons, blankets and sheets. Then she moved to the few dresses Emmalee had. Emmalee had begun to think of Lifee as a companion. In loneliness and desolation, as Emmalee became more distraught, she began to depend on Lifee, to talk her life over with Lifee.

Everyday Emmalee talked of going home to North Carolina. She spoke of her hatred of Alabama and Georgia and how she felt her husband, Jason, had let her down. Emmalee's loneliness and fear had finally crystallized into a sort of hate for her husband, whom she had dreamed would romantically carry her off to his plantation mansion. She had seen herself in Society with the other wealthy planters and their wives. Serving dinner with servants all around, dressed in livery, and herself, a shining light and Beauty from North Carolina. "Then . . . the negras caused the war and ruined, just ruined everbody's life . . . and I am poor and alone and my husband is God knows where. Or dead."

It was the thought of his being dead that sobered her up, at last, to the point of finally looking through his papers for deeds or a will. "Everybody knows it was his'n and mine cause I'm his wife. But, he's gone now."

At last she believed it was final, he was dead. As she gathered and looked through his papers, she thought, "Oh, how can I sell it without them papers?" She flopped down on her davenport, ready to cry. "And sell it, I will! No negras means no farm, no work, no money comin in! No negras means no nothin!" And she kept looking until she found those papers, a deed and a bill of sale.

A few days later Emmalee spoke to Lifee about selling the farm. It was in early February. Lifee was eight months pregnant, large with child. Lifee hesitated a moment, then said, "Mz Emmalee . . . I know you hate to give up your husband's land, your land. But, I know how important it is for you to get back to civilization and decent folks, as you say."

Mz Emmalee threw one hand up and answered, "Yes, Lord, yes. And to my real family. I miss my own mammy and my pappy!"

Lifee chose her words carefully, "You don't need to tell me your main business, but . . . you know I do a little work, now and again, for some other ladies, and their husbands still have a little money. Mayhap I can help you find someone to buy this farm."

Emmalee looked at Lifee with hope, "Yes, you could, couldn't ya?"

Lifee, as she talked, moved on, doing her work cleaning the kitchen. "How much you think you want for this place? You know, nobody is gonna pay too much."

Emmalee shook her head in her confusion, "They can't pay too much no way."

Lifee, still working, "How much you askin? Fifty acres, ain't it?"

"Yes, it's fifty good acres with a man to look out over it."

Lifee finally said, "Well, you don't need to tell me. They can ask you their own self."

Emmalee shook her head again. "No. I don't want em to. I'm a lady and a lady does not talk about money."

Lifee stopped and put a hand on her plump hip. "Mz Emmalee, I have tried to tell you, you livin in a different time and you have got to look out for yourself . . . and plan your future. We got your clothes all spruced up with new buttons and bows and your hair looks very nice and you are ready to land on North Carolina and break every rich man's heart."

"I can tell ya, I know I got to get home. I don want to stay another winter here. And if you all get the crops in . . ."

"Mz Emmalee, I have told you we may not stay here. Mor gonna plow the ground for you and we can even plant some crops, but not fifty acres. And we are not going to be able to stay here and help it grow and pick it. We have done a whole lot for you, in appreciation, and to use your slave shacks. You have got no pay and we have got no pay. We exchanged. And I don't have to tell you, you are way better off than your closest neighbors, all of em."

"I knows, I knows. But what will I do when ya'll are gone?"

"Well . . . I told you, we don't have to leave you here. We gonna be walking, but you can leave here in a carriage to the town where the coach stops . . . in class . . . if you sell this place."

Emmalee whined softly, "But, who gonna buy?"

"How much you want?"

Emmalee took a deep breath and decided. "At least fifty cents a acre. Fifty times fifty . . . hmmmm, let's see."

Lifee began wiping the counter again. "It's twenty-five whole dollars."

Emmalee looked up at her. "Is that there enough? Twenty-five dollars?"

Lifee just shook her head slowly. "In these days . . . it's good. Most people don't need another poor farm. Even ole rich man Mr. Pippin from the town. He ain't gonna give you nothing for this farm. Just cheat you, a woman, and give you almost nothing. He can't find enough Negroes to work the farms he got cause he cheats em so much."

Emmalee sniffled and wiped her nose with a dishtowel. "But it's got my house on it, and some shacks."

"Then add another ten dollars."

Fear, anxiety and spunk made Emmalee stand up, saying, "No! Another fifty dollars. Make it one hundred dollars in all!"

Lifee stopped wiping, "A hundred dollars?! Wheee!"

Emmalee sat back down, looking worried, "Too high?"

Lifee looked thoughtful, "Well . . . no. Not if somebody running round here with a hundred-dollar gold piece."

Emmalee laughed a little, "Me and my husband never even seen one . . . as I know of."

Lifee turned her full body to her, "Mz Emmalee?"

"Yes."

It was Lifee's turn to take a deep breath. "How bad . . . do you hate Negroes?"

Emmalee blushed, "Well, I . . . I . . . well, I don hate em, least not like Rufus, but they took his leg."

"Aw, Mz Emmalee, the war took his leg. Probably shot by a white man. It was a white man's war, Mz Emmalee."

"Well, they was the cause of it."

"Mz Emmalee, them Northern people don't love us Negroes. It's some good people there, just like there are a few good people here. And I don't know it all yet, but I bet there was some money at the bottom of that war. I'm sure of it."

"Lifee, of course ya say that. But . . . I don't know . . . how much I hate negras."

"Mz Emmalee, if one of them had one hundred dollars, would you sell this farm to them?"

"Lawd a mercy, ya talk so strange. Where a negra gonna find, get or steal one hundred dollars?"

"Would you sell it to them?"

"No . . . no, I couldn't do that to my husband."

Lifee turned back to her work. "Alright. I guess North Carolina and that handsome man husband can wait."

"Well, I let em rent it . . . til I come back."

"You coming back, Mz Emmalee?"

"I might . . . My new husband might want to."

"If he want to come back here, he won't be rich, then, Mz Emmalee."

Mz Emmalee sat back, took a sip of cold coffee, thinking.

Lifee looked at her, said, "You'd have to sign a paper."

Emmalee looked up, "Sign a paper?"

"Yes. I showed you how to write your name better."

Mz Emmalee got up in a huff. "Whoever learned you how to write should'a been killed. Ya know that?"

"I only help people with my learning. Now, I'm trying to help you."

"Well, get me one hundred dollars and . . . I'll do it! I ain't comin back. But don ya tell nobody white!"

Lifee did not smile, "I won't and don't you. Cause we need your protection. If Mr. Rufus thought this was our land, he would burn it to the ground."

Emmalee looked alarmed. "Sho would!" Then the word "our" sank in. "Your'n?"

Lifee gave Mz Emmalee her full concentration. "Mz Emmalee, I know you might not believe this, but, you know we walked here from Texas."

"Yea."

"Well, you know that's a long way and a many a things happen on them roads since the war ended and all these different kinds of people are coming South to rake her clean."

"Yea . . ."

"Well, I don't know what happened, but somebody must'a been running away from something because they dropped some of their money. I found it. But I don't know just what to do with it, because, you know, white folks, dishonest white folks, not like you, would take it away from me and I rather swallow it first."

"Yea . . . ? You found it?"

"I found it. Lord's truth. And I can pay you with that."

"One hundred dollars was all ya found?"

"Just about. It's all you are asking for this farm."

"How much did ya find?"

Life thought a quick minute, not wanting to antagonize Emmalee. "I found two of em gold pieces, just enough to swallow if I had to. And I need the second one to get the things we are going to need to work this place . . . and it still won't be enough . . . if anything goes wrong with the weather or something."

Mz Emmalee grunted her reluctant agreement. "Well, I don see how I can protect ya. I ain gon be here. And I need more money."

"Just don't tell anyone you sold the farm to us. You can't. I want everybody to think we are working for you. Then maybe we can make it."

"I need more money."

"Well, if we have a good year . . . and get a good start, I'll send you more money. Just as a gift for you being so good to us and letting us stay here . . . in exchange for our work . . . and food. But you said you wanted one hundred dollars for this farm, and that is what I will pay."

Mz Emmalee shook her head slowly, "But I din't know ya had more money."

Lifee shook her head slowly, "But you do know that nobody else will give you even fifty dollars for this farm right now or maybe ever." Lifee put her towels and rags away. "Now, if we don't stick to our first agreement, like honest women, then I won't bother you anymore. I'll just do what I'm supposed to do and leave when it's time. It's getting to spring and traveling is easier. And maybe you want to stay on here til someone comes along to give you what you want so you can get home . . . at last . . . to North Caroline. Don't know how long that'll be."

Emmalee sat quietly, thinking.

Lifee moved to the kitchen door, preparing to leave for the day. "Mayhap Mr. Rufus can help you get more money."

Emmalee said quietly, "I can't abide that Mr. Rufus and he don need to touch my money."

Lifee turned to go, "Well, what you want to do, then?"

Emmalee got up to follow her, "I want to go on and leave here. Tell me what must we do to get this here thing settled?"

One day, soon after that conversation, Emmalee and Lifee sat down together over the legal papers and the new blank deeds Mz Emmalee had gotten from the local notary. They copied the description of the land from the old deed and made out a proper deed of sale and a contract of agreement. When it was all done, Lifee told Mz Emmalee to buy a horse, since she had that old carriage in the barn, to ride to the county seat to notarize and record the papers. "If I change this other gold piece, I can pay for the horse when I come back."

It was about ten miles away in Mudville, a pretty good-size town, where two banks and three lawyers thrived.

So Lifee got Mz Emmalee to buy a horse and mule on credit,

explaining her tenants would bring the money she sent back and pay in two days. Lifee, also, got two milk cows to be paid for in the same way because she knew the seller would treat Mz Emmalee right and fair, and would cheat Negroes.

They hitched up the horse to the wagon Mor had repaired and cleaned up preparing for this event, and went to Mudville to take care of their business. Lifee and Mz Emmalee went in the courthouse while Mor waited in the wagon.

Lifee promised Mz Emmalee ten more dollars because then Mz Emmalee would have to help cash Lifee's other one-hundred-dollar gold piece, so Lifee and Mor could then have smaller change to spend without bringing attention to themselves.

As they had previously discussed, at the courthouse Mz Emmalee explained to the record filing clerk that the buyers were her neighbors and they were going to pay her a little at a time. The clerk only said, "Well, good luck to ya on that!" The papers were taken, notarized and filed.

Mor and Lifee were now the duly noted owners of a small farm. Unrecognized as such, but there it was; in black and white.

Next, they went to the bank and Mz Emmalee changed the second gold coin, which Lifee needed for themselves to buy things without bringing unwanted attention and to pay Mz Emmalee the ten dollars extra. It wasn't long before Mz Emmalee was on her way home with her hundred-dollar gold piece and ten dollars extra plus her own nine dollars she had kept in her secret cache. She left Lifee her address in North Carolina "just in case," as Lifee said.

In town, Lifee bought some things she needed for her family. Bolts of material for curtains for all the shacks. Bolts of inexpensive material for dresses for all and a suit from the pawnshop to be altered for Mor. Dishes and towels, even silverware, cheap, but satisfactory. Two sacks of white flour and four of cornmeal, salt, pepper, onions, garlic, molasses, green vegetables, some fruit for everybody.

Mor bought chicken feed, nails, a bale of hay, oats, a few pieces of lumber, coal oil a'plenty, and seeds for the crops. They filled that wagon up. Along the road to home, Mor picked up some chickens and two young hogs.

The method they used to purchase things was to say, "My Mistress Emmalee say she want . . ." and no one asked any questions about the money. One white store owner even said, after they left, "Now . . . see . . . them some good niggers. They smart, too! They probly still livin on their ole plantation workin for they ole master. Cause niggers cain't feed and look afta theyselves. They needs white folks care."

Lifee didn't have to stop at the Bingly farm to tell them anything because Mz Emmalee had gone over to tell Mother Bingly good-by and she was leaving. In front of Lifee, Mz Emmalee said, "The negras'll be takin care my land for me in exchange for a home and some of the fruit of their labor. We done worked it all out. I'm satisfied I can trust em. I be back in a few months, I reckon."

Rufus had been anxious, exasperated and angry, which he tried not to show. "Mz Emmalee, I could have looked after yo place fo ya! Them negras ain got sense nuff to see to all yo bizness. Negras need a master, a overseer, to get anythin done! They's lazy and theys dumb. Like little animal critters. You let me run em and I bet ya ya'll have somethin when you gets back!"

But Emmalee didn't like Rufus, so she had said, "Now, Mr. Rufus, ya got plenty enough to do without me botherin you. I trusts Mor and Lifee and, sides that, there ain nothin they can mess up with of mine." Then she remembered about property. "Ceptin the land and them few new animals they got to work the land with."

Mother Bingly, sitting in her rocking chair, just nodded and let Emmalee kiss her cheek good-by and whisper quite a few words. Mother Bingly listened as she nodded her head. After they were gone she sat there like that, thinking for a long time.

Lifee was thinking, also, about the whispering. So when Lifee returned from taking Emmalee to town to catch a stagecoach to the nearest train, she stopped at the Binglys by herself, for the first time. Rufus opened the back door with a frown. Lifee asked, "I'd like to speak with your mother, please?"

"What fer?"

"Mz Emmalee sent her a little something as a remembrance."

"What?" Rufus reached for the package. "Give it here to me." But then Mother Bingly called from her rocking chair in the kitchen near the stove. "Naw, she can give hit to me. C'mon in, girl."

Lifee stepped through the door as Rufus moved back. "She asked me to give you this bag of cookies and a bag of hard candies to let you know she was thinking of you, Mz Bingly."

Mz Bingly reached for the things with a smile. "Ohhhh, she didn't have to do that. She just a sweet woman." She looked up at Lifee. "What's yo name, girl?"

"Lifee, Mz Bingly."

"That's a funny name. But yo must be a good worker for Mz Emmalee to trust ya with all her earthly goods."

"Yes'm. I try."

"Well, ya'll let me know when ya needs some help plannin and makin cisions oveh there. I be glad to do what I cain. Umm-hmm."

As Lifee backed out the door, she said, "I thank you, mam. Now, good-by, cause we got lots of work to do."

As she turned away from the door to get into the wagon, Rufus called after her, "I be oveh there to check on ya."

Lifee stopped her climbing into the wagon and turned back to Rufus. "Mr. Rufus? We don't need no checking up on us. We will do just fine. I told Mz Emmalee, if we have problems with people tellin us what to do, we will leave her farm just like it is. She say she trust us, Mor and me, to do all the right things, and we will. So I thank you for your offer, but we won't be needing you to do anything. If we do, we will ask. Thank you, sir."

When Rufus angrily closed his door, he turned to his mother and said, "Gad danged uppity niggers! They gon ruin that farm, watch what I'm tellin ya!"

His mother laughed a little at her son. "Welllll, it now lookin better'n our'n. See after this land, son. See after yo own."

Finally, Rufus laughed a little, then laughed with glee, slapping his thigh, "Ha! Ya got to give it to her, that Emmalee, she beat the negras out! She got em workin for nothin but a shack! She a smart one. You know what she told me, Ma? She tole me she was gonna apply up for a paper for her to allow her to marry again. She say it takes three years and then she be back and we will talk about marryin. Ast me, 'Don let nobody bother my Negroes,' so I won't. I thought she was dumb, that Emmalee, but she wasn't, after all."

That night, when they were alone, Life showed Mor the papers. He could read a little now, but there were so many words, long words. Life told him, "This means the land is ours. Yours. We have bought it with that money we have been hiding that I brought from Morella's plantation. You are the owner of land, trees, springs, a house, a barn. Yours . . . all yours and mine."

Mor smiled at Life. "Mine? Mine? Woman, you must . . ."

Life threw the papers in the air jubilantly. "Yours!!! Mine! Ours! Forever! Even if they burn everything on it. The land is ours."

In wonder, Mor looked at Life very seriously. "That's what ya done with the gold?"

"Yes, and I'm gonna do more. I didn't spend it all. This is for now. This land isn't where I wanted our land to be, but it isn't all there is. For now? It's enough . . . for now."

Astonished, Mor looked at the papers that had fallen on him. Life smiled on him with great pleasure. His head was down, looking at the papers a moment. Then she saw his body shaking and saw the tears dropping from his face onto the paper. He cried softly as he asked, "Land? Is our land? Our trees? Our own farm?"

She placed her arm around his shoulders and pulled him to her. "Yes, Mor. Ours. Yours . . . and mine. She held him close, tightly, as her tears joined his. It took several moments for her, who had lived in a house, to realize the enormity this was to him, and finally, to herself. She had been so busy thinking and working things through, she hadn't stopped to realize the profound thing happening to her in the midst of all the white hatred and the freed-slave poverty. Her tears were also in relief.

When their tears had slowed in the joy of the thing, she continued speaking, "Yes, it's ours, and we have more money left. I have hidden it away. You want to take it and hide it? You can. Or I'll show you where I put it."

"No, mam, I don want to take it and hide it. It been worryin me ever since you tol me when we got here. But ya betta show me where it is, case I needs to know someday."

"Alright. Just don't ever act like you got money anywhere. We can't let anyone know the land is ours. It could mean our lives."

"I knows, yes, mam, I knows." Then he shook his head in amazement. "Lawd. This here land is ours. Thankee Jesus. Thankee Lifee."

Lifee did not want Mor to misunderstand their situation. Tears slowly ran down her cheeks as she cupped her hands around his tear-stained face, saying, "Mor. This land would not mean a thing to me . . . I could never handle this land all by myself. You are the farmer, I am the seamstress. You are the only reason this land will mean anything to us. Don't overestimate me and do not underestimate yourself. We both are important to this freedom."

Later, when the lamp was out and they were preparing to sleep, Mor murmured, "I want my son to have a education."

Lifee sleepily answered, "We are working on that. We just have to keep ourselves, and him, alive." A moment later she raised her head to say, "It's time we had that talk with everybody living here."

Mor answered softly, "Yessum, it is time."

Lifee raised her head again. "And I have a letter to write."

But Mor was asleep.

EIGHT

Lifee called for a little meeting at the shack used for school. Everyone came: some frowning, some curious, smiling. When everyone was there, Mor stood in front of his "family" and spoke, holding his head up high, proud.

"We got to get some things here we can all do to see that we be alright and safe. Ya'll know the white man is our first worry and the land crops is our big job."

Everyone nodded, some moaned softly.

"We got," he continued, "this here land and we gon work it and, with the Lawd's help, we gonna make it and live free. These shacks ya'll livin in, you can fix em up good as you wants on the inside with them curtains and that paint Lifee buys you, but we gon leave the outside lookin worn down as they is. Lifee gon get some locks for the doors, so when we out in the fields, nobody can't get in em to see how good we doin. Ya keep the same poor clothes, clean, wear em everday. Put yo best on on Sunday when ya goes to church."

Everyone stirred in their seat, listening intently.

Mor continued, "Now, I don like to lie to nobody, but we cain let the white man know the truth of us cause then we gon lose everthin we got. We gon make us some good crops. Bout fifteen acres only, cause we don want nobody to think we tryin to get riches. We gon most plant for us to eat and the farm animals to eat so we don have to starve nor beg. Be mighty careful what you say to the white man, cause you could be costin us our life. Me and Lifee gon share everthin with you. We hope we gon have us a future. A life. These here white folks done already took most from us; this here for us. We don want to cheat nobody, but if they takes any more from us, we be dead."

Everyone nodded in agreement.

Mor said thoughtfully, "That there Mr. Rufus, he be lookin over round here and we gotta be careful. We say we workin for Mz Emmalee."

Lifee spoke, "And he must never, never know that anyone of us can write or is learning to read and write."

Everyone nodded their head vigorously.

The meeting broke up and everyone went to their jobs. Lifee went into her shack to write a letter. She had bought some decent paper, not the best, not the worst, and now she used it for the letter. When it was finished, she did not give it to the coach that passed down the road to stop at Mr. Winston's store, where it picked up the mail. She lay it aside, patted it, then went to do her own work.

Lifee had been told by the Freedman's Bureau man, Mr. Winston, that there was an old lady, Widow Carbon, who wanted some sewing done. She took the wagon and rode to the old widow's house to see about it.

Lifee stepped up to the front door of the modest, clean house. Mrs. Carbon opened the door almost immediately with a frown on her face. "Don't come to my front door. You know betta. I don't 'llow negras at my front door. Now, step round the side there and come on in the back." Lifee did as she was told because she did not care. Her pride did not depend on front and back doors.

When she entered the back door into the kitchen, which was clean, Mrs. Carbon pointed to a chair and sat down herself.

"Now, I understand from Mz Winston at the store that you are a pretty good seamstress."

"Yes, mam."

"Well, I got some mendin I want done, but I don want it messed up. Times is hard. I ain got nothin to waste. What you spect to earn for yoar labor?"

"May I see the work?"

"Well, that's it in that there basket. Some nightgowns and a few everyday dresses cause I ain going to let you do my good things til I see how you do."

"Yes, mam," Lifee said as she looked through the basket. "I reckon one dollar will be fine."

"I'll pay you half. That ain no whole lot in that basket."

"One dollar. I do good work."

"All negras say that. Ya'll lie so much. Alright, but it betta be good work and you got to do it here in my house."

"Yes, mam. I'll get started now."

"Good. Are you close enough to go home for yoar lunch?"

"Brought some."

"Good. Then get started." After a moment, Mrs. Carbon asked, "Where you learn to talk so proper?"

"Worked for a teacher."

Aghast, Mrs. Carbon asked, "You mean somebody taught you to read and write and speak so clear?"

"No mam. Can't read nor write. Just talk."

"Well, I declare. Where you from?"

"Don't know where I was born. Just coming now from Texas."

"Ummm-hmmm. Well, you sound proper. Ya'll negras can really copycat everything. Now, I got some truly proper relations. I'm kin to some of the most aristocratic folks there is in the South." Lifee just kept sewing and did not answer. So Mrs. Carbon continued talking. "Now that ya'll free, I bet ya'll miss bein round fine people. Ya'll used to work for people that was so far above you. Was a good way to learn how real people really should live."

Lifee asked casually, "How was that?"

"Well, clean, of course! And real marriages! Real families! Not like ya'll, just anybody ya'll meet or work with! And all them different colored babies! My Lord!"

"We were all the same color when we were first brought here. But, you know, ya'll made the rules and you all had guns and whips. Ole Master had to be mighty busy out in the slave cabins to make all these light-skinned babies and people, cause they weren't usually made in HIS house. We did try, honestly, Mrs. Carbon, to have proper marriages and families, but we thought, honestly, that white folks didn't really believe in proper marriages because they kept selling husbands away from wives and children away from mothers and all like that."

A grunt and "Wellll" came from the pursed lips of Mrs. Carbon, "You be careful with yoah fast lips, missy, slavery ain't ALL over!"

Lifee put a finished garment down and picked up another as she spoke. "Mam, you know what? They just didn't let us do anything we thought was right. We tried to be clean, we even cleaned ya'lls houses and clothes so you all would be clean. We kept you all clean. But most of us lived on dirt, in dirt, around dirt, and it takes time to be clean sometime. If there was no creek around, there was no bathtub either. We did as good as we could in a handbasin."

"Wellll." Mrs. Carbon knew Negroes were dumb animals, so she thought she must be wrong about Lifee sounding so smart. Still . . .

Lifee continued speaking, easy, casual, "And we sure did want a real marriage, many of us loved our mates, but you know, it's hard to have a family when they kept selling our wives and husbands from us. Yes, we most certainly wanted our families, but, I know you know they took and sold our children, too."

"Are you tryin to be smart?"

"Heavens, no. But I want to ask you a question, please. About all the different-colored children. Do you think that slave girl took and raped that white massa on her own?"

"I won't have that kind of talk in my house. I am a Christian woman. I'll leave you to do your work. And hurry on it." Mrs. Carbon nearly flew from the room, but was back in about three minutes, saying, "You may talk a fine speech, but you still haven't learnt how to speak to yoah betters."

Lifee smiled, "What is 'betters,' Mrs. Carbon? I really want to know, because I want to be better. In the eye of the Lord, that is."

Mrs. Carbon left again, and this time she was gone a long time. When she returned to the kitchen, she sat watching Lifee as she sewed the items by hand. Lifee realized Mrs. Carbon was lonely, ignorant and just wanted to talk to somebody, so she decided she would not speak to her in anger.

But the first thing Mrs. Carbon said was, "If you have knowledge of the Lord, tell me why do all ya'll ack like animals? I know for a fact that all negra women are unchaste. But maybe since ya'll are like animals, it ain a sin for ya'll to consort with whomsoever comes to hand. Even tempting white men. Scuse me, Lord."

Lifee took a deep breath and said, "Mrs. Carbon, I know you have seen many cotton fields and cane fields and corn fields and the like. I know you saw all the women working out in those fields. These women had children and didn't even get to eat sometimes til late at night, when they had to tend their own gardens to be sure they ate wholesome or any food and that their children were fed. When do you think those women had time to do any 'consortin' with anybody? And as to white men, as you say, you think these Negro women went into the Big House and got THEM out to tempt them? What did she do, the slave woman? Go put on one of her store-bought gowns, ribbons and bows and perfumes and strut around to entice the master? I think the animal is the one who has the power to make human beings do whatever they, the masters, want to do no matter who is looking or who is there. Even their white wives sitting in the Big House knew and their men still didn't care."

Mrs. Carbon stood up, "I sure don't have to sit here and hear this. You a negra and you are lying."

"Yes, a light-colored liar. Think I stole this color, too? Who told you we lied, mam?"

"My husband had to deal with ya'll, he told me. All the men in our families told us. Sides, I know for myself from negra women workin for us."

"Yes, your husbands told you we lied. About what?"

"Why, everythin."

"Alright, mam."

"I see you are a light-skinned one, not so black, but even with one drop of that black blood in you, you can never understand the true meaning of life and are sure to end up badly. You will never understand the civilized and Christian ways of white folks."

"Yessum." After a moment, Lifee added, "You do know Africans didn't get in boats and paddle their way over here to bother you good Christians, don't you, mam?" The widow just sniffed and cleared her throat.

Soon as possible, Lifee finished the work and asked for her money. Mrs. Carbon handed her a half-dollar.

"It was a dollar, Mrs. Carbon." Lifee held her hand out.

"Wellll, I told you I could pay one half."

"Well, I said I would work for one dollar, mam."

"Well, there you are."

"Did you like my work, Mrs. Carbon?"

"Well, it's fair to middling. Good enough, I spose."

"Do you think you will ever want me to work for you again?"

"Oh, well, yes, I see you can do my good dress, so I spose I will."

Lifee put her hand down, saying, "Well, I will probably be too busy. I am going to get customers who pay me the little I ask, mam."

Mrs. Carbon was silent as she looked into Life's eyes for a moment. Then she took a deep breath, saying, "Well, here! Here it is! Uppity nigras! Ya'll are cheating us always!"

"Yessum. Thankee, mam."

And then Lifee gathered her belongings and was leaving, when Mrs. Carbon hollered behind her, "I will let you know when I need you again."

"Yessum." Then Lifee was gone.

Lifee drove to the Freedman's Bureau store to see Mr. Winston. She waited for the store to nearly empty, then with a small smile handed Mr. Winston the letter without the envelope. "I would like for you to read this to me, Mr. Winston, please."

Mr. Winston, a big man, but a kind one, took the letter and smiled back tiredly. "Well, let's see what you got here." He read a moment, then said, "It's a letter from Mz Emmalee."

"I thought it was."

He read another moment, then said, "She hope ya'll are doing well and keeping busy. She is gonna be delayed in coming back here and she wants you and Mor to move into the main house so it won't be empty and a temptation to somebody lookin for somethin to steal. Then she say give you what you need, but not too much, to keep the place goin til you get a harvest in and I will get my money when she sends it to you very soon. She tells me she trust you and ain't worried none, but help you when I can. And she say tell ole Mz Bingly her regards and all. That's bout all is in here cept she say the traveler who brought it is a friend of her family." He handed the letter back to Lifee, who folded it up and placed it in her bag.

"Well, Mr. Winston, we don't need nothin much right now, we pretty well set. I will let you know if somethin comes up. Thank you for reading my letter to me."

On her way home in the wagon, she hoped she hadn't gone too far, but she believed it was a good idea, because Mr. Winston would talk about it in the store and the other white folks would feel better knowing what Mz Emmalee really thought and would leave them alone on that farm. Maybe settle that Rufus Bingly down. The baby was about due and she wanted to have it in the main house in comfort. So everything was working out well. So far. She hurried home to begin moving to the main house.

Mor was always excited these days. He often spoke to Life in their quiet moments alone. "Jesus! Jesus! I gots land of mine own!" Lifee would smile and answer, "Yes, you got land."

"Oh, I's gon make crops and things for you!"

"Yes, you must. We got a mouth coming."

Mor, laughing, would answer, "We got some already here!" He could hardly wait for spring. He roamed over his land, looking for honeybees, touching the trees, sifting the soil between his fingers, tasting the fresh spring waters running through it. He loved his land. He spent a great deal of time in the barn cleaning and sharpening the old tools he found there.

He began stripping the oak trees, shaving them down into strips, to weave his baskets. He mended the chair bottoms in the main house and everything else he could find that needed repair. He wove the fish baskets, carved ax handles and hoe handles and sold them to Mr. Winston. He made fence posts for the chicken yard and fenced the yard because he didn't want the chickens getting used to sleeping in the woods and losing their eggs to the marauding wild animals. He fed and cared for his farm animals with love because they were his very own. It was still cold early in March, but he still got help from his little group when they decided to brave the cold for a while; searching, digging, just looking.

The school had been set up in one of the last three shacks. They had cleaned it up and Mor cleaned and mended the fireplace there so it could be heated for classes. Then Lifee took one of the tablets she had bought and started making the next ABC book. Capital letters and small letters. She brought in Luzy, Meda and Ethylene to help her. They were joined by Mema when she wasn't gone off working for some of her "folks."

They made the pages, then took thread and, placing it through the little holes on the sides of the paper sheets, made a book. They learned as they worked and loved the learning. Happy to learn to read, understand and write. The main house had three books, an almanac, a Bible, and a cookbook, and two old ladies' magazines with pictures. They started reading with these.

Lifee had Mor make a mailbox to set out on the road so she could get her "mail" from Mz Emmalee. She counted on Mz Emmalee not telling anyone the truth of the matter and prayed she could trust her that far. At least Mz Emmalee was not living in the area; talking would have been easier than writing, and Emmalee did not write well. "Now, I just have to pray she does not marry a greedy husband and he want the land back." Even with the deed signed, she knew white folks could do anything they really wanted to because they worked together, judges, sheriffs, courts and all.

NINE

Mema had bought some paint with her earned money and painted the inside of her shack pale green. Made the curtains from the dark green material Lifee had given her and even a cloth for the small table in her "house." Ethylene asked for some paint and got a pale pink, did the work herself, refusing Mor's help, then made white curtains to hang and a little skirt around her bed to hide what she put under it. All the outsides remained the same weatherbeaten, dry wood with chunks placed in cracks by Mor. From the road the place looked just the same as always, except cleaner.

Abby said she wanted to build her own house way out in the woods on the land, so "Don see no sense no how in fixin up this here shack!" But Meda and Luzy wanted a pretty shack like the others and did the work their own selves. Abby let them, smiling. They chose pale but warm green walls, and Lifee helped them make the pale pink curtains for it. Abby still smiled, saying, "Well, it take the place of spring green. And now I know when I make us'en a new house, they gon sure work on it, too!"

After Mor and Lifee moved into the main house, Abby did all the cooking on the woodburning stove there, easier than cooking in a fireplace, and because there was more room to move around in and store things. Now she had the slightly better pots and pans, even a frying pan. All of them could eat there or take their food to their own places, but mostly, they all ate together in the main house. They bathed there because that was easier, also. The outhouse to the main house was better, too, and Mor was always working on it to improve the smell and keep critters from moving in it from the cold.

Everything was going along very well in the school and all were proud, though they were not allowed to tell anyone what was going on in the school shack. They were proud inside their hearts and minds.

Mema was growing plump and went around smiling, happy to have her "fambly," but still sad because she had no "husban" like Lifee did. She always wanted to rub Lifee's swollen stomach. She helped Abby with the cooking when she was not working on some small outside job. Abby did the cooking for all of them except when someone wanted something special of their own which they shared with the others.

One day, as Mema sat sewing baby clothes from the material Lifee had bought from Mudville, she said, "I so happy I found ya'll. I never did even dream I would ever have me a fambly like this one. Ya'll ain lazy and you don steal and you gots love all round all of you. And I can read . . . a litty bit and write . . . a litty bit more."

Lifee, big and uncomfortable, was spitting into a small can. She just couldn't stop spitting. "I will sure be glad when this baby gets here. I'm tired of all this spitting and carrying all this weight! Feels like I have ten babies in here!" She spit again. "We glad we found you, too, Mema, cause if we hadn't, we might not have anything like this right now. The winter would have been hell."

Mema grinned in pleasure. "Yea, you be gon on down that road some else place. I's glad you stayin here."

Lifee lightly laughed and groaned, "I'm still going on down that road . . . someday. This is not the place for me."

Mema slowly shook her head, "It might all be someplace betta, but I shore don know no place I be pleased to be as this. I's home."

Lifee could only say, "Good."

Mema leaned toward Lifee, saying, "Now, all I needs is a good man for a husban and I be fine again. Like you and Mor."

"That ole Luther you brought by here a few times seem like a good man . . ."

"Oh, Lifee, he maybe is. He want to come move with me. Live with me. But . . . he don make my love spark none. I likes him, but I don want him doin nothin to make babies with me."

"Well, Mema, that is your body and that is your decision to make."

Mema smiled, "Yea . . . I makes my own cisions now."

Mema got up to leave, stretched, yawned and turned back at the door to face Lifee. "I prays to God to send me a husban. I pray to Him to send me a fambly and I got ya'll. So, I see what He gonna do this time. At church, He say ask and you receive."

Lifee smiled, spit and said, "Well, He got the power."

A few days later, after a particularly hard rain with fat, heavy clouds still filling the sky, everyone went to bed earlier. Some to study, some to just think, some to dream. Half asleep, Lifee heard noises in the yard near the main house. Sounds of moans and grunts. "Could one of the pigs have gotten out?" she asked herself. She pulled and pushed herself out of the bed, kicking over her spit-can, said "Shit!" and tried to look out of the window. Everything was black outside. She could still hear the moaning.

She turned back to the bed, trying to miss stepping near the spit-can and nudged Mor's shoulder and in a loud whisper said, "Mor! Mor!"

Mor groaned trying to wake up and said in his half sleep, "What, Massa! Yes, Massa!"

She shook his shoulder again, "Mor! It's me, baby! Lifee! Wake up! Wake up! There is something outside, moaning!"

He was awake now, raising up on his elbows, wiping his eyes with one hand. "What is it, baby? What is it?"

Lifee went back to the window, stepping in her spilled spit on the way. "Shit, now!" Come look out here, Mor. See if you see anything. You hear that. Be quiet!"

Mor listened, then moved to the window near Lifee, stepping in the same spit, saying, "Oh, damn! Lifee!"

"Shhhhhhhh. Your feet so big you had to go and step in it! Listen!"

He stood quiet and listened. He heard the sounds. "Cain see nothin out this window. It too dark out there! I get dressed and go see what makin that noise. Maybe somethin got hold a one of my animals, but I cain see how."

Mor dressed quickly and went outside with a lighted faggot. Shortly he returned with a worried look on his face. "It a man. He hurt. He bleedin somethin bad. I's gon have to bring em in."

Lifee gasped, "Bring him in?! Suppose he do somethin to us?"

Mor waved his hand, dismissing that thought. "I needs some help and ain no other man here and you too big with child and I don want you to get hurt carryin no big man. That's okay, I try to do it by myself." He went back out, saying, "Spread somethin out in that room by the fire and light a lamp in there."

Lifee stopped cleaning up the waste she had spilled and hastened as fast as she could to light another lamp and find a ragged old flannel sheet of Emmalee's to spread out before the fire. She also spread some old school papers over the sheet, mumbling, "He's bleeding!"

Mor dragged and pulled the man in as gently as he could. A trail of blood followed the man's legs. When they had him stretched out on the floor in front of the fireplace in the parlor, Lifee went to heat some water and find some rags to wash him with.

With one hand holding her side, Lifee declared, "We better call Mema, because I can't keep rushing like this and carrying this big pot of water. He's gonna need some good washin. You go get Mema or Abby and I will find some old clothes he can put on when we get those bloody ones off him." Mor was gone even as she finished speaking.

Mema came in tying an old robe around her she had found rambling in one of the old dilapidated houses in the area. Abby came with her dress over her nightgown. Mema rushed to the moaning man, Abby slowly walked over to him. Both bent down and began undressing him to see where the blood was coming from.

The gash across his face had stopped bleeding hard and was only staying moist. His chest and back had stripes and cuts across it and one of his legs had a very deep wound from an ax.

Abby was the first to speak while Mema squeaked and uttered little moans of empathy. "This man here hurt bad. Somebody done whipped him and cut him. Where we got that medicine salve? The turpentine. Alcohol. We got to fix that leg like a snakebite. Tie it up. Shut up, Mema, and get some hot water and get to cleaning up this blood off em!"

Lifee spoke, "The water's heating in the kitchen!" Mema flew, saying, "I get it, I get it! I get the terpintine and the alco'l. I get the whisky, too. I seen em pour it on a body to kill somethin! Mayhaps he need to drink some, too."

The man was still not fully conscious, but continued groaning now and then. They worked over him til they had done all they could. The man was now cleaned and wrapped in an old quilt. Mor stepped back, saying, "I blive that leg betta come off, it cut mighty deep to the bone; like they was cuttin a tree! But I don know how he gonna get it off. Cain call no docta, ain no docta would come out for a nigra. We done done all what we could. It tied up and the bleedin slowin down."

Lifee poured them all a small glass of the whisky and they sat around to wait for the man to awaken. He had fainted when the alcohol was poured into his wound. After an hour or so, Lifee suggested, "We ought to go to bed and sleep, it might be a long day tomorrow. He's warm now and the bleeding seems stopped."

Mor nodded his head. "When he wake up, he gon see ain nobody tried to do nothin but help em here."

Abby was already on her way out the door to her shack. Mema said, "I stay here with em. I ain sleepy. I can sleep right chere on this sofa anyhow. I keep the fire goin."

They all nodded and went their way to bed to rest. Mema sat there awhile, then poured herself a second glass of whisky, stared at the man another while, then fell asleep, snoring.

Lifee lay in bed falling asleep as Mor rubbed her swollen belly. He said thoughtfully, "I wonda who is the people who done that to him? Is they gonna still look for em and come here? He done trailed that blood and ain gonna be hard to fin. I get up in the mornin and get out there and sweep ova that trail on out to the road. We don need no trouble here. Maybe I betta go out now."

Lifee turned on her side, her back to Mor, and snuggled closer to him, smiling, thinking, "Please, no! You stay in here. You can't see the blood and neither can they. We'll get it early in the morning."

His sleepy voice said, "You right. It's way dark out there."

The last thing Lifee thought before sleep overcame her was, "Lord, I am so glad I have a man like Mor."

The injured man slept through the next day. Mema kept fresh alcohol on his wounds throughout the day. By then Abby had gone through her roots and made a poultice for his leg. He was resting easier, but Mema would not go away and leave him. She stayed at his side. All her little jobs flew out of her mind. Late in the evening, when he did groan and stir, beginning to awaken, she was there beside him.

She placed her hand on his chest, looked into his eyes and told him, "You alright now. We done took care for you. Now ya lay there and I fix ya some soup. Ya need to eat. Then you can tell what happen to ya."

The man nodded his head, felt the pain of his movement, closed his eyes and started to cry silently. Mema saw the tears and understood them to be tears of relief that she was black-skinned. When he had, painfully, swallowed each spoonful Mema gave him, he slept again. She stayed by his side.

The next day, he was awake for a longer time and tried to talk. "I is Benjamin. I's comin from Misippi. Had a mule and a pack. I din bother nobody, no white man. They wants my mule. It was dark. They beats me, cuts me. Took my mule. Throwed my pack all round the road and lef me there. I crawl, I crawl, I crawl. Don know how come I to come here, but I could't crawl no more. I stopped crawlin and jes lay out there to die. Want to hide, but cain get up to find no good hidin spot. So I jes stop, I goin be ready to die."

Mor, already having covered and swept the blood tracks over, went out with his wagon to see if he could find the pack for the man, Benjamin. He found a few things on the side of the road and looking farther in the high weeds, found a hammer, shears and a measuring rod. Mor smiled. "A workinman."

When he took the things back to Benjamin, Benjamin said, "My clock, my glass, my hooks is gone. That alright. I gets me some more."

Lifee was expecting her baby any time now and did not want Benjamin to occupy the parlor when she was in labor, so they talked about what to do with him. That last shack was not ready for anybody, much less a sick man. Then Mema spoke up, "I take em home with me. I take care a him."

Lifee looked at Mor, Mor looked at Mema.

Mema pushed out her chest, "That ain what I wants with em. He need a nursewoman. He a sick man. I'm just gon help em get betta. It ain all ya'll say so, no way. It my say-so, too! I's grown woman and that's my house. So . . . I am taken em home with me til he get well and go where he want to go!" And that's what she did.

In a few weeks Benjamin was up and limping around. He was not a lazy man, and everything he could do, he did. He became a good help to Mor. Lifee teased Mema, "He ain't so sick no more. He tall, he smooth, cept for that scar on his face and that hole in his leg. He clean and he talks gentle. You can't tell me you and that man are not sleeping together! Are you falling in love with him?"

Mema smiled a little and murmured, "Done already done that since I watch him when he first came."

Lifee smiled with her, but spoke seriously, "He isn't making any move to clean up that last shack and move out of your house."

Mema poked out her chest again, declared with spunk, "I don want em to! We nice company to both of us. I don want em to move to that shack!" No one argued with Mema if they didn't have to.

Lifee decided, "I had better have a talk with Mor and he had better have a talk with Mema. We got young girls here and we want things right."

One day soon after that talk, Mor spoke to Mema. "Mema, I blive it's time we have a lil talk.

Mema turned her head to the side, saying, "A lil talk. Bout what? You sounds just like a white massa."

"Ain no white massa, but anybody what got sense can have a lil talk."

"Well, suh, talk. But if'n I wants to do somethin, I can do it.

Mor nodded his head, said, "Alright. But . . . we got us a nice lil place here, Mema."

Mema agreed, "Sho do."

Mor continued, "What's good bout it is, we have peace and a cleanness and a goodness and, I hopes, God's blessin."

"Praise the Lawd."

Mor spoke on, "We has to keep that. So we cannot have mens movin in with womens. That can't be no way startin, cause we have a lot of women here is alone."

Mema turned her head to the other side. "Ummm-hmmm."

"So . . . if ya wants Benjamin, loves Benjamin, and he lovin on you, you gonna have to marry up with him, decent. He gon have to love you nough to make you hisn wife fore God."

"Marry! Who gon marry us?"

Mor laughed a little, "We take care that when ya'll decides. But we got young girls here now. Learnin how to live life and they gon take they lesson from us and we got to learn em right."

"Thems Lifee words."

Mor nodded, "What blongs to Lifee, blongs to me. Theys our words."

"Well . . . ya'll right, Massa Mor."

"Don call me Massa Mor. I's talkin to you like a papa . . . not a bossman, cause I care bout all ya'll what is here in my family."

"Well, I's sure gonna talk to Benjamin next time I see's em."

"He be in some-at soon, cause we just clearin up a field over yonder. Ground still hard, but we workin em what we can. I blive he be in soon, cause the cold make that there leg pain some."

Mema laughed happily, "He come in soon cause he like to kiss and hug on me."

"And I hope that be all."

"It ain all! I's a grown woman."

Mor nodded his head. "I knows. You do as you please. He just cain keep livin in yo shack lessen he have right good tentions and move in right. I means that."

But Mema was mellow when she talked about Benjamin. "I knows that. Preciate that. I's a pertected daughter like them white folks use to pertect they daughters, some of em."

"Call it whatsomever, but I's pertecting this here place.

Ethylene was quietly busy, always helping where she was needed. She was happy in her freedom and pleased with her family. But, sometimes, she was lonely. She lived alone in her shack that was

painted on the inside after Mor had scraped and sanded the thou-
sand-splintered raw wood, as he had done with each shack. She
decorated it with rocks, feathers, curtains and a small spread she
had made for her bed. She was working on a quilt for the next
winter.

She had seen very little of love, happy love between men and
women. Love very seldom had time to grow before one was gone or
the master decided he wanted her for himself or someone else. She
had heard tell some masters didn't mind, but, mostly, they seemed
not to like you to get too happy even for a little while. But she had
watched Mor and Lifee when they were together and, now, she saw
how happy Mema seemed to be even with the limping man. Ethylene was lonely for someone of her own. Often she lay on her little
pallet and thought about men and life.

Of her memories of men, the only ones she had, she was trying
to run from and she didn't always get away.

Sometimes Ethylene looked longingly at Lifee's body and its
bigness with child. She always offered to rub her stomach and her
back. Sometimes Lifee let her, but most times she wanted Mor to
do it. "I don't blame her, I would want my man to do it, too," she
thought sadly. "This freedom is why they can do that. God bless
Freedom."

She saw men at the Winston store sometime, but they looked
tired and old or they were young and not really looking for a woman
to burden them down because they were so poor. She turned over
on her back, laughing to herself, "I keep lookin, though."

Ethylene didn't go to the store much because sometime the white
men there stared at her as they spit their tobacco juice thoughtfully.
"I's still afraid of white mens. They do whatsomever they want to.
Ain no law, still no law, for Negro womens to hold white men
back."

She heard Abby holler her name and jumped up to go answer.
The milk was ready to be churned. She carried it to her warm
shack, set it between her knees and began the chomp-chomp-

chomp of the churner. Her thoughts kept time to the beat churn. "I wants me a man who ain scared of no white mens!" She thought again. "He be a fool, though, if he didt be leery of white men and I don't want no fool. I guess I just keep lookin. I gets me a fine house. All painted nice. And I sleeps through the whole night and ain nobody botherin me. I can sleep past sunrise, like now, and my work is my own. As the Bible say, 'The sweat of my brow and my labor is for me' and if I shares with others, well, they shares with me. God bless everbody, but specially me. God, I needs me somebody to be with me. Laugh with me. Smile to me. Help me live."

She finished churning the butter and carried the churn back to the main house. She set the butter in the butterbowl, put it in the cooler, cleaned the churn and sat down to talk to Abby awhile.

Her voice was full of her discouragement, "You know that Mr. Winston at the store done sent me word that white man doctor who is building that house up the road wants him a cook and housecleaner."

Abby kept moving about her work as she spoke, "I knows. You could use the money, chile. You likes nice things for yoself."

Ethylene twisted in her chair, "Yea, but . . . I don much want to be goin down there with no white man less I know he gon have somebody else there with us."

Abby looked at her, "Ya ain got to stay down there no nights."

Ethylene and Abby talked a great deal, so Ethylene could look Abby in the face and say, "Mens don wait for no dark night!"

Abby turned back to her pots, "He don sound like no bad man. He raised in the South, but he some kind of a Nothern college man what done come here to vet the animals. Say he like to dig in the mountains lookin for somethin blong to them Indians what they usta fight and run off from they home here."

Ethylene looked up from pulling at a fingernail, "He a school man?"

"I don blive you can tell him you is learnin to read none."

"He got a wife with him?"

"Don know."

"That sure would help . . . a little."

Abby turned to look at her, "You can ask that Winston man, he a nice man and he will tell you what he think. I think."

Ethylene got up to go, saying, "If the doctor man was a Negro man, that Winston man would tell me what he thinks, but since the doctor man is a white man, he might not tell me what he thinks bout him."

"Whateva way he do it, ask him and see what he do say, then you have somethin more to think on. Cause we can use all the money we gets, but ain nobody gon make you go nowhere, chile."

Ethylene smiled, "Yessum," and was gone bouncing down the steps feeling better.

Abbysinia was busy and pleased to be. She had never had time to rest, though as a cook she worked at her own pace most of the time. It was just all day and some nights before freedom. Up even before the rooster and he crowed at daybreak. Oh! How she loved her two girls, Meda and Luzy. "And they learnin how to read! And write! Oh, Lawd! Your blessin in abundance. We all full and I got my own shack. My own!"

Abby didn't think of a man. "I ain bringin no man in no house with me and my two girls! When they all grown up and gone married, maybe then I get some old widderman to rockchair with and talk with in my later age."

She dreamed of building her own house. "Right chere on this here land! I can do it! I can carpenter good as Mor, I swann. I wants my own kitchen and I wants my own pots and pans. I got to think of the way to make me some money. I needs my own money cause them girls gonna need more than that schoolin what come out that shack. I want em to go far as they can! I think of a way, please, Lawd."

⌒

It was middle March when Mema went to Mor and Lifee one evening and said, "I blive I done made up my mind. I's goin to marry up with Benjamin. He ready and I's ready and, sides that"— she gave them a wide, happy smile—"I's goin to have a baby!" She put her hands on her hips, saying, "And sides that, I got to marry up soon cause we don want to be no bad zample for our young girls round here. Now! Who gon marry us's?"

Lifee, who had been groaning from the weight of her stomach, now smiled in her discomfort and said, "Oh, good, Mema. Congratulations!"

Mor, smiling, said, "We got a Bible round here and I can read nough to say a marriage. We get a broom and you can jump over that, too, and Lifee can write you up a real licens and you be married up for sure!"

Lifee struggled to sit up, "We are low on white flour, but we'll get some and some sugar for a cake." She turned to Mor, "See can you sell Mr. Winston some brooms and trap baskets."

"I already got someat made." Mor smiled.

Lifee clapped her hands, "We going to have a party! It's a good thing it's still winter. That venison Benjamin brought you, Mema, can freeze and last til the party.

Mema turned her head to the side, said, "Ain got to last too long no way."

"How long?"

"A week."

"That's enough time, Mema."

In short time, Mor and Benjamin built a fire in the dirt floor of the little smokehouse. They got bark from a hickory tree and old corncobs and let the meat cook til the grease dripped down and the smell just spread out all over. When the meat was, finally, half smoked, they cut part away for the wedding and left the rest to finish cooking and dripping so they would have meat later on if winter lingered. That way, they wouldn't have to get out in the last snows and cold winds. They prayed the good smell of the cooking meat did not go so far as to get over to Rufus Bingly's house, because he was always scrounging food for his family and mostly for himself.

One morning Mor hitched the wagon up and he and Lifee rode over to Mudtown for supplies they did not have. Still saying they were shopping for their mistress, they did not have any trouble. The one hundred dollars Emmalee had helped Lifee change had lasted a long time. It was good that things were cheap.

They bought more flour, sugar, potatoes, salt and other things you learn you need as you go along. They wanted a nice, though small feast for the wedding supper. Lifee wanted a ham.

Since it was still winterish, Lifee went to the fabric store and got, "for her mistress," whole bolts of flannel and white cotton, a few of bright blue, yellows and greens, and one red. She went to the pawn-shop again and got two black suits; one to be fixed for Benjamin to marry in and one for Mor to do the marrying ceremony in. Benja-min had earned it and it would be the first suit he had ever owned and "He must be at least forty years old," Lifee thought. "And Mor? I want to do him proud because he will be doing the reading after long, long, steady study. He deserves it. Besides he's going to need it if we keep going to that church up the way."

She thought of her dear friend, Abby, and bought her soft, com-fortable shoes for houseshoes and soft-soled warm ones for outside wear. "Everybody's feet were ruined with them tough shoes the massas used to give em. They wouldn't bend if a horse wore em." The same for Ethylene, Meda and Luzy, though their outdoor shoes were more sturdy. Ribbons and some lace were on her list; some for Mema's wedding dress, such as it was, and some for Ethy-lene and the girls. A small piece of white satin was bought to make a wedding bow for Mema's shoes. Then she was through. She already had bought things to make for the baby, and Mor had built a crib-bed.

When they went home, Mor made a quilt bed on the wagon floor and bade Lifee lie down and rest her back. She had picked up a Sears, Roebuck catalogue, "So I can order things without people knowing so much about my business." She looked through it as they rode home.

Mor was always concerned about the house. He longed for the days of good, warm weather to come. He was aching to get started on "his" land. Every day he thought to himself, as his eyes roved over the land, "My land. I gots my own land." He imagined and pictured all the things he would do; a bigger smokehouse, a toolshed, fix the pigpen. He wanted to build the bed for his child to be born in, but the weather hadn't permitted him time to do it as beautifully as he wanted it done. He wanted, he wanted, he wanted; and his fingers ached to get started. The wedding gave him a way to use that dormant energy.

Getting ready for the marriage, Mema ran around like she was crazy. One minute she was sewing her red wedding gown. She had been so happy when Lifee gave her the red piece of material. It was cotton, but she never gave satin a thought, except for the white satin bows for her shoes; she loved that, too.

The next minute she would be making her new set of sheets from the cheap cotton Lifee had bought. She was, also, quilting her blanket from scraps. Everyone had to watch their scraps and rags or they would be in Mema's quilt. Ethylene hid her scraps for her quilt under her bed.

Ethylene was alternately sulking or happy. She was busy with helping Mema, helping Abby in the kitchen, doing her schoolwork with everybody. She had gone to see about the job with the white man, Dr. Ben Wright, who was building his house. He had seemed nice, but who knew? He didn't have a wife, but he didn't seem to pay Ethylene much mind at all. His interest was taken totally with his house and his work. He was, also, a nice-looking man around thirty-five years old. Most important, he didn't talk to his Negro helpers as if they were fools. He had hired Ethylene, but didn't need her until the house was complete. She was happy about that.

Mema was really cleaning and trying to fix up her shack for her new husband even though Benjamin already lived there. Mor had moved him out, temporarily, until after the wedding, saying, "Bad luck to stay with yo bride befo the wedding. You need to be goin somewheres kinda new after the wedding, not going back somewhere you just left."

Benjamin was going around grinning all the time. "Married! I's gettin married! Brother!" He was already making the cradle for his coming baby. "I gets to keep this un!" Mema, grinning, too, switched around, patting, smoothing and taking things from other shacks and the house to set in her shack. "Make it more pretty, ladylike and all," she said. People left some of their things there or went and got some of them back, as they saw fit. They were all excited for her. It was cold and bleak weather and this was something good to break the monotony of no work. So as the day came closer, they all washed, cooked, baked, cleaned.

They were going to have the wedding inside the main house. It was large enough for all their little family group, but Mema knew other people and had invited them all, against Mor's wishes. But Mema knew some would bring small gifts. "And I wants them gifts!" Neither Mor nor Lifee wanted any whites to think they were having too good a time. "Whites don like that," Mor groaned, "Lord, it's so many links to the white man's chain."

Mema cried off and on all through her wedding day, thinking of how everyone was doing something for her. "My fambly! My fambly." The wedding cake was beautiful. White icing with little pink sugar rosette flowers on it.

Mema told Mor, "I wants you to give me away to my husband cause you part of my fambly."

Abby asked, "How he gon give you away and marry you, too?"

Mema answered, "Just keep walking and stand in front when he through givin me away."

Benjamin had made Mema a ring from one of the silver-looking dinner forks, so one fork had two prongs missing when it was put back in the drawer.

They had baked venison, fried chicken, baked yams, stewed apples with molasses and cinnamon, canned string beans, hot biscuits and rolls, buttermilk, lemonade and the men had some white lightning before the wedding and some after the wedding, too.

Everything went as planned. There were no mishaps. When Mor, slowly, because he was still learning to read, reached the place to say, "Now, I pronounces you a man and his wife," Mema kissed her new husband and said, "Amen, Jesus!"

The festivities truly began then. There were about fifteen people there and they all sang. About Jesus. About Freedom. They sang some homemade blues as all the first blues were, about love and marriage. They shouted with joy and love and passion for their God and these newlyweds. This was the first real marriage for any of them to attend that they, alone, had planned and worked toward in their own way; under God, not over a broom. Meda and Luzy whispered together about what they thought the wedding couple would be doing that night. The couple's new name was Benjamin and Mema Dollar. Mema's choice.

A bit stout now, the little bride shone with joy in her red cotton wedding dress, her white veil trailing and flying behind her. She danced the white satin right off her shoes. Her face beamed at her husband right up to the time all her guests were leaving and her family was ready to go to bed. Then her new husband said, "Let's go on home, wife." And they did. That night, as they all slept, Mema hugged her husband, Mor hugged Lifee, Abby hugged Meda and Luzy, and Ethylene hugged her pillow.

TEN

March passed, and Mor started breaking the ground, in April, as the earth thawed and softened a bit. He had turned over the ground he planned to plant and was waiting for the right time to lay his seeds. His fish traps were out every night. His regular small traps for little critters were always out. Mor was not using all the land, fifty acres. He decided to use twenty acres of the best land and grow mostly what they themselves needed, to avoid white jealousy and envy. Plenty food for themselves: onions, potatoes, greens, tomatoes, green beans, watermelon, peas, corn, some velvet beans for the two cows, some sugar cane for syrup. Garlic was planted close to the house, also turnips, beets and carrots.

He and Ben had built a crib of oak and had built a hardwood bed for his child to be born in, and it was placed in the main house with the crib. Lifee always kept one large room upstairs empty of everything but what personal things Mz Emmalee had left in order to prove the house was Mz Emmalee's.

Lifee was still making tiny shirts and diapers from the soft white flannel and cotton she had bought. She had clean rags and sheets for her laying-in, and all was ready. Abby watched Lifee closely, very solicitous for her. They all tried to keep her from any work, even the lightest. "But I can sew. This needle isn't heavy!"

Lifee sat long hours thinking of her dreams and hopes. "This ole piece of broken heart of mine which was lost out in the world so long has a place of its own I can call my home."

One morning the sky was dark with clouds and it was raining, a steady, gentle rain. Thunder rumbled across the sky now and again. The magnificent, newly leafed trees swayed in the wind, like dancing. Birds making their sounds, flying through the air against the sky were beautiful. Mor liked that. He was out in the fields and Lifee was in the house alone. She was in the bedroom, piddling over the crib: smoothing the blankets, fluffing the little ruffled pillow Ethylene had made for the baby. There was one each from Meda and Luzy.

The trees were beginning to bloom. Blossoms showing between all the new green leaves in the woods. Honeysuckle blooming, the sweet smell wafting everywhere. Everyone, even Abby, was out in the fields with Mor, turning and breaking soil, but Abby was about to come out of the rain and bring her two girls with her. "Ain nothin but monia out here in this weather."

Lifee was singing songs to the Lord and praying in between. "Send your blessings down on me, Lord, I need em so." A thought crossed her mind of something she wanted, and she turned to move across the room and felt the first pang of pain. She placed her hands on her lower belly and bent slightly until the pain passed.

She smiled to herself and made her way to the bed. "I will lie down and feel my baby preparing to come to us." She lay, easy and gently, upon the bed, still holding her stomach in her hands, waiting for the next pain.

She thought, "In freedom . . . to freedom . . . my baby is coming into a different world. I have plans for you, dreams for you, my child. That's why we have struggled and lived, little black baby, so you could be born. So you could live, dream and do your dreams.

The dreams we could not do. But . . ." Another pain cut across her hips. She gasped and waited a moment, then continued talking to her child. "I love to feel you. It hurts, but I can bear it because I love you . . . already. I have loved you from the beginning when I knew you were there. I loved you even before I knew you were there. I wait for you." Another pain stopped her, but when it was over, she smiled, a sad, happy smile.

Abby had left the girls at the shack and come to the main house to look over the food situation. After she had been inside for a few minutes, she suddenly stopped and listened to the silence from upstairs. She moved to the doorway of the parlor, looking up, then she moved to the stairs, looking up. No sounds, just a feeling she had. She went back to the kitchen to continue her work.

She began to make little cookies for Meda and Luzy. "If they gon have to stay in that cabin all day from this rain, they gon need somethin nice." But she also prepared some garlic, chopped it, cooked it and added a little sugar for taste. "They gon need this here garlic tonic for worms and such. Make em sleep good, too."

Lifee lay in bed, feeling the pains that were coming more often now, about every ten minutes. She lay still between the sharp cuts of pain across her stomach that seemed, to her, to have a life of its own. Now the pains were harder when they came. Tears gathered in the corners of her eyes, rolling slowly down her cheeks.

She felt something like a knot being untied in her lower belly, and her water broke. She tried to raise her body up, "I should'a thought of that and put those towels under me." She was pushing and pulling herself off the bed to get the towels and fold her quilts down, when Abby stuck her head through the door, saw Lifee, gasped and ran downstairs to the yard, screaming, "Mor! Mor! Run get Mor, Luzy! Meda! Run get Mor." Then she turned and ran back into the house to Lifee.

Abby undressed Lifee and changed her into an open-backed nightshirt. She rolled her over and pulled the quilts and covers down to the foot of the bed. She stuck a big, clean rag between Lifee's legs and stretched papers all over the bed under her.

Mor, Mema and Ethylene had run from the fields to the house, up the stairs to Lifee. Meda and Luzy tried to run up the stairs also, but Abby stopped them with a sure hand and pointed downstairs, saying, "Put some water on to boil. Lots of it!"

By that evening Meda and Luzy had run up and down the stairs a thousand times, it seemed. Fetched water to boil from the well a hundred times, it seemed. Ethylene and Mema also fetched hot water, washed the rag towels several times, hanging them around the blazing fireplace to dry quickly. Mor wouldn't leave Lifee's side. She started out holding his hand, but soon didn't want to be touched by anybody. Just wanted that baby to come.

They did not have a midwife, but most older Negro women knew how to help at the birth of a child. Abby and Mema kept Lifee clean and oiled to help the baby through. Finally, they had to put Mor out. When Lifee moaned or screamed out in pain, he screamed out, too. "Wait in the kitchen. Ben done come in now. Have a glass of whisky. Go!"

Around seven o'clock that night, on April third, 1867, Mema caught the little brown baby, a boy. They all smiled, and Lifee breathed a painless moment of relief. She was exhausted, as were Mema, Abby and Ethylene. Ethylene had been running up and down the stairs, since she was the youngest. Mema, growing big with child, had been washing the rags and wiping Lifee's brow and body that glistened with sweat. Abby, crying softly at her friend's pain, kept saying, "It got to be like this. This the way it is, oh, Lawd." And now it was done. The baby was born.

When the baby was cleaned and wrapped in a blanket, Mor was called in, and when he saw his baby he had eyes for no other. He stood, beaming down at his free baby. The others were gathered around Mor, smiling at the new father and child, glad it was all over.

Now, of a sudden, Lifee was screaming again. Startled, they all turned to see what the problem was. Her legs were raised, opening wide again, and another head was coming through.

"Twins!"

"Another baby coming!"

"Oh, my Lawd!"

Mor exclaimed, "Jesus!"

Abby moved first, rushing to the bed, "More towels, gimmie them clean rags there!" Then to Lifee, "Push easy now, don't, you gonna hurt yoself!"

Mema said to herself, "Betta get some nother blanket ready!"

Mor said to himself, "I should'a build another crib! Jesus! I didn know!"

Abby caught the baby as it finished coming from its mother. There were gasps from Mema and Ethylene. Mor turned to look at the new baby. He frowned. A long moment, everybody waited. The baby was a boy. The baby was white.

They were all stunned. Lifee was gasping for breath, her body relieved at pain being, finally, over. Then Mema moved quickly and took the baby up in a towel, to clean and oil him. Both babies had started crying without being spanked. They had lived together for nine months without harm: and now they were in this world.

Everyone was strangely quiet. Lifee asked, "Why is everybody so quiet? What's wrong with my baby?"

Mema answered, "Ain nothin wrong with em. He just a diff'rent color from the first one. Cain get shed of them white folks."

Lifee, exhausted, raised her head. "What do you mean?"

Mor answered, "Our first one is brown. Our . . . second one is white. That . . ."

Lifee cut him off, "White? What are you saying? Let me see."

Mema spoke from across the room, "In a minute, in a minute. He almos clean and ready." She spoke to the baby as she lay him in Lifee's arm, "You ready for yo mama, boy?" Mor was holding the first one.

Abby spoke, "Let's us all go on out and let's leave the new mama and daddy alone with they new babies. We got to get the new mama some soup and the new pa a drink! We been had a long job. I have me a drink of that white lightnin my own self!"

"Me, too."

"I blive I will, too." And they left the room, taking the dirty towels and sheets with them.

Lifee looked up at Mor and burst into tired tears. "His baby! I hate him!"

Mor bent to put the brown baby in her arms, then picked up the white one. "Hush, woman. That white man ain here. These our babies."

"But he . . ."

Mor shook his head, "Hush talkin like that. Mayhap a long time ago he had a little . . . little somethin to do with it. But he gone now, left far behind us. These here is your babies . . . and what's yours is mine. These our babies. I wish I could'a gone through it for ya. I's proud of you . . . and I's proud to have em. This our family. These babies . . . I hoped big and you gived big."

Tears running down her face, she moaned, "But I didn't know and I give you this . . ."

Mor sat on the edge of the bed, "Lifee, baby, it was a time I was so alone I was misable and dint know it. That's misable sides bein a slave. I dint even dream of havin a woman like you. Wouldn'ta dreamed of havin a dream. Dint even hope for nothin! You come . . . in a little while you took this piece of broken-down man with a dead, empty heart. Lookit here, woman, I got a piece of my own land on this here earth. I got you and now . . . I am the papa of two fine babies. This here baby ain just a white baby, he got his African blood in em, too. Just like us. He ours. God made these babies and give em to you and what is yo's is sho nuff mine."

"Oh, Mor."

"What we gon name em, baby?"

They looked at the babies. Lifee pulled them closer to her. The white one asleep, the brown one looking at Mor with serious, round, bright, brown eyes.

Lifee softly smiled, "Well, I wanted to name a son Loam.

"Loams? What kinda . . ."

"It means 'earth, dirt, soil,' and everything of any value comes from the earth. Everything!"

Mor lightly laughed, "Well, let's call one that Loam name. What we gon call the other one?"

Lifee turned to the other baby and softly laughed, "Well . . . he mighty white."

"We could call him Mighty."

"No, he might not take it right. We can name him Air, maybe Airiel. Then we have earth and air."

Mor stood up, clasping his hand behind him. "You knows I like reading that Bible and I likes the names in it. I thought I would like a son named Able."

"Able and Aman! Yes, I like that!"

"Aman! Yes, let's name the brown son Aman, so he don't never forget he is one, and let's name the white son Able, cause he is gonna be if we raise em right!"

The after-birth pains were beginning, and Lifee groaned and lay back on the bed. She smiled at Mor through the pain, saying, "Sure wish you could go through this for me, too." Abby and Mema took over and Mor was banished from the room. He did not go back to work though, he went into his woods and thanked God for his sons, for them being safe . . . and free, for his wife coming through the childbirth in fine condition. "Just thank you for life, Lawd, for life."

And the African blood of Suwaibu and Kola were joined through Mor and Lifee and was still rushing, striving, pulsing toward the future. And the future had slowly rotated, changed, like the world turns, time moves. From African native to slave, to freedmen, to landowners, to parents, until there was now an even broader view in its scope. Oh, the African blood was moving on.

The twins settled comfortably into the family. Negroes were used to accepting the many-colored children the white masters left behind. This was part of their life in the white man's shaping of America.

As time passed, Lifee settled happily into motherhood. Mema settled happily into waiting for her child to be born. Abby, Meda and Luzy even enjoyed working in the fields because they were working for themselves. The hours were shorter for work and they could leave and go to the house whenever they felt like it. There was no angry red face glaring at them, no whip threatening to eat into the flesh of their backs.

Benjamin was glad to have a wife, a home and a joy . . . all in the twinkling of a beating and a painful leg. He had been going up the road with his mule, not knowing where he was going. Just looking for a life. Now he had one; it was here. The school still went on most evenings, and now Ben came to the class.

Mema had her baby amid a great deal of screaming, "Lawdy, Lawdy, mama, mama!" Kicking enough to break the bed post Ben had carved for them. And then . . . tears of joy. A girl! She held her baby, at last, proudly to her one remaining breast. She could stare at her baby for hours. Later, as it grew, she carried the child from chore to chore. She and Ben were happy.

But now, Lifee asked her, "What you going to name your baby?"

Mema smiled her huge smile, "Her name is Babe."

Babe nestled, even smiling, in the warmth of her mother's arms. Alone with Babe, Mema stared at her and smoothed her arms and legs, often holding the child fiercely, close to her breast. Her tears often fell on the baby's head as it slept in her arms. "I gots me a baby that is mine and I can keep it." Too soon, Mema was doubly happy, because she was pregnant again.

Mor paid Ben for his work. Lifee told him, "We are paying you out of what little we have so you can save some to buy your own farm someday. We don't ever know what is going to happen and we may not always have this place." Ben dug a hole in their floor and they started saving their little money. Mema made clothes for her baby out of every scrap big enough she could find. The others started putting their sewing baskets away, otherwise they would look up and see something they had planned to use for themselves on little Babe as a dress or shirt or something.

Mema asked Lifee, "Why don't ya'll sell some of this here produce we done growed? (She seldom came to school now to hear their continued plans for safety.)

Seriously, Lifee answered, "We work to eat and survive. We don't need the attention from white folks, who might think we are making money. Mor sells some to Winston for his store, but we don't want to go round in everybody's sight bringing attention to ourselves. See? Nobody makes any money off us and they might resent that."

Mema thought a moment, then nodded her head, "Yea, that ole man Mr. Coral raise all that tobacco and it look like him and his lil wife and babies was gonna be alright. But, he shouldn'ta painted his house . . . cause them nightriders sure did burn it up . . . and all what was left of his tobacco fields, too!"

"Poor Mz Coral. With a new baby coming and no house."

"They sure will do it. I bet I know who is the riders."

Lifee thought she knew also. She often took a few squirrels Mor had caught and a large basket of vegetables and fruit from the harvest over to ole Mz Bingly. She and the old woman were friends now . . . of a sort. She did it to make Rufus think twice about taking food out of his mother's mouth.

Once, in Rufus's hearing Mz Bingly asked, "How ya'll doin over there? I hope them riders don bother ya'll none. They just terrible."

And Lifee answered, "No, mam, they haven't bothered us. And if they ever do, we will be leaving . . . that day. Mz Emmalee just have to let her farm go, cause we won't stay."

Rufus did not believe Emmalee was coming back to him, but good food growing right next door to you was better than empty fields, even if he did have to sneak and walk way over yonder to back fields to steal any. "That negra planted them last three acres in back! Whyn't he just plant close to the road like everbody else?" And, too, he liked the squirrel meat that Mor sent. He didn't shoot it, so it wasn't full of buckshot, and you could chew it easy, even if you had sore gums and teeth.

After Lifee made clothes for Winston's children, his wife, Anne, became friendly to Lifee. Anne was a gentle woman, kindly and nice to everyone. She stayed close to her house next to the store. She would go over and help her husband when she was through with her own work, but usually she was home. She spoke to Lifee one day, "It's so quiet and nice out here, but it's not too many women to talk to, cept for a quick minute."

Once Lifee had given her a pie of Abby's and since that time Anne would walk over to Lifee's about once a month and buy a pie, which helped Abby to save toward her dream house. But, it also gave Lifee an idea. She spoke to Abby about it.

"Abby, you know you could open a little pie shop right up there next to the road. Mor could build you a little shed and a case of shelves. You could sell em now and then. Make a little spending or saving change. Meda and Luzy could help and they could use something to keep them busy and put a nickel or dime in their banks too."

Abby nodded her head thoughtfully, "I got all the sugar and flour I needs now and them fruit trees was full. I ain got no lemons, though. But we got plenty milk."

Lifee was excited with the idea. "These white folks miss that Negro cooking like they used to have it. You'll do good!" They looked at each other and smiled as Lifee continued. "We will even put up a little sign. Ethylene will help us. Sign can say MISS MAMMY, and we will tell them it means they miss ole mammy, but they will really be calling you Miss. They laughed a little at the joke, but now even Abby was excited.

In the next few weeks, between working the fields, Mor and Ben worked with Abby to build her a shed for the store. They had already cut trees for lumber in the last fall, and it was stored and ready to use. Three sides and shutters in front. A counter with shelves beneath it and shutters for it to be closed until a customer came. The customer could stop a wagon and take a few steps to the pie shed. Abby was on her way, Luzy and Meda at her side. They were still in school and doing well in math.

When it opened, they kept only a dollar in change. People began to come and they soon learned to bring the correct change and the pie pans back. Soon they ordered their favorite pies in advance. Abby sold at least seven or eight a day on the weekends unless there was a special order on a weekday. Whites and blacks bought. More whites had more money. The Negroes could make their own pies anyway. It was a little business, but it was their business. Abby thought to herself, "Magine that! Bein paid to work!" Then, a little later, "And workin for me. Myself!"

Lifee had her hands full with the twins, who were full of energy and growing fast, when she discovered she was pregnant again. She was happy again. "I hope it's a girl this time, because I believe it's the last time," she told Abby. "Mema's is due any day now."

When Ethylene had started working for the doctor, she thought she would hate the job and him, but he was easygoing and focused on his business, his plans. Dr. Wright loved animals and loved his work. People learned he was there and good at what he did. And cheap. He loved books and now Ethylene had access to them. Sometimes he talked to her, answering her many questions about the North, West and East and how life was different in all these places, yet, still . . . somehow the same.

Ethylene didn't think so much of a husband now. When she would help Lifee with the babies, Lifee would tell her what she knew of the world. They sat in the parlor one day, each holding a child. The babies were eleven months old: fine, healthy babies. Ethylene stood, hugging a plump baby, and handed it over to Life. "These babies sure getting heavy, chile. You better quit feeding em so much."

Life laughed with joy, "Oh, I have to feed my babies!"

Ethylene sat back thoughtfully, "I wonder what they gonna be when they grow up. One thing, sure won't be no slave!"

Life smiled as she lay one baby down, "Everything they can if I can help them. How is your job?"

Ethylene sighed, "Oh, it's fine. I like it. But, I'm thinking of things. I want to be somebody else. I don't want to be a teacher. I wants to be a nurse."

"Well, you keep moving along in your studies and you can."

Ethylene sat up, "I can?!"

"Sure. It won't be easy. Remember how they used to have Negro women nursing slaves on the plantation? And in the war? Sure did! They didn't always go to any school, and certainly no special school. But they worked on real people and saved lives."

"I want to be a real nurse."

"Well, we have to find a school, but I don't know if they have a school for Negroes. We have to press harder on your arithmetic. Get you ready."

Ethylene fell back with another sigh, "It take money, don't it, though?"

"Some."

"I ain't save but a little."

Life lay a baby in the wide crib. "Haven't saved!" she corrected Ethylene. "Well, keep saving . . . and we can make it. Quit buying all those little trinkets you like so much."

"I'd buy books, but Winstons don't have much to choose from, cept baby books for ABCs. There still isn't any school coming round here."

Life sat down, took a deep breath, "Well, you work for a man who can order you whatever books you want."

"I read his medical books, but I don't understand em."

Lifee sat forward, "Tell him. Tell him you want to understand more so you can be more help to him with the animals. Ask him where Negroes can go to school to become a nurse. I think that would be wonderful for you. It's more to life for a woman than fields to plant and a baby to birth and a husband to feed."

Ethylene laughed lightly, "Girl, Minister Prattle would die if he heard you say that."

"I'm not talking to the Minister Prattle. I'm talking to you!"

Soon after that, one day when everyone was in the fields and Mor had taken Lifee and Ethylene to town, Mema had her baby all by herself. The only evidence was another broken bed post. The bloody sheets were rolled up and put out of sight; the baby was cleaned and Mema was in the bed nursing her baby, grinning, with Babe asleep beside her. "It's another girl! I got two girls! I was gonna name her Betty. Always like that name. But I cide I'm gon name her Bettern, cause she better'n all babies I ever seen cept Babe." So, that was that!

Mor made a good harvest from his twenty acres he decided to use. The barn was full of wheat for the two cows and their calves, the two horses and the mule. The corn crib was full of corn for the hogs and the family. Abby had canned, dried or salted everything that could be and the shelves were loaded in the basement and pantry. They didn't kill their livestock, but the smokehouse was full of Mor's fruitful hunting trips.

They had raised only two bales of cotton. Mor had told the sad and angry stories of other Negro men trying to farm who had taken their produce to the mills and been cheated right in front of their faces and given almost nothing for a year's work. So Lifee sat down and wrote another letter to herself from Mz Emmalee, asking Mr. Winston to take Mor to the mills and oversee the weighing and the paying and he could have ten percent of the total paid, which was a good incentive.

Mr. Winston went with Mor. The white weighing man cut fifty percent of the weight, turned to Winston and winked. Mr. Winston didn't need enemies, his position as Freedman's Bureau manager placed him in a precarious position among the whites for speaking, when possible, on behalf of the Negroes. He spoke softly but firmly to the weight man, "This here is Mz Emmalee's produce. This Mor works for her. Now . . . we cain't cheat a white lady." They got the correct price and Mr. Winston got his ten percent. In addition, Lifee made a pinafore each for his two daughters and a plain nice shirt for his son. She wanted to count on Winston's help in the future.

Mor was happy watching his family and his farm grow. Everyone had plenty to eat, few but decent clothes and good shoes.

Everyone, except one, went to church on the Sundays the preacher came. One always had to stay behind to see they had no unwanted nosy visitors. Preacher Prattle came every third Sunday to preach, saying, "I comes to feed the Lord's sheep!" And after the sermon he fed himself very well also, sometimes at several houses of his parishioners.

Preacher Prattle was very interested in the Freemans. They seemed prosperous. They didn't contribute too much, but more than the others who were barely eking out a living on their land. The whites would sell them dried, rocky land at the highest price, then wait to take it back from them when they couldn't make it pay. Sometimes, most times, they took any tool and the mule or cow the Negro man had, to "make up the diffrunce" they said. Then wait to sell it again because the ex-slaves did work hard and save money and wanted some land of their own. But they could buy only what the white man would sell them. Sometimes, seldom, but sometimes, an honest former slave owner would sell or give his ex-slave a piece of land to farm and it would be good land.

⌒

The heat of summer was cooling down and Lifee, always busy, was tired and uncomfortable with the pregnancy and the romping twins. Preacher Prattle came bringing a couple, man and wife, with him. "They is tempraly without a home and they needs somewheres to stay for tonight til I kin git a place for em. I pick em up tomorrar. Ya'll is good peoples and God done sent ya a lil test. I tol God He could count on ya'll! Praise the Lawd!" He smiled a snaggletooth grin. "I wouldn't bother ya'll, but these good people ain got no-wheres to go. They needs only one day cause I'm gonna go round and fin em sompin. They don know nobody round heah! But me and the Lawd is lookin out for em! They got to get a job . . . and a shack, jes anythin they kin."

Mor had come into the house and heard the preacher. "Well, I reckon they can stay here just one night because we don't have so much room." He looked at Lifee.

The preacher smiled, "Thank the Lawd. The Lawd will bless ya!"

Mor nodded, "Oh, He do. He do."

The woman, Ann, was a plump, sloppy-looking woman who smiled all the time and talked about nothing much, constantly; picking, probing. Nosy. The husband, Dave, was a thin dark man who seldom spoke.

The woman plopped down in a chair when Preacher Prattle rushed off to do the Lord's will. She said, "Oh, this here a beeuteful place here. And all them pigs and chickens and things! Ya mus have plenny eggs and bacon! Yo house so niiiice. Oh! Jes lookit them fine babies!" She held her arms open, but they didn't come to her.

Lifee urged them, "Say good afternoon, mam."

They tried, "Goo mam."

Ann forgot the children even as she smiled at them. She looked around the parlor. "Well, ya'll such nice peoples to help us. We trust in the Lord and He done led us to ya'll. Ain He, Dave?"

Dave hummed, "Ummm-hmmm," looking down at the floor.

Mor turned to go back to his work, saying, "Well, Mr. Dave, you come on go with me. We finishin up the last of the harvest. We working in the lower east field on the last of the corn and cotton. The kids is workin on the peanuts, cause that's light and their favorite. But, we ending things up."

"Ummm-hmmm," he hummed. "I sho hope it light work, cause I's got a bad back and cain do much bendin and pickin."

"We will find somethin easy for ya." Mor led the way out the parlor through the kitchen to the yard.

Ann smiled, "Oh, theys gettin along fine."

Lifee said, "We're just cleaning up after lunch. Come on in the kitchen."

Ann rose slowly from the soft chair. "Oh, ya'll just ate yo lunch? I sho wish I was," she laughed as she followed Lifee. "I ain et since las night and it wasn't much at that!"

"Are you hungry? Abby? You already saw Ann and Dave. They are going to be stayin with us tonight."

Abby hummed, "Mmmm-hummm."

Ann exclaimed, "Ya'll done et and still got all that food left over?"

Abby hummed again, "Mmmm-hummm."

Lifee spoke to Ann, "Fix yourself a plate and sit and eat."

Abby turned from the washpan. "Where they gonna sleep?"

Lifee shook her head as Ann helped herself to everything. "I was trying to think of that. Ethylene could sleep in here with us and they can use her house for one night. I reckon."

Abby put a hand on her hip. "I don think Ethylene should have to . . . Your house is your own private selves place. She got all her private life in there."

Through a mouthful of food from a heaping plate, Ann said, "Naw, naw, we don want to put nobody out o' they house. We c'n sleep jes anywheres. Dave got a real bad back, but he can make it, Lord willin."

"No, we'll find a place." Lifie spoke as she listened for the twins. "I hear Aman and Able. I'll be back."

Between mouthfuls, Ann spoke to Abby, "You the cook round here?"

"Yes mam, I do most the cookin."

"Ya live here, too?"

Abby sighed, "I live here, but I got my own cabin outside."

"You goes outside to sleep? Lawd, chile, that like slavery. And these peoples is blacker than you! How they got this here nice place?"

Abby grew a little angry. "I don feel like no slave and I'm a grown woman what does my own thinkin. I got a house and I ain lookin for no place to sleep and no meal to eat. And this place nice cause we made it nice!"

Ann reached for another biscuit, "They sure must have plenny money with these fields full as they is and settin a table like this un."

Abby put her hand on her hip again, "You worry more bout their business than you worrin bout your own."

Ann smeared jam on her biscuit, "Oh, I's jest talkin. What friends do."

Abby turned back to the washbasin. "Mmmm-hummm."

Just then Dave came into the kitchen, holding his back. "I done done too much and hurt my back agin. I cain stay out ther workin in the sun like dis."

Ann reached out to pat his arm. "Oh, sugar, here, sit down. Lets me fix you a plate. They got plenny. You eat a bit and ya feel betta if ya lay down and res."

Abby was finished washing the dishes. She had cleaned all but Ann's plate, which was still on the table. She moved aside to let Ann wash her plate. But Ann said, "I jes use this here plate for hisn. He cn eat after me." She piled his plate high and the poor, tired man, in pain, ate every bite and asked for another baked yam. He finished the yam and drank a big glass of buttermilk. Then he pushed his plate away, leaned back and belched.

Ann patted his back, "Ya alright now?" She picked up the plate and turned to Abby, who was standing peeling squash. "Does ya have some dessert sweets? He like sweets."

Abby looked at the pies that were on order and said, "Be some dessert for supper. Ain none now."

Ann pointed at the pies, "Whats them there? Cain he have a lil piece of em?"

Abby shook her head, "They blong to somebody already."

Ann shook her head, "Well, I declare! Refusin people a lil piece of pie!"

Abby put both hands on her hips, "I am not gonna cut those pies! Now! If you want to make a pie and give him a slice, I will give you some apples so you can."

Ann set the plate down in the washpan, leaving the glass on the table, and started opening cupboards, peering in.

Abby spoke, "Wait til you finish clearing off that table fore you start making the pie. Maybe Dave can bring you in some wood for the stove so you can use the oven. And you got to wash that dish and that glass and utensils, so you can start clean."

Ann said, "Let it soak for a lil bit."

Abby did not relent, "It don't need to soak. And what you lookin for in them cabinets? I'll get you what you need."

Ann turned to Abby in anger, "This ain yo stuff! Why you got to watch it so much?!

Abby matched Ann's anger and then some, "You don't have enough in your mind bout our busines for nothin to be comin out yo mouth! Clean them things up!" She pointed to the dishpan. "He can wait til tonight, if you still here."

Ann sauntered out of the kitchen, "I don need to fool round in yo kitchen that blongs to somebody else!"

Abby snatched the dishrag from the counter, wiped her table and threw the rag in the pan on the dirty dishes. "Mmmmm-hummm! Too lazy!"

When Lifee came downstairs a little later, Dave, body drawn up tightly, was asleep in a chair, arms crossed over his plump stomach. Ann was lying on the divan. Both snoring as the odor from their traveling sweat permeated the room.

Lifee thought to herself, "I don't know many Negroes like these, but I suppose it all depends on who owned you and what you learned from them. They won't stay here long." She went into the kitchen to see what she could do to help Abby. That night they all ate dinner and Dave got his sweet dessert.

It was decided the newcomers would sleep on the floor in the parlor of the main house. Lifee loaned Ann a nightgown from the few she had, saying, "This will let you take your clothes off and wash them out."

Ann took the nightgown and mumbled, "In the mornin."

Lifee answered, "Minister Prattle will be here tomorrow and your clothes will need to be dry."

Ann did not answer. Dave slept in his clothes.

Sometime during the night Lifee heard sounds from downstairs and thought someone might be sick. When she went down the stairs Ann and Dave, he in his underwear, which was gray and smeared with dirt, were sitting at the table and it was full of food. The last of the dessert just disappearing. Ann saw Lifee first.

"Oh, Mz Lifee, we done woke you up! Lawd I tole Dave don talk so loud. We got a lil hungry and membered all this here good food here, jes goin to waste, and came on in. We gon get up early, early and clean up in the mornin. Dont mens make a mess?! And now, we gon be quiet so ya'll can get yo rest."

Lifee was just outdone. The kitchen was a mess! Who were these people in her kitchen? She just turned around and went back upstairs.

The next morning when Abby came to her kitchen all the dirty plates were on the table. The lunch, made ahead for today, was almost all gone and so messed up she wouldn't serve any of it to anyone. She started to turn around and go back to her cabin, but she took a deep breath and went into the parlor, where Ann and

Dave were, thinking, "Ain nobody gonna run me out my own kitchen!"

She banged a pan near Dave's head, his eyes flew open in alarm. Then Abby proceeded to Ann and banged the pan near her head. Said, "Get up! Wake up, woman! Get up and get in there and clean up after yoself!"

Ann did indeed wake up. Still fuzzy from sleep, she yelled as was her personality, "Whoa, woman, who you hollerin at? I ain no slave like you is! Ya ain tellin me what to do! This here ain yo house!"

The babies started crying upstairs. Lifee came to the stairtop. "What is going on, Abby?"

Ann hollered up to Lifee, "This here bitch want me be a slave like she is! I ain gon do it!"

Lifee started downstairs, "You ate! You made that mess!"

Ann mumbled, "Huh!"

Lifee spoke to Abby, "I'll clean up the kitchen, Abby. I don't know what's going on around here, I didn't expect anything like this. But Minister Prattle will be here today and take them away."

Ann jumped up, "No, no. Don nobody needs to clean up after me. We clean up ourself. Cain nobody say we don pay our way."

Abby took the last word, "Cleanin up after your own self ain no pay to nobody after you have done ate up everybody's food! Now, get in there and clean that place up!"

Ann cleaned at the kitchen with her lips puffed out. Lifee came down to try to cook lunch for all because Abby said she would not come back in while "them strange triflin people" was there. "I got a place to cook in my own house!" Ethylene said she was not coming to lunch. "I blive I'll eat with Abby."

Lifee, Mor, Dave and Ann ate dinner together. Mema came in with Bettern nursing and Babe on the other hip. She had been talking with Abby. She watched the strangers eat for a moment, then she looked at Mor and Lifee. She made everybody uncomfortable. She turned to leave, then turned back, said to the strangers,

"White folks worked you for free . . . nothin. Now, after freedom, you think Negro folks gonna feed you free? For no work?" She looked at Mor and Lifee again, said, "These po'ass folks ain got nothin and they happy moochin, but they ain gonna eat nothin Ben growed! Let em eat what they growed they own self! They been free long as we'uns!" Then she strutted out the kitchen door without a goodby.

Later, Ann spoke with a smile, "Havin babies is hard on ya, make you mean. Like her."

Lifee answered, "She is one of the sweetest, hardworkingest, kind woman I know. She is part of my family."

Ann scraped the dishes and put them in the sink, then went to sit down in the parlor with her husband. Lifee cleaned up the kitchen then went to sit with them as she watched the babies.

Mor went back out to work, looking at Dave as he went. Dave saw him and said, "I betta not go witcha now. I cain get to hurtin now, cause I gots work to do if we finds us a place. I needs to work for money, cause we ain got nern, like ya'll."

Ann spoke up, "Ya'll rich! Ya'll got everthin!"

Mor had to answer, "Naw, we ain rich. We work! All of us!" Then he went on out to work scraping the fertilizer up from the cowshed and the pigpen.

Lifee cleaned the rest of the house in between looking after Able and Aman, thinking to herself, "Well, that Minister Prattle coming to get them today!"

But, Minister Prattle didn't come. And the evening and night were a repeat performance of the last one. Mor and Lifee talked during the night and the next morning Mor got up, hitched his horse to the wagon and prepared to drive Dave and Ann to the church.

In the house Ann was trying to talk Lifee into letting them stay. "We got plenny room for us here. Don need much."

But Lifee answered, "We do. We got two babies here and one on the way. And you have hurt Abby's feelings and run her out of her kitchen."

Ann puffed her lips out, said, "Huh! Don she work for ya'll? She need to give ya'll more respect! I know she was no good slave! Ya'll need to let her go! I stay on and help long as ya need me!"

Lifee laughed kindly, "Abby does not work here. This is Abby's house, too. And she is a hard worker. We don't even need to talk about that."

Ann didn't know when to stop. "Ya'll ain runnin this here place right. Where the lady ya'll work for?"

Lifee sighed, "She is gone to visit her mother."

"Where she go to?"

Lifee was trying to stay calm. "To tend to her business."

"Where?"

"To tend to her business."

"Well, ya'll sho gon have trouble when she come back here."

Lifee stood up, finished with the conversation and wishing Mor would hurry. "We'll handle it."

Dave asked, "Do ya got some othern shacks here?"

Exasperated, Lifee said, "Mr. Dave and Mz Ann. Everybody black is poor. We all have to work for our keep. They work or they starve. You worked for white folks in slavery. Now you're free and you've got to work for yourself. Work is a joy to me. Everybody needs some fruit from their own labor."

Dave spoke again, "We workin folks. Bettern the ones ya got."

"We don't see that. You haven't cooked one thing you ate. You haven't washed one thing since you've been here in two days."

Ann took up for him. "He a sick man . . . and I was yo compny. I was raise right. Compny don work when theys visitin."

Lifee started to the kitchen door to call Mor, saying, "Company that appreciates what you are doing for them does. You got to go! You can't stay here."

They sidled to the door and looked longingly at the food started

in the kitchen. Mor came in to get them and their few pathetic
bags. Mor felt sorry for them, but they were sorry people. They
didn't do anything to help themselves.

They drove to the church, but the church was closed, empty. Mor
drove to the house where Minister Prattle usually stopped, Sister
Welcom's. Minister Prattle was gone, supposed to return in three
weeks. Ann said, "Well, I guess'es we jes has to stay wit ya'll til he
come back."

Mor answered, "Minister Prattle ain your keeper, far as I know.
You grown people. You got to look out for yourself."

Mz Welcom agreed. Mor looked at her, said, "Well, he left Dave
and Ann at our house. He sposed to get em yestiddy."

Mz Welcom mumbled, "Well, ummhumm, Mr. Mor, he gone."

"Well, what must I do with em?"

Mz Welcom spoke a little louder, "Umm, I reckon they can stay
on there with you til he get back." She raised her eyes to look in
Mor's eyes.

Mor answered firmly, "No mam, they can't. We are full. They
sleepin on the floor now."

Mz Welcom looked down at her feet again, "Well, that be where
they sleep here if I could find a place. They just ain none."

After thinking a moment, Mor asked, "You got the key to the
church?"

"Yes, but I cain . . ."

Mor insisted, "Well, least they be warm with that stove there. I
bring some wood to em."

Mz Welcom went to get the key, came back saying, "Well, umm,
I don know . . ."

Mor followed up, "And they can work cleanin and paintin the
church . . . and wash them curtains in there."

Mz Welcom spoke up again, "I keeps the church clean."

Mor reached for the key, "Good! You can tell em what to do." Mz Welcom didn't hand him the key, so Mor turned to leave. "I'll drop em off at the church. You let em in when you have time."

Mz Welcom wasn't quick enough to think of anything to say, but she tried, "I don know but what it . . ."

Mor turned back to her, "We Christian folk and we can't put these people out. The church the onliest answer to everthing. The Lord's arms are always open." Then he was gone with Sister Welcom looking after him.

On the short ride to the church, Ann spoke, "It be cold in that ole church."

"Oh, I bring you wood and they got some outside the church you can cut."

Ann moaned, "Ain nowheres to cook."

Mor laughed lightly, "Everbody, all the members will bring what they can. We will, too."

After his wife nudged him, Dave spoke up, "Brother Mor, if it all the same to ya, we likes to stay on visit wit ya'll."

Mor stopped laughing, "Family visits; strangers work. I work. Sides, it too crowded. At the church you cain stretch out and be alone to yourself." He pulled in front of the church.

Ann spoke, "We don need no space. We is OLD married people."

Dave added, "Was plenny room at yo house for us. We was fine."

Mor turned to them, "I'ma tell ya the truth. You lazy. You lookin for a home like the boll weevil. You want'a eat, but you don want to work. You ain nobodys children. You too old for your own mama and daddy to care for now. All us slaves that ain no slave no more . . . is poor. All we got is strength to work so we can take care ourself. Ain got no strength to work and take care nobody else. This a hard, hard world. It don seem like it thinks it owes nobody nothin. You mighta stayed on at the house for a few days more, but you treat us like we fools. Ain no fool got enough to give none away and we gave you plenny. I think ya'll is fools . . . mainly cause you thinks you smart. You even done run Abby out the kitchen and she cook all the food you ate. And that her house, too! So . . . get on out my wagon and get on bout your life."

By that time Sister Welcom had arrived at the church with the key and a small package of biscuits and potatoes. "I's sorry, Brother Mor, but I done already had em for a few days and I was tryin not to get caught again." She turned to Dave and Ann, said, "Here is a little food to keep ya for a while. I'm gonna tell the other members what ya'll needs, but I think you betta get on round here and find some little jobs to do, cause everbody here is poor and workin hard, hard. I's a church woman, but, Lawd knows, I cain do no mo, right now."

Dave and Ann got off. Sister Welcom let them in the church, then Sister Welcom came out rolling her eyes at Mor and shaking her head. Said, "It's too early for beggars! Ain nobody got nothin to beg yet. I ain never, in all my born days, seen Negroes as triflin as them."

Mor waved a hand and drove back to his home, sitting on his land where he and his family did some hard, hard work.

ELEVEN

Abby and the girls were making a little savings from their Miss Mammy pie shed. Abby saved every dime because she had a dream of making a better home for her girls and their education. They were not lazy. They helped her, but they weren't sure of their dreams.

Meda and Luzy were growing, healthy girls. Meda was the serious one who took her schooling very seriously. Luzy was the laughing, playful one who learned to read and write, didn't like arithmetic, but counted money really well.

They both liked the boys, but Luzy was the bold one. Their social life was centered around the church. They belonged to the choir and the one youth group in Sunday school. Luzy made eyes at the boys, flirting even though she didn't know she was flirting: she just loved the boys.

Meda was more reserved. Quiet in her shy way. Blushed around boys. Consequently she was not as popular as Luzy and that was the way she seemed to want it.

Mor told Life one day, "That there Luzy is gonna be marryin up pretty soon now."

Surprised, Life asked, "She has a friendboy?"

Mor laughed, "Not one . . . a hundred! All of em like her."

Lifee with lowered voice, "Is she . . . does she . . . ?"

Mor's laughter stopped, "I don blive she do. Abby right on em, watchin as they go. Everbody just like Luzy and she enjoy it."

"Well, good. But, don't they like Meda?"

"Sho they do. She just more stand-back kind of girl."

"Standoffish."

"Yeah, she stand off."

Lifee, though always conscious of all her extended family, began to pay more attention to Meda and Luzy. Mor was right; they weren't doing very much wrong, but all the possibilities were there. Lifee knew Abby was thinking of having the girls she thought of as her family with her all the time, but it was obvious, time was bringing about a change. They were growing up. "We have to do something about their continuing education to keep their little minds busy and keep them from making mistakes. I want them to be independent for their own good."

Lifee and Ethylene were by now checking into schools and colleges for continuing education and nursing. They knew there were many white ones on the East and North coast. Many little colleges for Negroes were trying to get started and many Negro families in the East were beginning groups and paying their own teachers to teach their children. Hampton Institute was one training school, but it was in Virginia. Atlanta Union, Fisk, Talledega, Toogaloo and Howard were a few of the others.

Lifee pored over all the information that came from her written inquiries to the few Negro newspapers she had located being published. "But which schools teach nursing?" Lifee asked herself.

In time she came to the conclusion that Ethylene could prepare herself by taking higher math, English and other general subjects. "But how do I get her there? Somewhere?" Lifee asked herself.

In the meantime, Lifee suggested to Ethylene, "You work with that vet, Mr. Ben, and learn all you can watching what he does. All nurses didn't go to school or have the chance you have now. Some just worked for doctors and received a certificate from him. Some just picked things up along the way. We'll still work on a college, but we have to face that there may not be one that will accept you. I know Negroes have been free a longer time in the East and North, and I know they have been preparing for their children and their education. Because Negroes love education and they know what it will mean to the future of anyone. We'll keep looking. And you keep watching that doctor, Mr. Ben, even if it is mostly with animals. I know some sick people even come to him when they can't get a regular doctor. Watch him and learn."

Other things were bothering Mor and Lifee lately. Now almost all the Yankee soldiers were gone back to their homes and the government was not making effective new provision to protect the freed slaves. More and more black bodies were being fished out of the rivers, bloated, scarred and broken. Lynching was becoming more frequent, men and women. The poor white class was hungry . . . and angry. Many of the wealthy whites were also very angry at their loss of revenue, empty land and no one to work it. They were directing some of the mayhem from behind the scenes as they ran or had people run for public office working to pass new laws to keep Negroes down and keep them as close to slavery as possible. It was a tense and terrifying time. The Negroes watched in a cautious silence. Lifee and Mor thought of their children.

Then Lifee had her baby, a girl, with only the help of Mema, who was carrying her daughters on her hips. Not from worry, just from love. Lifee named the new baby Pretti Ocean, pronounced "Oshe-an." When Mor came in from the fields covered with sweat, he was excited and happy to have a daughter. "Now, we's got em all. Boys and girl." The twins, their little eyes bright with awe and delight, stared over the rim of the little crib at their new little sister.

They were settling in for the winter. The firewood was piled high, the corn crib was full, peanuts piled up high for dark days in the winter. Abby had canned vegetables and fruit and it was stretched over long shelves in the basement. Sugar and flour packed in barrels, safeguarded as much as possible against bugs and ants. The winter cold would keep them from spoiling.

Old Mz Bingly had accepted her sacks of greens, corn, onions and squash and a few jars of homemade molasses, a small bag of eggs and a ham. "We split the ham with you, Mz Bingly. Mz Emmalee told us to share what we could with you. I brought you these other things cause it's winter and times is hard for us all. But God is blessing us with these small crops and we thought we would share our blessins with you all."

Mz Bingly's daughter, Wanda Sue, smiled at Lifee with tears in her eyes. She liked Lifee and Mor and Ethylene. She tried to visit Ethylene, but Ethylene was always busy, running somewhere to work. Rufus just looked closely at the provisions from his distance. He had been watching the emptying fields and wondering about the coming winter.

After several weeks Lifee received answers to her letters of inquiry to schools. It was going to be harder than she thought to find a nursing school that would accept Negroes and it would be far away. Even many doctors used any remedy that might work, sometimes using Indian and African recipes of herbs and spices. With their, mostly false, college-learned cures; seldom washing their hands even. There were some good doctors, but they were mostlly self-made after learning what there was to teach them.

"Just keep learning what you can from that Dr. Ben Vet." Lifee frowned as she spoke to Ethylene. "We'll bide our time and see what comes along. You will have to go away to some school for Negroes."

When Lifee spoke to Mor about it all, he frowned, saying, "Why don that girl get married? Settle down to keeping a house for a man and giving him children? Runnin up and down these roads and diffrent places is not good for a woman."

Lifee smiled, placing her hand on his arm. "I fell in love with you, Mor, or I would be running up and down looking for some way to earn a living, my way, independent."

Lifee told Ethylene what Mor had said about marrying and being a wife and mother. Ethylene replied, "But I am not ready to be a mother and a wife. I can read and write! I want to do anything a man can do, almost. White folks can . . ."

Lifee stopped smiling, "No, don't think like that. That's wrong. You always want to do what YOU want to do. Nobody else has anything to do with it. I hope you will do what will take care of you and yours when you do have children. Don't go trying to prove anything to men or women. White folks are not a good example. There is no need to consider them in your dreams. They sin as great or more than anybody! Make your own world. Forget white folks. Work to please God and make your own world without what white folks think or do. They don't know themselves and nobody else. They made this place like it is and nobody has any peace and sometimes, no life."

Before the light snows began, Lifee drove the wagon to Mudville and inquired of a few Negroes which lawyer worked with Negroes and was as honest as possible. She located his office and stood looking at it as her thoughts swirled in her head. Then she went to the bank and said her Mistress Freeman wanted to begin a bank account and needed the necessary things to fill out. She returned home, filled out the papers and wrote a letter to the lawyer.

A few days later she drove the ten-mile trip again. She took five gold pieces to the bank with a letter signed by "L. Freeman and

Mordecai Freeman," opening the account and received a letter of credit.

"My mistress say her account balance should look like this." She held up a paper with "$500.00" printed on it. She showed them, also, the letter to the lawyer asking him to check the letter of credit for her servant. She had given the correct balance in the letter of credit, saying she trusted her servant implicity, and said servant would pick up withdrawals for her and make deposits.

She took the letter to the lawyer, who accepted it for his files and to make a note of the signatures. She had changed another gold coin and paid the lawyer a retainer fee. He was satisfied.

Now Mr. and Mrs. Freeman had a bank account and a lawyer even though the lawyer didn't know his clients were Negro.

She stopped next at a store that carried a few books and purchased two dozen of them. Smiling at the salesman, saying, "My mistress say bring some books home. Can you tell me what these is? And would you please put a list of the prices so my mistress can check em, please?" There were two or three art books. Lifie thought, "These children don't know a thing about art. They need some extra beauty in their lives and to know they can make beauty."

As a last thought, she purchased two children's flutes and two harmonicas. "These children need some music in their lives even if they can't play it good. Somebody will teach them. That piano teacher at church can start on Luzy, Able and Aman." She was very pleased with herself and life. She was actually thinking of the future: planning it for herself at last. A future!

Later, she gave Ethylene fifteen dollars to get the vet, Dr. Ben, to order books from a white college for nursing and a beginner book in biology for a doctor.

Meda took one of the toy flutes and Luzy took the other. The twins were given one harmonica to share and Mema's babies were given the other harmonica to play with to listen for the sounds coming from the instrument. Lifie cuddled Pretti, saying, "You are going to learn to play the piano. We'll buy you one when we get to where we don't have to move again. You are going to know some of the beautiful things about this world! Because it is not all ugly. Which is all they will show you down here deep in the South!"

At last, she began to plan a trip to the Carolinas. "It's still South, but coast people are different from these inland folks. They are exposed to more of life and they work and are not starving to death as they envy others who work and have things."

The weather was becoming colder though and the baby, Pretti, was still small. "Don't want no sickness, so I guess I won't invite it in my life. If anything happen to any of my family, sickness might become my master. Lord, I have to put life off another six months or so! But Pretti will be older and can travel better. So . . . I'll wait."

Another body was found burned, still smoldering amidst the logs even though snow was lightly on the ground. The penis had been cut off for someone's souvenir. The poor man hadn't had much else. No one could identify the body and no one seemed to be missing in the small community. Then one house in the community was burned and the husband shot when he ran out of the burning house with a child in his arms to show them people were in the house. He screamed, "What is I done! What is I done?" just before they shot him. Then they rode off, taking the man's mule, laughing at the baby crying as it lay in the snow, reaching for its father. And these were the superior white people: They say that of themselves.

The winter passed slowly, but steadily, as usual. Mema had her two girls. She and Benjamin seemed satisfied together. Ethylene was learning, eager to go to her job or staying holed up in her shack studying her books over and over. Meda spent a great deal of time in Ethylene's shack, reading whatever was there. They were so proud of being able to read. Luzy preferred to bake with Abby. She saved her share of the money because there was nothing to buy anyway. She planned on a million different ways to spend it when she had a chance, usually something to make her prettier to the boys.

Abby was biding her time, dreaming of building her house. One day Lifee talked to her about it. "Abby, you can build anything you want here on this land, but . . . Well, I don't think you should unless you really want to stay here. We may be gone."

Abby turned from the sink to look at Lifee. "What chu mean?"

Lifee smiled and sighed, "All our children are getting older. They are going to have a life of their own. You want to build a home for Luzy and Meda, but they may be married and gone. Meda needs to get to better schools and Luzy does, too. There are none round here. They don't even have a school started around here yet, though they are talking about it; say a teacher from up North would come to teach. But, we know, they might kill him . . . or her."

Abby leaned back against the sink board, "What you gonna do with this house? You ain gonna just walk away are you?"

"This is just a house. We talking about life. The future. There will be another house. I'm going to try to find another farm somewhere else and we can all live there where these children will have a chance."

Lifee's face glowed, "Abby, there are places where free Negroes who been free longer than us have started living like people. Have schools and small communities where they hear music and have art. Better white-owned stores that have more books and supplies."

Abby leaned forward, "But, they still got white folks and they still scared."

"Abby, we're in one of the worse states in America. The lynching here is every week almost. One day they gonna turn their face to our place. They're gonna wonder why Mz Emmalee doesn't ever come back here. And once they believe this place is ours . . . we don't know what will happen."

Abby looked thoughtful. Her dream had been here in their little world. "White man just won't leave Negroes alone. He hate us, but he can't get us off his mind, and we ain bother him nare bit." With a deep sigh, she turned back to the sink. "Well, ya'll our famly. We gonna have to go where ya'll go. I will kill em if they bothern my girls and my girls is gettin up and real pretty and it won't be long."

So that was settled. Lifee sighed in relief. "Thank God." They were silent a moment, each with her own thoughts. Then Lifee said, "I won't go searching until the spring when the roads are kind of clear. I'll go first and try to get a place. Then I'll come back before Mor plants too much. He is going to act just regular, but not really do too much. Then if everything turns out like I think, we will all take off early one morning like we are going to visit somebody. Mor going to build another wagon and get another horse. Mema and Ben might want to stay here. We'll see."

But Mema balanced her babies on her hips and said, "No you ain't gon leave us here. I beeeen wanting to leave here. I did want to go Northern, but ya'll my fambly and we goin wit chu. Ben love it chere, but I ain gon let Benjamin stay here and get killed."

The winter was no harder than usual, especially since there was plenty to eat for all. Life told Mema, "Don't get pregnant again on these cold winter nights when you all tucked up in a warm bed."

Mema answered, "I ain't. I got my two babies again. Ben want a boy, but I tole him we'll have em when these girls brings us they husbands!"

Abby began to set little things aside that she wanted to take with her. Tentatively packing. Meda and Ethylene were very excited. "Real schools!" they said as they laughed together secretly. Luzy was in love with a young boy and said she didn't want to go, but she was excited about going somewhere else, too. Her sense of adventure outweighing her puppy love. No talk about the move was to be done anywhere around anyone at store or church.

Mor talked to Ben about it. "Lifee, Mz Freeman, think she goin by herself with the babies, but she ain't. I'm goin with her. She think folks'll get spicious if we both gone, but I ain fixin to let her go nowhere on no road by herself."

Ben nodded, smiling, "Mema, Mz Dollar, say we goin with ya'll. I was rekoning we could stay here and run this farm for ya'll. Make it pay even."

"Don't need to make it pay. You can just stay if'n you wants to. I think things is not lookin too good, right round bout now, for Negroes to be hanging round Missipi, Bamma and Georgia. We don know what it gon be like somewheres else, but it sure cain be no worsen here! It ain safe. Negroes is dyin almos everyday now. These white folks is actin mighty evil. They don want you to have a thing lessin they want it for themself! My boys ain't but goin on three years now, but I'm thinkin I betta start teachin them bout white folks fore they get killed for bein born!"

Ben nodded, "Well, I got it a little betta cause I got girls, but they gonna have them other troubles. Mema, Mz Dollar, she know what to tell'em though. We got to teach em!"

Mor scuffed the ground with his foot, then stooped to pick up a handful of the dirt. "Man, all we wants is for them white folks to leave us alone. They think we needs em, but we don need their help. We don want their help. We can do for ourself if they just go away, cause they the bigges problem we got. Get rid of them, we be fine."

"Sho is right bout that."

"Lookit this dirt. Fine growing dirt. Cain even stay here and do my own work on my own land. And, Lawd! If they knew it was mines, I'da been dead! And maybe all my famly, too!"

Mor's sons, Aman and Able, were always underfoot now. They were about three years old and growing fast. They loved to think they were helping their father as he tended the cows, chickens and hogs. They got sick eating peanuts and he let them eat all they wanted so they would learn on their own. Later, he told them, "Stick to the fruit off them trees, that's good for ya!"

Abby loved all the girl-babies. Babe and Pretti were her favorites. She had faced up to the fact that Meda and Luzy would soon be stretching out to their lives. She loved them, of course, but the new ones, now, they would be around awhile.

And so life went on. The winter passed, but Lifee did not get to go searching for a new home. So many things had come up with the farm and the babies, summer was gone and fall was slipping by fast. She looked up from her work one day and snow had started falling again. "Oh, God, another year gone and we are still here. This next time, I'm going for certain."

She had been back to Mudville several times to put money in the bank for her "mistress." She had forty gold pieces in the bank and fifteen left in her possession with some smaller silver pieces. She had her certificates of bank credit tucked safely away. "I don't know what's next, but . . . I think I'm ready."

The church was the meeting place for most all the Negroes living in the area. It was where you met all newcomers and caught up on the latest gossip, whispered words of the latest lynching or burning and planned to send something to the surviving widow. Although women were lynched also, they were much fewer than the men. It was also where you borrowed or loaned a needed tool or a bit of manpower. In other words, they brought their joys and their woes to the church.

It was at church one Sunday that Abby was speaking to Brother and Sister Mostly and found out they were losing their farm. They were in their sixties and were too old to keep up the work required to pay the white man who had loaned them a mule and some seed.

Joshua Mostly, back permanently bent, eyes dim and runny, shook his head sadly. "I tell you, Sister Abby, I done tried to think of everwhichaway I can to hold on to my farm. It ain but fifteen acres and I jest caint do it."

Abby, a hand on each bowed shoulder of the man and wife, said, "Ohhhhh, Brother Joshua."

"An how I'm gonna take care my wife? In all the years I been with her, I ain nevah let her down."

Sister Mostly spoke softly, "We been married forty-five yeahs now. He ain nevah let me down. An I ain nevah let him down neider."

Abby squeezed Sister Mostly's shoulder tighter. "Ohhhhh, Sister Mostly." She turned back to Brother Joshua, "What you gonna do then?"

"Ain nothin we can do. That white man gonna take it. Gonna take my pappy's land for use of a mule. I ain't got the mule no more; he already come got that when he seen I was sick and couldn't work the year out."

Abby shook her head in sympathy. "There ain't nothing you can do?"

"Could borry the money, but who got money to lend? And how would I pay em back? Naw . . . caint borry none."

Abby thought of the money she had saved from selling her pies. She was about to open her mouth and ask, "How much you need?" when Brother Joshua opened his mouth and said, "I ain nevah gonna be well enough to work it no more. I'd sell it, but what colored person got the money to buy? Sides that, I don know if that there white man would let somebody else buy it. They make the laws and they got the power, ya'll know! He say I got twenty-five more days to come up with HIS money; and he done already got his mule. Seed still in the ground. Lawd, I is losing my land for a bag of seed." He shook his head sadly again. "My pappy's masta give him that land when he bought hisself out of slavery. I was raised right there. Been there fifty years now. Free! But they won let you make no money, much lessen save some. Won let you plant what you wants to plant cause you know what you doin and can make money to keep the land! They done had they eye on that land since that ole masta died."

Abby patted his shoulder and hugged Sister Mostly's shoulders. "You got twenty-five more days? Let me see what I can do. How much do you owe?"

"I owes him fifteen dollars, he say, and least one hundred dollars for a crop I didn't bring in."

"Sometime the good Lord finds a way for you, Brother Mostly."

"Well, I hopes He lookin for a way for us now."

Abby said a few more greetings to a few more people on her way to the door and went to sit in the wagon to wait for the rest of her family. She was thinking about the home of her own she had always wanted. "Woe is me, Lawd. I ain got but forty dollars!"

TWELVE

Several things happened around that time that changed Lifee's life. A young white woman, Tricia Tims, about twenty-five years old, moved from the East back into her family's abandoned house which was not far from Mor's and Lifee's property. She brought with her a Negro child of seven years, Laval. She said Laval was the child of a former favorite slave who had died during slavery. He had no home, no relatives, so she had raised him herself.

Her old homestead had been burned partially and was badly decaying. She was referred to Mor as a very good carpenter by Dr. Ben. They made an agreement and Mor began doing inside work on the house first so she could live more comfortably as the outside work was done.

The white men in the area complained to Tricia that a white man would have to work with Mor to supervise. When she told Mor, he smiled, but said, "Let's just let em do the job, cause I got too much to do already." He went home. Tricia spoke to Dr. Ben about it and asked him to supervise, because she knew what was really the matter anyway; they did not want a Negro man behind those walls with a white woman.

Dr. Ben, who really liked and respected Mor and knew how he was with his family, told the white men that he was the supervisor and everything was going along fine. They became suspicious and stopped liking Dr. Ben then, but he was the only vet within fifty miles either way and they all patronized him, so they accepted his word. And those who had nothing else they cared to do began watching Mor very closely. Lifee worried because she knew what white narrow-minded men could do.

Then Abby came to talk to Lifee about Brother Joshua's land to see what she could do to save it and at the same time get a piece of her own land. "They can keep livin in their own house and I will build me a new one for Luzy and Meda and me." Abby was already full of contained joy at the very thought.

"I'll ask Mor to talk to Dr. Ben. I think a white man better buy that land if another white man wants it. It could mean trouble for you, a Negro, to buy it and mess up his plans."

Abby agreed and stressed the time. "Alrighty, but we ain't got but twenty-four days now."

Lifee was still trying to find a school for Ethylene to continue her schooling, with an eye on Meda to follow in Ethylene's footsteps.

At the same time, her sons, three years old now, and little Pretti were demanding more of her time as well as Mor. Mor was finishing off the summer-fall season on his own farm before winter closed in completely so he could take Lifee across to North Carolina. He, also, had the job for Tricia Tims, which he had taken because they could use the money. They wanted to leave most of the money in the bank. The rest of the money Lifee had was for education. Somebody's.

Life seemed to be closing in on everybody. The only ones on the farm who weren't in some state of flux were Mema and Benjamin. They were doing well, happy with their two children. They had connected the shack closest to them to theirs and now had a larger house. Benjamin worked hard with Mor everyday but Sunday, when they all went to church.

Tricia Tims was on Life's mind. In a few conversations with her when Life had taken Mor his lunch over to Tricia's house, Tricia had been very sociable. Life had learned that Tricia had been living with her mother, who was from the Northeast. Tricia's father was a wealthy Southerner and slave owner. Tricia was sent East yearly for her schooling, returning in the summers to the plantation.

Tricia didn't like the Southern ladies in the area. Well, few had had her education. Those who had had left with their families when they abandoned their plantations. So she grew lonely in this forlorn part of the South. Once, when she had been imbibing a little Southern bourbon, she became more talkative with Life. Life did not pry; she had already had her taste of white friendship and she did not know this woman.

But Tricia had called Laval over to her and in a maudlin way looked at Life and said, "He is all I have. My mama and Laval. They are my family."

Life tried to soothe her, "Well, someday you will fall in love and get married to a fine prince of a man and then you will have your own children and you will have a fine family of your own."

This seemed to anger the young woman, she frowned and said, "I have already fallen in love. I had my fine prince of a man. And now . . . he's dead."

Life started to sympathize with the young woman, but Tricia continued, in anger. "My daddy killed him. Right here. Right down there! He locked me in my room and then he beat him to death and then . . . he shot him."

Life moaned at the thought. "Oh, why would your—"

Tricia cut her off. "Some ole biddy must have told him. Or some stupid slave . . . That they had seen me with him and that the baby I was carrying, the baby his daughter was carrying, belonged to a nigger."

Life was startled into silence.

"So my daddy killed my love. Right . . . in . . . front . . . of . . . my . . . eyes. He knew I was watching from my bedroom window." Her anger seemed to be lost in her sorrow for a moment, then she was angry again. "I had seen him visit the slave quarters for his favorite women. My mother knew his favorite was out there. She was hurt and in pain every day and night. Especially the nights. She wasn't young . . . but she was a woman."

Tricia poured herself another drink, then looked at Lifee. "Are you ready for one yet?"

Lifee shook her head no.

Tricia took a drink from her glass in the midst of a sob. "So then, I myself fell in love with a handsome slave man, with a beautiful, kind personality. He was gentle. He was a gentleman. And, though he was frightened . . . eventually we found a way, I found a way, for us to make love. We . . . made . . . love. While the war was going on. Guns shooting, cannon roaring, death everywhere. We made love. Everytime I could get him away. I was a virgin." She smiled. "And he loved me." She frowned. "Then someone told my father and he killed my handsome buck. I saw all the blood on the ground. I saw all the flesh of the man I loved swollen and torn . . . and dead."

Lifee didn't know what to say or whether to say anything at all. She hadn't expected anything like this.

Tricia was calm as she resumed speaking, "About five months later, we moved back East to wait out the war. He knew the South was going to win, he said; they just didn't, that's all. When my little child was born and was a beautiful deep tan, my father looked at him . . . and had a stroke as the horrified nurse held the baby up."

Lifee couldn't help shaking her head and saying, "Mmmmuh! Mmmmmh! Mmmmmh! Lord, Lord."

"We had moved back East before anyone could know what had happened. But not before I paid one of the slaves to dig a proper grave for my lover and move his body there from where they had dumped it, rotten or not! And I told my mother I would live on the street if they hurt or killed my son or gave him away. So we raised him, my child, as a child of a favorite slave who had died. Which is true! I'll show you where the man, the father of my son, is buried. I came back to put a real tombstone on his grave. And to rebuild my son's future home for when he is old enough to protect it. My son will own! the house his father was a slave in! I demand it!"

Lifee listened in silent wonder as the white woman told her about her private life. She did not like to hear personal experiences of others not her family and she knew Tricia would never have spoken to her of these things if she had not been drinking and deeply hurt and lonely in her heart. Lifee did not know what to say. She decided to say nothing, but to rise and go to this woman and touch her in empathy and concern. Tricia looked up at Lifee with tear-filled and sorrowful eyes. She was grateful for the touch. Then Lifee left the woman . . . still sitting there, drinking and thinking.

Joshua Mostly lay on the bedraggled bed in the bedraggled room (which was a mirror of the rest of the house), staring at the ceiling with the paper hanging down in ragged sheets gently dripping dust and fragments of paper and flour flakes on him and all else. He thought to himself a question: "I have been livin? Here, in this house my daddy and mama built, fifty years. I been poor all that there time and that's what have kept me right here. But, bein black is WHY I am here; worser off and cain do no better."

His eyes were rimmed with blue. Not from white blood, but from staring into and under the sun for most of the fifty years since he was nine years old trying to plow a row to build a line of cotton, or corn, or greens or sugar cane. Yet . . . at the end of every row, and every planting season and every year was no nothing. Nothing. "Always back where we started or behind where we started. Deeper in debt." He sighed, a tear rolled down his grimy, wrinkled, sunburned face, falling on the thin, ragged fabric used for a sheet.

"I knows on judgment day . . . these people . . . these people who hates me will try to tell God it was my fault. But one thing I know, God knows the truth and the truth will set me free. God knows it ain my fault. It is white folks finding fault with the colors God had done created and God is perfect. How can He do somethin wrong? And if you thinks He did, you is going to come under His judgment." Joshua was at the end of his life, his ragged dreams and his worn-out hopes.

How can a person say white folks defeated the Negro, especially in the South? Because they did. They knew he was a man . . . which is why they tried so hard to make him not one. If a thing is not a man you don't have to work so hard to prove it.

Now Joshua lay thinking of his wife. When he first met her it was at one of the secret meetings of folks, slaves, who wanted to gather about God. She sang, softly, with the group, each one making up the verse as it came their turn. "I saw that there tall, strong woman; high behind and low-breasted woman. A good strong color, but that dint matter no way. I kept a-comin to them meetings as I could and then I knew I loved her. Loved her. I was young and strong and hadn' had enough of nothin. And Lawd, behold! she love me back. My daddy was free, so I was free. She weren't. I worked all them years to buy my wife, Viry." Then he spoke the one word outloud, "Viry."

His thoughts continued. "We done been together forty-five years. She still in the next room. Just sittin. Just sittin and a-thinkin. She been a hardworkin wife. She thinkin bout when I bought her free. She could'a picked somebody other. But . . . she picked me." Then . . . softly, so his wife wouldn't hear him . . . he cried.

When his tears were drained, he dried his eyes with a corner of the sheet. He had made a decision. "I rather sell it off if we can lose it for seed and the use of a mule."

He rose from the bed and went into the kitchen where Viry was sitting in an old rocking chair that was broken and rocked crooked. As usual, her hair was combed and wrapped in a frayed and threadbare, but clean, headrag. Her once colorful print dress was washed bare of the print and hung uneven over the tattered stockings she wore every day because she said, "A woman sposed to cover her legs when she might go out mongst peoples."

She had puttered around all of the nothings they had in their tired house and put them in bags because she expected that white man any day to come put them off the land. "I don unnerstand eveythin, but I knows if that white man want this piece of land, he gonna get it! Even if'n we pays him."

She did not turn toward Joshua, she knew what he looked like and she knew he was in pain. She didn't want to see it. Anymore. Not today. Maybe tomorrow she could take it.

But Joshua said, "Sister Abby been talkin bout buyin the land. I done made up my mind. It's worth a try. She say we can still live on here and I can work with her on the land and, maybe, a little extra job. Get paid a little." He put his gnarled, wrinkled, swollen-veined hand on her shoulder. "I got to keep you a home and me a home. I'm gonna buy you a new dress if I have a dime lef over. And a new headrag! I wants to see you smile at me agin."

Viry drew up all her depression and grief that lay in her heart. Determined not to add to his already heavy load. She turned to him . . . and smiled a gap-toothed smile. Then turned her head away again. "Whatsomever you say, old man o' mine."

At the behest of Lifee, Tricia Tims wrote to a friend in Boston and inquired about a nursing school for Ethylene. Lifee and Ethylene waited, almost holding their breath, for the answer. It came in about two weeks; the friend knew of a school where she could join a small group of Negro women learning to become nurse's aides, but no nursing school would accept her at this time.

Immediately Lifee and Ethylene counted their money. Ethylene had saved around forty dollars in the two years she had been working for Dr. Ben. Lifee sighed and added another forty with Mor's agreement. Tricia wrote her friend again, asking for information about a place for Ethylene to live while she went to school and perhaps a job to hold until school started and perhaps to keep through the six months of school.

As they waited for that answer they cleaned, packed, trained Meda to take Ethylene's job for Dr. Ben and held their breaths again.

When the letter arrived the friend knew only a Negro woman who worked for her who would help. The friend said, "If you just say the word 'school' these Negroes will do anything to help their own kind."

Finally all was ready. Mor and Life loaded Ethylene into the wagon and drove her to Mudville to catch the train to Boston, which cost about six dollars. Life made her buy a round-trip ticket. "Always have your way to get back to people who love you."

They had sewn the other money to Ethylene's underwear, which was then tied on her. Tears flowed from apprehension, fear and joy as they put her on the train with a group of Negro women traveling on the same train.

Life had been to see Dr. Ben about buying the land from Joshua before the white man took it for seed and the use of a mule, which he had already taken. Dr. Ben did not want to get involved. So Mor went to talk to Dr. Ben.

"Dr. Ben, sir, it's just a little ole piece of land. Bout fifteen acres is all. They a old couple and ain't, don't have nowhere else to go. Now . . . Abby wants that land and she is gonna build her own house on it and let them old people stay there free cause it's really their land."

Dr. Ben began shaking his head slowly, but Mor kept talking.

"And another thing, you know, I hear you talkin bout some of these fine dogs and cows and horses you sometime have to keep for a few days and nights and you gettin wore out doing all that by yourself with just Ethylene helpin. Now . . . Meda, she don't know too much yet to be much help . . . yet."

Dr. Ben began thinking about what Mor was saying.

Mor continued, "Well, I could build you some kennels over there on the land, cause you know I'm gonna help Abby build her house. Anyway, it's just up the road and it's got a sizable barn and shed. I build you the kennels over there and you have a built-in animal keeper in Abby who is mighty smart and sponsible and will watch um for you. And she have some help cause the old man gonna be there and he knows about feedin animals and things. One of em can raise a flag or come down here and tell you if a mergency come up . . . for a mighty low pay . . . and she a good cook, too!"

In the end Dr. Ben agreed. "Well, it might work out. I'll try it. What do I do?"

Mor smiled at him, grateful because you couldn't ask too many white men to do you a favor against another white man. "Sir, Mr. Winston at the Freebureau store can tell you the whole thing and Abby will give you the money. They wants a hunnerd dollars, but the county will take twenty for the land; fifteen acres, cause that's all Joshua owes in back taxes. But it got to be soon. Today even."

Dr. Ben started walking away. "I'll go today. I believe I'm getting a good deal here. Thank you, Mor."

With all these things going on, Lifee wouldn't get to go on her trip to see where she might want to move her family. Mor would not let her go alone and she appreciated why. Also, he was working good and winter was almost on top of them once again. Maybe there would be less lynching and burning, or stealing of men for the prison gangs, since there was less field work in the winter. Anyway, she had finally seen Ethylene off to her new life in a real school. So she put her own dream off one more year. She thought.

THIRTEEN

Benjamin and Mor rushed through the job of cutting trees for Abby's house. "Use MY trees!" she proudly requested. They put the foundation down for a three-room shotgun house. The weather gradually became too wet to do too much more than frame it. But Abby was over on her land working on her own house whenever it was dry enough. She was anxious.

Luzy was in "love" for true, at last. She didn't care about school any longer, "I knows how to read and write and count enough!" She had been slow, but steady.

She was in love with a young boy named Torchy Biggers and they wanted to marry. NOW.

Abby tried to hold her off from rushing. "Are you knocked to have a baby with that boy?"

"No mam." Luzy laughed, embarrassed.

"What you in such a hurry for then?"

"I loves him."

"He love you?"

Luzy put her hand on her hip. "He wanna marry me! I spect he do!"

Abby shook her head at life. "Well, I want you to marry in our new home on our own land."

"Ohhhh, Mabby! That a whole ole year."

"No it ain't! Can't you see I'm goin fast?"

"Ohhhh, Mabby." Luzy wailed, throwing her body around one of the studs on the house foundation.

"You can wait! That little fast butt of yours can wait til we can do it right."

Luzy stopped moving and thought a moment. "I'm tryin to keep my dress down."

Abby got the point. "Is he got a home to take you to?"

"No mam, he live in a three-room house with eight people sides him already."

Abby sighed and stood up from her bending work. "There, you see? You need to wait til we get our own house. That will make a nice celebration marriage."

Luzy understood Abby's point, too. Her voice kept the wail in it though. "Will it be a year, Mabby?"

"No, Lawd, chile. Long fore that. Long enough to give you time to make a little wedding dress since your aunt Lifee done taught you sewing. If we sell enough pies. Don't you see, girl? We are gettin our own house. When I am dead . . . you and Meda will have some land of your own."

Luzy danced a few cold steps, "Torchy say we gonna go to a big city someday."

Abby stood up with her hands on her hips. "Torchy ain't got plank, pot nor wheel. How he gonna tell you where he gonna take you? Hand me that rock there for this fireplace, and do something with yourself to help me get this house up. Bring me them rocks from over there."

"Mabby, it's fixin to rain out here."

"I know it. Hand me that flat piece of wood with the clay on it and mix me some more clay and straw."

"Mabby, we gon catch the new monia!"

"We can work on the inside of the fireplace in another minute."

"Mabby, when you termined, you termined!"

Abby laughed, shaking her head. "Somebody gettin married can't even say 'determined'!"

Luzy laughed, "Torchy ain't marrying me to hear me talk!"

Abby reached over to bap Luzy on her head for talking such talk to her, but Luzy ducked and ran over to the clay pile and began preparing clay for the fireplace.

"I sorry, Mabby, scuse me, but I a grown woman now."

Abby shook her head, fixed her mouth in disgust. "You ain grown, you just ready. Your behind is runnin head of your head!"

"I been good."

"You been kissin."

"But I been good."

"You been a good kissin."

"I gon be a good wife."

"Chile, I bet you cain spell wife."

"I done learn from you how to be a good wife."

"Well . . . Go on chile, hand me that board and hush."

"It gon rain on us, Mabby."

"When you gets married to that young boy, it sure nuff gon rain on you."

"Awwww, Mabby, I loves em."

"Chile, chile. And I loves you; I guess we both fools."

The winter passed slowly as Abby waited to finish her house and Lifee waited to hear from Ethylene. A letter had come to say she had arrived safely and met the woman she was supposed to meet. "The woman helped me get a domestic job that was live-in so I have no rent to pay, but do work hard for every hour I am in the house, and I am there every day I am not in school, for twenty-four hours. The lady I work for loves to give parties. She sleeps when I work. I sleep when I can. But I'm here! Going to school! Becoming a nurse's aide! Someday I will become a real, true nurse. You watch and see! And I don't mind the hard work because I am working for myself! Oh, Lifee, reading and writing have changed my whole life. But I do miss my family. I can never thank you enough for what you all taught me. I can cook, I can sew, I can clean and I can read and write. And I am going to be a nurse's aide, something instead of a slave."

Lifee read the letter to Abby and they sat in silence a moment, thinking about the old plantation and how life had changed for them all. Abby wondered out loud, "How can anybody have freedom and don't do nothin with it? Little as it is, I even has my own bizness bakin these pies. And now . . . I has my own land. I can't hardly think of how all o' us was nothin but dumb slaves."

Lifee smiled fondly at Abby, "We didn't make ourselves slaves. And we weren't dumb. We weren't allowed to learn anything better than the work they wanted us to do. No one can know what they are not taught or are free to learn on their own. That is why ex-slaves speak all different kinds of ways. They learned from all different kinds of people; some intelligent, some educated, most ignorant and uneducated. Ex-slaves speak mostly like their old masters and overseers, mixed with their own backgrounds from Africa, if they could remember them."

They just sat there; Lifee looking in the direction of the future and Abby looking in the direction of her house.

The Yankee soldiers had long been gone from the South. The Freedman's Bureau had lasted awhile, but now showed signs of collapsing. The federal government was changing. The Southern men who blamed the Negro for the loss of their land, money and comfort were now leading in Congress and the legislature, so laws were being brought forth through which slavery could be brought back under a disguise. Pay for Negroes was absurdly low, yet if freed slaves tried to leave the South, landowners and the envious would kill them. They used any pretense, until they covered themselves with sheets, then they didn't need to pretend. If you wouldn't work for the pittance they wanted you to work for, they would take what you had and still kill you. Then there was the prison-gang work. They just took you, made up lies for your offence and sent you to work on the very place you had refused to work for so little pay; and then you worked for no pay. A black man could not call a white man a liar on point of death, so he had no way to prove his innocence.

Sometimes the Negro would be out in the fields working and the white man he was working for would be in the Negro's house with his Negro wife. She could not say no because her husband needed the work and it was hard to find a job. They probably "owed" the boss and they had children to feed. The white man would leave with a smirk, "Them black-nigra sluts." Purposely confusing her need for survival with desire for him.

All white people were not full of hate for the Negro. They were intimidated and fearful for their own lives from their own people. But there were a few who helped when they could; there were few.

There were signs of violence everywhere in the South with the stronger emergence of white protection societies and the Ku Klux Klan. Mor and his little group of family lived in its midst trying to avoid trouble . . . and survive.

Mor was bringing in a small steady pay for his inside-work for Tricia Tims. He gave Benjamin the little work he had been doing for Dr. Ben, so Benjamin was building the kennels on the land Dr. Ben had contrived to buy for Abby with her own money. So Benjamin and Mema had a little income for extra. Everyone already had plenty food they had grown themselves. Mor and Benjamin always saw to their land being cared for and worked first.

Mor and Benjamin had looked ahead to the time the white man would turn his eyes to their little farm and think "them Negroes" had more than they deserved. So during the season, in their spare time, they had dug a deep hole far in back of the acreage among the tall trees and brush. It was ten by twelve and lined on the dirt sides with tin. They had stowed many canned goods, fruits and vegetables. They stored vegetation that kept well, as it was cool in summer and cold in winter, as well as dried meat and sundry other things. Closed it by covering it with wood smoothed over with dirt. Just a little insurance if someone was to come take what they had worked so hard for or burn down the storage sheds. Burn in malice or jealousy. Or both.

Both were rather silent men, but they sometimes talked as they worked. One day when they were just finishing the food storage hole, Ben wiped his brow, leaned on his shovel and told Mor, "I'm learning a heap from you, Mor. I'm learning bout how to be a freedman. How to take care my fambly. I can even read and write . . . some."

Mor took advantage of the moment of rest, wiped his forehead and leaned on his shovel, too. "You a big help to me, Ben. I'm sho glad that ole Mema kept you alive and then fell sweet on ya! I couldn'ta done all we have done without you."

Ben waved his hand at Mor, brushing the compliment off. "I is full. I am full. What is 'at right way to say it?"

Mor waved his hand at Ben in the same way, "It don't matter. Just longs I understand what you sayin. I try to talk better round Lifee, but I can't always remember what's right either."

They laughed, then Ben continued. "But I am full. I is a daddy and a real husband. Even had me a real weddin! I is got everything!"

Mor grinned. "Me, too." They laughed and went back to work. For themselves.

When the winter was over and spring planting began, Mor had Lifee put the trip off until the crop was put in. Then, each week and month there was another period to wait "jes a little time more, baby."

Able and Aman were just almost four years old when Mor began taking his sons out to the fields with him. He would keep them a little while, give them a few peanuts or a sweet piece of fruit and take them back to their mother. "They gonna learn early how to take care themselves," he said. Neither Mor nor Lifee laughed or thought it was too early. It was spring 1871.

Lifee did all the cooking now. Abby was over on her own land, working on her house on the inside and living in it at the same time. Luzy and Torchy got married at the church house "Because," Luzy said, "it's taking too long, Mabby. I wants my marriage NOW!" Abby let them go ahead and she baked the cake and everyone contributed to the wedding party. Wasn't very much gift-giving because people stayed closer to their houses and land. They didn't want to be seen spending even a dime.

Mr. Winston still had the store, but most white landowners paid in scrip and would redeem it back from Mr. Winston. He didn't like it, but he had to live there, too. He was a kind man. Sometimes Mr. Winston just tore the scrip up and took a loss rather than let a boss know what his "negra" had spent.

Lifee took on a little extra work as a seamstress. Pretti was a well-behaved child and her mother gave her plenty patch material to play with. The white people who hired Lifee didn't want fancy clothes, just good, solid go-to-church clothes.

Now and again, Minister Prattle came by to visit with his church members, but he never brought any other people to stay there except an occasional man or woman to help in the fieldwork for a few days, good meals or a fine good night's sleep as they continued on their way looking for their family or a place to make a home.

Minister Prattle told Mor, "I never did meant to leave nothin bad on ya'll. If'n they'da been good-intention people it was a good chanct for 'em to pull theyselves up a step or two and help theyself. But they sho did't, so . . . now they gone."

Mor still worked for Mz Tricia Tims. She always had something for him to do. He usually came home for lunch, but had lately stopped. Lifee knew Tricia liked Negro men, at least, she had liked one anyway. One evening when Mor came in from his day's work, she asked him, "Mor?"

"Yes, mam." He exhaled an exhausted breath.

"You don't come home for lunch anymore?"

Mor didn't seem to be paying attention. "Don' I?"

Lifee was. "You know you don't." She waited for him to answer. He didn't. "Why?" she asked again.

Mor was taking his shoes off, sighing and leaning back in his chair, his boys climbing over him at the same time. "She always fixin somethin at lunchtime. She offer me, I eat. Saves time. Stop that boy! Put that down, little girl." He hugged the children, turning to look at Lifee.

Lifee set dishes on the table. "What you saving time for?"

"I got all this work to do. We jus finish up with Abby's house and I had to help old man Joshua mend up that house'a his. It's bout to fall down."

"But you spend a lot of time working for Tricia."

"Mmmmm-hmmmm. She pay."

Lifee stopped all her work. "Does that white woman like you, Mor?"

"She like my work. Mmm-hmm."

"You know what I mean, Mor."

"Awwww, Lifee . . ."

"Does she? When are you gonna be through there?"

"I don know. Everytime you think you might be through, somethin else shows up. That house in a bad way. Needs more'n I can do, I think. She wants to be real comfortable in there. Wants everything real nice. And she pays." He took his shirt off and went to wash up. Pretti followed her brothers following her father.

"Com'on, ya'll, you better wash up, too," Mor hollered over his shoulder.

When he came back to the kitchen he sat the children down and then sat himself. Lifee was not through talking. "Mor?"

"Yes mam."

"Have you ever wanted to be with a white woman?"

"Lifee? I don't need anything from no other woman."

"But, I ask you have you ever wanted a white woman."

Mor thought a moment. "I honest don't know no Negro man who wants one. Sometimes your curious comes up. But, me, I wouldn't want to love a white woman."

Lifee persisted, "Have sex?"

"Well, now, Lifee, you have ask me and I got to tell you the truth. I blive it would be good to have sex with one of em, just because the white man done lied so much bout they are better women than Negro women. But, I know, you couldn't keep the white man out the Negro woman's cabins. And their own women, sposed to be so specialty, would be lonelying around inside the house, sometime cryin. And another thing, if I was to do that, it would be so I could pay the white man back, but . . . I wouldn't be raping the white woman. Lots o' white women wants to do it cause white man done told her so many lies, but she see Negroes ain't animals when HE want to do it."

Lifee listened carefully, appreciating Mor's logic.

Mor continued. "But . . . if I hunched up a white woman, it would be so I could be gettin back at him. He done misused me, all our women and many a woman's child. And I can't respect him as no father. He sold his own, he slept with his own. Then he lie and say 'we the animals.' " The dinner was getting cold, but the children were eating.

Still, Mor talked. "I ain't not ever known no Negro who want to rape no white woman. Not just cause you gonna die, but they just don't look done. Like they ain't cooked enough or whatever you want to say. And I know one thing more; they gonna always, no matter what, feel like they better than you. It's been bred in em. They believe the lie. Someday, it might be better. But, I'm talkin bout now." He looked at Lifee and said, "I need the money for my family. I loves you and my family. Now . . . alright? Can I eat now?"

So Lifee didn't worry about it, but she took to showing up with his lunch on some days when he was working at Tricia's house. Mor just laughed at her, slapping her behind, saying, "I got mine and I'm happy with it. It done gave me my sons and my daughter. This here is mine!"

But Lifee decided, by herself, not to take her trip by herself.

Each day Mor wanted to stay close to his land and each day Lifee wanted to explore, seek for a new home. She did not like the limitations of the deep, ignorant South. She wanted more freedom, broader horizons; which horizons Mor did not know about so was not pushed to move by any inner compulsion. So the next year passed and they did not move because she loved him and loved watching her children grow and the land yield.

But she never lost her fear of the white men of the South and her concern for the safety of Mor, her sons and Ben. They all were in constant danger. Even in the middle of the night when they were all in bed asleep she feared for them. She kept them, as much as possible, to a very low profile; to seem poor and ignorant . . . so they could live.

When Ethylene had written she was finished with her training and was now a nurse's assistant, she had also asked if she should come home. Lifee knew Ethylene was barely surviving in Boston. They didn't pay Negroes very much. But Lifee knew by the question that Ethylene did not want to come home, so she wrote her to stay there if she thought she had a future there, but to prepare to help Meda get into the same training program. Ethylene heaved a big, grateful sigh, stayed where she was and began preparing for Meda.

Lifee forgot to worry about Mor and Tricia because it was not enough to worry about. Her Mor was her man.

But the future . . . the future . . . the future stayed on her mind. She still dreamed of leaving to search for a better home. For the moment, she had taught her sons what they could understand. But each inch grown, each inquiring look from the upturned face, made her think of their education. "I need schools for my children." There was a school in the area now. But the teachers were always being run off or even killed. And it wasn't always safe to let white folks know you wanted to learn. But many old, freed slaves went and took the young ones.

But every minute was not spent in terror. They all found pleasure among themselves. Family moments were especially enjoyable and satisfying. Lifee and Mema often laughed about Able always coming over to play with Babe, Mema's oldest daughter. He wanted to play with, work with, eat with, learn with Babe. Babe could be serious, even so young, because her mother saw to it that she was in every class Lifee had for the children. But she liked to laugh and play and was much more fun. Besides, Mema always had something good to eat in her little house. Able's mother always knew where to find him.

Lifee was not jealous, she loved Mema and her children. Aman was usually trying to read one of his books; almost five years old and he was already learning to read. He liked to be alone if his brother was not there. He would play teacher or preacher. His class or congregation would be trees, bushes and animals. Aman liked his books, his crayons, his harmonica, the piano and Dr. Ben's animals. When Able went to Mema's, Aman begged his mother to take him to the church where the piano was so he could play with it. Both Aman and Able were taking music lessons. Lifee wanted to buy a piano and have it at home, but she knew it would be noticed and remarked upon. She did not want any attention as to what they could afford.

Aman, also, loved the Bible, to preach. Able would listen, then take the book from Aman, try to read what Aman said he had read, then nod his little head, saying, "Yea, it sure do say that."

Their colors meant nothing to the boys because they had seen them from birth. They began to see the colors only when other people did, but wondered why it was so remarkable to some people. Able thought Mor was his father and loved him as his father, as he loved his mother and his brother. He saw other very light Negroes, so he did not feel different. He did not think he was white. He was right; he was not white.

Mor studied his sons as much as possible and was pleased to note they were removed from the turmoil of color. They were young, but they seemed to live in their own world of brotherhood and they had so much love bestowed upon them, it was what they lived with in their minds. When they were with him, he had to find things for them to do "like you, Daddy" and they tried hard to do a thing right.

Life was always concerned about the men in her life. Negro men and boys in the South were always in danger no matter what color they were. But it was their minds whites wanted to control. Life wanted of all her family thinking for themselves.

Ethylene had written she was working and had a small room with cooking privileges. She was ready for Meda. So plans were made for Meda to go and Meda was very excited about them. She liked working for Dr. Ben, it was different, but it was still domestic work and paid little. Meda was almost nineteen years old now. She was still very quiet, head usually in a book; even ones she had already read. She did not want a boyfriend, her education was foremost. Life had done her job well. They all wanted more than they were told they could have.

Life smiled as she thought of Luzy. Luzy had married at sixteen years of age and already had a child on the way. But she was happy, so far, and it was her life, after all. They lived with Abby, who was mad about it one minute and in the next minute, happy another child was on the way. She said to Lifee, "Well, that there is what families do; grow."

The next year was 1872. Lifee still dreamed of leaving to search for another, freer place to live. The money was still intact at the bank in Mudville. Always thinking of the twins and the future, she pressed harder on Mor.

Both Mor and Lifee watched their sons grow. Lifee watched them at play and study and at their little chores around the house and immediate yard. Mor watched them when they playfully followed him to work in the fields or "helped" him in his carpentry and animal care.

Both boys were smart and quick, but Aman was quicker with his hands at carpentry. Able was quicker with his skill when working with his father on leathers; holsters, saddle repair and chair seats. Both liked weaving baskets and, certainly, loved the animal care.

Mor noticed that Aman liked to tend the hurt chickens or disgruntled cow or horse, and dogs hurt in fighting. He was small and could hardly reach up to the horses, but he had a soothing voice and way about him. Both always wanted to accompany Mor to Dr. Ben's place. Both loved the beauty of birds and things wild. Neither liked going hunting, setting traps or any killing, which was unusual for boys. Often an animal caught in a trap would be "accidentally" released after its removal from the trap.

Mor also noticed when other children at church or school teased Able about his white skin, Aman always spoke up to say, "He ain no white boy, he's my brother!" Able would say, "Hell on you!" like he heard his father say sometimes. Then add, "I like all the colors God made; my mama said so!" Mor noticed when the boys had any dealings with an outsider who was white, Able stood forward.

When the outsider was colored, Aman stood forward. So the brothers joined forces to the world.

The boys had their little disagreements about possessions or friends, but those were easily forgotten in moments. The boys were their own best friends because they were taught that love and family were the most important things on earth.

Over time the local white people took to thinking that Able was the illegitimate son of Mz Emmalee and the soldier who didn't burn her house down, left behind by her when she went to visit her family. "Lordy! When ever is she a'comin back?!"

They were good-looking, strong, healthy boys. And it was not unusual for children of Negroes to love school and learning since they had to fight to have the right to do it. Lifee spoke to her children, often, of them moving one day so they could continue their schooling and go on to college. They didn't know exactly what college was, but they wanted to go. Aman wanted to be a vet like Dr. Ben. Able wanted to be a doctor or a carpenter or a cattleman, and lately, a lawyer, though he wasn't sure exactly what that was, just knew his mother had one.

Pretti would follow them wherever they went, whenever she could. She just wanted to be with her brothers. The twins were kind to each other and especially to their little sister, Pretti. She kept up with them as fast as and wherever her little legs would take her, but Lifee gave her limits. No farther than Mema's house at home and no farther than her father was, when she was with him in the fields.

All the children were good children, but their parents were kind, thoughtful people, so they thought that was just the way to be. Mema always said, "They just young, chile. I'm restin up for when they gets out here in this life."

That year on the twins' birthday they planned a small celebration. Mema's children, Babe and Bettern, came. Abby and Luzy brought a cake and their new baby. Other five-, six- and seven-year-olds came from the church families. There was a good little supper of boiled ham, hot baked yams with the brown, sweet juices oozing from them and corn on the cob dripping butter. Steaming hot biscuits and homemade preserves completed the lunch. Peach and berry cobbler and Abby's coconut icing cake sat waiting on the sideboard.

Gatherings were still done on the inside of buildings, the house or the barn if it was a summer picnic, because of the hostility and malevolence of others who would have resented them for being able to be happy. Tension was growing worse. The times seemed to be getting harder for everyone. Every month there were as many as three or four lynchings. It kept the Negro women in a constant state of tension and stress worrying about their sons and husbands. Mor and Lifee were careful. Well, everybody was. Unknown, their freedom had brought them hypertension and high blood pressure; which both Mor and Benjamin had. But they tried to live normally, so a birthday party for the children was arranged.

As the party was winding down, babies asleep, toddlers getting tired and cranky, a timid little knock could finally be heard from the back kitchen door. Lifee went to answer and when she opened the door there was Rufus Bingly's sister, Wanda Sue. Wanda Sue had a small package in her hand, homewrapped in a towel, tied with a piece of knitting yarn.

Wanda Sue was around twenty-eight years old now, still a gentle person. She was not ugly, just uncared for. Lifee still gave them much of their food.

She spoke hesitantly as she tendered the little package to Lifee, "My mammy say she want to send this over to your little ones, cause it's they birthday. She didn't have so much, but . . . you all bein so good to us and all . . . we wanted to let you know we sure thanks ya'll." Lifee, smiling, reached for the package. In her nervousness Wanda Sue did not realize she was still holding on to the package. She continued speaking. "My mammy, she gather every sock she could find in our house, washing it and unknittin it til they all clean and ready, then she knit it into two pairs o' socks for em. It don't all match up, but they be warm . . . and they very clean . . . and nice." She exhaled as if she had rehearsed all the words and now, at last, it was over. She let go the package.

Lifee took the gift with a smile, "Ohhhh, you tell Mz Bingly she didn't have to do all that work for these two boys of mine, but that it was so kind of her, so thoughtful. We can sure use em and we surely do appreciate it."

Lifee didn't want Wanda Sue Bingly to come in the house and see the remaining piles of food as evidence of plenty, but couldn't just close the door in her face, so she turned to call Luzy. "Come in here and say hello to Wanda Sue. Talk to her a minute while I cut them a piece of birthday cake to take home for later."

Wanda Sue wanted to come into the bright, warm food-smelling house, but allowed as she hadn't been invited she would talk to Luzy on the back stoop for the few moments it took Lifee to cut large pieces of cake and wrap them in a little paper and the towel the socks had been wrapped in. She would take them back to the peaked, drawn woman whose youth was dry and disappearing in the wake of nothingness she had at home every day.

As she handed her the package of sweets, Lifee had a sudden thought. "Have you ever thought of having a job, Wanda Sue? You know, Dr. Ben really needs someone over there to help him in his work. Would you be interested in doing something like that?"

The Binglys knew almost everything the Freemans did outside their home. Wanda Sue had often envied the Negro girls who had the nerve to work out and for Dr. Ben. Her face broke into the prettiest, sad smile. "Oh, yessum, I surely would be."

"Well, I'll ask him, or Mor will, and maybe that will be something you can enjoy and be a help at home, too!"

Wanda Sue turned to go, she was so embarrassed. Then she

turned back just as quickly, "But, Lifee, I don't know how to write, nor count nothing more 'n money."

Lifee frowned, "Why? You haven't gone to the school that's been opened, up the way here, for you all, at least two years now?"

"No'em. I . . . I . . . so much bigger and older than the children goin there . . . I just couldn' . . . I. And my brother says—"

Lifee stepped down from the steps, "Nobody pays any attention to things like that very much. Don't pay them any mind if they do! You go get what you need! You are a person! You have to do for yourself! Tend to your business and forget about those others! You know, you are a nice-looking woman, and you are not old. What are you doing with your life, Wanda Sue?"

Wanda Sue turned her face away from Lifee and frowned a little, she was uncomfortable. "My mammy need me at the house."

Without really thinking, Lifee said, "You need to come out of that house and go to school. If you learn enough you will have a way to get out and maybe get married and . . ." She saw Wanda Sue blushing and hesitated. "Don't mind what I say. We are women and sometimes women talk like this."

A frown flicked across Wanda Sue's brow as she thought, "Is Lifee trying to tell me what to do? Like a child? Or a slave even?" But on second thought, the girl smiled briefly and turned away to leave. Then she stopped and turned back to Lifee. "Mz Emmalee told us, me and Mama, you think you bought her farm, but she really jest lettin you take care it for her while she gone. That she be back to get it by 'n by. We didin tell Rufus that buyin part, so Rufus don bother ya'll none."

Wanda Sue liked Lifee and didn't know why she was talking to Lifee like she was. For one thing, Lifee didn't say "Miss" when she spoke her name! Wanda Sue wanted to throw the cake back at Lifee, but . . . she was hungry. And her mama would so enjoy it. Uncomfortable again, Wanda Sue smiled, trying to say "I'm sorry," but she couldn't say "I'm sorry" to a Negro! So she said, "Thankee for the cake." Then blurted out, "My manners are showing poorly. I . . . I am surely sorry." Amazed at herself, she turned and walked hurriedly down the worn path to the road, to get home, to enjoy the cake and whatever else might be in the package. But she thought about the job and the school. Her mother had been telling her to go to school, too. But her brother, Rufus, who thought he was too old to go, had stopped her from going to the "Yankee" school. "Cause you jest a female girl."

As she walked along the road, the sun was starting to set and the world seemed to be in a golden glow mellowed with a pink haze. She felt some kind of joy in her breast and her mind. "I am surely glad I said I was sorry. I am sorry." She smiled to herself for no reason at all.

She spied, at that moment, a turtle, slowly making its way across the bumpy dirt road. "What you doin out here away from your water, all by yourself?" When she reached the turtle, she picked it up. It was a young turtle, its legs struggling to get back to its search on the road. "I'm gonna take you and put you back in the water! Don you know somebody will pick you up and take you home and eat you!" She thought of doing that herself. Her brother would do it. But she took the turtle near the biggest creek and set it down. "Now! Git on with you! Go on." And the turtle struggled away, slowly, toward the water it smelled.

When Wanda Sue went into her house, her eyes searched for her brother. He was not home. She gave her mother the package. "It's a piece for both o' us. Lifee seem to be real pleased with the gift. She said 'Thankee' to you."

Wanda Sue went to the broken mirror over the dilapidated bu- reau in the bedroom and looked into her face. Trying to see how the world would see her face. It looked familiar to her at the same time it looked strange. "I am a real person," she told her mother from the bedroom. Later, with her mouth full of cake, she turned to her mother and said, "I blive I'm a'goin to that there school." After a few more mouthfuls, she said, "And I'm a'goin get me a job. Maybe."

Old, tired, Mz Bingly looked at her child she worried so much about, for a long moment. Her old body straightened a little. Her heart lightened a little. "We got to fin some cloths round here and git some 'o em ready." They both giggled; Wanda Sue in embarrassment, Mz Bingly in delight. Then they took another bite of the coconut cake. "I'a knit plenny more good socks for this here kinda cake. Lawd!"

Lifee spoke to Mor, Mor spoke to Dr. Ben and Dr. Ben agreed it might be a good idea. Lifee went over to the Binglys to tell Wanda Sue to take herself over to talk to Dr. Ben and then to take herself over to talk to the teacher for lessons after school, when the smaller children were gone.

In about three months or so, Wanda Sue, studying very hard, was stumbling through a few books loaned to her, marveling at the lives in the books. Her face relaxed, her eyes brightened, her heart lifted and soon she was sitting in the little schoolhouse all through the day classes. It helped that she was trying to teach her mother.

Mz Bingly cried silent tears when she thought she failed the homemade lessons. Said, "I's too old, not able to learn." Then, one day that Wanda Sue was in school, she had to trudge slowly to the store herself for some snuff. She would not trust her son with the money to buy it for her. In the store, without thinking, she looked up and the words on the walls that had always looked like crazy designs made sense to her. She asked Mr. Winston, "Do that sign say 'open' out ere on that thar door?" He nodded.

She pointed to another sign. "Do that sign say 'Do not put somethin, somethin, hand in the somethin'?" He laughed and nodded, saying, "It say somethin like that!"

Mz Bingly trudged slowly home, sucking her snuff, trying not to smile. But her mind was going over and over like wheels on a railroad track. "I is readin. I is readin. I . . . am . . . readin!"

In six months Wanda Sue was working for Dr. Ben. Lifee fixed up the two dresses she had kept hanging in the empty room of Mz Emmalee and gave them to her. Wanda Sue wore one a week and washed the other. Then she did the same thing with that one. She was slow, but she was determined. She made a life for herself even under her brother's nose and disapproval.

After all his disapproval of school and even work, Rufus tried borrowing money from her, but their mother kept Wanda Sue's money for her. She wanted Wanda Sue to have a better life than hers had been. She loved her son, but she'd smile a toothless smile as she shared a meal with her daughter, who had bought the ingredients, saying, "Don you let that ole fool mess in yoah life. That ole fool cain even read!" And they would giggle together gleefully.

FOURTEEN

Soon after the birthday party gathering a young Negro boy, nine years old, had been killed by beating and burning because someone said he had accosted a little white girl. She had dropped a penny in the store and he had picked it up to give it back to her. He was then roughly handled, dragged out of the store and beaten. Mr. Winston could do nothing about it, he was outnumbered.

The further the civil war receded into the past, the more abusive and cruel the Klan and other racist groups became. More lynchings, more burnings of people and property to combat freedom for former slaves. To control the ex-slave's freedom, landowners and sheriffs used the prison work force to bolster its needs and to replace the workers in the fields, on railways, on roads.

Men were arrested for cursing, for daring, even softly, to answer a white man back. Whites told lies about Negroes owing them and it was a legal offence for a Negro to say a white man had lied. Negroes were killed many, many thousands of times for an imaginary rape of an imaginary white woman. Children as young as seven years old were taken and sold to landowners for a ten- or twenty-year sentence. To be "accused" of stealing a dime was enough for a ten- to twenty-year sentence in a work camp where the conditions were atrocious. Negro men with families were taken, and once this family had no wage earner, the children were declared orphans and taken by the state and sold to white farmers to work in horrifying conditions; some, all their life . . . until death. This was sanctioned by the towns, cities and state because they all made money from it. It was a way to have their slaves back; hundreds, thousands of them.

Mema, Abby and Lifee worried almost constantly. They were grateful they worked for themselves and were careful not to give any white man reason to be jealous of them.

Abby said of a neighbor, "They tortured that there man first! Cut his ears off, cut his tongue out and cut one finger at a time off. One by one, Lawd! Then . . . last . . . they cut his privates off of em. All of em was laughin at em in his pain. Was a crowd gathered. Always a crowd is gathered . . . at most of them lynchin's; havin dinner and laughin! They even bring their children! To laugh at death!"

Mema, who often traveled walking to her work in the area, saw the remains sometimes. "But, ya'll knows, you can't stop and help em! Can't touch em! Do, you be the nexes one out there. Got to move them bodies at night after a day or two. Poor families. Poor children."

They were afraid for their men and children. "Oh, damn! Damn this white man, God! His ignorant, damnable hate is destroying us as well as himself. Why can't they leave us alone, Jesus?"

Even though Aman and Able were only five years old, Lifee began to reckon more on her life and family, dreams of the future and leaving. One night, after the children were in bed, windows open to let any fresh evening breezes flow through the house, Lifee approached Mor as he stretched his body out in weariness in search of rest.

"I can't keep putting this off. You don't mind staying here with your farm, but I do and I don't want my sons to grow up midst all this lynching. They're going to be older soon and white folks already looking at them strange. We are going to have to go. And this time I mean it!"

She was convincing and Mor already knew what she meant.

"Mor, I can't even make my children pretty clothes! These white folks round here are poor and jealous of everything. I can't even keep them too clean. They don't like you to do anything better than they do. And you know what you have to go through. Why, if it weren't for Mr. Winston staying down here after the Freedman's Bureau closed, and Dr. Ben with jobs and such, you'd have way more trouble just because you don't need them folks for nothing and don't have to beg them for nothing. I don't think this can last. And times are getting harder. Money is scarce. They notice more what you have and they never did like you working for that white woman, Tricia." Mor nodded his head, tired, he worked hard, everywhere.

Lifee continued, "I see these white men looking at Able. Some laugh at him, but the ones who frighten me are the ones who hate him for having that skin most white as theirs! And my children don't look like they are dumb and going to be 'good nigra workers' on some white man's farm! They still have these prison scouts always looking for somebody to lie on and take off to work for nothing. They're still beating and burning and lynching Negro men and raping Negro women and even children. Killing them! I'm not worried about just getting ahead. I'm worrying about staying alive! All of us!"

Mor nodded his head in agreement again. "But where we gonna go that it will be betta? I know what you say, but you don't know, cause you ain been there in no new place where white folks is livable."

Lifee was almost in tears. "All I need to know is it sure isn't better in Alabama or Georgia where we are. It's got to be better somewhere. Survival is what we are after." She put her arms around his neck and sat on his lap. "We can always come back here to visit or stay. It's still going to be yours. They can burn it down, but they

can't take it away!" Lifee paused, because she knew, of course, that
the deed didn't mean anything if the white man wanted the land.
"Hell!, they made the laws. Well, we just got to try. If they want it,
they're going to get it whether we're here or not!"

Mor nodded his head again and patted her plump behind nestled
in his lap. "You right. We got to think of the children. That Pretti
getting awful pretty and getting to be a big girl. Time just seem to
fly on way from here."

She knew Mor was overprotective, but how could you be overprotective of a Negro girl in the South? He didn't want anything
happening to his sons, but most especially what could happen to his
daughter.

A few days later Mor came into the house visibly upset and
angry. "Lifee, you know what they done done? They done killed
Lester Royal just cause the man built a fence round his house!
Killed him! And burnt up the house. His family staying in the
church. We got to take some things over to em. Lord have mercy! Is
this killin ever goin to end?" Lifee grabbed her shaken husband and
held him.

Mor eased Lifee's arms from around him, reaching for his hat.
"You right. We goin. Soon. I talk to Benjamin now, see what they
want'a do."

Lifee went over to Abby's to tell her what plans they were making. "They aren't clear plans yet, but, this time, I don't think they
will fade away."

Benjamin and Mema still had only two children. Two clean and
well-fed children. Mema worked in the fields at field time and did a
little domestic work here and there for her favorite customers. But
she was mainly a housewife, still in the little three-room, now,
shack. She was surely Benjamin's woman and he was just as surely
her man. They loved their two girls, but Ben was hinting about a
son.

Ben scratched his head, then shook it, looked at Mor, said, "No. We reckon we just gonna stay where we are. Life ain not a happy thing away from our house, but life ain never been so good for us before now. For the firstest time, we can keep the fruits of our labor."

When Mor had finished stating his case, "This here just a searchin trip, but the nex trip, I don blive we comin back here. Least til things change." Mema answered, "We just black and minds our own bisness. Ain't fixin to have no truck with white folks ceptin them I works for. We gon work and keep on like we doin."

Benjamin agreed with Mema. "Lawd, I blive we's home, Mor. Who would'a magined what ya'll was bringin to me? Two childrens, land. Naw, we gonna stay here. Look afta things for ya."

So they talked a bit more about the land and Mor left to go home. As he started walking toward his house, Mor stopped. Standing still a moment, then he turned slowly around, looking at all the labor of his hands. All the land stretched around him. A place of his own where he could be somebody. A place he wanted, one day, to belong to his children. There was plenty room to build on for all his children. "Lawd, Lawd, they won't leave us alone. What did we eva do to these people. Didt they work us for more'n three hundred years? Didt they rape our mamas and kill our daddies enough already? They done taken our childs who we never see again. Ain that enough for em? They don seem to care bout nobody. I can't paint my house, can't fix my fence too good, can't build a extry shed or a bigger barn. I can't love my own things in front of everybody." As he had shed tears when the land first became his, now his silent tears rolled down his face, dropping onto his dirty shirt; dirty with the dirt of his own land. Good dirt.

When Lifee talked to Abby, Abby wanted to go with Mor and Lifee. She didn't really know how old she was, but she was several years older now than when she had walked across all the states. And she was in her own homemade home, with grandchildren in it. And it was her land! That kept her from leaving.

She had become friends with Viry, Joshua's wife, before Viry died. She had enjoyed being an older lady sitting in the sun of an evening, eating goobers or tea cakes with another older lady. Both knowing the darkness they had come out of. The light they were in.

And now she and Joshua sat every evening out on the tilted porch they had built together. He had been in such misery and loneliness when Viry died, Abby had reached out to him in sympathy. They worked the kitchen garden together, an acre or so. They were happy with the new life growing around them.

Joshua was even happy because he believed he had reached an age where the white man did not worry about him anymore. Didn't fear him in that way that white men feared black men. And . . . he was still sitting on his land. "I don't have no money, ceptin the little I makes carin for Dr. Ben's animals in the kennels, mostly hunting dogs. But that money pays the taxes and a little mo; chewing tobacco, a shingle for a leaky roof, now and then, and a good knife to whittle with. What more I need? I got all the wood I'll eva need right chere!" He waves his arm at the tall trees around his land. Abby's land. "And Mor done remind me how to make them basket traps to go with the brooms I makes and sell sometime. And I know I will be buried with my folks, next to my wife on this here land my pappy worked so hard to keep."

They didn't want to go. Neither one.

FIFTEEN

Over the past years Mr. Winston had grown to trust Lifee and Mor. He liked them. They stayed out of trouble. Kept to themselves and worked hard. "Don't look like to me, Mz Emmalee is ever going to come back here. She sho lucky to have somebody she can trust on her land," he said to his wife.

Then Lifee brought the letter to him "from" Mz Emmalee.

Dear Mr. Winston,

Surely hope all your family is doing well.

I am having Mor and Lifee to come up here to pick some things of mine up and take them back. My new husband does not want to come live there right now, but maybe someday. Please see that they get off alright and safe. Add a letter, if you will, please, to my letter so they will have safe passage, cause you know they got that white-lookin boy.

Thankee. Will send you all something.

Mrs. Emmalee

Lifee thought it was best to leave off any new married last name. So Mr. Winston wrote another letter and Lifee added it to the

new safe-passage letter Lifee "had from Mz Emmalee." The letter
Lifee did not give him to read because he would be able to check
out whether there was such a man who was supposed to have signed
it. The private safe-passage letter said:

Whoever you are,
   These are my servants and they are bringing my son to me.
Give them safe passage, for I will someday soon be coming
through that way. Let no one bother or take anything of mine, or
theirs, from my trusted servants.

                                            Thank you,
      Mr. Elihu P. Sattler, Attorney, Sheriff's Dept. America.

Mor and Lifee did not have a farewell gathering. They were coming
back anyway. They didn't want any notice taken of them in any
way. All said quiet good-bys.

Aman was eager to go, just hated to leave his pet animals. The
piano would be there in the church when he returned. Able, young
as he was, only hated to leave his smooth, dark-skinned, sloe-eyed,
dimpled, plump little friend, Babe, with white pearly teeth she
loved to sink into food. Babe had a strong little body with long legs.
Everything promised she would be a lovely little lady when she
would be grown. She and Able would just look at each other and
laugh happily.

Able cried when the wagon Mor had made a cover for pulled
away early one June morning. They had used most of June helping
Benjamin put a few crops in. They now skipped cotton, didn't plant
it at all. There was not much money in any crop for some reason
now. But there was plenty pork meat hanging in the smokehouse
and food in their secret hideaway in the ground from the last No-
vember, when the weather had been right for preserving meat.

Lifee had plenty fried chicken, bacon cracklins and beef jerky in
the wagon. Jars of preserves and homemade breads to last as long as
possible to a good distance away. They would cook at night and

sleep out under the stars. The children in the wagon, Mor and Lifee stretched out on a homemade bed on the ground. Lifee was happy as the wagon pulled away. Mor didn't know what to feel, but he thought he felt good.

They were stopped on the second day by two young white men who wanted to search the wagon for whatever they could take from the helpless Negro people. But Mor gave them the letter and Lifee told them what it said, going heavy on the sheriff's dept. When they looked at Able they thought he was white and it must be true.

But they took the bottle of white lightning Mor had brought for tired, cold nights, and a handful of the fried chicken Lifee had. Laughing, happy with the liquor as they rode away on their tired horses. Mor had a rifle Mr. Winston had given him for hunting and was relieved they had not looked under the driver's seat.

All of that brought about the circumstance of Mor talking to his sons as he drove across the beautiful, blossoming land. He had always spoken to them of their survival, even young as they were. Going as far as he thought their little understanding would hold. But, now, on the road, with nothing to protect them, like a door; nothing between them and death but their actions, he talked to his sons as men and to his daughter as a woman.

He put the horses in a comfortable, steady gait, leaned back on the extra plank built onto the seat for a backrest, and spoke.

"Now . . . we goes to church and we know there is a God. Bible even say his name is Jehovah, Psalms 83:18. And we know He created man and woman. We know He loves what is good. From that we just have to know there are some good white people in the world. Dr. Ben, Mr. Winston, Tricia and that old white lady, Mz Bingly, who made you the socks . . . like them. But we also know there are plenty more bad ones and they seem to have the power what give them the rights to do whatever bad thing they can think of to hurt us, kill us, stop us from makin a livin and be satisfied with the work of our hands. Your mother say this America white men is not like the other peoples all over the world. America white men is full of hate. Sons? And you listen, too, little daughter. They hate us for no good reason me and your ma can think of. They lie, sons, they lie so much about everything. Anything. They lie on us so much." He turned to look at his children. "Are you listenin to me?" They, solemnly, nodded yes, their little eyes looking earnestly in their father's face. "This here means your life. You got to know em, cause you in the world with em and your life depends on what you know."

"Well . . . they say we lazy. But the African peoples worked for them for more'n three hundred year, I blive. Now we want to work for ourself . . . since freedom, and they try to stop us. We don't stop, all of us, but they still call us lazy." He looked at Lifee for agreement. She nodded approval.

He continued, "White women PAY Negro women to come into their dirty houses and clean it and feed their own white children, but they don't say THEY are lazy, they say we are." He looked at Lifee again, then back at his children.

He continued, "They say we dumb, CAIN'T learn, like animals. But they won't let us go to school. Use to kill us if we somehow or nother learned to read. And now, if we get a schoolhouse, they will burn it down. Kill the teacher even, white or black, don't matter." He shook his head in disgust. The children were struggling to understand, but it had been everyday enough for them to sense the tension in the air of life.

He continued, "They say we don want nothin. But if we get somethin . . . they take it away from us. Fair, unfair under the law, but they make the laws. If they can't get it and it will burn up, then they burn it up . . . or down." He turned to his sons, "You see what I mean, sons?" They nodded, slowly. Little minds trying to grasp this thing that seemed so important to their father.

He continued, "They say Negro womens are whores and tramps." Lifee raised her hand to stop him, but Mor turned to her and said,

"Lifee, they hear them words at the store already and I want them to understand what it means when they hear them pointed at Negro women. Let me do this."

He continued, "They say Negro womens are whores and tramps. But ain no Negro women I ever heard of, in my whole life, ever run them down and raped them. They can't let our woman alone. They will take a Negro man's wife right in front of his face. MAKE her go. Cause it could cost her husband his job, and you know they poor. And it could cost him his life if he say something! But, they say we the ones have no moral, don't do right." He looked at his sons, heard the sounds of the horses' hooves, felt the breeze winding its way through his wagon, felt the sun's warmth on his family; saw the trust and love in his family's faces; and loved his family so much.

He continued, "They say this white woman is the best of everything. But, they tell this white woman making love is dirty. She too good for it. So they can only do it mostly with Negro women they rape or force in some other way. But they don tell the white women they are rapin. They tell em the black man wants to rape. They say Negro men make bastards. Ya'll remember what I told you a bastard was? Well . . . most the bastards in the world was made in slavery in the slave quarter and they was the bastards of white men. And them white men made them bastards and left em. Sometime sold em and sometimes, when they might'a got grown, them same fathers made babies with they own daughters. They beat em sometimes. They killed em sometimes. But they very seldom loved em and treated em like a child of theirs. Very seldom."

He was silent for a while, then, "You see all these light, white children in the world? Well . . . they not from African men."

Able looked down at his skin and frowned. Mor saw him and said, "Cept a few, cept a few." Able looked up at his father and smiled uneasily. Mor changed the subject until he could learn how to explain it.

He persisted in his spoken thoughts, "But a black, African man got to be a man in his own way, no matter what the white man lies about. If you do nothin for yourself and your wife and children . . . you are nothing. So, sons, be a real man. Work for yourself if you can. And you can. I am a carpenter, which you are surely going to learn, already learnin. Little by little. I am a cattleman, which you are learnin, too. I build wagons, make saddles and harnesses, which you will learn when we get all the leather and cowhide we need and be in one place where it is." He looked sidewise at Lifie. Lifie smiled.

He continued, "I can do a multitude of things the white man uses and needs. He got to pay me cause I don't work for him no more, I work for us. Learn to do something he needs, and everything you need. That way, you support your own self-respect. That means you gettin to be a man. Cause . . . no work means no home, no wife, hungry children. No life."

The sun was getting hotter as it shined down on the steady-paced wagon. Mor took off the heavy wool shirt worn for the cool mornings, leaving a lighter cotton shirt. Aman and Able did the same. Lifie gave everyone a drink of water from the water can and, everyone refreshed, Mor started talking again.

"White men don't only just hold Negro men down, they hold other white men, too. Poor white men who wants to work, like miners and some mill workers. His own color. So, you know he don't care nothin bout you. Yea, he lie to us all. But we the most sufferers, cause he put the white man he holds down on top of us, head of us, and if they at the bottom . . . where that put us? It's some things you GOT to have; God bless your mama, one is a education. Education and the control of yourself. Bide your time."

Lifie spoke softly to Mor, "Maybe that is enough for today. You are giving them so much to try to understand. They're young. Save some for another time."

Mor nodded, smiled and agreed with his wife. Soon the children were playing in their small space and making games with the scenery. Then Mor turned to Lifee and said, "But this just the beginnin. I got to say it over and over, til they got it."

Lifee, serious, "I know."

Another day, it rained lightly, but the wagon cover was up and it was kind of magical, riding down the road with all the beautiful trees and colors. The birds and a clean, fresh smell in the air. Mor decided to teach his children again. When they were settled and quiet, he began.

"White men, most of em here in the South, I don know bout the North, but, most of em don like us. Hate us even. But, they always where we are. Watchin. Enjoyin our food, our music, our singin and our laughter and our lovin, if they can. I notice that in slavery, too. But they don want you round them. They scared. They need to pretend they better'n you . . . More lies. So they pretend like they is too good for you, but they lyin again. We got plenty blood mixed right here in this here dirt, soil and ground of America. Our blood from all our peoples. All our dead people. This land is our land, too." He turned to his sons, pointing his finger at them. "Don you ever forget that!" Then he reached for more water.

"You got to watch em. Watch and remember. They ain even half great in the Bible. Cause they full of lies and God hates a liar. It says that in the Bible, don it, Aman?"

The little boy spoke right up, because he often read the Bible so he could preach better. He stumbled over some words, but his mother was a good teacher. "Yes sir, Daddy."

"That's another thing they lied about; there ain nothin in the Bible that say being black is a curse. Nothin!"

They rolled on across the countryside. Driving during the days, trying to get through the towns in early mornings, when not too many people were up and out. As they crossed over deeper into Georgia, going toward North Carolina, they stopped sometimes in the colored business sections of the town. Lifee found some Negro newspapers, which she did not know were in existence. She bought them. Good reading practice for the children and they needed to know more about what other Negroes were doing.

They spent the nights out under the moon and black broad sky. It was the first time the members of Mor's family had been alone together. Traveling. And, too, this time they were riding in a wagon, not walking.

When they had to stop and shop, or feed the horses, they had to show the letters which granted them safe passage. Many people, especially children, stared at Able. Some threw rocks at the wagon full of Negro people as it passed their way. Able began to see he got a different look or respect from people. So when the rocks were thrown after the first time, he looked out of the wagon cover and threw a few rocks back at the white children, saying, "These my papa's horses!" Mor said to Lifee, "I nearabout died. I whipped them horses up and got on way from there!"

The children loved the wagon riding and the nights out, even under the wagon cover. Each day the weather grew warmer. Late afternoons after lunch they were a little drowsy and agitated, but soon fell asleep in the back of the wagon, where it was hot, but shielded from direct sun by the wagon cover.

When they first left the border of Alabama near the Chattahoochee River, they traveled across Georgia close to the coast of the Atlantic Ocean because the coast was what Lifee wanted to see. But the way was longer that way so they turned East to head toward North Carolina. "That ocean will be up there, too," said Lifee with a smile toward her children.

In a store, one afternoon, after she had shown the letters, she was told, "Ya'll better get on out'a here, cause yo color ain't welcom here. They jes had some trouble which you will see down the road a piece. Don't stop, cause they may tear up yo wagon even if it do blong to a white man! They ain't gonna take no time to read no letter!" They followed the advice, hastily.

As they rode through another side of the hot little town out to the countryside again, Mor, whose horizons were steadily broadening, commented, "They done had all this their own selfs and they don want to share none."

And, of course, Mor's afternoon talk began. "They full of hate and sickness. I am glad you can't hear what all they done done, and do, to Negro people; men and women and children. So pay em no mind to follow or blive. And don look em in the eye, they don like that. They know you will see them lyin and they know they will see that you know." Mor swatted at a mosquito.

"Now, I give you an example. You and the white man can see somethin happen. See the same thing! But, when ya'll talk about it, he say it wasn't what you saw. He say it was somethin else that you know ain true. And he got all them words and he can confuse you ever which way you go. They do it to each and other, too! He want his way to be right."

Lifee shook her head and laughed. "They sure will."

"Then," he continued, "when ya'll go to talkin bout it, he will use up a lot of words, to esplain what he say both ya'll saw. Use up so many words that don add up to meanin nothin at all. Is another lie. And he expect you to believe him. That's when you tell em he's right and leave it alone. Cause if he get mad about it, he'll kill you do he want to."

Lifee had to laugh at all her lessons gone awry. "Mor, you are tearing up all those English lessons you have learned, or were supposed to learn. I'm trying to teach our children how to speak correctly and you—"

"But, see, Lifee, I'm out in the fields or workin somewhere else where most people just talk any kind o' way and sometime I just pick it back up and talk any kind of way. Ya'll children listen to your mama, she right. Don copy after me."

They rode on awhile, then Mor continued. "I want you to know, now, white folks came down here from the North and fought that war that freed us. And some of them white teachers that come down here to teach the freed slave end up dyin for it. It's some white folks that got good in their hearts. They was raised better. They blive the Bible, maybe. But they do treat Negroes like they was human beings. Heard was a underground railroad helped plenty slaves to freedom. Risk their life! Knowin the white man who was after em, I'm sure some of them good white men did lose their life. But they was white. See? And good people! That's why you got to pay them attention when they got anything to do with your life; cause you need to know what kind'a white folks you are talkin to."

Aman touched his father's elbow to get his attention. "Why, Daddy, why they so mean sometime?"

"Cause they ignorant. See, everybody got a mind. You got one, Able got one, Pretti got one. A mind can be narrow and you ain got too much in it and ain got sense enough to want to put nothin in it. So you can't have enough sense to reason things out and think. No matter how old you gets, your brain, your mind, just don never grow and your mind holds on to things you might'a learned when you was a child. Lies or anything. Can mess up your life. Or somebody else life." Mor pondered a moment, "Then you got people that have broad minds, like your mama say, and a broad mind got lot of room in it for sense. And you fill it up with sense and you use it. Like when you learnin new things. Your brain holds it, you remember cause you got sense. You got more to use cause you got more to reason with. And you got sense enough to use it. Understand? Sons?" They nodded their little heads. Pretti did, too. Her father smiled at her over his shoulder and said, "You, too, baby, cause you gon be a woman someday and they be after you. Strong. Gonna try to make you a loose woman. Your mama tell you more bout that later. Woman's talk.

"Like, white folks say the slaves loved em. That's another lie, cept for a few good masters, but who can love a master over your life?

Only Master is God. But, God freed slaves by not really making white men masters over our minds. We still had our minds. Even us slaves knew what the white man was made of. He even lied about his own God. He broke every one of His laws. Slaves didn't respect him or love him . . . but for a very few whites who were fair to blacks and whites alike. Freedom had to come; I study my Bible, too. Evil last a long time, sometime, but not for all time." Everyone but Pretti thought about that; she, still almost a baby, was playing with a homemade pink doll.

Mor moved his buttocks on the seat to a more comfortable position. "And I'll tell you this last thing for today, then you can rest if you want to. Remember now, cause this is for your day, your time. The white man never forgets you was in his power one time. And he keep tryin to test you out, over and over again. He want that power back. But, you watch him, smile at him, but he don need to know all what you thinkin. Remember, he love money. So you got to get your own money; even from him. But it be yours . . . and you will keep your own power. Most times. And be careful. Live right. Be careful cause white men got the prisons and the laws. Them prisons built for you and a few real bad white men, a few Indians and some Mexicans. We don have no laws of our own. No law men, as I know of. And even though they tell us we are free; some of em, we are only free to obey their laws." He looked back at the children, seeing if they were bored and falling asleep on him; they weren't. They didn't know anything about lawyers, but they were thinking they would like to make laws, whatever they were. They knew laws because their mother had house laws they had to obey.

"Last thing today, sons. Laws can be good. God got laws. Laws can be fair. Only God's laws truly are. But, the average white man ain no more thinkin of God as a polecat is. I bet Jesus Christ can't count no more God-fearing men in the America South than he could in . . ." He turned his head to Lifee. "What's them names in the Bible?"

"As Sodom and Gomorrah."

Mor nodded and smiled, "That's right. Though every single one of them claims to be a Christian. I have heard it told that they call it the Bible Belt. If it is, that belt is wrapped around the Bible to keep it closed! Negroes have died, been killed, for nat'chel human rights that God gave everybody. The white man want em for his own private use. But thank God, he don own God. Never has." Wiping his brow with his blue print handkerchief, he said, "I blive that's enough to put on your minds for today. I just want you to know to keep the white man clear in your mind. It means your life. And maybe mine and your sister and your mother's life. You hear me, sons?"

The sons nodded solemnly, "Yes sir."

"Well then! Let's eat somethin!"

Later, the wagon rolled on toward North Carolina through the beautiful countryside. Lifee held Mor's free hand. Able looked off into the distance and back at his skin, then at his mother and father and twin brother. He began to cry quietly, but didn't know why. Aman noticed and placed his hand in his brother's. He reached for his sister, she was asleep. He looked at her a moment, thoughtfully. "We are all Negroes," Aman sighed, "I'm glad. Cause that's what Daddy is. I wanna be what Daddy is." Able nodded in agreement. "Me, too."

Later, Mor and his family had settled down for the night after their evening meal. It was warm, but a fire had been made for cooking the little meal. The children, already tired, were now full and stretched out in the wagon. They had wanted to sleep under the open sky and stars, but their parents wouldn't let them. "If anything comes up happenin round here, we want to be able to move quick as possible. Not have to run round gatherin children from every bush round here." So the children were gone to bed. Mor and Lifee had coaxed the little fire down into smoldering ashes and were lying back, arms folded beneath their heads.

Suddenly, Mor placed a hand on Lifee so as not to alarm her and slowly sat up, looking in the direction of the trees close by. He sat still a moment, listening to the sounds of the night for that one strange sound he thought he had heard.

There! He heard it again. He sat up straighter and reached for his gun. Mor waited, then rubbed his hand over his wife, saying very softly, "You just quietly get up and move on over to the wagon and get in. If somethin happen out here, you just drive off fast as you can down this road and don stop for nothin!"

"I'm not going to leave you!" A fierce whisper.

"You take my children and do what I tell you!"

The reminder of their children pushed her body up slowly. She rose and walked casually to the wagon. When Mor saw that she was seated at the driver's place holding the reins, he slowly got up with his gun and walked carefully toward the place where the noise seemed to have come from. "Is somebody in there? Somebody? Somebody betta speak up . . . fast. Don't, I'm gonna shoot my rifle off in there and keep shooting til I hit somebody!"

Then he heard a low, frightened whisper; loud enough for him to hear, "No sah, no sah, don't shoot! We colored men, like ya'll. One o' us can't run and we's tired." Two men slowly came out of the brush, one limping, the other helping him along.

"See? It's only us's. Is you alone here? With yoah woman?"

"Who want to know?"

"Is it any white mens here bout?"

Mor relaxed a little, then thought, "Is this a trap?" Then asked, "What ya'll doin out here you got to hide?"

"No sah, us ain don nothin. Us hungry . . . and tired, is all. Does you have anything ya'll can spare us to eat? It done been a long time since we done et."

Mor could see them as they limped out of the brush. He looked them over and then behind them to see if there was any other movement among the night-black trees. Seeing nothing to alarm him, he turned to the two bedraggled, scrawny, dirty men. One was in pain, you could see it on his face. Mor reached to help the lame.

"Come on over to the fire; we start it up again." The men nodded and moved a little faster.

Lifee was getting quietly down from the wagon. When the small fire was started, she put the beans and rice they had left over on the fire and threw some smoked pork on top of it to heat for the men.

One of them said, "I's Lemuel and this here is Sicky, least ways that's what they calls em." The other man looked up and spoke, "I's Henry Vern. Henry Vern my name." He turned to Lifee, said, "That ere vittels ain got to be hot, mam. I ain haved no hot food since I's a chile no way." Lemuel added, "Thas so, thas so! Us take it like it is, mam."

Lifee served them.

As they ate, Mor talked, "How come ya'll to be out here like this? The two men looked at each other, questioning whether to tell or not. Finally Lemuel said, "They is our color. Us can tell em." He looked back at Mor, "Us is runaways."

Mor exclaimed, "Runaways?! War is over! Ain no slaves no more.

"Us is peon runaways. From the prison camp."

"Ohhhhhhh." Softly from both Mor and Lifee.

Lifee asked quickly, "Are they far behind you?"

"Don know, mam. Us lef this here mornin when they sot us to work by the river. Sicky here . . . Henry, here, his feets are rotten and he can't go fast. I couldt leave em."

Then Mor asked, "How come you to be there?"

"Henry, here, was a orphaner at freedom time. They killed his mammy, done already sold his pappy, and then they got all his sisters. He be the one boy."

Henry spoke up. "I was nine years old. They say the law say they can take us orphaners and give us's a place and a job. I is sent on to the prison work gang."

From Lifee, "A little boy."

Then Lemuel spoke up, "Five year ago, by the Christmas count, they say I stole a peppermint stick candy. I go to the stoe for my wife and chillun; I had three chillins, and they say I stole that candy. A stick of candy! I dint have no lot of money, but I work, I had a job! But they sent me to th prison work camp, dint have no trial even! The sheriff lie on me, too." Lemuel looked around the woods fearfully, as though the sheriff might still hear him defend himself. "They beat me somethin fearful, but I swears by God, I never stole no candy nor nothin. Nothin!"

The men had eaten greedily. Lifee stooped to fill their plates again. Mor admonished her, "Don give em too much, it'll make em sick."

"Give me more, mam, don care do I get sick. Us ain had no decent food in least five year."

Mor asked, "What way is the prison farm?"

"Over that'a way."

After a moment, Mor asked, "Where ya'll headin?"

Henry answered, "Us don know. Us don know where us is. Us jes wants away from there. Ain goin back. Will die first.

"Henry can't run nor walk good. I speck I's goin have to leave em sometime . . . or us both get catched."

Mor said thoughtfully, "I don spect they lookin for ya'll. If you left by water." He turned to Henry, "How are you sick?"

"I ain sick! My feet jes is sore and rotten! I been standin and workin in water for six, seben year, since I been in that prison camp. I been there fore Lem came."

Lifee knelt down to him, asking compassionately, "Let me see your feet."

"Naw, mam."

She became firm, "Let me see your feet. See if I can help you. You got to start healing . . . or you won't be no good to yourself."

Henry hesitantly stretched his legs out. The smell of his feet was nauseating, they were beginning to rot. Lifee looked at them, gasping, then went to the wagon and got a tin basin, which she filled at the river. Good thing Mor always stopped by water. She placed it on the fire to warm the water. Then she got some powders and unguents from the wagon and a towel, which she handed Mor. "Tear this into strips. It's old." She took the worn-out pair of soft houseshoes of Mor's from his feet, then sat to work on Henry's feet. He grimaced in pain, but stared at her like she was an angel. "A uman bein," he breathed.

While the work on Henry was being done, Mor and Lemuel talked about a plan.

Mor, rubbing on his chin whiskers, "What you goin to do?"

"Where is we?"

"You in Georgia on the line of South Carolina."

"I's goin on up to'ard the East, me."

"Where you from?"

"Born in Georgia."

"Uhmmm-humm. What bout Henry?"

Henry spoke for himself, he was about fifteen years of age, counting by Christmases gone by. "I's goin way from here. I's goin East, too."

Mor took a deep breath and said, "We goin that way. Can hide you in the back of the wagon. We will ride out tonight and drive all night. Horse's tired, but they done rested a bit. I got three children in there sleep, but we can do it. It's tight but it's room if you willin to squench up."

Eagerly they answered, "Us willin to do everwhat it take to get way from round here!"

Lifee spoke, "You need a bath and some clothes. You can't be found like that."

Henry whined, "Ain gettin in no water. My feets is fixed. I's tired of water."

But Lifee insisted, "I'll bring you soap and water and you wash your bodies and heads." Mor added, "Stir the water some, to scare off the snakes."

Everyone got busy. Mor bringing soap to Lemuel, already in the dark water; Henry whining as he took the ragged clothes off and slid off the bank into the river. Lemuel looked at him and said, "Sicky . . . Henry, us is gettin in the water freemen this here time. That make it diffrunt."

Lifee called to them softly a short distance from the shore as she went to look for old pants and shirts of Mor's. "Mor is going to cut your hair and you shave. Then you won't look like peons anymore . . . so much."

Mor's clothes were worn, but had very few holes because Lifee kept them mended. These were old on purpose and packed especially for the wear and tear of the road travel. Henry was puny, so the clothes hung on him, but tied around the waist, they worked for him. Lemuel was not much better, but they made things work for him, also.

Then the children were wakened and moved drowsily nearer their mother and father. The men got as far back as they could go, and facing each other from each side of the wagon, stretched their legs out. They were covered with blankets. The horses hitched again, the wagon started. It was almost midnight. The darkest hours. As the wagon started, both men burst into tears of relief and thanksgiving, whispering, "It's human beins out here."

They rolled on at a steady pace so as not to tire the horses any more than necessary because Mor planned to travel all day. They rolled through the usual small villages and a town or two and in the morning stopped by another stream for washing up and feeding the children, who were agog at the strange men, but so well raised they did not say a word to them.

Mor told Lemuel and Henry, "You in South Carolina now. Passed the sign way early this mornin."

Unloading the breakfast utensils, Lifee told the men, "Mor going to cut your hair this morning, while I cook." The men were eager to look like human beings.

Mor pondered about unhitching the horses. "Mayhap I let them stay hitched case somethin comes up, just put em close to the water so they can drink and rest a lil more." He returned to the men. "Now you rested a bit, ya'll can make a plan."

Later, they drove all that day heading up South Carolina. The men slept again and Mor stayed awake to drive.

Along the way Life had been picking up Negro newspapers in the colored sections of the larger towns, reading them and seeing the progress some Negroes were making. Their own newspapers! Only one or two, but their own! This was 1872 and Negroes had schools and even colleges started up! She spoke excitedly to Mor, "I may be making a mistake! There are colleges opening in Georgia coloreds can go to! I can't take Georgia and their hatreds and keeping Negroes down, but we may have to stay there; just move up toward Atlanta. I still want to live in the country though. We got too many mouths to feed and we need to keep growing our own food. But, I did want to start my business in a place where women like to dress up and they have a social life that gives them occasions to dress for."

Mor nodded his head in agreement, "Well . . . we gonna try to do the best thing. I told you I think I am goin in a bizness of my own; carpenter or rebuild wagons, or make saddles and harnesses."

Life nodded to him, "We got to do this thing kind'a fast, because Mz Emmalee has told that we bought that farm from her. Even if she is planning to come back to get it, Rufus may not continue to leave us alone."

"I know." Mor sighed.

Life placed her hand on Mor's leg nearest her. "Mor . . . you could be one of those men back there. They take Negro men all the time . . . and we have two sons."

Another deep, heavy sigh, "I know."

When night fell, they stopped by a small river running through a myriad of trees. When all was settled, Mor fished, the men stretched and Lifee showed Henry how to tend his own feet, put new strips on them and wash the old strips for the next time. He was pitifully smiling at her as he said, "I wonders where is my motha."

Lifee didn't answer him and left him to cry in privacy. She thought angrily, "A fifteen-year-old child stripped of his family and life!"

The children sat eating, staring stealthily at the men who still gobbled their food from their plates. But, soon after the meal, they forgot the men and went, within sight, to discover the woods. The adults spoke together over the campfire about what to do.

Mor finally acknowledged, after having talked it over with Lifee as they drove, "We going back home, cause we done made another plan. So, what ya'll want to do?"

Lem shook his head vigorously, "I ain goin back. I reckon I jest get along on home see is it still there. Ain got no money, but I sho wish I could pay ya'll for your help."

Mor laughed a little, "We don expect no pay. We glad we could do somethin."

Lifee smiled, "You all help somebody else."

Worried, Henry spoke, "I cain walk far on these here feets."

Mor looked at him and thought outloud, "We passed a right good-size town back not too far. We go back there and find the colored part of town and maybe a place ya'll can stay and start from."

Lifee pointed, "Keep those clothes."

Mor nodded his head, "Ya'll sure look different with a bath and a haircut and a shave. Now nobody won't think you just comin from a prison camp."

Lifee added, "But don't show out none, because you still show a little prison shadow over you. Get a good rest tonight. You will fit in with plenty people because they all got hard times now." So that's what they all did; get a good rest.

Mor hugged Lifee very close all that night. Before he fell asleep, he whispered to her, "Woman, you have kept my life from bein like that. You have made me a home. Give me a chance to prove I am a man and not no animal like I been lied to be. I am a man . . . and I am proud and happy you are my wife."

Mor started out early the next morning. A quick warm breakfast, for the benefit of the prison men and the children, and they were ready to go.

When they finally reached the town they were heading for, they just looked for the poorest part of town and then they looked for the church. Found it and found the minister, Mr. Liggett. He heard the story as he nodded his head, it was a familiar one. "Sure. We find some way. Can they work?"

Lem wanted to separate hisself from Henry's feet holding him back. He nodded in the affirmative and said, "Yes, suh, just sore feet need time to heal up."

But the minister had an answer to that, "That's alright, I know just the widder woman needs somebody to cut wood and things like that . . . in exchange for food and such." He looked at Mor, saying, "Leave em be here. We take care of em. Onliest job I know for Lemuel is fieldwork right now. Lessen he got a trade?"

Lem cut right in, "I knows how to make shoes."

The minister brightened, "Well, now! Right there you got a good thing! We find somethin for you."

So Lifee and Mor left the two men with the minister and started back to Georgia. They had been gone two weeks and had just reached South Carolina, and now Lifee was turning away from one of her dreams; the ocean. She thought, "I have children. I must think of their education or they won't have a future. There are more colleges starting in Georgia and they are less expensive than some others."

Mor got the wagonload of family home in less than two weeks. He had driven longer, stopped less. "Pee in that big can; eat that cold biscuit with a little meat, we eat better tonight fore we sleep."

They had decided they were going to move up near Atlanta or Savannah, where there were plenty Negroes and an established society of churchgoers and people trying to go into business. And schools and colleges.

When they returned they found everything going on as usual. Mor spoke to Benjamin and Mema again. "We going to leave this farm for good this time, I blive. If you want to have it, it's yours. But, I tell ya'll now, it's dangerous. These nightriders and hoods are gettin more dangerous everyday, everhour. They lynchin for fun. We been doin alright, but it can't last. Cause white folks gettin poorer; crops is bad and ain got nobody to work em. They gonna come here one day. If not to get us . . . yet . . . then to get our food and stock. What ya'll want to do?"

This time, Mema spoke up, "We goin. If ya'll go, we goin."

Ben sadly nodded in agreement, "I sho would like to keep up with this farm, but . . . like she say, we goin."

Mor was glad in his heart, but this was too serious to dwell on, "We can't all go at the same time. We got to have a plan. They been killin colored men cause they be tryin to leave here. And this here new sheriff that come here from Mudville time to time, he helpin them. Me and Life got to find the place, so we goin first."

Benjamin was feeling the excitement, and the fear, "I'll start buildin a wagon for us and the chillun and things. Lord, I hate to leave my little home; I'm uster it. Even got my fav'rite chair. I just built that new outhouse. But, what bout all that food we got in the ground back there, put away?"

Mor had thought about that, "We figure out a way to get most of it. We ain goin by train, we goin by wagon. And we ain tellin a soul we goin. Not a livin soul, ya'll!"

Mema puffed her lip out, "Of course not! Not a soul. We got children ourself now!"

Lifee spoke to Abby. Abby was very happy to see Lifee again, but she was also happy with her new little house and land and Luzy's little baby. "I don like that boy Luzy married, but he tryin out alright. Lease he work the land with me and Joshua."

Lifee, anxious, "Abby, we are going to leave here and we may not come back."

Abby took her hand, "I know that. I thought you was already gone."

"I mean, for good. We givin up the farm."

Abby, aghast, "Givin up ya'll's land!!!"

"We'll get another farm! But these white people are gettin too wild round here for Negro blood and Mr. Winston doesn't have the power he use to have now that the Yankees are gone."

Abby had to agree. "I know that is true."

"So . . . what do you want to do?"

"I'm gonna stay here with my family."

"We are your family, too. But . . . alright. I will write you when we are settled and you can come on if you want to. Wherever I am, you always have a home."

"I blives that, Lifee, but what bout Luzy?"

"Luzy is married. She got a man and a whole new family now. They are welcome, but she will have to do what he says."

Abby's troubled face seemed ready to break into tears. "Lawd'a mercy! White folks, black folks! Reckon they gonna bother me and my children any? My family?"

Lifee took her friend-mother in her arms. "They are never going to let Negroes alone. They have hate in their hearts from somewhere. They came to this country with it and slaughtered the Indians. And now they have to use it on someone and they got us where we can't fight back. But, I don't believe it will stay that way. Negroes got newspapers now. Only a few, but it's a start. We got schools coming up now, too. Colleges." She held Abby away from herself, "Now . . . you got yourself working for Dr. Ben and they think this is his land, so you will probably be alright. They might not bother the old man Joshua either, I don't think. He can't do much work anymore."

Abby started to cry again, "Lawd, Lawd, Lawd, all we want is peace. Peace, land and to be let alone to work and live our lives til we die. This ain their land. This is God's land!"

Lifee hugged her friend's shoulders. "Don't tell anyone what our plans are. You are going to hear that Mor is very sick and I am going to have to take him off to a doctor and a hospital where they will take him in."

"Oh, my poor chile. Poor Mor." Her tears flowed this time.

Lifee shook her gently, "He won't really be sick. I'm telling you so you won't worry."

Abby smiled through her tears, "Lifee, you make more plans than a doodle bug."

The friend-mother-daughter hugged each other as they laughed; not loudly, but quietly, as Negroes had learned to do. "We have to plan. We have to." Lifee sighed after the laughter.

SIXTEEN

Mor began to get sick.

Meanwhile, Lifee wrote to the colored newspapers in Atlanta and Savannah for someone to direct her to someone who could find a farm-home out of the town, but near enough to shop there. When she got her answer, Mor was very sick. Benjamin was doing all the work. Slowly, the farm was running down. They were giving Abby most of the food that was buried and living off the rest.

Mor was not lazy and, in the beginning, hated all the good workdays going by while he languished inside the house. Then, he discovered that at last and for once, he had time with his children. He romped with his sons, played with his daughter, studied with them all. They ate together and he even took a few naps with them. He made more love to Lifee, which usually pleases a woman, and it pleased her. He had often been so tired and sleepy. Now they had day moments and night moments.

Mr. Winston, at the store, believed Mor was deathly ill. When it was mentioned in the store, laughingly, that the farm didn't look so "pros'pres" anymore, he said Mor was down low, sick. "He might have to go off to find a hospital that will take him in."

"Welll," someone would say, "they work for that horse doctor; he can work on him, too!" amid laughter.

Benjamin's wagon was almost completed, just needed a few things he could do alone. They worked on it in the barn.

Mor told Benjamin, "When the time come, borrow a horse from somebody. Send em back money enough to buy another one. Don you buy nearn horse round here and say you leave coming to see me cause you hear I am dyin. You will hear from us where to come to."

"Yes suh," came the ready answer.

Mor and Lifee left with their children about ten o'clock one night. Lifee was driving; Mor lying down sick in the back of the wagon. The wagon filled as tight as could be with cooking utensils, bedding. They drove long days and made the trip in a week; it would have been sooner, but the horses had to rest at night. They decided on Savannah, finally. Lifee would have her coast and the children could be sent to Atlanta when it came time for college. It was fall, 1872.

They were shown, by a colored realtor, an abandoned farm being sold for taxes. It needed a lot of work, of course, but it had been a good farm. Twenty-five acres of rested earth ready for planting. A main three-bedroom house, kitchen, parlor, full porch and a few extra rooms probably used for quilting or spinning.

Mor mused, "He must'a built this here house hisself; it's personal."

Then there was a smaller house. Not a slave shack as Mor and Lifee knew them.

Lifee said, "Perhaps a son, a married son, probably gone to war." It had a kitchen, two bedrooms and a small parlor and a small extra room probably used for storage of food. The house was square shaped.

The farm, also, had a barn and shed for tools and a chicken house that was falling to pieces, a small corral for horses attached to the barn.

Lifee turned to the realtor, "We'll take it. Right now. I have a letter of credit from the Bank of Mudville. I will write you a draft and a letter to my lawyer. If you will take care of the necessary things to get the land deeded to us. We have children, as you saw, and we must know whatever we need to know as soon as possible."

This was a colored man, dealing in real estate among the colored population of Savannah. He was used to these types of sales and requests in these new days. So many people coming and going since the war. The dead, also, leaving property behind and some others not liking the new laws, left the Southern states completely. There was plenty abandoned land to sell for taxes and a small charge.

The realtor saw that all looked legal and he took the draft and the lawyer's letter. In two days he had the papers from the courthouse and the deal was done. It cost $300. Three gold coins of Lifee's in the bank.

She cashed a draft for another three hundred dollars and in a week they had new furniture for the cleaned and painted house. Mor was busy, also. He bought a mule, chickens, four young hogs, two cows, seed, tools, plows. He even bought extra wood for building wagons and leather for making harnesses and a saddle to show his workmanship and start his business.

There was no plumbing from the city, so Mor took one of the small rooms in the main house and cut a hole in the floor and sat a toilet over it. He sat a tin tub in the room for baths and fixed a pipe from the pump to enter it. You had to catch the water in buckets and heat it, but it was better. Under the house and hole he sat a large tin tub, filling it with water and lime. It had to be emptied every day or so, but it worked. They could go to the toilet inside the house. He did the same for the other, smaller house. They both stood back and grinned over his work.

Now one of them had to go back to tell Benjamin and Mema and

Abby where they were. They decided letters could be dangerous. They decided not to drive the wagon, but to go by train and get a ride over to their old farm just ten miles from Mudville. Lifee did not want Mor to go back "well," so it was decided she would go alone. And that's what came about.

Lifee looked at the money they were spending and worried a little because that money had been for future college costs. "The children have to go to school. Even my girl." Mor answered, with a laugh, "She probly be married long fore college." They had thirty-four gold coins worth of money left in the Mudville bank.

But Lifee retorted, "If she don't have to be, she won't. My daughter is going to college and get to what I could never get to. She is going to be somebody where white folks can't hurt her."

That night when they finally said good night, Mor asked, "Lifee? My woman, why you keep me? You could have a way better man than me. Somebody who speak better English like you always tryn to teach me; better manners, oh, all the things you tryin to teach me. Why? Why?"

"Mor, darlin, you keep me satisfied with everything you do. Don't change. I could never leave you in all these times of trouble. You've been always right beside me. You've been right with me in all our troubles and what we are trying to do. I want you just the way you are. I'm satisfied all day, I'm satisfied all night. Now. What about you? Why do you stay with me?"

"Cause. Cause you my woman! With all I ain't, you love me anyway. Keep me anyway. In the night, don you think you don give me much as you say I give you. See? We match. Neither one of us can't get no better. I want you just the way you are. You smart. You sweet. And you done showed me . . . you mine."

Lifee's sadness at leaving Mor and the children stayed with her all the way back to their old home. She carried one large suitcase, shabby by design. When she finally arrived there, it was dark night as she had planned.

Benjamin and Mema were more than glad to see her. There had been so many questions from friends and neighbors at the church and Mr. Winston had stopped by once to see how Mor was coming along. They had told the truth; "We ain heard nothin. I hope he still livin." Mr. Winston hoped that Lifee was doing alright, all alone wherever she was.

It was night when she went to see Abby. Lifee saw her in the lamplit room, the baby was asleep beside her. Abby looked so much older. In the six or seven years since slavery, the children, her business, the new farm, had taken a toll on her; Abby with the big heart and welcoming arms. Joshua lived in Abby's house now. He sat, fallen asleep, in a rocking chair.

Abby was knitting for the baby. Lifee thought, "Here is a woman who was a slave from birth. Worked all her life, sunup to sundown and more, and still working. Everybody's children are her children. Hands red and dry from being in water, cooking all the time; same hands helped build her own little house. Making a home for somebody, anybody."

Abby did indeed look old, tired, but content with her own. Not happy. She had seen too much cruelty and grief to ever be happy again. Had she ever really been? From a baby in a slaveholders sight; probably not. Usually slaves hadn't. Had she even ever been a young, laughing girl? Probably not. Laughter, the humor at their own expense, helped slaves to survive, but laughter; to get through what? Through tears? Through a daily dying.

And now . . . then she was a mother and a grandmother and a friend or aunt. Steady as a rock. But, Lifee could see the rock was grinding down. Still . . . Abby was happier and more content than she had ever been in her slave's life. Now a freedwoman, living daily in fear of those who resented, first, her freedom, and now her land.

As they embraced, it was the first time Lifee had ever called

Abby "mother" and Abby acted as though it was natural, because she was the mother. It filled the empty place Lifee had in her heart where her true mother had never taken place . . . a little.

"Mother, I am back for a very short time. I come to see you to tell you where I am so you can find me, write me, come live with me, whatever you need, little mother."

Abby, eyes brightly shining with love, hugged Lifee tightly. "Lifee! My chile. You back!"

"Not to stay. Just come after Benjamin and Mema. We're leaving, Mother. You sure you all want to stay behind here?"

Abby felt behind her for her seat, said, "Chile, I'm gittin too old to run now."

"Are you sick?" Lifee asked with alarm.

"I don feel bad, not sick. Just . . . settled . . . and tired; and I can't leave Luzy and that boy." She smiled and pointed to the baby sleeping in its homemade crib. "And my grandbaby!" She stooped to lightly lift the knitted blanket from the baby's face. "Look'a there. Ain he sweet? Chile, I can't leave him here alone with the chilrens."

Lifee smiled at the sleeping baby as she placed her hand on Abby's arm. "Well, Mother Abby, this time I don't believe I'm coming back unless something so big happen; white folks let us really be free."

"Well, where is you?" With no school and constant conversation with those still illiterate, Abby was reverting to her old way of talking.

"We're in Georgia. Savannah. In the country on a farm again. It's what we wanted."

"Savannah. That's a good-soundin name. What kind'a people?"

"Well . . . they are not so country and ignorant. And it's a coastal city, so they've had contact with the outside world and that makes them more reasonable. But, we are still in the South and it's still Georgia. But we have a good country church and when we drive into the city, them city colored folks have themselves some small, grand churches . . . and the ladies dress up and look pretty. And they believe in education for their children! They build their own schools! Pay their own teachers! Til the government comes along and takes it over; they want to be sure they control what our colored children learn. But they still cheat us. Still cheat us. Anyway, you have to bring your grandchild up there. Have you heard from Meda? Or Ethylene?"

"I hear from Meda through Dr. Ben. She send my mail there. She print big so I can read it easy. She got a beau, chile! She ain said nothin bout no marriage though . . . yet. Ethylene tryin to get to be a real nurse, still searchin."

"God bless em! I have to send them my address case they need me."

Abby put her hand on Life's arm, "Yes mam, I want my grandson educated. Luzy ain never goin back to school now she got a man. Meda workin, domestic right now, but she gon graduate soon. Say she want to be a doctor, but ain no poss'ble chance."

Life pressed her friend's hand, "They have a Negro doctor up in Savannah. He serves the colored people. I don't know how he did it, but I will ask him."

Abby covered her mouth with her hands, "Well, God'a mighty! A colored doctor!"

"Mother Abby, I can't tell you all that the colored people are doing up there; monst themselves, but they are striving. Some live in very nice houses, too."

"Well . . . no po' negras!"

Life smiled a little, "I didn't say that. There are plenty poor Negroes. If there weren't, the white folks wouldn't have the domestic help they need and they wouldn't allow any more progress for us. But, they don't mind a few getting ahead. And in a city, they don't need field workers, so they need you to know city things. I had a colored agent get my house for me. Real estate man they call them."

"Lawd'a mercy. A real estate man! Oh! I miss you, Lifee. No-body round here talks bout things you talk about. Not many, any-how."

They talked a little longer, then Lifee hugged Abby good-by, stole another peek at the baby . . . and was gone. Praying under her breath, "Lord, please let my friend be alright. Let me please see my mother Abby again."

Plans were rapidly made for Ben and Mema to move. They had already taken care of many things. The wagon was ready and Benja-min had let it be known to Mr. Winston in casual conversation when Ben was in the store one day. "We's pretty broke, but I done built a wagon for a Mr. Wilson and I sposed to deliver it in a few days. I hate to go cause I got to walk back bout thirty-five miles. But, I needs the money, so I got to go. Facts is, I'm glad he needed another wagon."

Mr. Winston rubbed his chin, "Wilson, Wilson . . . Don't know no Wilson got that kind'a money now, but so many people comin back South now."

Benjamin knew they were killing Negro people who were trying to leave, or putting them in prison to be in work gangs, so Mr. Winston had to be talking about white people coming back.

"Well," Mr. Winston continued, "right smart of you to get that job. How is Mor, Ben? You heard from um?"

"No suh. We wish we knew where to get to visit with um. Don know how far she had to take em to find a doctor and a hospitle. He was down so low sick, don know if'n he gon make it."

Mr. Winston shook his head in sympathy, "Well, you let me know. If they can't write, you'll never hear less'n they send some-body with a message."

Ben nodded his head, "We hope that, suh, we sure hope that. Well, I'm goin on. Got to get ready for wagon deliver. I know you busy, suh, but keep a eye out on Mema cause I can't take em wit me and make em walk back that far."

"She know where I am if she need me, but don't worry bout that Mema. She can take care herself."

"Yes suh, thankee suh." And Ben rushed home, smiling inside his chest, ready to leave.

Lifee had stayed in the main house during the day and came out a little at night to help pack the last things in the wagon, eat with Mema, then back in the house with no lamps lit.

On the third day the wagon was packed as full as possible and still carry two adults and two children with Ben on the driver's bench. They had given all they couldn't carry to Abby; tools and things she might need and she had the keys to come take whatever she wanted.

Benjamin told Abby, "Better do it soon. That Rufus gonna notice fore long and be over lookin around. When he find ain't nobody there, he gonna come right in and clean it out."

Lifee added, "That's right, Mother Abby. So you and Joshua get all you can; pots and pans, tools we forgot. Everything. We aren't coming back for nothing!"

Ben had already carried some heavy tools he couldn't pack in the wagon with people in it, over to "lend" to Joshua, that he knew would be a problem for the two old people to move. Didn't want to count on the two young people, Luzy and Torchy, to get things before Rufus did.

On that night, the third night, they planned to roll out. They left about eleven o'clock; wagon covered almost flat because it was supposed to be empty. Lifee, Mema and the children lay flat on the wagon bed amidst provisions and household thngs Mema wanted to go with her; sheets, quilts (I ain leavin my hard work behind me), towels, face rags, curtains, favorite pots and pans, clothes (there weren't many anyway), the children's colorbooks Lifee had bought them, toys.

Tears rolled down Mema's face as they pulled away from the houses. She raised up and peeked through the cover for a long time, til she could not see her house any longer. Whispered with tears in her throat, "Thas the first real, honest-to-God house I ever had in my whole life, and now, look at it, it's goin away from me."

Ben didn't turn his head to her, but he whispered loud enough for her to hear, "Hush now. Don cry, less'n you make me cry. Hush now, Mema baby, we gets another home. A better'n."

When they rolled far enough to know they were really on their way, Mema turned her face away from the direction of her old home and faced the direction the future was. She whispered, "I am still goin home, ain't I, Lifee?"

With a smile, Lifee whispered back, "You are still going home!"

The children had been carried onto the wagon asleep. They slept til the early morning, when they were about fifteen miles from their old home. They woke to the sound of frying bacon and the smell of their father's coffee. They ate among the bird-filled trees with sweet magnolia blossoms falling around them to the sound of a bubbly creek.

They traveled all day. The ladies slept during the day off and on, between meals and toilet stops. Ben wouldn't let them drive. At night, when they were supposed to bed down, Ben made them sleep on the wagon still. He was so nervous he could not sleep much, so sometimes they rolled along all night. They went the back roads, by swamps and "dangerous critters" Ben said. They were making good time on the road.

One morning, early, as they rode along, they saw a man lying by the side of the road. When the man heard their wagon he raised his head up, raised a hand weakly and moaned. He was ragged, but Lifee leaned over the wagonside, staring at him. "Stop, Ben, stop a minute."

Ben kept moving, "It a trap. It a trap." He raised a whip to spur the horses on.

"No! Stop a minute, I believe I know that man! Let me out."
Lifee was climbing out as she spoke. Ben stopped the wagon, un-
certain what really to do. Lifee stumbled a little, but kept her foot-
ing, then she ran back to the man, who had lain his head back
down.

"Is that you, Henry? I recognize your feet all wrapped up like
that! They're in rags now. What are you doing way out here? You
laying there like that; snakes are out here, and wildcats, too!"

Henry raised his head and focused his tired eyes on Lifee. He
reached out for her with a weak arm. "I's lookin for you and Mor. I
knowed you in Georgia. Ya'll said so. I been walkin a year seem
like."

"What you looking for us for?" Ben got down from the wagon
and came over to where they were as Henry answered. "I cain fin no
home. Ain got nowhere to go to. I kin work for ya'll, hep ya'll out
some for my keep. Lemuel gone. I don know what all to do now."

Lifee looked back at the wagon, then at Ben, "We are almost
there now. Help me put him somewhere on the wagon. Mor knows
him. He helped him once already." She bent to help the man get
up, Ben helped her help the man. When they had pushed and
pulled him into the wagon, pushed and piled some household
things to the side as much as possible, they settled him in.

"I am hungry," Henry said.

"What we got ready he can eat?" asked Lifee of Mema, who was
crying and moving her children back from the dirt of the strange
man.

"Here, give em this." She handed Lifee something from a bag
she kept handy for her children.

Lifee handed the man the dried food, "Here, this will hold you til
we stop to feed the children."

She watched him as he ate the food, then said, "I don't know
how you thought you were going to find us. You aren't anywhere
close where we were."

Henry's eyes teared, but he didn't cry, he smiled, at Lifee and the children. Said, "I was close. I was close cause here you is. Right chere."

A few days later a motley, tired group of people turned into the drive of their new home.

Mor came out of the house first with arms out waving, mouth wide grinning. Aman and Able were right behind him with Pretti bringing up the rear. "Mama! Mama! Aunt Mema! Uncle Ben!" Able sounded the happiest of all when he hollered, "Babe, Babe! You sposed to been here already!"

Mor was surprised to see Henry, but took it in stride. "Man, I don't know what we gon do with you, but sit up there in that rockin chair for just a minute. I be back."

Henry struggled on his poor feet to the porch and the rocking chair. "I do somethin to help. I am usable. I be usable to ya."

Benjamin and Mema were shown the little house, which was a real house, not made from a slave shack. Mema was overjoyed and radiant. She went through the small house with cries of "Got a real door! Got a real sink! Got a real bed! Got a real kitchen! Got a real back door! My babies got a real room! With a real bed!" It was when she opened the door to Mor's homemade toilet that she screamed, "Lookit! Lookit here, Benjamin! We got a inside out-house! Lordy! Lordy! No more steppin through, nor over them snakes at night! Oh, God, You is so good!"

Then she turned to Lifee, who was vicariously enjoying Mema's joy, and said, "You got to go now, Lifee. My little family got to get down on our knees and thank God for what He done done and done helped you to do for us. I talk to you later. Got to thank God first. And I thank ya'll, too. You and Mor. Thank ya!"

After they had prayed, Babe and Bettern, also, Mema heated up plenty water and they all bathed, one by one, in the new long tin tub, with the door closed. Everybody used the new inside toilet.

Ben laughed and said, "Not too much, cause I got to empty that 'ere thing." The wagon was emptied of all they needed for the night and beds were made. Then they went to eat the good meal Mor had prepared for them.

Finished with the meal, everybody nodding in sleepiness, Ben and Mema rushed good-nights and went back to their new home. Put the children to bed, ran Able off, smiled at each other and went to bed themselves. They meant to make love, but were asleep before you could say "jackrabbit."

Henry had bathed and eaten with the family, then Mor took bedding and laid it out in the barn. "It ain too cold out here, these blankets keep you warm. But I ain planned for you, so this will work til we find out what to do. You get a good sleep and tomorrow we get a good breakfast and see what work you can do. We build a small shack and you make it a home for yourself."

When the time came, Mor showed Ben all around the farm with Henry limping behind or staying in the wagon. Ben was impressed, as Mor knew he would be. Henry was even more amazed and, once, as they rode along, Henry asked, his eyes big with amazement, "How you got this in this world? Is white peoples round here? Do they knows you got it? This a white folks house! Is I got to hide again? Oh, Lawd a'mercy!" he groaned.

Mor stopped the wagon and turned to Henry, "They ain sposed to come here and do nothin. Slavery over, Henry. We bought this with our money. But, it take hard work to keep it. And pay taxes. That's all."

But Henry was still overwhelmed and astonished. "End of slavery mean this here? Mean this yourn? Mean you ain got to run hide?"

"End of slavery sposed to mean you ain got to run and hide no more. Sometime you have to, cause the white man ain satisfied with havin no slaves. But we tryin to work around that there." He raised the reins and started rolling again, looking at his farm with even more pride. Henry sat and stared with his eyes and his mouth wide open in amazement.

After they had talked over all the possibilities and were back at the house, Ben asked, "How is the white folks out here? Is they mean as them back home? They got lynchin out here?"

Mor placed his foot upon a stump as Henry leaned in closer. "We still got white folks don't want to leave the slaves be free, but close to the town, they much better. If you work hard, they leave you alone pretty much. But any ways you go far out in the country parts, they out there. They hates Negro people to have anything. They lynches, but they lynch monst their own selves, secret-like, the Negroes who live close to em. Don't too many Negroes live out round the county in small towns too much, if they can get away. But some of them white folks that had slaves still got their Negroes as still slaves, right now, today. And most of um never had a slave even when slavery was still goin on. They was poor then and they poor now. But they holdin on to that land the gov'ment gave um homesteadin. Just don't go that way," he pointed away from Savannah. "Only go that way." He pointed toward Savannah. "You ain never gonna be a hunnerd percent safe, but you sure do better there."

It was too late in the season for much planting, but they worked the soil so the earth could be softened up for the coming spring planting season. Winter would soon be upon them. Henry cut wood for all of them. They all cleaned and sharpened old tools and polished the new tools. Then, because winter was coming, Mor began work in the barn on the wagon he was going to build to sell.

"This one for sale. I make this wagon out of good, strong, pretty wood I got right off this here place. I fix it special and I can charge pretty good for it." He was silent a moment. Then, "What brings me to what I want to talk to you about, Ben."

Ben gave Mor his full attention because of the seriousness on his face. Mor took his gloves off and waved Ben to a seat and took one hisself. He looked around, from habit at times like these, took out a package of chewing tobacco, took a small knife to cut two small plugs to chew and offered one to Ben.

"I got this stuff when Lifee was gone. It was company for me. And when ya'll got back, I didn't stop. Anyhow, I don let her see me." They smiled together. Mor took another few minutes, savoring the taste of the tobacco, smelling the hay, the chicken feed and all the other wholesome farm things. A few chickens wandered around, picking at any and all specks on the ground.

Mor handed Ben a tin can, said, "Spit in this; I'll throw it away later."

Mor started slowly. "Ben, I know you a hardworkin man and you prize your family. And I can use your help for long as I live and tend this here farm. But . . . I know you need to have your own land. Now . . . I been thinkin, you need to make you some money so you and Mema can have your own land someday. You a land man. Now . . . we can't just keep on workin for food. You got to work for money, too. We don know how times is gonna be, but land is cheap now and this the time to work at it."

Mor spit in his own can. "Liked to forgot and swallow it!"

Then he continued, "Me, I'm goin to work this farm and get a start on it, but in all my extry time I'm goin to start building wagons and making harnesses and such. I want me a business. It's time, I blive, for you to think on somethin you can do to have your own private money so you can save for some land of yours."

Ben sat nodding his head in agreement at all Mor had said. Now Ben said, "We been thinkin on that thing. I don have no special trade sides cotton ginnin cause I work with my old massa on ginnin the cotton and I knows them machines pretty good; fixin littl things on em, sharpinin them and such."

"Ever build one?"

"Naw. Not complete."

Mor nodded understandingly, "Well, it must be a builder round hereabouts somewheres. Find one and maybe you can get on to work with em and that be your joy and we work this farm for food while we save. Lifee say they got a penny-bank buildin for freedmen, where you can put in a nickel if that all you got. Get ya'll a bank account and save. Won't be long, if you steady, fore you can buy that land. You ain got no rent to pay with me. We works together."

"Thankee kindly."

"Don thankee me. We work together. You helpin me."

Ben smiled at his friend. "You helpin me, too."

Henry just listened to his two new friends and wished he was a whole man with two good feet. "But my hands is good," he thought to himself.

Mema was so happy! She was living in a real, honest-to-God house! Not a shack or a lean-to, for the first time in her life. Her children really had their own room! This was not another dream of hers. In a moment of visiting with Lifee she said as much. "Chile, my life done change for the better ever since I came to meet you!"

Lifee laughed gently, "You work at it, Mema. And you got a good hardworking husband and beautiful children."

"Ain't they beuootiful?!"

Lifee got serious, "You know, Mor and Ben are making a plan for Ben to work out extra and save for some land for you all."

"Yes mam! I don know what I do if we get some land of our own."

Lifee laughed again, "Work! That's what you will do! But I was thinking of going into my own business of making clothes. Kind of a small business, because there are no people going to pass by here and look in a window and order nothing like they do downtown. I have to figure a way."

"Well, I knows you will. You smart!"

Lifee nodded, "So are you. I was thinking of you going into a business for yourself, too."

Mema gasped, "What kind of bisness I know? I don know nothin but cookin and chillins."

"Wellll, it's lots of these women who work in the fields or even go to town shopping sometimes. You could have you a little baby-care business where you take care of them while their mothers are working or shopping, by day or by hour."

Mema started to say no, but then, she thought, "Ole Sister Hope use to do that for the church members. And even in slavery, they was somebody to stay back and watch the chillin for free." So she said, "I sho could, Lifee. But these here poor folks ain got no money do they?"

Lifee shook her head sadly, "Not much, but their job could be done quicker and easier if they didn't have babies running or sitting at the end of a row, crying."

"Yes mam, they sho could."

"And you can't charge much, but whatever it is, you could save it. Put yours and Ben's together, you have already thought of that, and you will have enough for a deposit and down payment on a piece of land in a year or so. They selling for back taxes not paid now and land is cheap. We all are going to eat what we grow, as usual."

Mema was thinking hard about all this, "How will peoples know to come to me?"

"We just hand out handbills at the Negro stores and tell our neighbors. Have to be all Negro cause white folks don't want to mix their children with ours. That Freedman's Bank even pays five percent interest so your money be making money, too."

The winter months passed with everyone absorbed in their plans. Mema and Lifee printing by hand the handbills that would be given out in the spring. Mor and Ben and even Henry worked in the barn honing down wood, setting up plans for the wagons and even starting work on two.

Lifee sent for a few hundred dollars of the Mudville bank account, then ordered it all transferred to the Freedman's Bank in Savannah, "Where I can go my own self and ask for my own money."

With the few hundred dollars Mor bought good leathers for his harness making. Lifee picked over fine materials, but didn't buy much, just enough for two fine ladies' dresses. One, a day dress and the other an evening ball gown. She didn't know what size to make them in, so she put the material away and just pulled it out of its safe resting place now and then, handled it, smoothed it; her fingers chafing to get out the scissors and needles.

Benjamin had located a cotton gin manufacturer, but it was at least twenty miles away and he wouldn't have any time at home with his family. He began to cut everybody's hair, practicing to be a barber. All the males were almost bald. One day he put on his black wedding suit and went the five miles to Savannah and inquired at a Negro barbershop if he could become a barber.

The answer was "You can be a shoeshine man, but I ain't got time to train you for no barber."

Ben went home, talked it over with everyone there and three days later went back to the barbershop man. Said, "I will pay you to learn me. Three dollars a week."

The answer was "I will teach you for three dollars a week."

So Ben went to town three days a week. One dollar a day and by spring, he was a good barber and was working three days a week making twenty-five cents a haircut.

Mema was going out of her mind with ecstasy. "My husban is a barberman, chile!" Her handbills had gotten her three women who had, all together, seven children. Ten cents a day each. Mema was truly happy, but she wanted a dollar a day, so she handed the handbills out twice as hard. The yard was nice for them to play in. They took naps in the children's room and their tired mothers picked them up at dusk. "Only five day a week," Mema insisted. "Chillins is work! I needs a litle rest!"

Henry was a little slow, his limp was worse than Ben's because every time his feet touched the ground, they hurt. He told Lifee every evening, "Theys gettin better though, theys gettin better." He loved his new home. They were building on a small shack for him, with a floor and a real bed on posts he made himself. "God, I thanks Ya, but don let me lose my home You done give me. Please God."

Mor and Ben had gotten the ground ready and had done as much early planting as they could. They covered most of the acres. Henry following behind, doing what part he could.

Things looked good, very good.

Then . . . the 1873 depression hit.

No one knew why. Everyone asked "How?"

Banks closed; all money therein was lost. Lifee liked to have died.

Haircuts went down to a nickel; still, few came. Ben stopped going to work. "No use. The owner need all who come in for hisself."

Mema lost the babies she had taken care of: her business.

Very few could afford a wagon. Mor finished his wagons anyway and covered them from the chickens. For the future . . .

For the first time in her life, Lifee went to the fields with Mor, Ben, Henry and Mema. The twins were six years old and they went to the fields, too. They carried water, brought tools they could carry and any other job their father found they could do.

They helped to set traps in the creeks and springs for crayfish and turtles, rabbits and squirrels, coons and all.

By the end of the year, 1873, they could not afford to feed all the livestock. They slaughtered and smoked what they could and kept what they could feed. They shared with closest neighbors and their community church.

Lifee and Mema insisted on all the chickens and cows being kept and fed because the eggs and milk were so important to the children and them, too. "We grow their food, too!"

Nights, Lifee left the fields early. Tired, dirty, worn and frustrated. She went in to fix supper, usually one thing at a time. A big pot of cabbage or greens, or peas, or beans. They grew much corn to feed the two hogs and the horse and to make bread for themselves. No more white flour for biscuits.

They all worried about Abby and Luzy and Old Uncle Joshua. They worried about Meda and Ethylene, but, though they earned very little, at least they had jobs.

Lifee talked to God. "Thank you, God, we paid this farm complete. All we got to worry about is taxes, and someway, we will take care of them. I care about the money we lost. Allll our saved money. But if something had to go, I am glad it was only the money. Thank you, Lord."

Mor toiled fourteen, fifteen hours a day, worried about his wife and children and his farm. He spoke to God, too. "Lord, what they done done that everbody done lost all they money? Why the gov'ment need to borry all that money from the Negro Freedom Bank? Ole Frederick Douglass, the president of that bank and even he couldn't stop em. It's somethin goin on here, but I am glad you didn't let us go all the way down. We still got the land. Lord, it ain no fun down here. If'n You ain gonna take us up there where You is, then let us have a little more down here and make all this dreamin and work worthwhile. Not disrespectin You, just tellin You the truth and that what You love, ain it?"

Everyone had their own private worries, worrying about each other. Henry was scared everyday they would tell him he had to go, until Mor told him, "That ain how families do things. You here. You ain done nothin wrong, so you family. We got to stick together in these hard times. It gon pass. I blive it gon pass. But we cain wait for it to pass, we got to help it pass."

Henry was so relieved, he went into his little one-room shack and every pore in his body shed tears. The sweat of fear, poverty and aloneness again.

In the darkness of night they would sit exhausted at the dinner table. Whippoorwills, crickets screaming at the top of their voices at the hardness of the times. At strangers always stealing the growing vegetables and fruit from the trees.

Lifee stared out the back door. Mor stared at his children. Benjamin stared at his plate. Mema sighed and said, "It ain over. We workin hard as we can. Somethin good got to happin."

Then everyone would begin to move about. Lifee to put the children to quick bath and bed. Sometimes the children fell asleep even as they bathed. She dried them and dressed them as they slept, gently laying them in their beds. Mema went to her house and did the same thing. Bettern, too young to be anything but a problem in the fields, would be ready to play as she was used to do with her mother. Babe, like Pretti, so young, yet who worked hard doing whatever they were told to do, would fall out like Aman and Able. Then in the morning, everyone would have to hit the floor and start all over again.

Henry barracaded, locked and put bells on the chicken house, the cow and the hog pen to alert them to thieves in the night. Everybody slept half awake.

All the children were tired, and as much as Lifee wished to lie down and rest after church on Sunday, she insisted on school in the parlor for all the family, but especially the children. She gave them homework to be done, when it was possible, for the next Sunday lesson. There was no public school close to them and they couldn't do without the larger children in the fields at this time.

Now when Mor reached for Lifee in the night, Lifee moaned in weariness and turned away. When on another night Mor patted on her shoulder and reached for her, she would say, "Not now. Not tonight." Mor would turn away with a tired sigh.

Even Mema, in the darkness, the feel of a searching, asking hand, said, "My Gawd! You knows I'm tired!"

But Ben needed something to make him feel good. He remembered the ladies in town looking for a husband. He went one tired night, bathed and in clean overalls. He returned several hours later just before daybreak and came to bed. Mema, rested, put her hand on him, tried to kiss him. He said, "My Gawd, woman! You know I's tired!"

Mema answered, "Yes, you tired. Mmmm-humm. The next time you leave this here house like that, I am goin with you!"

Of course, Mema told Lifee.

So the next time hands went searching cross the beds, they got a tired, but welcome answer.

SEVENTEEN

Slowly, slowly the years crawled by. Slowly, in five years or so, Mor and his family crawled up out of the slump. The main money cache was gone, but new money, hard-worked-for money, began taking its place. In the closet, in a hole. "No more banks," sighed Mor and Lifee.

"I ain puttin my money nowhere near a white hand," said Ben and Mema.

A few more years strolled by, not rushing. Mor's business of building wagons, making harnesses and now saddles was started again. Someone able buying now and then.

Lifee still didn't have her dress business, but she lovingly cared for the bolts of material she did still have. It was good fabric; European fabric and it had lasted with her smoothing with her field-roughened hands, cleaning care. She would look at it and sigh, "Someday. Someday soon now . . . maybe."

Ben was cutting the hair of most of the countrymen and one or two of the poorest whites. Mema had eight children she kept for fieldworking mothers again. Ten cents a day, each. In the last ten years Ben and Mema had saved enough to put down on a small farm, but were waiting to find one they wanted, close.

Babe was a smooth, walnut-brown, pretty, plump fifteen-year-old with sparkling white teeth that showed off her ready smile. Her mixed Negro and Indian hair spread wide around her pretty face until her mother made her tie it in with a ribbon. Babe loved laughter like she loved food, but she could be serious at a moment's notice; life on the farm and poverty made her think seriously about her own future. Though they often saw the beautiful golden and brown colors of Pretti and Babe as they played a moment in the fields, Babe was still Able's best friend right along with his brother, Aman. Babe liked them all, but she loved Able, though she declined to fawn all over him.

Time had seemed to crawl like a snail, but it was 1883 before they knew it. Aman and Able were going on seventeen years of age; were good farmers, wagon makers. They had even learned barbering from Ben, but never tried to do it professionally; didn't want to cut in on Ben's little business. They were all just beginning to relax from ten years of hard labor and thought.

Lifee and Mema were sitting on the front veranda one morning, when a fancy-looking carriage turned a bend and could be seen coming down the road that passed their farm.

Mema, lazily pushing herself with one toe, was on the porch swing. Lifee was sitting back in a rocker. They no longer had to work in the fields, but the years of toil in the hot sun had taken their toll; wrinkles around the eyes from squinting and sun-dried skin around the back of the neck, darkened from their bending over under the same hot sun. But, they looked content, satisfied. They had kept the farm going, their children fed and husbands satisfied for the most part.

They watched the carriage come slowly, but steady, saw it slow down as it reached their mailbox, saw it pull the horses up to turn into their driveway.

They sat up in their seats, watching closely. It was not a poor carriage and it was a large one.

When the carriage finally reached the wagon-parking place and stopped, the door opened and Abby, tired and worn, stepped out holding a young boy, half-asleep, in her arms. She sat him on the ground, woke him completely and turned toward the house.

Lifee and Mema were stunned. This was so unexpected. They had heard from Abby just a month ago! She said things were fine; Old Joshua was still holding on, still working the garden with her; Luzy and her husband, still together, had had two more babies before Luzy punctured her womb with a knitting needle to keep from having more children. Luzy was very ill for a while, but she survived . . . and there were no more children. She and her husband had taken the main farm work over with Joshua and Abby helping at important times.

But now . . . here was Abby and she didn't look like she was on a trip of joy.

Lifee and Mema suddenly came to life and ran down from the porch, arms opened to grasp their old friend and family. Thinking, as they ran to her, Abby looked so tired and beaten down.

Abby spoke first. "I done left my land ya'll. I left my land. I ain got no home; me and this chile."

Lifee held her, saying, "You have a home here with us anytime and all the time." She turned to the child. "Oh! So this is Luzy's boy?!"

As they were talking, another young man around nineteen years old got down from the driver's seat and walked around to open the passenger seat door and Tricia stepped down. Tricia, the white neighbor Mor had worked for, it seemed so long ago.

Lifee was more surprised. "Tricia! How are you? How good of you to bring Mother Abby to us on your travels." She took Tricia's hand and turned to her son. "And this is your fine, handsome son! I'm telling you, we have almost grown men, all of them. Doesn't time fly?!"

Mema was leading Abby to the veranda. Abby looked at the clean, wide porch with the swing and rocking chairs on it. She said, in a sad voice, "Oh, ain this beautiful. You got ya'll a nice, nice house." Abby sat down and started crying softly. "Mine gone. My house is gone, chile, gone."

Mema patted her back, said, "Lemme get you some cool water. You tired. All you travelers is tired."

Lifee was still talking to Tricia and her son, Laval, as they walked slowly to the house. Tricia was saying, "Oh, my, that poor woman."

Laval touched his mother gently, saying, "Mama, we better get that medicine Dr. Ben made for her."

"Get it, son."

Lifee had moved quickly to Abby. "Mother Abby, what's wrong? Why are you crying? What happened to your house?"

Abby shook her old gray head. "They burned it down. They burn my little, ole, poor home down. That white man wanted Luzy; followin her when she at the store or goin to church. Watchin her, starin at her. That chile was going nearabout crazy. But he couldn't get her. Then . . . three days ago, she went home from the fields for food for the children and all us. Torchy and Joshua and me was still workin the field, but the land wasn't that big so we heard the screams. We all ran in from the field. That white man had beat her cause she wouldn't obey him and he was rapin her."

Mema's anger and defeat was in her voice. "Did they try to catch him?"

Abby began crying again, louder this time, "He was still there. Didn't think he needed to run."

Lifee, aghast and aware of the danger, "Still there?!"

Abby nodded as she spoke, "Yes mam. And when Torchy was goin to his wife, the white man, you know him, was Mr. Bibitch, he shot Torchy. And Old Joshua was only steppin into the house, trying to catch his breath, he old you know. Wasn't nothin he could do, but Mr. Bibitch shot him, too. Evertime he shot that gun, Luzy scream louder cause she worried bout her babies. So . . . he shot her, too. I didt get to go in the house, but I saw him when he got the fire from the stove and threw it on the bed and curtains; them same curtains Luzy saved for and made with her own hands. I was at the back of the house and seen him run out the front of the house. I went in there to get Luzy out and my grandchillins, then I was gonna come get Joshua and Torchy, but he stopped me, the white man did, and told me to 'Leave em be!' or he would shoot me, too. So I tried to put out the fire, but wasn't nobody there but me and I couldn't haul the water from the well fast enough. I tried, but it had got too far. I couldn't do it. And my babies was cryin, screamin. I started to go in anyhow, but if he shot me, who could help em then? That fire was burnin up all my life, all my little things I loved from my freedom days. Gone. Gone with my chile and her chilrens." Her tears flowing faster down her strong, but tired, wrinkled face as tears began falling from the eyes of the listeners who held and tried to comfort her.

"I saw Luzy was dead, clothes torn all off'a her. But, my boy, here, Roland, he was gone after some fertilizer at the store or he be dead, too. His mama read that name in some book, so she named him that. She could read. Now, it's just us two is left. Meda paid us a visit and just left bout two weeks ago goin back East or she be dead, too! Oh, Gawd, oh, Gawd. They still is rapin us, killin us at they will."

Lifee gently lifted Abby up, "Come in the house, Mother Abby. I have a room for you. You have a home always." As she walked into the house with Abby, she talked to her. "I'm going to draw some water for you. You take a nice cool bath and lie down and try to get some rest. Maybe eat a bit. Then . . . we'll talk. Get some rest now."

Abby allowed herself to be led. Glad for someone to give her direction right now. She still cried softly, "My life was all made.

Knew where I was gonna die and be buried. Right there next Joshua, by Luzy. Now . . . that's all over. They done come in my life and smashed it to pieces again. For a little piece of pussy that blonged to a black woman and a black man. If they hate the Negro people so much, why don't they hate every piece of em? If they own white woman is so wonderful they kill for em, why don't they stick with em, why ain they own women enough for em?" Abby was finally quieted, bathed and resting, sound asleep after she took Dr. Ben's medicine.

Mor and Ben had come in from the fields to eat lunch. They all sat around the table. Ben and Mema were more uncomfortable around the white woman, Tricia, at their table than Mor and Lifee were. Ben could hardly eat. "This could mean death if anybody know it," he thought.

Tricia was talking, "She was quiet on the trip here. Holding it in until she felt free with her own folks, I guess."

Lifee reached to pat Tricia's hand, "It was so good of you to bring her to us."

"I had to. I couldn't stay there anymore right now . . . and she could have gone to your old house, but it's about all run-down now. Emmalee never has come back, I don't think."

Mor and Lifee looked at each other sadly. Ben saw them and looked sadly at Mema.

Tricia continued, "Besides, I was planning to leave. Laval is filling up their eyes now. They know he goes away to school and they have a lot of reasons to hate him; staying in a nice house with a white woman at his age. I was going home; my mother is not well. I'm needed there."

Mor asked, "Who is watchin your house now you gone?"

"Well, we have a old yellow Negro who was always hanging around years ago, asking if he could work for me. Said he use to work there during slavery. I gave him a job and found out he was honest, so I moved him in and he has been caretaking for me for about ten years now. He seems to love the place like I do, so I left it

in his hands. He can stay there long as he wants to, I'll pay him. I
don't think anyone will bother him because I told Mr. Winston he
worked for me."

Lifee smiled, "Old Mr. Winston."

Mor smiled, too. "I remembers that ole, bent, yellow man piddling round your house. He helped me a little, now and again."

They talked a little longer, then prepared the beds in the twins'
room for Tricia and Laval. The twins slept on a pallet in the living
room. The twins asked, "Golly, Ma, that's his mother? She's white?
And he's brown?"

"I know you don't usually see a white mother with a brown child.
They usually get rid of them, in some way. But, yes, she is his
mother; she is white and he is brown. I'm your mother and you are
white and you are brown and I am brown. Negro people come in all
colors because we didn't have any choice. And besides, I think you
all are beautiful. Someday, soon, sons, we will have a little more talk
about life and all the strange things that can happen that are not
really strange at all. Just, sometimes, sad."

Lifee didn't sleep well that night. She and Mor had talked about
the solution for Abby; there was no need to wonder what to do, just
to plan on a bedroom for her and one for her grandson, Roland.

Mor mused, "I was plannin on building somethin better for
Henry fore now anyway. We have to put em in one the kid's room
for a while til me and Ben and Henry can build a room on our
house for her."

Lifee patted his arm, "Every woman likes her own. Just build her
a large room with a fireplace and things for a kitchen sink and a
bedroom big enough for her and Roland. Put in a extra wall so
Roland will be separate from her for her privacy."

Mor turned to her, "I can add on to the one we got for Henry.
Then he can feel part of a family better than he does now. Everybody got somebody close by, but him. We got plenty room and I
got plenty wood cut. Ain makin no wagons right now."

"You are a good man, Mor. I love you."

"I got a good family, Lifee. I love you."

Lifee smiled in the dark, "Now you got another boy to be your son. Roland."

Mor laughed softly, contented, "I know he already know how to work if Abby his grandmaw."

Lifee grew sad instantly, "Oh, Mor, I am so sad and sorry about Luzy and her husband and Joshua and the babies."

Mor nodded his head in the dark. "I tole em, get on way from there."

Lifee turned to him, "It could happen here."

"Happen anywhere. But when you know it's right on you, you change places."

"If you can."

Mor insisted, "If you can't . . . you still can. Some kind'a way.

EIGHTEEN

The next morning Life, who usually woke before Mor, built a fire and then went back to bed to sleep until Mor wakened. Then she got up and fixed a breakfast he knew would be a really good one because she had company. Breakfast finished for her household, she let her guest rest longer. She was sitting on the veranda with a cup of coffee, cooled now, when she heard the screen door open behind her. She turned to say "Good morning" to Mema or the twins, but it was Tricia.

"Well, good morning! You up early aren't you?"

Tricia yawned and sat in the swing. "Well, it's a different day. Good morning." She had a cup of coffee in her hand. "I wanted to talk to you alone. I made myself wake up early."

"Well, you go right ahead. Talk."

Tricia took a sip of her coffee, looking at Life. "Well . . . you know I have money. And I believe my mother is about to die . . . so I will have even more money."

Life remained silent. There was nothing to say.

Tricia continued, "I want to make a deal with you."

Life set her cup down on a little table nearby. "Yes? A deal?"

"Yes. I know you love your children and I know your boys are smart because you have an education and you are smart."

Lifee nodded slightly, "We have some pretty good schools here now, too, for Negroes. Negro teachers and white teachers."

Tricia nodded and continued. "That's nice. But, see, I am going back to Boston. Laval is going to have a hard time there with me, and he does not know enough about his people. His father's people. I've tried to make him white, but he isn't white. His skin is brown. A lovely golden brown."

Lifee sat forward, her full attention on Tricia.

Tricia continued, "Now . . . he is my son . . . and I love him, but he needs more than I can give him right now. And I want him to go to college. He has got to go to college because he is a Negro and I don't want him to be controlled by anyone. No one."

Lifee said, "That is exactly how I feel about my children."

Tricia sat back, "What do your sons want to be?"

Lifee did not smile, she said, "Able thinks he wants to be a lawyer. Aman can't decide between a lawyer"—she shook her head—"or a meterologist. He likes rocks and metals he sees his father work with. And he wants to study the Bible. Not to be a minister, I think, but because he is interested in the truth of the matter."

Tricia leaned forward again, "When will they be ready to go to college?"

"They are both A students. Aman seems to glide through, but Able is determined not to be a poor Negro, so he makes it. And, thank God, we have several colleges to choose from now. Spellman, Howard University, Fisk, Talledega. Howard is sort of far away for us, but Georgia has several colleges and universities for Negroes now. We are just trying to get and keep the money together for TWO . . . and Pretti isn't far behind. She wants to be, well, she is settling for getting a teaching credential."

Tricia leaned back and pushed the swing a little, "Well, here is my plan. See what you think of it. I want to leave my son with you

. . . because he will have less trouble in school if they don't see a white woman."

Lifee laughed, "Oh, there are some white people who send their 'favored' servants to college."

"But I am his mother. I think that is different."

"No. Many of them are the mothers, also."

Tricia shook her head, remembering her own life, "Well, I want my son to go two or three years in this country to a good Negro college and then I will send him to Europe, if his grades stay good, and he can do graduate work there."

Lifee leaned back, comfortable, "Well, I think that is wonderful for him. What does he want to be?"

"A veterinarian. Dr. Ben's influence. Can you imagine? All this money at his disposal and he wants to be a vet!"

Lifee smiled, "Well, now, that's not a bad thing. There are several animal illnesses that need to be studied. He can be a scientist, too."

"That is what he wants. I really only want my son to be happy like his father never had a chance to be."

Lifee reached for Tricia's hand, "You are exceptional. Caring for your son like you do; bringing Abby here to us. You are kind."

Tricia laughed, "Sometimes I see things so much the way you people do that I think I am a Negro, too! But, knowing my father, I know I am not. Anyway, now . . . you have a white son. A white Negro. Why don't I take him, at my expense, and get him into the best university for becoming a lawyer that they won't let a Negro in?"

Lifee, aghast, "To be your son?"

Tricia shook her head, "No. To be a friend's son."

Lifee thought a moment. She knew she would have to ask Mor, but, she also knew she would not keep her son from something that would be of such value to him. Though they had saved every dime they could, still it wouldn't be enough for all three of them. And then, there was Babe and Bettern and, now, Roland to send someday. "I . . . I'll see. Let me think. I have to ask Mor . . . and Able. And there is Aman, I have never made a difference between them, they have never felt a difference. And I can't, cannot let white folks' mess come in between them now. Let me think."

Tricia nodded, "Good. Then I would like to pay for Aman's education and get him into the best university for what he wants to do. Though it may have to be a Negro one. And Laval, of course, I might not need you if he did not want to go to a Negro college in the United States. But, I know he does. In fact, it's the only kind he can go to here in America right now, no matter how much money I have. We've talked about it. Now that I am going East, I intend to work on it more."

Lifee was thinking already, "I don't know about your sending all my children to college. We want some part of it ourselves. We are the parents."

"Oh, Lifee. You've worked hard. Mor has worked hard. Wealth and work is not distributed evenly or wisely. Why not do this? I cannot take your son's love from you. And you can't take my son's love from me. And we don't want to. Friends don't have to grow up together. I feel like you all are my friends."

Lifee nodded, "You are right; friendship is a character thing. You know, I didn't really hate you, but I didn't like you. I thought you liked Mor."

Tricia smiled and touched Lifee's hand. "I did. But I liked you better for the woman you were and are. I've kept you in mind when I have made some important decisions."

Looking at each other intensely, without smiling, both women leaned back, silent, with something each had with the other that was intangible while at the same time, tangible.

Finally Lifee spoke, "You should stay a few days; rest yourself and the horses before you start off again. Eat and sleep good."

Tricia threw her head back and smiled again. "I would sure like that and I know Laval would. I'm not taking these horses any farther, though. We will go by train from Savannah. I am leaving ya'll the horses and carriage."

Letters had been dispatched to Meda and Ethylene. After they received them, both took leave from their jobs in Boston, scraped the money together and came to the farm. Their arrival was excitement for everyone.

Lifee was making suits for Tricia from the fabric she had hoarded and cared for so well. She wanted to see if she could get orders from Tricia's rich friends. All she needed were their measurements. Tricia had assumed the clothes Lifee wanted to make for her would be something she would fold away when she reached home and just tell Lifee nothing had happened by way of orders. But she did not know Lifee's expertise and taste.

When the clothes were finished and duly cleaned and pressed fresh, she was astounded at their art, so flattering to her figure, and their tailoring was not to be compared to anything but the best. Tricia took the clothes away gladly, knowing she would be envied for her seamstress.

"I might even buy a place in Savannah," she thought. She had liked what she saw in the beautiful little town of Savannah as she rode through its streets.

Then she was gone, clutching her bags. Henry took them to the train station in the carriage which she sent back to Mor and Lifee to keep.

The house had been very crowded. Tricia had taken up a room which Ethylene would not share with her. "I'm not used to white folks that close to me; makes me uncomfortable." So Laval, with chagrin, took the room with his mother, but spent all of his time with Aman and Able and sometimes teasing Pretti. Mema made room for the boys while warning them about, "My beautiful daughters!" Meda and Ethylene took their room.

Henry, Mor and Ben were busy cutting and hauling boards, building the room for Abby, Roland and Henry. In little over a week, it was ready with only a little inside work remaining to be done. Abby, again, helped build her fireplace.

"Mor, I want it this big!"

"Mabby, you don need no fireplace that big. You won't be cooking for everybody this time."

"In time I will!"

Ben, standing by with stones and mortar, said, "You need to rest, Mabby."

"I ain used to restin. Rest when I die."

Lifee smile and shook her head. "Give her the fireplace ya'll, please."

So it went.

Abby was very happy to have Meda with her. "My daughter, my daughter, we done lost Luzy."

Meda placed her arms around Abby. "I'm here, Mabby, I'm still here."

"I got her son, though. He a fine boy, just like ya'll were."

Both Meda and Ethylene had jobs as practical nurses in Boston and they wanted Mabby to return with them. They had not realized how much they missed her and everyone else.

Lifee hugged Mabby as she told her, "You do what you want to do. This little house here is yours. Whenever you want it, won't anyone but Henry be in it."

Abby, who really wanted to go with Meda and Ethylene and, also, wanted to see a big city, said, "Wellll, I reckon I'll go for a bit, just to see how they livin and all." So, when Meda and Ethylene returned to Boston, Abby and Roland went with them. "It be crowded a bit, but it won't be the first time. We'll make it alright."

Now that everyone was gone, Lifee waited for a warm, quiet morning to speak to Mor about Tricia's offer. She was rubbing his tired back when she said, "Maybe we shouldn't let her do it. We can still help her with Laval, but maybe we better provide for our sons ourself."

Mor stretched, turned over and wiped his hand across his face, smoothing the last of sleep away. He thought a moment, then said, "Listen, Lifee, the black man been in the cotton and cane fields and every other kind of field for least up to two hundred years, you said. I believe you. I didn't have a free day til I was most goin on thirty somethin years old, close as I can count. Tricia's daddy was a slaveowner; killed em sometime; least one we know of. Our sons got to have a future, cause white folk, some, most, tryin to figure a way to make life for em what it was in slavery time. Now . . . here come a gift, what we always prayin for, a miracle or somethin, and you got to think bout takin the gift? Yes! Let her help us educate our sons. We . . . could . . . do it, but why should they suffer and we suffer through it if we don have to? It's like a payback to us; to our sons. We still got a daughter to educate cause she nigh on fixin to be ready for college herself."

Now, this was the way Lifee wanted him to think, so she asked further, "But, what about Aman and Able being separated like that, through their color?"

"Lifee, my boys been with me workin and learnin since they could hear me and understand my words. They not no fools. And they love each other; as men and brothers. Aman won't want Able to miss this here chance. Specially since he gon have a chance, too. Able already use his color to help Aman and me sometime. And Aman use his color to help Able sometime. They pretty well understands this world. Trust em! You made good sons. They know bout life and they gonna know a good chance when they hear one. They both know what they wants to be. They each be doin that with this chance." He raised himself up on his elbows, "Lifee, baby, I'm gettin old. I been tired a long time. Let that woman help us fore I die."

Relieved, Lifee threw her arms around him, "I agree, but don't say that!"

Mor laughed softly, "You mean, don't DO that. I'll try, but I'm tired." He lay back down. "Not too tired to do what I have to do, but . . . I'm tired all the same."

And so it was almost decided. But, Lifee had to talk to her sons, first and last.

On the next Saturday morning, Lifee woke her sons up with cups of hot coffee taken to their room. She made herself and them comfortable as she told them she wanted to talk with them about their future.

Aman and Able sat up in their beds, giving their mother all their attention, as was the way in those days. Lifee got directly to the point. "Your daddy will be here in a minute, but we can talk til he comes. You both know what Ms Tims has offered us; your college education. You know you will be separated. But, your colors do not make that necessary; it makes it possible."

Mor had come in and Lifee beckoned him to his cup of coffee, saying, "I'm telling them what we talked about." Mor nodded, and said, "Ya'll been fine sons and young men. Nobody rushin to get married." They all looked at Able because they knew he wanted to get married. Mor continued, "And, now is time for the next chapter in your life. What work you want to follow. Don't just let money be your guide. Make happiness your guide, because there is more to life than spending money."

Mor thought a moment in silence. Then said, "Now . . . it's your turn. What do ya'll plan to do? What you decide to study? Are ya'll goin to separate for school?"

Able looked at Aman; they both smiled and shrugged their shoulders.

Aman spoke first. "I already know what I want. I want a place like this one we got. I want to be out in the open, free to do what I like. I ain thinking bout marrying right now. But, I do want to go to school to learn more about things. Able, he want to cut a road in life cause he probly gonna have a big family; lotta children and all."

They all laughed.

Able spoke, "Yes, Dad, I want to know the law. Cause that's why we don't have any of our own laws. We don't know nothin about it. I don't want to leave Aman, but I would like to go to the best law school there is because I need to know how white folks think, the highest white folks. If we have to separate, it ain gonna be but three or four years, and when we get married we gonna separate anyway. But we'll always be close cause we brothers."

Aman spoke again, "Yes, I know I want to study the Bible, not to be a minister, just for my own information because I think it's about life . . . and I got to live it. Maybe I'd like to be a vet cause that can be outdoor work, and I can already build anything I want to cause Daddy taught us. I'm already a carpenter and he has taught me about cattle when he bought that Longhorn cow and studded her. We raised em from a baby calf. Only two, but that was enough with all the other work we had to do. And I think if Ms Tims wants to do this, it's alright, cause you all done worked hard and saved hard and if we go to college that means four more year of hard work, Daddy, without us." He turned to Able, playfully hitting him on his head. "Goin separate is alright, I'm not goin to lose this old nuthead!"

Able laughed and ducked the next blow. "That's right. Let her send us. Save yourselves. Do something for yourselves. And, even, you still got Pretti. Though she don't need much cause she a girl and she's just gonna end up married anyway. If she can get a husband; she so quiet and hiding all the time."

Aman nodded, but said, "She'll get one, but she need to know how to look out for herself if he die. She can sew, but, well, we'll take care of her, but I know she likes to have her own, like you, Ma."

Lifee waved their talk away, "Don't worry about Pretti, she has her own plans."

Mor, satisfied and proud of thinking sons and a planning daughter, laughed and said, "Well, that's settled, Lifee. The boys agree and I'm glad. I can do it, but I'm sho nuff tired. But, don't think I'm fixin to die; I ain't. And what we done saved for ya'll we can help Ben and Mema send their girls off to school college."

Able sat up straight, "Good! I want Babe to continue her education."

Lifee stood and laughed lightly, "If Bettern gets that far, I'll be surprised!"

They were laughing and talking about Bettern as Mor and Lifee left the room. Mor hollered over his shoulder to the boys, "Don forget we got to set that trap for whatever is bothern the livestock tonight! We got to stop that bugger!"

Both boys hollered back, "Okay, Dad! We're ready anytime!"

Able added, "I done already checked the guns!"

That evening near dark, Mor left a young cow, no longer a calf, out in a field near the wood at the back of the farm. The cow mooed, crying to be put in with its mates. Mor said, "That'll call em in. He think he got a free meal."

"They all been free meals, Dad."

"Well, they fixin to stop."

Mor and his sons took their rifles and each found a close place, lying on the ground hidden among the brush scattered about by nature. The cow quieted now and eating grass as the men waited. Henry had wanted to come, but Mor wanted to be alone with his sons.

After a few hours there was still no sign of any animal stalking her. The men came together for a cup of cold coffee Mor had brought in a jar, along with a jug of water. They talked in the warm night air; whippoorwills and other insects calling their sounds out into the night. The wind was not high, but branches of trees whispered together as another day was done and night fell. The men forgot to whisper, but voices stayed low as they waited.

Aman asked, "Daddy? What was it like being a slave? Why did you remain a slave?"

Able spoke, "Yea, why didn't you run off? Get away?"

Aman reached to touch his dad, who was close, "Yea, Pa. From all you and Mama have told us, wouldn't it have been better to die trying to get away? Than stay and suffer? Not be free?"

Mor took a moment to answer as he felt the wind's breath on his face. Then he said, "Ya'll ain free now and I don see you runnin and dyin! We are not free yet now. But, it must'a been a hundred times worser then." Mor took another long moment as he pulled a piece of the dried grass and put it in his mouth to chew. Then he spit it out and rubbed his head in thought; not of "why," but of how to tell his sons so they would understand.

"I could'a run off. Been killed. But at first, for a long time, I had my father. He was teaching me his skill of raising Longhorns, just like I tried to do ya'll, but we had hundreds then; leastways, the plantation owner did. My mother was gone . . . sold. Didn't even know her, but my daddy knew I was his'n. I blive. He use to try to tell me bout her, but the years passed before I was old enough to understand. He had to have other mates for babies cause they thought his babies would be good cattle raisers. So I know he got mixed up in his tellin me bout my mama. My mother. But I sho loved to hear bout her. But . . . after I learned and was most grown and could work like a man; I was bout fourteen years old, I reckon. See, my daddy could count, cause he had to count cows and things was to do with em, so he was taught how to count and write figures, that's all. No words. But he knew how to do that a little, too." Mor spoke with pride of his father in his voice. "But, my papa was sold, cause I was old enough to take over and he was gettin old, couldn't work so good no more. Then . . . I began to hate the white man . . . more.

"They gave me a woman, for my own, twicst. The first one didn't have no children, that lived, cause they worked that woman too hard and too long. So they sold her and gave me another'n. I had two children with her. When she was with child again, they sold her and moved my children out my shack to the community house and later, sold em cause they was girls; no cowherders. I think I loved the second wife, Clorine, and it hurt me. Lord, it hurt me when they took her away. And, Jesus, when they took my babies, I like to died! I hated the white man more. That's when I decide for myself; no more woman, no more wife, no more children."

Able persisted, "But you stayed . . . and took it."

Mor looked at his son through the darkening night, shook his head slowly and smiled, a little, at his son. "I thought of runnin. Yes, I thought of runnin. But I saw what happened to them who ran. I didn't see none who got away! I saw em chopped up! Pieces of their body cut off. Manhood cut off! Killed! Dragged by horses cross the rocky ground for miles and miles . . . while they was still alive! Til they died! And they family was whupped, too! Til the blood ran. You'ed a thought we lived on red dirt! Blood ran til it made mud out of hard ground."

Able and Aman looked at each other and at the pain on their father's face.

Mor continued, as though talking to himself. "I didn't want to be no slave . . . but . . . I didn't want to die either."

Both Aman and Able reached an arm out to their papa.

Mor spoke on, "We talked. Us slaves. About God. Not the white man's God. He was like them and we knew the real God had to be better'n that! We talked about God, the few of us who could read a little, they told us, through the years, the truth about God; so we had . . . hope."

The young men were quiet and thoughtful. Aman staring into his papa's face through the darkening night.

Mor spoke on, "Was a old woman used to say, 'White man ain even favorite of his own God. God send the rain to clean the earth, and white man keep on covering the earth with peoples blood, so even the rain is offended. They offend the rain . . . forever. God don like it!' "

His son's eyes were upon him, straining to see him clearly midst the darkness. His voice continued through the silence. "So . . . I had hope. And I was free in the dark of the night. You learn to close your mind and heart and move on to the next day. Only my body was a slave when the sunrise came. My eyes and mind and heart were free in the night. And . . . I'll tell you another thing. My papa taught me and I learned to know it; the slave was everythin to the white Southern man. Your mother say, 'inde . . . indespen' . . . anyway, they couldn't'a lived without us. They couldn't'a tamed that wilderness, built no grand mansions, nor great herds, no nothin! They couldn't'a done nothin! without us. We . . . we did the conquerin of this America. They conquer us cause they had war stuff, guns. And ships, where you can hold all them people. Our people had boats and rafts, I reckon, to do little things round they own country. Anyway, cause of all I knew, just from seein things and hearin the news from their newspapers, I knew we was more important than anythin else they had. Even money, cause we WAS money. So I had a value to myself. And I learned all I could to be more. My pride gave me more hope. I HAD to hope."

Mor sat up straight though he still spoke softly. "And I'll tell ya'll somethin; I hear people talkin bout how the Bible ain nothin but the white man's tool to keep us down, but they given the white man too much. White man didn't make the real God, they only made themself a god. White men didn't write that whole Bible either,

Hebrews did, with God leadin em. I have learned that. And the white man ain gonna be the one separate the sheep from the goats on judgment day, the real God is gonna do that! And when you think bout it, white men, nor no man, controls anything on this earth don't God want him to. Not wind, nor water, nor sun, nor storms, nor floods, nor nothin! You hear me?! So I ain fraid of em no more. The truth will set you free, you can blive that!"

He settled back and took a few breaths to relax himself. "I get exited ya'll." He wiped his brow. "And my work was the work I loved; horses, cows, dogs. I could spend hours brushing, rubbing, leading them where I wanted them to go. I am a cattleman from the beginnin."

Mor's sons looked toward each other and smiled at their father, as Mor continued. "Negroes, most, know we had to be important because when we got news of their newspapers, all their news was mostly about us . . . slaves. We had to be important to the white man, the Southern white man. And the Northern white man, too. Cause he started that war what freed us. It was money . . . and we was money. We filled his mind, night and day." He stopped a moment to wipe his brow. "Our minds were full of freedom. We never forgot it!"

He pulled another blade of grass, stuck it in his mouth. "But, what do you do? I'll tell ya'll. You live." Mor spit the grass out. "And in all my years of refusing to have a wife or child . . . I don have no way nor words to tell you the loneliness . . . the cold, hard loneliness . . . I felt. But . . . I lived. And . . . look! I found your mother in my life! And Freedom was near. so I could dream. Dream . . . cause I never thought she would be mine. And what I have, her and ya'll, is a bigger dream what I could never have thought would be. That's why you have to live . . . cause you don't know what could be there in your life down the way a piece."

Mor reached out for their hands that were stretched toward him. "That's why we want ya'll to go on to this college. Get you'a educa-

tion to be what you want to be. See? We ain truly free yet. But . . .
we are free-er. And look what I got; two fine sons and a fine daughter. My own farm and good friends. A wife . . . a wife who I'll kill
death over if it come to take her. Take what ya'll want in school.
Dream. Cause ya'll don know . . . it can come true. But ya'll got
to get that education. I used to had to stop being free at sunrise.
Sunrise was the end of my freedom til sunset and night. Ya'll never
have to stop bein free. From sunrise to sunset ya'll will be free. Ya'll
never have to stop."

Mor took a deep breath and sighed it out. "So . . . there ya'll
are. I didn't run. I tried to live. I had dreams . . . and I had hope.
Them made it possible for me to endure; as the preacher say. Endure."

Mor then hesitated because he had been, also, listening for
sounds from the cow. He didn't want the cow hurt. He realized she
had been quiet for some moments now. Had she sensed a presence?
A danger near?

Mor whispered, "Let's get ready, sons. I blive it's near us."

As quiet as possible they took their places in the tall grass. Almost immediately Mor touched Able and pointed near the edge of
the woods. Whispering, "It looks like two pair . . . I see four eyes!
Wildcats!"

Mor aimed in a way sure to miss the cow. The cats were creeping
on their bellies toward her. Mor aimed at the one in front. He could
only see the eyes. He whispered, "I'll take the one in front." He
knew Aman would hate to kill any animal and would aim for a leg
or shoulder; it was dark and he would probably miss. So he whispered loudly to Able, "Able! You take the one in the rear."

Mor inched forward on his belly an inch at a time. He didn't
want to make a sound! Wild animals hear exceptionally well.

Once in place, Mor knew the wildcats would soon leap and even
if he killed the cats, he would have to put little Bessie to sleep too, if
she was hurt. He could not wait too long. He took a deep breath,

aimed, waited a split second to be very sure, and . . . pulled the trigger. The gold-purple eyes flashed then the wildcat fell over. The other wildcat, shocked, in a second had turned to run back to the woods to hide among the trees.

Mor stood and shouted, "If he gets in there, we'll never get em tonight! Run! Get em! Watch out!"

His sons were up in a second, racing toward the escaping wildcat. They could not see him so well without view of his eyes, they had to follow his sounds as he ran. They heard another shot behind them; Mor was making sure the first wildcat was dead.

Able and Aman sprinted across the field, over the fence, listening for the sounds of the wildcat's escape.

Aman shouted, "He's in the trees!"

Able was in front. Aman a close second.

They reached almost total darkness among the trees. They slowed, then stopped. Able whispered, "He can see us; we can't see him. We better stop."

They stood there in the silence, now, for long moments, listening. Then Able raised his eyes to the treetops. He raised his gun slowly, holding out a hand for Aman to be still. Able waited a second too long and the big wildcat leaped from the thick branches of a tree, toward them, first. Then Able pulled the trigger as the animal rushed through the air toward them, legs distended, claws out.

Bang! Bang! He had two shots. One hit. When the large wildcat hit the ground, it was dead. "Whew!" was all Able could say. Aman had more to say, "Thank God you're a good shot! You got him!"

Able, who always got the animal he was after, smiled at his brother and handed Aman his smoking gun. "You take it this time, Aman. Tell Pa you got him!"

Aman took Able's gun, smiling happily.

By then Mor had reached them. "You get him?! I heard the fire!"

Able turned to his pa, saying "Aman got him, Papa. He got him as he was jumping at us from that tree." He pointed.

Mor looked at his son, Aman. "Well, by Gawd, son, you can shoot when the time comes!"

Aman shook his head and handed the gun back to Able. "No, I didn't, Pa, I didn't do it. Able got em. He shot him in the air!" He turned to Able, "Thank you, brother, but I ain gonna lie. It means as much to me that you got em as well as if I had done it myself. I'm always proud of you. You can shoot! I got other things I can do, I don't need to lie. But, thank you, for the chance to make me look sharp in front of Pa."

Mor spoke now, "Let's get him outta here. I don't like the woods in the dark. You sure he dead? Shoot em one more time, Able."

"Got no more shot in this gun, Pa."

"Well, you shoot em, Aman."

"Pa, let me give ya'll my gun. Ya'll know I don't want to shoot nothin less it's after ya'll!"

All done, they started tramping and dragging the animals out of the woods onto their farmland. Thoughtfully, Mor spoke, "You know, I was looking round the edge of the fence line and I found some old bones and some new ones. They're hog bones. Now, I ain got no hogs out this far and I ain lost none; that means somebody been layin bait for to draw them cats out here to my cows."

Both sons spoke, "Who would do that, Pa?" and "You think somebody settin us up for trouble?"

"I don know what to think. But, I'm thinkin on it."

They walked awhile, now leading young Bessie back to the barn. Mor, breathing heavily from helping to pull the cats, which his sons tried to stop him from doing, and carrying all the guns and leading Bessie, said, "You know, that ole white man, Jackson, who done moved round back of our land, he don like us here."

Able spoke up, "He is poor. Got that land pretty cheap and, maybe, he doesn't like us having all our stock."

Then Aman said, "We see him driving his wagon real slow down the road here by our place. He always lookin over here at us workin." After another minute, "Papa, we gonna be gone off to college in a little while. We won't be here to help you."

Mor nodded his head, said, "Ben is here and Henry is here. We can take care ourself. Might not be nothin noway."

"Well, I sure would watch out for em." Able worried aloud.

In the excitement at the house over the two luxuriously furred animals, any impending danger was forgotten by everyone but Mor. He put it in his mind to remember and think about. And watch. "I'm gonna tell Ben and Henry first chanct I get."

He also, thought about his sons. He was proud. Proud of them both. Able had been a good shot and had been willing to give up the glory of such a good shot. Aman had not been willing to lie for the glory. He thought to himself, "You sure is a good God, God."

He spoke aloud to his sons. "I'm sure gonna miss my sons when ya'll are gone off to school! But, you got to go!"

With the time for leaving for college coming closer, Lifee was with her sons more than usual. Measuring, sewing, cleaning and preparing clothes, packing for them. They were always close to their parents, each in a different way, of course. They talked to their father about personal "men" things more.

One day after much hustling and bustling around the clothes strewn everywhere, in a moment alone, drinking afternoon tea, Able had asked his mother, "Mama, we are all almost grown now."

Lifee answered in a saddened voice, "Too true, too true."

Able spoke hesitantly, "Ma, there is something I have always wanted to ask you."

"Why haven't you, then?"

Able scratched his head like Mor did when he was thinking. "Because it is hard . . . to ask . . . you."

"Well, son, hard never stopped you before."

"You are different . . . sometimes, Ma; not approachable. You and Dad don't discuss all things with your children."

Lifee smiled to herself. "Well, today I am approachable. What do you want to discuss?"

Able swallowed hard, took a deep breath and said, "Well . . . I know I am a twin."

Her heart seemed to tremble a little in her breast. "Yes."

"But my brother and I are different colors."

Lifee bent closer to the material she was sewing on. "Most slaves, at the end, had white blood in them."

Able sat, drawing his chair close to her. "Because the white men . . . bothered the Negro women?"

Lifee held her head up, "I can say yes to that, every time."

Able looked into her eyes, "Is that why my skin is white? And why Aman's is brown?"

Lifee set her work down, "You have been wanting to ask that for a long time, haven't you? Aman, too, I reckon. I'm sure."

Able placed his hand over the stillness of her hands, "I love you, Ma, and I love my father. But, WHY do I have white skin? I know light Negroes and I know white Negroes, but the white Negroes had white fathers. But . . . how would I be, could I be a twin and have white skin and he, brown?"

Lifee thought a long moment, then pushed her work farther away. She looked at her son, who she knew was intelligent. She respected him because he loved and respected Mor and his brother, Aman. She thought, "But, if I tell him the truth?" She spoke out-loud, "Baby, son, life, nature is so strange sometimes, we do not always understand it. The only thing I know for sure is . . . you are mine. My son."

"Yes, Ma, I know, but . . ."

Lifee thought to herself again, "Go with me, God, go with me, please." She said aloud, "On the day your father, Mor, and I came together as a man and his wife . . ." She took another minute, thinking; there were seconds as her heart and nerves strained to find a way to say what she had been practicing to say for the many years she knew this question would come. She hadn't known for sure which son would ask first; "So . . . it is Able."

She looked down at the sheet she had pulled into her lap without knowing she had done it. Then said, "On that day . . . I was raped." She looked up into her son's searching earnest eyes. "I mean, truly raped by someone I had been running from for a long time. It only lasted a moment, thank God, but in . . . that moment . . ."

He finished the line, "I was conceived."

Life shook her head, a single tear flew from her face to the hand Able was holding out to her. "I can't say that. I think, maybe . . . a piece of you; the color part, maybe. But then Mor, almost immediately after, took me, we made love, true love . . . and then I think you were completed, son. Because you are good like he is. You have all his ways. And the white man's rape was so fast, he didn't leave enough behind to finish you and make Aman. Mor did that. So . . . you have the color my womb held, but you are OUR son."

Now Able took her hand, saying, "I know I am your son, Ma. Yours and Dad's. Thank you for telling me, like that. I can live with that. I don't want to be white and lose Dad and you. But, I intend to use what the white man caused me to have . . . because I cannot give it back. I will use it to make a way to make everything better for all of us, after my education is done."

Life grasped his hand on hers. "Do you not wonder about the man who left the white skin to you?"

"No. I know he was a rapist. I know he hurt my mother. I cannot care about a rapist. Dad was right; they say we are the rapists and the liars, but, all the light and white Negroes I know of is pure evidence that they have lied and taken advantage of women they owned and didn't own and those women could not say no."

Life reached up to encircle his neck. She held him as a few tears rolled down her cheek, which she hastily brushed away. "My son, my son."

NINETEEN

True to her word, Tricia made arrangements for colleges for all three young men; Laval, Aman and Able. The sum of money it had taken was nominal to her, not worth speaking of.

Pretti's education was prepared in advance for her because she would be going in another year. Babe was going with her. Both to get their teaching credential. Babe, also, wanted to study home economics; cooking was her dream as well as teaching. She wanted to be able to cook everything. They were going to a school in Savannah because the Negroes there were very forward looking and had established just such a school for their daughters' continuing educations. They would live in Savannah with friends found through the church so they would not have to commute the five-mile stretch by wagon every night. They would come home on most weekends if possible.

Lifee had asked Babe, "Honey, you sure you want to study just cooking?"

Babe, always mannerable, answered, "Yes, mam. I'm going to be a housewife and I love to eat. I think my husband (she grinned) will, too, and I know my children will. So, when he brings home the food, I will know what to do with it. You taught me how to sew, but I can't make those dresses and suits like you make Ms Tricia, but I can make most anything else. The school will teach me the rest of what I need."

So . . . that was settled.

The house was so quiet when the boys were gone, at last. Lifee and Mor started bathing and going to bed early after farm chores were done.

Mor would come in, wipe his brow and say, "Whew! I didn't know how much them boys were doing!" But they were so proud. Mor would say now and again, "I got TWO sons in a college! Now!"

Lifee would laugh and say, "And a daughter on the way!"

"Yea! And a daughter on the way!"

Lifee would nod her head sagely, "And a daughter-in-law on the way, also. She sure is smart to go on to that teaching school and not wait for Able to finish and marry her. She needs to improve herself and keep up with him!"

Mor laughed lightly, saying "Lifee, you think that boy is gonna come back here and marry her? After he out there where all kind'a women is? Pretty ones, too."

Lifee laughed with Mor but said, "Yes, I do. That man has been loving Babe about since he first laid eyes on her. And she is a sweet girl; good to her mother and her daddy. Clean, too. And she can cook! That Able love him some food!"

But Mor persisted, "Humph! It's more in life sides food."

But Lifee had her answer, "There is more to life than a lot of things. We'll see."

"Well, we sure will. I ain sayin he won't, I'm just sayin . . . we'll see."

"Hush up and put that dish in the sink."

"That dish too heavy."

"Well, if you can't lift that, I might as well give up on my plans for the night."

Mor threw his head back, laughing. "There the dish go, right in the sink. Wasn heavy at all."

They laughed together as they had many, many times.

Tricia had come back to Savannah with magazines and pictures, some measurements of friends in Boston who really only ordered because she browbeat them. Though they liked the dresses she had worn, there were so many good tailors in Boston they didn't need to order so far away; unless it was from Paris.

Tricia bought a grand mansion in Savannah and soon Lifee was going over there to service any customer. At first, Lifee was glad to have something to do that would bring money to the farm home. Something she loved doing. Often they talked simply as friends. One day Lifee stayed for lunch at a well-set table with the finest foods available in Savannah placed before her. Tricia's brown servant-girl looked at Lifee askance for sitting at a white person's table. Lifee smiled at her.

Often, after lunch, they retired to the drawing room with a glass of Madeira wine to wait for Henry to pick Lifee up in the wagon. Lifee did not like to use the carriage too much. "Creates jealousy. I don't need problems. Life is just now settling down for us."

As time passed, Lifee was beginning to realize she didn't want to work at the dressmaking business away from her home, after all. She had been noticing certain things about Mor that made her believe he was not his normal self. She wanted to be home with him. They were able to be alone more often now, something they had seldom had. She was just preparing to break the relaxing silence and tell Tricia that, when Tricia stopped staring out of the wide window and turned to Lifee to say, "You know what I told you, one day, about how much my dear mother said I was like a Negro? Cause I liked ya'll so much?"

"Yes, I think I remember."

Tricia took a sip of her wine, "Well, you know, before my mother passed on, I told her that, too. Just joking, teasing. You know what she told me?"

"Of course not, what did she say?"

"She looked at me, so sadly, and said 'My poor child with a Negro child.' And I said, Well, Mama, I am happy anyway. And I might want to get married someday and have a white child, too. I'm still young enough for somebody to fall in love with me . . . I reckon."

The two women started to laugh, but the laughter didn't come out right, it stumbled. So Tricia continued, "Then Mother said, 'I hope you do, child. You are a nice person. I'm glad I had you after all.' Well, when she said that, I was shocked, 'After all?!' Then Mama said, 'Well, Patricia, I started not.' I said, 'Mother!' "

Lifee started to say that sometimes happened to young women, feeling that way. But Tricia cut her off.

"Mama said, 'I will tell you something, because I remember what you experienced with your father . . . when you were pregnant with child. I remember what you told him about seeing him going out to the slave cabins.' And I said, Yes? And she looked at me a long time then told me, 'Well, I could understand you . . . because I had seen him doing that myself.' Then she was quiet a long time, but finally she said, probably to herself, 'Oh dear, what am I doing? To my child.' "

Tricia drank the rest of the wine in one swallow. "I asked, What is it, Mother? And she answered, 'Patricia . . . that old yellow man you say was always around looking for a job after slavery ended? You told me his description and I know it is him; he used to be the butler in our house. A fine handsome Negro man. Did a fine, regal job.'

"I got a little frightened from her tone and the way she was looking at me. I rushed her, 'Yes? Yes?'

"So Mother continued speaking, 'Well . . . in my jealousy . . . and anger at your father . . . Well, Patricia, I am sure he is your father because I turned to that fine, regal butler. I had known him all my life. He grew up here in Boston, a slave of my own father, and when I married your father, they gave me servants to take with me to the South. He had just finished training and they had their own. However all that is, or was, in time, we became lovers after those many years I had watched your father enjoy his life. Rashoman was his name. Did he tell you that?' "

Lifee was silent. Tricia continued, "I said, my God! Mother! Are you trying to tell me I am a Negro? She said, 'Of course not! You are my child, also!'

"But he was a Negro! That was all I could say. But she answered me, 'Well, it never showed on you and your father thought he was your father and so why should you be a Negro?' I screamed, 'The blood!' You know what she said to me, Lifee?"

Lifee shook her head no.

"She said, in her aristocratic way, 'The blood . . . poo on it! From what I know, my dear, there are many white people running around banks and even the White House that are Negro and act like they don't know it. But, I must tell you this also, don't let it be said you have Negro blood. We have a great fortune of millions of dollars. You would never be able to trust our lawyers and accountants to continue to be honest with nor for us . . . if they believed you were a Negro. I am only telling you now . . . because I don't hate and you don't hate Negroes. We have a brown child that you say is going to inherit all our dollars. I'm glad he is in college because he will need to know everything he can to hold on to that money. I told him to be sure and take banking along with whatever else he studies. That white-looking Negro you brought here, what's his name, Able? Well, he is smart, he is taking law. Law. I hope they stay friends. I wish Laval had that white skin!' "

Tricia turned to look at Lifee, who was looking at her silently, but not sadly. Then, of a sudden, Tricia started laughing softly, then it grew louder; then Lifee joined her in the laughter. Loudly, finally rolling around on the sofa. They laughed til they cried.

Then as suddenly, the laughter stopped. They were trying to catch their breath. But, when Tricia looked into Lifee's eyes and said, "It isn't funny! And you better not ever tell. I'll say you lied!" all the laughter began again.

Tricia said, through her laughter, "The reason I can laugh is because I have money . . . And they cannot hurt me . . . if I can keep it. Then she stopped laughing, and between gasps to regain her breath she said, "I understand, a little, now, why Negroes are so tense and frightened with white people. I am now frightened of what they could do to me, and I am white . . . and a woman. Tell your son, Able, to study hard, learn everything . . . hurry up and get his law degrees. I may need him one day. I'll send him anywhere he has to go to get the best. Right along with my son."

The year passed slowly for Mor and Lifee without their children at home. They saw Pretti every weekend, but after singing in the church choir on Sundays she and Babe left to go back to their schooling. Mema was proud, but lonely for her daughter and was secretly glad her younger daughter, Bettern, didn't want to go away to school. Bettern's attitude was "I don need none of that schoolin. I got a fiancé at church and we going to get married. Soon."

Aman and Able and, sometimes, Laval came home in the summer to work and study. They were involved in campus activities, but wanted to help their father and to get their heads together for their plans for the future. Their mother was proud to hear them speaking of stocks and bonds and money matters. They exchanged books each thought the other should read on the subject.

The young men were thriving on college education. Aman's face lit up with wonder when he said, "The information that is available on any subject! There is so much in the world to know!" Able would smile and hug his brother and say, "It's a lifelong process you can take as far as you like; and I know you will, too! But I don't think they have correct information on every subject. Be careful of believing everything you read."

Earnestly, Aman would exclaim, "You may be right. Well, you are right. There are even some books I cannot get."

Able would frown, "Well, let me know what they are and I will try to get them for you."

"I really enjoyed the last books you brought me. They helped me formulate the plan we were talking about."

"Good. I had hoped that."

They huddled in their room together most of the time; studying, talking, listening, arguing. When home, they ate food as though they were being starved. Even when Babe was home, Able spent many hours with Aman; "Getting ready" they said. Evenings were reserved for Babe.

Mor wasn't doing much farming. Ben and Henry, sometimes Mema, were planting and harvesting what they knew the family needed and, of course, Mor tried to put in his help. Lifee was bringing in a goodly sum of money sewing for Tricia and her friends, but she was getting tired of that. It was 1887 and she was going on forty-six years of age. Mor was fifty-three. His work had been harder for many years and it showed on him.

Tricia sent word that she had a few orders for Lifee. Lifee was glad for a chance to talk to her friend after a long summer during which Tricia traveled with Laval to Europe. She decided to ride in the carriage Tricia had given them, with Henry driving. "She lives in that fancy neighborhood so we can go fancy sometimes. Henry has no uniform, but, so what?"

Henry dropped Lifee off and then, usually, went shopping for her or Mor or anyone who needed something from town. She never took long measuring and displaying the swatches of fabric for perusal by the fashionable lady acquaintances of Tricia.

This evening on their way home, horses in a steady trot, Lifee was aglow, counting money in her head. Henry looked hard at her and said, "Mam, Lifee, I think you need to know that ole Mor ain doin so well with his health."

"What do you mean?"

"Wellll . . . bout two weeks ago he fell out, just plumb fell out right there in the fields. Was lucky we was round the same place so we could help em. He said not to tell you, but . . . we was pretty scared there for a bit."

"But, but . . ." Lifee sputtered, "he didn't say a word to me!"

"No, told us not to neither."

"He seems tired, but he said he was feeling very well."

"Wellll . . . he might be, but that ole sun is hot out'n here and fieldwork is still fieldwork . . . hard!"

Lifee began to fan herself with her handkerchief. "Well, don't tell him I know. I will take care of it. And how are you feeling?"

"Oh, I's fine, fine, mam."

A few moments passed in silence, then Lifee said, "Mabby hasn't come back yet, so you have a lot of time alone over at that house of yours. Is it lonely for you? Do you ever think of marrying, Henry? I know you meet ladies at church every Sunday when we go."

Henry tried to make a jovial laugh, "Awww no, mam. Don't nobody want nobody cripple like me."

"Don't say cripple, you just have bad feet."

"Yessum. But they sho is bad."

"But you feel fine?"

"Yessum, mam."

"Well, good, because I am going to get Mor out of those fields for good. We're of an older age now; I should have thought of that before now."

⌐)—

She made the ordered clothes and with the money she earned she bought good, beautiful wood. Asked Tricia to perhaps find a friend who would like a new, beautiful wagon so Mor would have to work in the barn out of the sun and any other harmful element.

When she brought the wood home, she told Mor, "Let the other"—she couldn't say younger—"others work those fields for a while, Mor, why don't you? We don't need all that food you all are growing anyway. And I need you to stay close to the house because I'm not feeling too well lately."

Mor had a chance to say something he had wanted to say for a long time. He didn't like his wife staying away all day on her trips. "Then you don't have no business out there sewing for that Tricia!"

"Oh, that is easy and I get to stay home with you most the time."

"You always running back and forth for them fittens with them ladies."

Lifee smiled at her husband, charmed by his wanting her home. "All that is easy, Mor, all easy, and you know the money is good and can keep us both home and not working so hard."

"Huh!"

She wondered if her being the money-maker was bothering him. "Mor, if you ever build a wagon, the kind you wanted, it would sell very good indeed. You will make more money than I do. That wood we bought is excellent; special ordered. I hate to tell it, but I used our money we set aside and don't put in the bank to buy it cause it was so beautiful and I knew you would love it."

Mor scratched his head as he always did when he was thinking, "Well . . . we'll see. I'd like to get my hands on some good, fine wood." And so he did.

As life would have it, one evening Henry and Mor were coming home from a late drive to get something Mor needed for his special wagon project. They rode under a darkened sky that was so full of clouds you could not see a single star. They had just left the city proper and were continuing down the dark unlit road. Mor spied, in the distance, what looked like a huge bundle.

"Look like somebody done lost part of their load, side of the road up a piece there."

Henry clicked his tongue to keep the horses moving and said, "Maybe just threw some trash off to get shed of it."

They were going to pass the bundle, when it moved and they both said, "Lookit that! It's movin!"

Mor sat up straighter, straining his eyes to see, "That ain no bundle, that a live body . . . I blive!"

Henry slowed, but obviously planned to keep moving along.

Mor touched his arm holding the reins, "Pull over, Henry, let's see if he alright."

They climbed down from the wagon and walked back carefully to the person-bundle. When they were close enough to see good, the bundle moved again. Looking up with sad, deep eyes, the woman pulled a quilt closer around her legs. "She a big woman," Mor thought, noting the head-kerchief, while Henry said to himself, "What's this chere? Trouble, I'll reckon!"

Mor bent close to the woman, "What you doin out here, mam? You waiting for somebody to come pick you up?"

The woman looked back down at the quilt and slowly shook her head no.

Mor persisted even with Henry tugging on his shirt to leave. "Well, are you alright? You sick? Lost?"

The woman continued shaking her head slowly no.

Henry, turning to go, said, "We better get on down the road, Mor."

Mor, hesitantly, took a step backward. "Is somebody coming for you? They might not can see you way back here."

Then there was a movement under the quilt and a soft sound, "Mud'dear?"

Mor stepped forward and pulled the quilt aside. The woman grabbed it back. "Leave it be! My babies is cold here on the ground." Her voice was low and her words gently drawled. A rumpled paper bag was set beside her.

Mor gently placed the quilt back, wanting to tuck it. "Somebody coming for ya'll?"

Again, she shook her head no.

Mor was getting a little exasperated, "Well, what you gonna do? Where you tryin to get to?"

She just waved her hand weakly at him.

Henry stepped up, "You got a home, woman? Where you goin with that chile?"

"Nowhere."

Mor stepped back, "You come on here and bring that baby and come with us." He reached and pulled the quilt from around her legs and reached for her arm. She grabbed the tail of the quilt and pulled back.

Mor wouldn't let go his end of the quilt, "Lady, you better come on with us, and bring that child."

The woman had to stand to hold on to the quilt. A child of about seven years, thin and small, struggled up from beneath the woman's legs, then a smaller child about three or four years old crawled to follow the first one, holding on to the woman's thin, worn dress.

Mor exclaimed, "Well, look'a here! Babies! Com'on ya'll. You come on here to my arms. That's a boy!" He reached for the other child as Henry took the first. Then he reached for the woman; she brushed his hand away and started following her children.

Almost in tears, but angry, the woman asked, "Wheah ya'll taken us? Gimme my chillens! I ain gon with no mens! Just ya'll leave me be! I ain bothern you!" At her full height, she was a big woman; big bones, big hands, breast and hips. "Give um back to me. I's the mother!"

Mor set the child down from his arms, then turned to the mother. "We ain tryin to hurt them nor you either. We tryin to

help. I got a wife at home. She wouldn't want you and these children out here either!"

Henry, holding the other child, spoke up, "Sho wouldn't! He got
a woman. A wife!"

Mor, in a low, kind voice, said, "Now, you can't be sittin out
here. It's cold. And you see them clouds? It could rain on ya'll
anytime. You come on with us now and eat you a good meal and
feed these children somethin hot on they stomac."

"How I know ya'll ain tellin tales?"

Henry piped up, "How you know he ain tellin the truth?! Ain
nobody gon bother you none. We a Christian house. We all goes to
church! Ever Sunday and some nights through the week!"

She looked at Henry, "Who you?"

"I'm Henry and this here is Mor!"

The woman looked at them a moment more, then began to cry.
Deep heaving sobs. She did not let go of her quilt that Mor was still
holding the tail end of. She took a few deep breaths, reached for her
children as she said, "Don ya'll hurt us, now. If ya'll gonna hurt me,
just leave me be, leave us be!"

Mor decided to say, "I am a ex-slave men. Henry is a ex-prison
labor man. We know what it feel like to be scared . . . and hurt.
Sister . . . mam, we ain gonna hurt you none."

It was now very dark and faint rumblings could be heard from
the sky. The woman looked at Mor as a long moment passed. She
moved to her children, pulled them close to her and started walking
toward the wagon. Once there, Mor lifted the children up to the
plank seat. Henry reached to lift the woman up, she stepped away.
"I can get up by myself, thankee."

She climbed up and they knew she was weak because they could
see her straining. But Henry stepped back and continued on around
to the driver's seat. When the woman had pulled her children close
to her, wrapping the quilt around them, and all were settled, Henry
geed the horses and they trotted down the long dark road.

After a few moments Mor turned around to say, "My name Mor, Mor Freeman. What is your name, mam?"

"Grace Mae."

"What's your other name? Your last name?"

"Nothin. Don't have no other name; just nothin."

Henry piped up again, "My name is Henry. Henry Freeman."

"Mmmmhm," from the woman, Grace.

"Well, we just let you rest and ride if you don feel like no talkin."

"Thankee sir."

When they arrived at the house, Mor helped Grace Mae down and into his home. Lifee had come to the door when she heard the wagon rolling into the yard. She smiled inquisitively and held the door open for them to pass. Mor spoke to Grace, "This here my wife, Ms Lifee Freeman.

Lifee had Grace Mae and her children bathe, saying, "It will relax them and they will get a good rest. You can bathe while I fix you all some food." Lifee looked into the crumbled paper bag to see what they had by way of clothes. The few pitiful garments, children's clothes, were worn and ragged. She went to her children's rooms, "Lord, it's been years since I had something this size." There were some clothes she had in old trunks from her children. "Well, all underclothes are about the same for boys and girls." Then she gathered things for Grace Mae from her own things.

Grace Mae was about twenty-two years, tall and large, smooth chocolate-brown skin, with wide, round brown eyes, beautiful wide nose, full lips, also beautifully shaped. A tooth was missing from each side of her mouth and her teeth were large and very white even though caked with a green plaque at their base. Her fingernails were short, below the fingertip, broken, ragged and cracked. She didn't smile much and her eyes had a sorrowful and brooding look.

Grace Mae spoke little, but handled her children with much care. She bathed them first, with Lifee's help, which seemed to embarrass and annoy Grace Mae. The children were amazed and delighted with the feel of water in the large tub. "First time they ever bathed," Grace Mae said with one of her rare smiles. "I mostly can jes wash em off."

Lifee smiled back quickly so as not to stop her from talking. "What are their names?"

"The girl, she Flower. The boy, he Dingo. Cause the ole master say my mama was a Mandingo slave. So he name after his'n granpappy."

"Where . . . is your mother? Do you know?"

"My mother was sold soon after I was borned. Say they had to pry me from her arms. I's glad to know I was in her arms . . . one time . . . anyhow."

It was an old story to Lifee. "Your . . . father?"

"I never knew my daddy."

"Sisters or brothers you know of?"

"Ain nobody but me and my chillins."

They had finished with the children by then and, after eating a good hot meal, they were put to bed. The old water had been thrown out because Henry's and Mabby's cabin did not have a bathroom like the main house. Then it was filled again for Grace Mae.

In the bathroom with the door closed Grace Mae stayed in the tub for so long, Lifee heated more water. When Grace Mae got out, the water was almost muddy with old dirt and dried skin. Lifee knocked gently on the door, "Grace Mae? Here is some fresh water for you to rinse in. Put on a robe, right there on the nail, and Henry will bring it in."

Done, the door was closed again and Grace Mae lingered in the tub til the water was cold. Lifee had been going through the house checking supplies and Henry was cleaning what he had long let go because he lived alone.

"Lord, Mabby would fall out if she saw this house like this. We gonna clean it up tomorrow, Henry."

When Lifee had picked out and set up the little stack of clothing for Grace Mae and the children, Mema had come to the cabin. "I want to see who you done dragged here now!"

Lifee smiled, "She'll be here in the morning. She's taking a bath and she looks mighty tired. We fed them already and they are going to use Mabby's room."

Mema grinned, "Reckon she gonna be safe. That ole Henry ain been round no women since I known him."

Lifee laughed a little quick laughter. "Lord, you know you are right. But, I trust Henry. He must be starved for loving, but he respects our home. She'll be safe. She does not look like she wants to be bothered in any way. Name is Grace Mae. She's a good mother. I like her."

The little cabin had a bedroom on each side of the kitchen and sitting room, which were in the middle. When Grace Mae finally came out, Lifee gave her the pile of fresh clothes. Grace Mae was dressed in a flannel gown, a worn but warm robe that had been Lifee's. It was a little small, but it would do, Lifee thought. The children were in the big bed with warm, clean quilts covering them. Grace Mae was going to get in the middle.

Lifee shook her head in commiseration and said, "I know you are tired."

Grace Mae nodded yes, but said, "I am tired, but I need somethin, please, to put on my boy's feet. They torn from all our travelin."

"How far you come?" Lifee remembered Mor said he had picked them up just a mile or so up the road.

"Bout five miles, I reckon."

"Five miles? I thought you were from far off."

"It sho was from far off."

Lifee did not want to worry the tired woman any further. She fetched the unguent for the boy's feet and started to leave. "You get some rest. We'll talk in the morning."

"I tell you now, mam, get it on out the way. I be gone early in the mornin. I's lookin for a work-job. I mean to look out for myself."

Lifee turned back to the woman, "Well, you can rest a few days. What kind of work do you do?"

"I does everthin. I clean house, I work kitchen gardens, I plow, I saw, I cut, I picks, I cut trees, clear stumps with a hatchet, but don't like it none. I cook and I sews. I won't be here on you long."

"Well . . . let's see. You may find what you need here. We don't have no fuss with people who work. But, how come you to be traveling tonight? Mor say you were just sitting on the side of the road."

"I runned away from my massa."

Aghast, Lifee asked, "Grace Mae! Slavery been over for about fifteen years or so. This is 1887!"

"My massa, he say no, he a poor white man, white trash. He got me when peoples was sellin off slaves tryin to get away from here. Was a good woman, Terrine, she half Indian and Negro, she was sold off and she grabbed me cause she knew I didn't have no motha and the massa in such a rush, he didn pay it no mind, mayhap thought I was already her chile. She raise me. I member her fightin that massa and I member I had to sit out on the cold floor when he was in my place in her bed when she just was tired and ain eat and just give over to him. I seen her whip, too, whip til the blood run down her body; she be tied to a tree. She died when I were ten or leven. Then he come at me. I has five chillen, but four is dead. I counts all my chillen to be mine even if they is dead. Then . . . the last one was my baby girlchile. Name Flower, cause they the only pretty thing I ever seen. Growin wild; we eats em sometime when we hungry. Now she five, I blive; you can count them notches.

"I must been bout twelve when the first one die. But the nex year that one live, that be Dingo. I don know no better and got nowhere to go nohow. He say work for him and he pay me in one year. I counts year by Christmastimes. But, after one year I got no pay and I's knocked with chile; sure his'n. And his'n wife know it, too. She beat me, call me somethin bout sluts, but she don send me away nowhere. When baby was born, I say I's leavin if no pay. He say, 'No, you ain! That my baby! You leave here, you got to leave that baby here!' I don want to leave my baby"—a deep sigh escapes Grace Mae—"so I stay. Take his wife beatin, nurse my baby and he die. Milk no good, don eat nough. After that there, me and Dingo, we eat veg'table right off vines or out of ground; wash em, that all, cause they don't feed us none much and we sleeps in a corner behind that stove. Me and my baby chile."

"Lord in heaven. Them bastards!"

"Yessum," Grace Mae said as she put some of the ointment on her own tired feet. "I fight that man mos evernight for all them years; four I blive. But, I got knocked again. I loves my baby girlchile, but I din want no more baby by that white trash man, nor no white man. But he say he keep my Dingo if I go, but Dingo all I has in the world what's mine. So . . . I stays. Then I has nother one and nother one; they all die. The las one was Flower, and she live. Then I knowed I was goin, cause I never let that . . . that man do to my daughter what he done to us's."

By now Lifee was sitting down, "You got away! With both your children! Good!"

"Yessum. Sho was. Was'n goin no other way."

"How?"

"Well . . . I made me a reckonin. Like when you reckon what you gonna cook for supper. You has to plan it, see what you gonna put in it. So I did right fine work. Start to please the woman-wife.

Say loud things to him, like 'Leave me be! Don touch on me!' The wife crazy, cause she say 'Don talk to your massa such like that.' But, I keep on. Ain no whippin gon stop me, cause I got a plannin, all this here year, from Chris'mas to Chris'mas."

"What was your plan?"

"Well, now, they gets lot of goins-on round from Thanksgivin to Chris'mas. They have two chillen of they own at home yet. They goin out to a sociable and I know I'm gon be home with them chillin alone. They's men, thirteen and fo'teen year old, mean ones. I just said to myself, 'Alright, I's cleanin up the kitchen.' Them boys was sent to bed early; they in they room. I already done gather my few lil ole things." Grace laughted softly. "I wrap my baby-chile up and take my son hand. I know he tired cause they works his little body so much. He done worked all day and the big boys hittin and teasin him til he cry, but I knows we all got to go at this chanct cause he ain goin to take her out to church, they very religious, til the nex Chris'mas sociables. So we, my chillens and me, creeps out. Dogs don say nothin cause I been the one feedin em lots of times. We take our time to the gate . . . then we flys. Flys like a hummin bird cept'n we on the ground. I know snakes out there by side of the road in the grass, so we has to run on that rocky dirt road. We plumb run that whole four, five miles til we get to that corner and it was real dark there and I seen the clouds. I knowed it would rain soon. I see my boy; he fagged out most to death; child don never get much of nothin to eat, cept what I pulls up or picks off some vine and feeds him in the fields in the summer. He ain but bout ten year old; I keeps account of that and use one notch every Chris'mas on a comb. You can count em, I can't. But I ask the storelady oncet; I reckoned she could count cause she work with money. She say 'ten.' I fold up my chillen up under my knees and throw that ole thin quilt I done made, what she let me keep, throw it over my legs so they be warm. Then . . . I wait . . . and I prays. I don know howsomeever God gon help me, but I just know He is; I hope. I's scared, too, cause I know it dark and I's alone and the rain comin.

That ground already a little damp and sho was cold. But I got four drawers on and my sack dress and a apron I made. Then . . . there yo husban was, and . . . here we is."

Lifee stood, took the woman's hands, turned them gently over in her own; her tears fell on the extended hands. "My poor, poor sister. We all went through things like that. All the Negroes. But least most of us have been kind'a free these last fifteen years or so. I got sons in college and university and a daughter going to teach school someday. And all that time . . . that lying devil kept you for a slave."

Grace Mae nodded her head in sadness. "Yessum. He sho did. But I reckon that over. Us ain goin back there lessen I die first." She thought a moment, then looked at Lifee questioningly, "Yoah daughter in school? She gon be a tea . . . cher? What is college? What is that there versity?"

Lifee smiled, "Education; all places for education. You'll know soon because when you are ready I'm going to teach you all."

But Grace Mae's thoughts had shifted. "He maybe gon look for me."

Lifee shook her head grimly, "Even if he find you, he can't take you. You are home here. You got a job and a home. Your job is just what you're doing; taking care of your family." Lifee looked aside thoughtfully, said, "Now, the lady who is supposed to be here is gone off to visit her grandchildren. She is an older lady, Mabby. She will be happy for you to take this room and this house. All you have to do is care for it. Don't worry about Henry, he is a nice man, a good man. You won't have any problems."

"He kind'a lit'le. I can whup him if he do." Grace smiled tremulously, "Ya'll gon let me stay here? And ya'll don even-not know me?"

Lifee spoke softly, "I know you, Grace Mae. You are my sister. I know your life and what it's been. God has blessed me to have a husband and a place I can share. It's only land and wood. The Lord made them and they are free. He made us free so we are free to help each other. So I'm glad to share with whomever I can help. We have rules here, God's rules."

Grace Mae's face looked like a child's as she spoke, "I don know nothin bout Him much, but I hear tell He sposed to answer prayers." Her eyes drooped as she tried to stay awake.

Lifee pushed her gently back on the bed. "Go to sleep now; get your rest. Don't try getting up early, just rest as long as you like. If the children wake up, send em over to me and you rest." Lifee turned to leave, turned down the lamp and blew it out. As she was going through the door, Grace Mae raised her head, saying, "Mz Lifee! He do answer prayers. I didn't even not pray for this here much, but look'a here, I's restin. Done had the first bath my chillen and me ever done had. And a clean bed? A real bed!"

"Now he is going to give you sleep without worrying about anyone bothering you."

The weary woman nestled under the covers, "Oh, Jesus! Thank you, God, for these here peoples."

The next morning Lifee waited breakfast for Henry, but he hadn't come by nine-thirty nor ten o'clock. She went over to the cabin to see if there was a problem because Henry was usually in her kitchen heating water when she got up. She had made Mor rest a little extra this morning. He complained, but he was glad; he felt very tired.

Lifee knocked gently on the cabin door. Inside she could hear talking and the laughter of children. She opened the door and looked in; Henry was playing with the children, still in their night-clothes. He looked around at Lifee with a big smile on his face. "Mornin!"

"Morning. Is Grace Mae still asleep?"

"Yea, she still sleep. But I done cooked for the chilren. We doin jes fine!"

Well, Grace Mae slept a whole night that night, all day the next day and the next night. Didn't even wake up to eat and Lifee didn't let anyone wake her. "She is tired. This is probably the first time there was no call for her to get up and get out! Let her keep on sleeping, poor child, she deserves it!"

Lifee had told Mor and, later, Mema and Benjamin, who rested at home a bit on Saturday mornings now that there was less work to do. Mema was eager to talk to the new woman "we done saved!"

"In due time, Mema. Remember, she does not like to talk."

Mema placed her hand on her hip, "It's a lot she don't know bout life, now, thinkin she was still a slave all this here time we been free! And never done had a bath! Lord'a'mercy! You take your time, Lifee, cause you don't know that woman yet!"

Lifee had to laugh at her friend, "Look how long we've been friends, Mema, and we didn't know each other."

Mema had to agree, "Yea, an we needed everythin just like her."

"Lord, yes!"

Henry and Grace got along in that cabin just fine. He loved having a young single woman living with him even without the loving he knew Mor and Ben had. He had never made love anyway, so . . .

The cabin was sparkling clean and with touches of branches of trees, leaf bouquets, here and there in the little three rooms. And laughter, mostly with the children. Grace had never lived around a Negro man since she was three. It was a new experience for her. But, she still didn't want to be any more than friends. Working friends, because she went out to feed the livestock, milk cows, gather eggs before she was asked. Many times when the others went out to do their chores, the work was done. There was no hard work to do because of the season.

Henry rushed home when his work was finished. In the past, he had always stayed, sitting with the others after they ate; he listened, happy just to be around, have a family. But, now, he rushed back to the cabin; to "his" family. Grace Mae knew he watched her all the time and she was flattered, but didn't know what the feeling was because she had never been admired as a woman before.

"You a nice, beutiful lady, Mz Grace Mae."

"My name is Grace Mae and I's no lady. I's just a girl-woman. White folks is ladies and Mz Lifee and Mz Mema is ladies."

"You is a lady." Henry remembered his lessons, "You a lady, too!"

Then Grace would laugh, but liked it. The man, Henry, did so many things to make Grace laugh or smile or be happy, she began to do little things for him. Though Lifee and Grace had made her a few nightgowns, Henry bought her some strong, pretty flannel for another nightgown. Grace, also, made Henry and her son pajamas.

Although the farm had plenty meat, Henry bought Grace an especially good piece of meat; she cut it up and put it in a stew for them all, Henry included.

He slipped her money from his meager savings; she just left it on his bureau or slipped it back in his pockets. He gave her an imitation diamond brooch from a dime store in town. She wouldn't wear it all day on her work clothes, but she pinned it to her nightwear to sleep in. She stared at it on her breast; it was worth more than real diamonds. And it was all hers.

One night, naturally, he, in a burst of emotion, reached out to hug her. She pulled back abruptly, so he settled for kissing her hand; that large, calloused, rough-skinned hand.

She told him, "Henry, I likes you. You is good to my chilren. But . . . I don't want nobody to pick me for their woman. I wants to pick my own man. I ain never choosed my own man. Never, not anytime, never. I wants to choose my own man the next time, cause I know things I got to think about. So . . . you nice . . . but, you go on on your own way."

Henry, embarrassed, answered, "Yessum. I is sorry. I am sorry." He turned from her and shuffled away on his feet that would never really be good feet again. "Yes mam," he repeated as he went into his room and shut the door.

Now, I don't know if Mor talked to him or if it was just his common sense, but, he kept bringing the little presents, only now they were just for Flower and Dingo and now and then, a sweet for them all. He played with the children, but cut it off when Grace Mae came around them.

Grace Mae started worrying, just a little, about Henry.

Then she stopped worrying about him and just thought about him. Just passing thoughts.

Lifee could not see what was happening in the cabin, but she felt some tension between them. She thought about the boys' room and decided she could put most of their things in Pretti's room so Grace could move in there awhile since Pretti was gone to school in Savannah.

"You know, Grace, you and the children might take Aman and Able's room so you will have a little privacy until we can think of something better." Grace turned to her with a smile, "Oh, Lifee, I would surely love that. I'll keep it clean and all and we will be quiet."

Lifee laughed, "Chile, quiet is something I want, but it's not what I am used to. Today we can skip the school lessons and get you moved."

Grace shook her head vigorously, "No mam, I don want to skip no lessons. I ain got that much to move. Won take but five minutes no how."

Later Lifee, when alone with Mor, told him about the change. Later Mor mentioned to Henry, "Now you got a better chance." He smiled. "Court her."

Henry frowned, "Court her?"

"Yes, court! Court! You don't know what court is?"

"I reckon."

Mor was enjoying this and, too, he wanted his friend to have a woman. "You can use the carriage to take her to church with the children. And stop at that little Negro store and get em a ice cream or soda. That's a start! She a good woman, Henry, put right in your lap near-bout. She clean, she quiet, she love them kids. She easy to get along with and she goin to school."

Sunday, they all went to church. Pretti and Babe came in from Savannah because they sang in the choir, but mostly because it was time to be home with mothers.

Henry wore the suit Mor had bought him from a pawnshop, cleaned and pressed, with a sparkling white shirt and old-fashioned blue tie. Henry drove the carriage with style and flair. Grace rode beside him with grace and a big quiet beauty in the new dress she had made with many suggestions from Lifee.

Lifee sensed she had a helper in Grace with her seamstress business. That could be a way for Grace to make money. "Well, we all have to have some and she has two children."

Henry took them for a ride after church, in the opposite direction of her old home, of course. The very thought of it made Grace extremely nervous. He even let Dingo sit on his lap and hold the reins. It turned out to be a grand day for the four of them.

There were no touches, no words of anything but friendship from Henry. Grace looked at Henry with a different respect. She smiled and talked more to everybody later that evening.

That happened several Sundays in the same manner. Lifee caught them casting furtive glances at each other. The one glancing would look away quickly when caught at it. Henry's glance was with admiration; Grace Mae's glance was questioning.

Grace, of course, saw the togetherness of Mor and Lifee, Ben and Mema. She had been lonely all her life, from birth when her mother had been sold away from her weeks later. No kind words except from Terrine, who had snatched her so she, herself, would not be so lonely. After Terrine died, there was no one but her children. But they were only children.

The months passed. The Christmas holidays came and went. All the family had come home. Even Mabby with Roland, Meda and Ethylene. Meda had finally fallen in love and was going to be married. "I want to bring him home here and be married around my family."

Able had spent most of his time with Babe, who walked around grinning shyly at his attentions even though she had been receiving them for years. But, always, finally, Able and Aman would be off to their room, door closed, huddled together over books and talking in low tones. They were not hiding, it was just serious time between the brothers. They were fulfilling a plan. They always came out with satisfied smiles. They traded books from their classes each thought the other should read; of law and money.

Pretti, Babe, Ethylene and Meda had spent hours discussing their work. Ethylene had said, "Wouldn't it be nice to have a school round here for girls to go to learn nursing assistance?" They all agreed. Babe said, "I'm tired of school, but I would go to that one. Then I could go to that job when I got tired of children and teaching."

Ethylene nodded, "I just get tired of a city life. I miss all this space and the animals and birds and trees and everything. The quiet at nights."

Pretti thought about that a moment, then said, "I think I like living close to a city, so if you want to go you can. But there are too many people always round you there."

Babe put in her few words, "I think I like a city. A big city. Negroes don't have a city, they just live on the edge of one. But, I can say, the Negroes in Savannah are forward-lookin people. And they say Atlanta is even bigger with more people and the Negroes there are way ahead of a lot more places."

And so it went with the girl talk.

Mor walked around full of smiles watching everyone, his chest full of laughter, love and memories. Henry still looking longingly at Grace. Grace still looking the other way.

Grace Mae and her children were encircled and drawn further into the family. Being surrounded with people, some her very own color, and love, so much love among them, almost overwhelmed her with what a family could be. In all the years of her life, always the refrain of "A mother I can't remember and a father I will never know" was all her history she knew. It had made her hold her own children dearer, closer to her. That was one reason she liked Henry; he seemed to love her children. They relaxed and played happily with Henry. She didn't care that he did not bring her gifts anymore. He brought them for her children. He had pestered Mor to teach him to carve toys out of wood. Which Mor did teach him; he liked knowing things and teaching them to others. Henry and Grace Mae lived in the cabin again, peacefully. And at the Christmas gathering, Grace saw what a "family" really was.

Grace had confided to Lifee, "I like em, but he too ugly. And he got them feets. I just happy to be free and my chillin learnin writin and readin. Don need nobody and nothin else; just ya'll stay my friends."

Lifee answered, "Your family. And Henry isn't ugly to me. And at least he has some feet even if they are sore."

Grace Mae grinned that big beautiful smile that lit her face and even brightened her large sad eyes. She was back in the cabin, but the doors were still closed at nights. Her children were bright and happy. Learning. Dingo was sweet, a learner who liked to work and followed Henry everywhere. Everyone loved Flower, she was a sweet, pretty child who wanted to be like Ethylene, a nurse. Ethylene spent a lot of time with her.

Lifee told Ethylene, "Get married and have one like her!"

"I'm just waiting to feel something, Auntie."

Everyone was charmed and amused at Lifee's gift to Mema; five separate little flower patches to stick over the breast that had been cut off. Mema was so happy with the flower patches she went home and immediately put one on. She wanted to wear one and show it off to the family.

Lifee laughed as she pushed Mema away from everybody, "They are for Ben, Mema! Keep your dress up on your shoulders!"

Mema laughed happily, "Ben love em, honey! He say 'What one you wearin tonight?!' "

When all was over and the family guests gone, things settled down and the household returned to normal. Everyone looked sad for a while then they would talk about who said, who did, and love and laughter would carry them on to their normal contentment.

But the holidays being over had brought a loneliness to Grace Mae. Her big body with the undernourished heart longed for more. She did not understand herself. When she felt down, she took a physic; castor oil or something else Lifee suggested.

She witnessed daily the bond of love between Mema and Ben, Lifee and Mor. "Ain that won'erful," she would think.

One early morning she went to the main house to start breakfast. It was the dark part of the morning, stars still blinking in the sky. She heard the sounds, she thought, of them getting out of bed. But the sounds continued long after it would have taken them to get out of bed. She stood still a moment . . . and listened. The bed-springs. Lifee and Mor still in bed. Then she knew, they were making love. She couldn't make herself leave to come back later; she just stood still . . . and listened.

It was not a wild ride; the springs clicked and squeaked every few seconds. It was a slow, deep, resting rhythm. Her own body stirred in spite of the fact she had never liked what people called "lovemaking." She had never made "love," it was, from the time she lost her virginity at ten years of age, a quick tussle in the hay or on a bed of rags. In fact, she had hated the act. But, now . . . her body stirred within without her volition.

Grace was ashamed of it even while she did it. "I should go on to the cabin and sit awhile and then come on back!" But she didn't. She stood there, frozen, listening, listening to the bedsprings' slow groaning, with her face turned up to the ceiling, to the room the sounds came from.

When at last she heard only the deep sounds of Mor's voice and the loving light wail of Lifee's pleasure as Mor talked to her, Grace tore herself from the spot, went home to the cabin and got back in bed with her children, pulling the quilt up to her chin. She lay there feeling her body calling to her. Love is a strong thing to be surrounded with. Later, around her children waking to the day, life resumed. Grace went back to the main house, where Lifee was bustling around the kitchen, smiling. Grace watched Lifee closely. In wonder.

After a while, Grace asked Lifee, "Do old people make . . . love?" It was a foreign word to her tongue aside from her children.

Lifee turned with a laughing smile. She had heard the back door open that early morning. "A woman can look up as long as a man can look down. And when things won't get ready and you still got love, even if you just lay on each other or next each other, you making love."

With the men on the farm being married, except for Henry, Grace began to look at him closer as the days went by. "He still ugly." She shook her head in sadness. "Lookin like a broke-foot frog goin somewheres."

Henry was not ugly; his face only reflected his sadness, his loneliness, his lack of fulfillment. After all, he was also among love and men who had their women . . . and home.

Now it happened that sometimes when Pretti and Babe were home on a weekend, Pretti played the piano, Babe and Henry played the tambourines, Mor the harmonica, Ben the fiddle. Ben had taught Henry how to fiddle, but Henry hadn't been able to buy his own yet. Lifee, Bettern, Flower and Dingo would dance to the sound of music and their joyful laughter.

Grace would sit and watch, enjoying everything but too shamed to join in. In time, she did join in and found she liked the feel of her body responding to the music and joy. Anytime they wished, one of the musicians would lay their instrument down and join the dancers. Henry would play in their place for a while, then he would join in the dancing. His feet would never be normal, but he could dance a good rhythm and he had little special steps of his own. He even looked good when he was laughing and dancing.

On one of these times, he gathered his nerve and went up to Grace, holding out his hand to ask her to join in. She never had danced with him. She shook her head no. But Lifee called out, "Oh, get up and dance, girl, you know you want to!" Then Mor called out, "Try it, Grace, it's fun!"

So she did. Right away the music slowed as she went into Henry's arms. Henry closed his eyes, almost. They didn't dance close like lovers, but their bodies touched, now and then. Little things trickled up and down Henry's spine and he could hardly breathe. He thought he was in heaven. He had never held a woman in his arms in his life.

Grace's body, which was now always stirring, betrayed her and warm waves moved gently over her body. She broke loose from his arms and commenced to dance in a rhythmic bounce, like for the jungle drums. The music picked up so Henry joined her in the bouncing step and at the end they all laughed with pleasure over the new member of their little dancing group. Grace was embarrassed at her actions, but joined in the laughter.

When Henry held out his hand again, she shook her head, and when the others told her to join in, she got up and went home to the cabin. They laughed at her for being ashamed, then continued in their own fun. Henry sat down til the music reached him again and he held out a hand to Flower and danced with her.

It was about two weeks later when Grace woke one morning with her hands between her legs, just holding herself. She left them where they were as she lay and thought. "I's . . . I am a grown woman with two babies livin and two dead, and I ain never felt nothin like Life do. Does." She removed her hands and pulled herself up, looking in the distance beyond the window, through the trees, at the flying birds. "Birds is doin it. Squirrels is a'doin it. Snakes is a'doin it, too. Everything and everybody, but . . . not me. I'm gonna see bout this here mess."

Henry usually had a glass of bourbon at bedtime and he offered Grace Mae some each time. She had always crinkled her nose up at him and refused, but, this time, she reckoned another plan.

Flower sometimes spent the night in the house with Life. Dingo wanted to, but hadn't yet, because his mother wanted at least one child beside her. This week when the workdays were over, Grace asked Flower, "You goin to stay the night with Aunt Life?" Flower looked up, glad to have the chance since her mother usually tried to get her to stay home when Life asked for her company, said, "Yes, mam, M'dear."

Grace looked away from her daughter, "Well, see do Dingo want to go stay the night with Mor. He deserve to if you do."

That night Grace bathed in the main house, powdered her body with one of her Christmas gifts and sprinkled cologne, another gift, on her body. Put on a decent robe she didn't usually wear. Life had made it, with her many patterns in mind, not just a place for arms and body that Grace knew. It draped a bit, very nicely complimenting her body. She took a few deep breaths, said, "Just this oncet," to herself and went into the central room in the cabin. It was still winter, wind blowing and all, so the fire was lit.

Henry was at the sink washing his hands and neck. He turned to see her and was taken aback by the prettiness of her, big and comely. She had brushed her hair back and tied it with a string to get it out the way; not flying as usual. She sat down and asked for a drink.

Henry threw his towel down, somewhere, and started to his room before he had turned his whole body around, consequently he started falling and stumbled all the way to his door. He looked back at her, embarrassed, but laughing at himself. She smiled and waved him on, thinking, "He sho want to give me that there drink! with his ugly self! I mus look pretty nigh good." Her heart giggled in her breast.

Henry returned, went to the sink, fumbled with the bottle top, poured the liquor, spilled some, took the glasses to the table. "I'm scared to hand it to you. Scared I spill it all over ya." They both laughed nervously. She reached for the glass daintily. His clumsiness made her more relaxed.

Now . . . Henry did not know what her plans were, would never have dreamed them. But she never had come out to talk to him alone and in her nightwear.

Well, they drank and they talked, a little, just running words they would never remember.

They had another drink.

Neither were used to drinking. Henry usually had only one or two in the evenings.

They had another drink.

Henry began to sing. He usually sang gospel songs, but seemed to have learned a few blues-love songs from the juke joint down the way which he and Mor would look into sometimes. Then, sometimes, he would go alone when Mor was with Lifee and Benjamin in the house with Mema. Very seldom, once a month or so. He remembered some of the sad love-song verses. The blues. He made some up as he went along.

I got a pretty woman, but she don't want me.
Lord, if she leave me, where will I be?

Or

I wants a woman, just for my own
So I can love her anywhere and go to my sweet home.

Grace laughed in her quiet joy and . . . drank. She was not drunk, just a little high by now. He was not drunk except with happiness. At last, Grace said she had better go to bed. Henry said nothing; his joy fell a little, but there was so much too good to be true his heart still held to the joy.

She wrapped her robe tighter around her amid the homemade room with the fire still burning brightly . . . and moved toward her door. Henry watched her go, longingly but quietly. She waited for him to speak. She didn't know exactly how things went when each person had a choice. He didn't speak, so she went into her room and closed the door, then opened it a little and left it that way.

Henry saw all this, but still sat there. He wouldn't even begin to believe she was inviting him in. He was happy, but he, slowly, became sad again, then happy again, back and forth. Finally he got up from his chair and put the glass in the dishpan. Splashed cold water on his face. It mixed with the tears that formed but did not fall. Then he, too, went to his room. He started to close his door, then said, "Hell wit it!" undressed, put on his sleeping gown and went to bed. The liquor put him to sleep almost immediately.

Grace Mae lay in her bed, alone, thinking, wondering, thinking. After about an hour, when she could see he was not coming through that door, she got up. She looked at herself in the mirror, then turned and walked slowly, pushing her every step, into Henry's room. She pushed the door gently open wider and looked in at Henry curled up in his bed. She knew the bed was clean even if a little ragged because she did the laundry.

She moved quietly to the bed and stood looking down at Henry, who was snoring softly. Grace touched his shoulder and stepped back. No response. She leaned forward and touched him a little harder. No response. She let out a sigh, then stepped around the bed and got in it. Thinking, "This here night is near-bout to be over. Daylight soon." She got in the bed beside him, but not touch-

ing. She waited for him to wake up; he didn't. She lay there thinking about what she was doing until she, too, fell asleep.

During the early hours of the still dark morning Henry tried to
turn over, but something was blocking him. In his sleep he just
stayed put, but in a few moments he, unconsciously, tried again.
Still blocked. By the fourth time he was waking up a little. In her
sleep, Grace, whose body had been drawn up tight, loosened,
stretched out, with one hand on Henry as it usually was on her
children. Henry raised his head and turned to look; and there she
was! Grace Mae! In his bed! "WOWWEE!"

He turned over, gently, to her, trying not to wake her. He hadn't.
But his hands, his hands! They wouldn't be still. They reached over,
reallll slow, and touched her ever so softly. He waited. His hands,
those hands, began to rub her gently. He caressed her arms, her
hair, her calloused, rough hands. He raised up, resting on his elbow,
and pulled the covers from her breast, gently . . . gently now. He
softly stroked her shoulders and gradually moved over her breast. "A
woman, a real woman, Grace."

Grace had awakened quietly, but did not move. She lay there
feeling the tenderness with which he touched her. She knew she did
not love him "this way," but there was fire in his hands as each
stroke seemed to burn through her body. Feeling good.

He languidly moved his calloused hands, that did not scratch her
skin his touch was so light, over her breast. She closed her eyes
tighter at the almost unbearable warmth and sweetness that came
over her body. She wanted to turn to him, but didn't want to break
the spell of the moment.

Henry moved the covers down more; her stomach and pubic hair
were exposed to him now. He smoothed her child-marked stomach
over and over and over again. Then his eye would catch the wonder
of her breast again, child-feeding breasts, and his hand would
wander its way back to them. He leaned down to kiss one and
where the thought came from, he didn't know, but he thought of

his own mother he had never known during slavery. He bent his head closer to her breast and a nipple moved effortlessly into his mouth. He sucked it gently, softly, oh, ever so lovingly. He could have cried with the emotion flooding his body. Grace Mae, a whole woman's body, here beside him, in his bed, to explore and enjoy, to love.

His lips moved over her striped stomach, still gently, as he kissed every inch and scar of her. Suddenly, he stopped! As Grace moved her legs, opening them a little. He waited a moment; very still.

Satisfied she was still asleep, he returned to the wonders of his morning. He would not touch her pubic hair, that seemed sacred to him. He removed the covers, slowly, from her thighs, thinking as he did, "I should'a put more wood on that fire." Then that thought was immediately forgotten in the wonder of her soft, round, firm brown thighs. He moved his body to kiss them also; "Ahhhhh, so smooth, so warm, so beaut'ful."

As he smoothed and caressed her thighs, he looked at the mound of hair where the thighs met. He looked up at where her head was, wondering how much farther he could go. The mound was sacred, but the wonder and magic was so great. "I ain gon rape her, Lord, I just want to see one. This one, Lord." He would not move her legs farther apart, so he just stroked the mound of hair lovingly.

Grace Mae could take it no longer; she yawned, stretched, moving her legs apart as if in sleep. Henry lay still, watching her, waiting. Then she turned her head and looked down at him. Their eyes met. And held. Held for long, long moments. She moved her hand to his shoulder and left it there, gently, while he looked into her eyes. They agreed on something silently, and he began to rub the body of her again.

His hand was on the sacred place as she slowly raised a leg to push the covers down with her foot. He never stopped looking into her eyes; nor did she stop looking into his eyes. Her fingers curled around his arm and drew him up to her. She thought, "I don't want to kiss him though."

Henry pulled his gown out of the way; off even, and moved, even as he held himself back from his urgency, gently, slowly on top of her, between her legs that were raising her body to him.

Well, it never got worse; it just got better. When daylight came they were these two virgins; one a middle-aged man, the other the mother of two live children and two dead ones, for the first time in their lives, alive and hungry for the beauty of the human body. Each other's body. At last.

Life knew when Grace didn't show up early as usual, something was likely going on in the cabin. She kept Dingo and Flower busy doing interesting things. Mor smiled at her with his eyes over his coffee cup as she smiled back. A secret, pleased smile for their lonely friends.

When Grace did come in the main house later that morning, she was smiling a secret smile of her own. Later, alone, she told Lifee, "I never did like that Henry. I thought he was ugly . . . and cripple. But he ain neither one. I likes him. A lot."

Wisely, Lifee didn't say anything, but she wanted to say, "Maybe when Meda come back with her beau to get married, maybe we will have two marriages!" She kept the children overnight much more than before and Grace didn't complain one bit.

Mor didn't say anything to Henry about what he thought he knew, and did know. But men have certain ways of saying certain things to each other about love and the three of them; Henry, Mor and Ben, had their way of talking also. Besides, Henry had a different way of walking now, even with bad feet, he nearly strutted as he did his jobs now and they caught him several times just standing still staring off into space way off yonder. Or looking back toward that cabin that he couldn't hardly wait to get back to every evening, never to come out again until the next morning.

Mema laughed happily for the couple because she loved love and she was glad they had some. "That ole Gracie Mae's long face ain't so long now. Henry done shortend it up and put a crack in it that smiles!"

Lifee had to prepare for the wedding that would be in about six months, the same time Pretti and Babe would be finishing their schooling, receiving their credentials for teaching.

The months passed and summer was nigh. All the preparations were made and all the family came down for the wedding. Meda's beau was a handsome young man struggling his way through college to be a doctor. He didn't see Meda much because his college was in Atlanta and she was still in Boston. But they met enough to know they loved each other.

Mabby was glowing with happiness. "All my childrens doing just fine." Then her face would cloud, "All cept my little Luzy. Gotdamn white folks and they rapin, killin selfs!" Lifee soothed her with words and got her mind back on Meda and the wedding.

Everything was going smoothly. Grace, who had finally said, "I loves Henry and I don't never want nobody else," was getting married at the same time in a lovely dress made by her and Lifee. Yes, Henry bought a ring for Grace. "I wants everybody to know she married and she mine."

Mor went with Henry to buy the wedding ring at the pawnshop. Had to go to the pawnshop because everyone was saving money for schools and college. Mor even sent a little money, now and again, to Aman and Able, who did not ask him to, because he wanted to be a part of their going to college, too; Lifee knew they were already part of the whole process.

The men looked through the window at the glittering rings, bracelets, watches and whatnots. Henry rubbed his head and said,

"I got to get her somethin nice cause she a fine woman and she gonna marry me; I jes ain got no whole lotta money."

Mor answered, "Money and costs ain't what's important right now. It's what that ring means that counts." An idea had been edging its way into Mor's mind for the last few weeks. Now he said to himself, "Me and Life ain't never been married cept over a broom. I know she is my wife, but mayhap she need a real ring and a real marryin in front of a preacher. I could surprise her with a little ole litty-bitty ring, since she hate to spend money."

So while Henry hesitantly stepped through the door and to the counter, Mor pushed him on and they both looked and pointed at the different rings, dusty in their cases, some with little sparkles and some with big sparkles. They did not chose by glitter, they chose by price. That's when Mor told Henry his was a surprise for Lifee and not to tell anybody, although he planned to tell Benjamin.

They came out of the store smiling all the way down to their worn work shoes.

Henry stood in a black suit, from the same pawnshop, proud as any man at his wedding ever was. "I got a pretty woman! Good to me as she can be," running through his mind. Flower and Dingo, growing fast and healthy, were flower girls and ring bearer.

Able had come into his parents' room the night before the wedding to speak with his mother and father. He stood straight and tall before them. His second year of college over, one more to go. He was first in most of his classes and no lower than second in the others. He and Aman had already been experimenting with their ideas and Able's allowance of which Able sacrificed much in order to invest it on the word of Aman, who was studying "money" and investment.

Very seriously he spoke, "Papa, Momma, Babe and I would like to get married also. We have waited this long, but it is hard, very hard." He looked at his father. "She will stay here and work at teaching while I finish my courses. But . . . we want to get married now."

Mor simply gave his son his usual big smile, "Boy! Man! Have you thought all this out carefully? It's'a many a woman, pretty and all, who is going to be out there where you gonna be working."

Able waved the words away. "I see many of them now. But I always knew I loved Babe and always would. She suits me perfectly."

Lifee did not smile. "Babe is dark-brown-skinned. A lovely dark brown. Are you going to continue passing for white after you graduate?"

"No mam, Mama! I'll be so glad when this is all over. My university . . . friends are all white. They know so little of life except for dollars and cents, which is why I'm glad Aman is studying economics. I'll know the law and he will know money and the stock market. Together we will be unbeatable and rich. And we don't want all the money, as they do, we just want enough behind us to keep our loved ones safe. Their interests are different from mine. One of my main interests is my family. They build families by marrying the money, marry the name, have the right number of children, live in the neighborhood someone else has chosen for the 'best' people. Their life is different from mine. Perhaps you would not, but I think you would be surprised how much vulgarity and cruelty are concealed behind fine manners. I have love, a mother and a father who care. We are close. They are often alone. Sometimes not knowing where their parents are; back from Europe or off for a month on some island or some affair. And Pa, they not only hate or mistreat Negroes, they do it to the poor of their own races. I do not know who has taught them what love is, but it certainly is not the God they claim."

He smoothed his hand over his hair thoughtfully, "Oh, I don't know, Ma, I sit with them at dinners, at lunch or in study period. I have some friends there; they are not all haters. Some are kind men, a few. They don't bother to hate people. They go about their business of living. Some dream of families which they want to love . . . love each other. I get so confused sometime; I know whites are our enemies. . . . But, Pa, from some of the things I study and observe, there are people who do not love America, nor do they want its ideals to prosper. They want us to hate each other. They keep poor whites poor and call them trash; and they keep Negroes poor and call them worthless niggers, then set them against each other for the pittance thrown to them. They are cunning and winning. But, yes, I know, Ma, there are some good white people."

"But, right now, Ma, I love what I have, Mama. And I have my family and Babe."

"Well, you sure do have Babe."

Able smiled and continued, "I will use the color of my skin to help me and mine. I'm going to dress that brown skin in the most beautiful clothes in the world and I am going to build for her a beautiful home that will house and protect all those kids I know we are going to have. Babe feeds my stomach, very well, and she feeds my very soul. She makes me laugh, she makes me happy. I love that brown-skin woman!" He threw his head back, laughing. When the laughter died, he grew serious. "White people think we want to be white, like they are. What we really want is to be free, like they are. When we say we want to be accepted, they think we want to be buddies, but we don't necessarily. What we mean is accepted in the fields of good education, jobs, voting, opportunity to progress, fairness and justice.

He spoke on, "I know kids at Aman's college are very color conscious. They say marry light to lighten up their children, lighten up the race. But, Papa, that is no reason to marry. Jesus! They are fools. They know all these light Negro people came from rapers. No, I don't relish the thought of continuing that line of forced life. What I want in a woman does not come in colors. And I am not ashamed of my African heritage and the black blood that flows through my veins. My parents survived because their parents survived all the way back to thousands of years ago. And in my studies, I read between the white lines and know why they are still raping Africa. My country. I want Babe; now, tomorrow and always. She makes me happy. I'll make the living, but she will make the living worth living."

Mor smiled, but spoke seriously, "That is how I feel bout your mother. So there ain't nothing left to say. Marry Babe, now, if you want to. You a man." Then Lifee smiled at her husband and . . . that was that.

The last thing Able said as he was leaving was "Ma, get somebody to help you with this wedding work. I have the money, I'll pay."

The wedding day dawned bright and promising. Pretti, the artistic one, and Babe, the happy bride, had ordered Mor to build them a wooden archway and they covered it with Lifee's beautiful home-grown flowers and homemade bows and streamers of rainbow-colored ribbons. Mema wanted Babe to have a store-bought bouquet to go with her lovely handmade wedding gown. Lifee bought a bouquet for Grace and Meda. Everyone was smiling all the time now.

The helper Lifee had chosen was running everywhere all at once; answering every call as fast as she could, with a smile on her face and laughter on her lips.

All the family came; all had saved for the event. Mabby came, getting older, but still bustling around, ruling the kitchen. She stayed up all the night before the wedding cooking and sending out beautifully roasted hams and chickens and even a turkey. Huge trays of candied yams, bowls of collard and mustard greens. The sideboard and tables were loaded. Aman and Laval took tastes, quickly, when no one was looking.

Meda had a lovely, inexpensive store-bought wedding gown. She was so happy and smiling with joy. Her beau was quite handsome, Lifee said, "and smart, too! Doctor smart!"

When all was as ready as it would ever be and the pawnshop

clock toned the hour, everything and everyone was in place. The pianist from the church began playing the wedding march.

The couples were to be lined in front of the minister; Henry and Grace on one side, Meda and Richard in the middle, Able and Babe on the other side. All the parents and family members were in the front rows each side of the aisle. Guests behind them all.

Mor, all spruced up for the wedding (especially his son's), had walked Meda down the aisle to give her away to Richard; Ben walked his daughter Babe down the aisle to give her to Able at last; Aman walked Grace down the aisle to give her to Henry. Suddenly everything got serious and quiet.

It was at this moment Mor leaned close to his wife, saying, "Lifee, baby, we have never been married cept by a old broom in a white man's yard, now we in our own yard and I got a ring and I want to ask you to marry me."

Lifee's mouth opened in surprise as she blinked her eyes at her husband. Mor continued, "We ain got to holler, but everything he tell them to do, we can say it to ourselves and hold hands. When they slip the ring on, I'ma slip my ring on your finger. And when he tell them to kiss, we gonna kiss. Okay? Now. Will you marry me, Mrs. Freeman?"

Lifee, thrilled, leaned closer to her husband, started to tease him, but said, "Yes, Mr. Freeman, I will be your wife."

So, quietly, as the solemn vows were taken by the couples, Mor and Lifee held hands, whispered all the vows, and were married in front of a minister. When the minister said, "I now pronounce you man and wife; you may kiss the bride," everybody kissed and Mema hollered out, "Oh, Benjamin. This our second time!"

The wedding was a huge success.

Now, the young lady from the church helping Lifee was named Alma. Lifee has chosen her because at sixteen years old was the sole support of her little eight-year-old sister, Tooney. Their mother had died about seven years earlier of tuberculosis when Tooney was one. No father had appeared.

Both girls had golden, honey-colored skin, hazel eyes and hair of tiny little waves Alma kept tightly pulled back and tied at the nape of the neck. She was a hard worker; always working or looking for work. She didn't keep jobs long because of the men in the family she worked for; black or white.

Alma lived, at the time, in a little back room of the church by the kindness of the congregation because she always attended church with her sister, ragged or not. They also helped her with food and some used clothes when they were able. Because of her steady vigil over her sister and steady work in kitchen or field, Alma was strong and moved quickly and efficiently. At sixteen her body had developed into a figure of womanly promise.

Lifee watched everything all the time and when Able and Aman came home for the wedding, she noticed Aman stop whatever he was doing to look at Alma as she passed to and fro doing some job. On their second day home, all the jobs she found for Alma to do were somewhere in the vicinity of Aman. But . . . she either called out to Alma (so everyone could hear) or told Aman to tell Alma to do a thing, so Aman could not think the girl was too forward trying to be around him. Because Aman was a handsome young man with serious intelligence in his face and was used to girls pursuing him to some degree.

Lifee made sure Alma had a pretty dress of Pretti's to wear at the wedding, too. Aman never stopped looking, but he never said anything to her either other than a few questions about her family and schooling.

He did say to Lifee, "Ma, you need to teach that girl, what's her name? Marie?"

Lifee answered, "No . . . Bessie."

Aman turned his head to his mother, "Bessie? I thought it was Alma?"

Lifee laughed lightly, "Then you should have said that."

Later, Lifee thought, "This may not go anywhere, but I'm going to do the best I can to make it go somewhere. I can't let my son know exactly what I am doing though, because that will kill love every time."

Lifee did not let Alma move back to the church; she moved them into her sons' room and everyday, after chores, Lifee was the best teacher she had ever been. She almost ran that girl crazy trying to remember everything. Alma stuck to it because her sister, Tooney, was learning also. Beside which, they had a good home.

After the weddings Mema, Ben and Bettern moved out of their house so Babe and Able could have a small honeymoon before he returned to the university. They had two days and Able was supposed to be gone. But, two days passed and Mema went to the house and knocked, tentatively. Babe answered through a slight opening in the doorway. Her eyes were bright, teeth sparkling through her smile. "It's too early, Mama dear, we'll be dressed and ready soon. We are not ready yet. Bring me a chicken so I can cook it for this hungry husband of mine."

Mema put her hand on her hip. "You ain got time for cookin no chicken. Eat with us in the house!"

"Mud'dear, bring us a chicken. My husband wants MY chicken."

"Well, you betta fry it quick and come on out'a there."

"Bring the chicken, M'dear."

Mema left and brought the chicken back. Babe stepped out to take it, kissed her mother and said, "Now . . . let us be. He's gonna be gone a long time and this is all we have together. We are married, Mama."

Mema drew closer to the opening in the door, "You sore? You hurt? I got some . . ."

"M'dear, I am fine. He is fine. We are fine. Good-by now."

"Babe! You quit feedin that boy! Don't, he might not never come out!"

The door closed and it was two more days before husband and wife stepped out. All Able's clothes were washed and ironed. He was smiling and happy and Babe was bursting with happiness. They were satisfied with the choice they had made, years, years ago.

"This is my life dream," Babe said to her mother.

"This is one of my life's dreams," said Able to his father.

And that was that.

Now Life was still taking orders for making garments from Tricia where she went to carry swatches of cloth, measure the customer and compare designs and patterns. All they had to do was show her a picture from some European or New York magazine. She loved making high-fashion garments.

One day Life arrived as appointed and Tricia was very excited for her. "OH! I have a very fashion-conscious lady for you to meet. She usually buys in Paris, but she admired my dresses and when I told her about you, she wanted to meet you and order a few garments. We will have a cup of tea while we wait or would you rather have a drink?"

"Tea will be just fine. How old is this . . . ?

"Mrs. St. Travail. She is . . . about forty years old, I think. She is a very lonely, slim woman; a calm, but joyful demeanor. She will be easy to sew for."

At that moment the door knocker sounded and the butler went to answer the door.

Tricia bounced up from her chair. "This must be her. She is here!"

Both Tricia and Life stood and turned to face the entry.

The very attractive, mature Mrs. St. Travail was removing her gloves as she glided into the room with an amused smile on her face, "Good morning!"

Lifee thought, "There is something familiar about this woman," but said, "Good morning, Madame."

Tricia, smiling, spoke, "This is Mrs. Freeman, Mrs. Freeman this is Mrs. St. Travail. Mrs. St Travail's brow wrinkled ever so slightly as she looked at Lifee.

Tricia was bustling around the room showing Mrs. St. Travail where the cloths were and a few magazines. But Mrs. St. Travail waved her away with a flighty hand, saying, "Oh, I have brought my own, but, later, I may look at those also."

Tricia gestured to a chair, "Would you like tea, coffee, lemonade, Ann Marie?" Lifee's eyes traveled to the genteel Mrs. St. Travail again as she answered, "I will have lemonade, thank you. I like a sprig of mint in it, if you please."

"It shall be done." Tricia left the room to call a servant.

Lifee had not changed much from her youth. She had not gained much weight, if any, because of the hard work in her life. Her features had only aged, but well, because her happiness balanced her hard times. Mrs. St. Travail moved closer to her, "You seem familiar."

"I was thinking the same of you, Madame."

Then Tricia was back with the servant close behind with the tray of lemonade drinks in her hands. "Now! You all can get started when you are ready."

And so the afternoon passed measuring and talking about their sons and their universities. When Mrs. St. Travail was ready to depart, it had been arranged that Lifee would come to her house for the fittings. "I wish you would come tomorrow because I plan to select a few more things after I look at these pictures Tricia is so kind to lend me."

Lifee said it would take two days and so they arranged a time. Mrs. St. Travail smiled, "So we may be alone and undisturbed for the great work."

Lifee departed soon after, with many thanks to Tricia for a new customer. At the last moment Lifee turned to ask, "Tricia, why do you not think of marrying? You are still young and very attractive."

"There is no one I know in this whole country I would want. Even Mrs. St. Travail found her husband in France. They don't stay here long at a time. He has business all over the world."

"Well, why not take a trip on an ocean liner yourself? Many handsome men travel."

"Oh, Lifee, it's all so mysterious, these people you meet during travel. You never know how they really are. But I am meeting some doctors and professors through your son, Able, on his campus. And I meet some at the campus of my own son at Howard University. Some are very nice. When Laval goes abroad for his last years of study, I might go. But I am not unhappy, my friend, except you wouldn't let me come to the weddings at your house! Laval went!" Tricia pouted.

Lifee patted Tricia on her arm, "It was just that Negroes are so uncomfortable around whites. They don't trust them. I wanted them to relax and enjoy themselves. You sent a lovely present. Thank you."

But Tricia persisted, "I don't think I should be left out of everything. I truly enjoy myself around Negroes."

"Well, at the graduation affairs you will be welcomed."

"I look forward to that, I do. And," she hesitated, "do not let Ann Marie get any . . . gossip from you. She can be very persuasive."

"And I always keep my word."

The two friends smiled as they hugged each other before the front door was opened and the Southern world could see. They looked at each other, understanding, and said good-bye.

Two days later Lifee rode the carriage to the grand mansion of Mrs. Ann Marie St. Travail. She was welcomed in, given a selection of refreshment and served. The servant had hardly closed the door to the sewing room when Mrs. St. Travail turned to Lifee with a smile bursting from her lovely face. "Lifee! It is you!"

"Yes, it is me. But, you! You! I always looked for you, but never dreamed I would meet you again. Mrs. St. Travail! A rich man's wife! You said you would do it when we were poor slaves together in New Orleans! And you did it!"

"Oh, I did! I did!"

They embraced with joyful laughter.

"Of course I did it! I was determined. I packed all my young mistress's finest clothing in two trunks. She owed me that much for the years I had slaved and taken her abuse for nothing! Then I stole money from her secret place. I had earlier enough for my ticket, and now I had enough to carry me until I could find a position, and I took the ship to France."

Lifee listened eagerly to her friend of years ago.

"I met him, Alain, Mr. St. Travail, aboard ship. I told him I was running away from my father, who would not let me go to get an education. I would give him no name because, I said, I feared he would know the name and send me home to my family. Oh, he is a good man, Lifee. He protected me in the finest mansion I had ever seen. I succumbed to his charms, naturally. He seduced me and soon I was pregnant; but going to school, *mon amie.* The child removed all his anxiety about his family not accepting a stranger (because we still could not contact my family)." Ann Marie smiled. "If they had only known my family had been slaves! In the end, the turmoil of our love and all, and the child and all, we married and I have been with him nearly twenty years now!"

"Oh, how fortunate you are!"

"Oh, but, Lifee, I miss the Negro from my life. It hurts to pass those in trouble by and not be able to do something! I remember so well my own life. But, I have a Negro attorney here I correspond with. I send him money when I hear of some injustice to a Negro who most certainly cannot afford representation. The Negro attorney cannot help him as much as a white one could, but I cannot afford to take such a chance. The blacks are so hated and feared by most whites here. Not all of them hate Negroes, and those are my closest friends, but I cannot jeopardize my life and my children's.

"That is good, Ann Marie. It is pitiful how we are still treated even as we try hard to better our conditions."

Ann Marie nodded. "They want us to look up to them, to try to emulate them, but they lie! They are not who they say they are, most of them. Some are, but they are not the ones who hate Negroes. It is the insecure ones who hate and need someone beneath them and they do all in their power to keep the Negro beneath them. In fact, I have noticed in my travels, we are all humans, we all sin; some more than others. Some, in very cruel ways. And not just in the South either, though nowhere as bad. Did you know lynching is the South's gift to the universe? And you have no idea how many wretched things are covered over by the screen of 'High Society' and its money."

They talked on as they pointed and measured and shuffled swatches to decide what to make out of which. Ann Marie spread her arms and said, "I want a full dozen ensembles; if that will help you, Lifee."

A few more hours passed as each talked about their lives again. Finally Life jumped up, "I must go, my family, you know. My husband. But I will be back in a few weeks."

Ann Marie stood also, "I will set up an account for you at the fabric shop. Get everything you need, whatever it is; and not just for me, get things for you and your family." She reached into a pocket, "I have some money for you. . . ."

"Oh, Ann Marie, I cannot take from you except for what I make you."

But Ann Marie pressed the money into her hands, "Do not be a fool! This money is much money that was made from slavery. On our ancestors' backs! Take it! Take it all! Use it; help 'us'! But, you must promise me, though I know you do not need to, never, never to discuss my ancestry with Tricia . . . or anyone. My life would be over as I know it. True, I have put much away should I ever need it, but, I'd rather not need it."

"I understand. You are, as always, safe with me. I will find a way to spend this money to help some of these poor and needy Negroes, there are so many. There are many well-to-do Negroes in Savannah, but they seem to avoid the poor; they call themselves 'society.' They want to be white. They even marry to lighten their skins."

"They are fools! I do not want to be white, I have to be white! To live decently in this world where they have killed humanity in order to rule."

"I have met some who have hearts."

"And I know some who are decent God-fearing humans. But, not enough, or this world would be a better one."

"I must go, Ann Marie. I look forward to seeing my friend again. It is so good to have accidentally found you."

Later, in the carriage on her way home, Lifee smiled as she thought of her friend, Ann Marie. "God bless her and hers." Then she thought of Tricia and Ann Marie. Two white women. Then she laughed and laughed and laughed, but discreetly. "Two of them! Living a white life. Well, they are white! They should if they want to! Nobody needs to suffer under the white man's yoke if they don't have to. But for them both to be part Negro and fooling each other; they are missing a great deal. A great, great deal. There is more to life than skin. Skin . . . and money. But maybe I would do it if I could. No, I don't think so. I must have Mor. And Aman and Able. And Pretti. I must have my life. It is worth it. I'll bear the white man's yoke. I make money to protect us from its weight. But, I am the better off, I think. I am me. And my own is my own; before me and after me. My ancestors were from Africa and they suffered to survive. For me, though they did not know it. For the future which they did not know. And I am here. Me and mine. I am me."

When Lifee arrived home, Mor was in a state of irritation. For two years now, he had been troubled at the little incidents happening on the farm. Livestock missing, burning of small areas of growing produce, burning of small field sheds, things such as that. Little troubles that could have grown larger and were growing worse, more often. Ben, Henry and he were good men but they could not be everywhere all the time.

They had sat out some nights to trap whoever it was, but had been unsuccessful. But Mor thought he knew who it was. His neighbor on the land right behind his. A white neighbor who did not make use of his own farm except for liquor stills. A white neighbor who hated to see the green growing fields and the fat, healthy livestock belonging to a "nigga," as he would most certainly say.

But, what to do? Mor did not want to tell his sons. "They got enough on their minds tryin to graduate," he said. "I will wait it out until they graduate, then, baby, I blive we gonna have to move again. We betta keep saving our money. Cause this here stuff gonna grow. Soon they gonna try to kill one of us, or more. I'm tired of this shit. They just won't leave us be. Don't even want us to make a livin!"

He talked with the men at church about it. They nodded their heads in understanding. Some of them had the same problems. But . . . what to do? "Jest have to watch em, close as we kin. And help each one as we kin."

Ann Marie had given Lifee two thousand dollars. Five hundred, she stuck in the hiding place, later to be spent on clothes for schoolchildren, repair of the schoolhouse, its heater and books and paper. One thousand she marked for her sons to find out the best place to put it to help other Negroes. "We are troubled Negroes here, too. I've got to look out for all these Negroes that are part of this place!"

But, life goes on. As usual.

⌒

During and since the second year of college, Aman and Able had been taking their allowance, putting it in an account of Able's to direct it under Aman's direction. With the money they saved, Able invested in stocks and bonds and certificates. Especially railroads and the ammunition stocks which lately had been growing unheeded. They lost a little on small stocks Able thought were a good risk, but they had acquired a great deal. Starting small and growing.

After the initial investment had been deducted from the profits, they divided the money for their own savings, but invested the initial money again, adding a bit to it if they thought it was a good risk. They never touched that money they had saved except for small gifts for their parents.

After the third year, Able graduated with honors and was on the dean's list. He had made good connections and was wanted for his apprenticeship in several huge firms in Savannah, Atlanta, Chicago and New York. He chose Savannah, "For a start," he said. "I have other plans." No one knew of his dark little wife on the farm he went home to. He encouraged no close white visiting friendships.

He worked in Savannah using Tricia's address, but he went home to Babe every evening. Their love was as bright and strong as ever. He loved sitting at the kitchen table telling his day to Babe as she cooked, stirred and prepared food for him. Often they caught their own fish, raised their own ducks, chickens and pheasant. He bought her cookbooks wherever he found them and they would work on things to eat together. He set the table, she filled the plates. And they loved.

Aman was graduated from Howard in business economics with honors. He remained away for another year studying theology. His interest in the Bible had never gone away. He often discussed these things with his mother when he was home.

"What are you gonna be? A preacher, son?"

"No, Mama. I just want to know the truth. God, the creator, must be the most important thing in our lives. Every intelligent being has a plan; God is beyond the epitome of intelligence, so I know He has a plan. I want to know the plan. I want to be part of it, that's all."

"Now, son, I always have believed in the Bible, but some say it's just a book of stories, fables. So why do you put so much in it?"

"Oh, no, Mama. Listen to this. This is no book of fables!" He went to get his Bible. When he returned to his waiting mother, he opened the book reverently. "Listen, and look, Mama, here at Isaiah 40:22, it speaks of 'the one who is dwelling above the circle of the earth, the dwellers in which are as grasshoppers.' Now, Mama, people still thought the earth was flat until not so long ago when they say Columbus sailed from Spain on that premise. How did this man, Job, a couple thousand years ago, know that the earth was a circle? Unless he got that information from someone who could see it or had created it. Who but God?" His mother opened her mouth to say something, but he held his hand up, "No, listen, I'm not through. Job 26:7 says 'He is stretching out the north over the empty place, Hanging the earth upon nothing.' Now, how did that man know that?! The Romans or the Greeks said Atlas was holding the earth up! But, right here, in this Bible, it says 'hanging the earth upon nothing!' Mama, thousands of years ago! God had to be telling these men something!"

"Oh, son! I've never heard tell of those things before."

"I know. These preachers do not know their own Bible. The Bible tells us not to seek in the soil of the human mind for the truth, but to seek in the Bible, His word. They speak of hellfire! There is no place in the Bible, that I have found, that says hell is where humans will burn forever! No place! Look, Psalms 146:4 says when a man dies he goes back to his ground (from which he came, Mama) and in that day his thoughts do perish. Now, how can a man know he is suffering if his very thoughts perish? And at Ecclesiastes 9:5 it says 'For the living are conscious they will die, but as for the dead, they are conscious of nothing at all, neither do they anymore have wages, because the remembrance of them is forgotten. Also, their love and their hate and their jealousy have already perished and they have no portion anymore to time indefinite in anything that has to be done under the sun.' It says that, Mama!"

"But, son, what about ghosts? What about spirits that people say they see?"

"Well, Mama, you remember the Bible said there was Satan. I seldom hear anyone discuss him, even in church. He has been lying on God since the beginning, with Eve. He is a spirit creature and he can do things we cannot understand. He does many things. Wait, I will show you." He was turning pages when Grace Mae came in with some problem in the kitchen and Lifee reluctantly stood up to go see about it.

"Don't worry, Mama, we are going to talk again. But you can see why I want to know my own God and my own Bible; because many people belong to Satan and they are not telling all the truth. If they even know it."

And so the session ended with Lifee's mind torn between the wonder of what she had just heard and the doings in the kitchen.

This was one of those times when Aman, Able and Pretti were all at home at the same time. Pretti had fallen in love with a mortician's son, John Rambo, and was now married with a baby on the way. Mema had exclaimed, "A mortician! Buries dead people?!"

Lifee laughed at her, "Makes good money. People always gonna die. Our little girl will be taken care of. Going to give us a grandchild, too, since Able and Babe haven't!"

Pretti didn't like living in the funeral home, but with John's income and her income from teaching, she knew they would have their own house soon. She would speak to her mother with a smile, "Well, it is quiet there and always full of flowers!"

Lifee smiled back to her daughter and thought, "Raised her right! She can see the good things and bide her time."

〰

On one of her trips home, Ethylene had talked about coming back to Georgia to start a school for nurse assistants. Everyone agreed it would be wonderful and Mor, Henry and Benjamin could build it right there on their land. Ethylene was excited. "I have saved most all my money cept for a few bills. I can buy books and some equipment and borrow the rest." So that was in the minds of all.

Later, Mor pulled Ethylene to the side, saying, "Ethylene, baby, save your money a little longer. I can't tell you why right now, but we maybe won't be here a real long time. But wherever we will be, they still gonna need a school like you are talkin bout. And I don't want nobody to know what I just told you til I am ready."

Ethylene didn't know what to think, "Can't talk about it? Why? We always all talked about everything!" But she kept Mor's counsel and didn't speak to anyone but Lifee. She just had to! But Lifee looked at her seriously and said, "We are a family and Mor is the head of it. If he does not want us to talk about it yet, then let's wait. But I will tell you I don't know much either, because he does not like me to worry. And I never have gone wrong listening to him. So, you listen, too. Keep saving. Keep planning and dreaming. Things may change, I hope not because I love my little home. But remember, in the past, changes have always been for the better."

Ethylene felt better but, thought, "I don't know what to hope."

Now, although Aman and Able were close with many interests in common and were a good team economically, their dreams were different. Able loved his life with Babe. He never forgot his plans for their parents, as Aman did not; they planned them together. But Able had all he wanted for the time; his food and his family, his brother and the money.

Aman, now that he could make money, even before finishing college, was seeking something greater than the money. He often thought of love.

He knew many beautiful and lovely young Negro women, even a

few lovely white ones, in his world. Most of these women were friends only. Aman came at a woman first by looking at her beauty of body, then he went directly to her mind. If that was empty or full of fluffy, inane thoughts, he discarded all thoughts of the whole woman.

He wanted children, certainly, now that he could afford them, but he must have a woman like his mother. A woman who thought and would survive; like his mother, his sister, Babe and Mema. He had grown up among self-sufficient females. His thoughts included, "I do want her educated though. A good education."

He spent most of his time studying charts, statistics, international business corporations and Wall Street. Through Tricia Tims, he and Laval, who was also quite astute in preparing himself for maintenance of his mother's fortune, often worked together in the same office.

Able had fronted for them in New York to acquire a decent office at a good address, simply to keep records and have at their disposal all things needed to keep up with the market. Through Tricia, they even had clients who had never seen them.

Tricia wanted Laval to travel, see more of the world, so Laval was often away. But, while away, he studied the market and industry of whichever country he was in and brought the information back to the office Aman maintained.

Once, in speaking of his dependence on his mother, Laval said, "I hate to think that we could not be doing this, as well as we are, without the presence of white people to make it possible."

Aman answered, "We could do it, it would just take us much longer and we would, no doubt about it, be cheated of much that was ours. But, they have white skin, and this being the world it is, white skin and green money control it. But, wait, Laval, if we have learned anything, we have learned green money controls white skin, many, many times. We work hard, keep learning everything we can, we will," he laughed softly. "Well, you already do, but I will have enough money and knowledge to say, 'Hey! This is me! Ole black me . . . and I can make you rich . . . too!'" Aman looked at Laval, who was smiling. "Then," he continued, "We will not need any white skin helping us along. My brother is part of us, I'm not speaking of his white skin, nor your mother's. I am speaking of those who would hold us back."

They were quiet a moment or two, then Laval said, "I don't know whether to tell you this, but, I am . . . attracted to white women. Or very light women. I've never . . . allowed myself to become involved with love . . ."

Aman had his own reasons to ask, "Why, Laval?"

"I don't know . . . I don't know if it was because I was ashamed to like part of a race that pratically demolished my people and keeps them down so, or . . . if it's because in my heart, somewhere, I do not really like them."

Aman leaned toward Laval, saying, "I think I can tell you why."

"Why, then?"

"Your mother is white. You love your mother. I want someone like my mother. You want someone like your mother. You have very good, strong memories of her love for you. So, why not love a white woman? They are not always like their white men. Remember, in a way, he keeps them down also. Fall in love with whomever your heart tells you to. Be damn to a world that is full of dumb shit!"

Abruptly Laval turned back to his work, saying, "In any event, I want to travel more before I settle down to any woman and babies."

And so their days passed.

TWENTY

On one side of Mor's farm there was another white farmer, Rafe Smith. He had been there about two years now and his farm was prospering. He had a wife, three almost grown sons and a young daughter. When Mor worked the field next to the Smith farm, they sometimes met and talked over the fence.

Rafe Smith had started the conversations by asking a question about how Mor did some of his planting. Mor was wary, but glad to talk about his work with a neighbor. Lately Rafe had told Mor, "I ain got no quarrel with you people. I admires a man who raises his family right, is God-fearin, and works hard. You don't bother me and I don't bother you none. But, you best be careful and keep a watch out."

Mor, alarmed, asked, "What do you mean? What should I watch out for?"

Rafe took his hand from under his overall strap, scratched his head thoughtfully and said, "I don't reckon I know right all of anything, just a feelin I been havin lately. It's some people who don't like somebody when they prosperin. Bible say they envyin and covetin. Them kind is dangerous people. Got to watch em."

Mor knew when enough questions had been asked and would be answered. "Well, thankee. I will be careful and keep a watch out."

Time passed quietly enough. Mor, Henry and Ben watched over the land, but the same small things kept happening and they all knew it was the neighbor on the place behind them. Deke Filbert, and his lazy sons. But they were white and the law was not going to do anything about the problems unless he caught them himself and he certainly was not going to come sit out on a Negro farm through the night, even once.

Able had worked in Savannah long enough to establish himself, straighten out all Tricia Tims's financial business and several of her friends', meet a great many important people and then decide to move on to Washington, D.C. He came home on weekends, but left on the train early Sunday afternoon unless he felt like staying over one more day.

He was working on some very important projects for his family. The main one being the home he was building for Babe and himself in Virginia and the baby he hoped would soon be on the way. The other was also a main one he had been working on with Aman; a home away from all the stress of the Deep South for his parents and other family members.

Both Babe and Mema were upset they would have to part, but both also thought it was inevitable. Able often thought, "But, how to get them to leave that little piece of land they love?"

When Able came home to see Babe one night, Mor decided to speak with his son about his problems. Lifee had urged him to, because, as she said, "Listen, we have raised them, helped put them where they are today. They are out of college and Able knows the law. He might know something we can do."

"Ain't nothin, baby. What can we do to a white man?"

"Let's ask and see, Mor."

So Mor spoke to Able, but Able's answer surprised Mor a bit. "I don't see why you and Ma want to stay here anyway. You don't have to work. Aman and I have enough to take care of you. Move! Move out of this state!"

"Son, ya'll was raised here. This here is ya'll's home."

"Papa, 'this here' is where the white man let us alone enough so we had time to get grown. This isn't heaven. This is the South! I thought they might let us alone if they thought I was white and owned this place, but I know by now they see me and Babe together and they see us all together and, even if I were white now, they don't like me either. I want you to quit working out in those fields. One day they may up and shoot you and we won't be able to prove a thing and we will have lost a father. I don't want to lose you! You just sit still long enough for me to take care of some business, then I want you to leave this place!"

"I don't want to leave 'this place,' as you say. This place is my place, Mine and your mother's."

"This place belongs to whoever is going to kill somebody over it. That's Southern justice!"

Later Mor told Lifee, "I told you, Lifee, he can't do nothin about this place."

Lifee just looked at him for a long time. Then she looked off in space for a long time. Finally she said, "We are just the same as slaves if we can't protect ourselves."

Mor grunted in disgust. "Well, we ain't slaves." Then he left the room, saying, "I will kill somebody bout 'this place.' Maybe that will make it mine."

A couple of months passed with no problems. One of the three men, Henry, Mor or Ben, stayed up each night patrolling the land carrying a shotgun. They were all tired, stressed, nervous and overwrought. All ingredients to promote the high blood pressure they all had an were not treated for because they didn't know they had the problem. Hypertension. It was a Southern hazard for Negro men.

Each time Able came home he was exhausted from worrying about them and relieved when he found they were alright. He and Aman had discussed the matter and came to their own conclusions. They were pooling money for the solution.

Lifee often heard from Ethylene, questioning her about the school building plan. She had no answer. She and Mor did not have the money to move where they could own their own place and didn't know where to move to get away from the white man anyway. "We still do not have any answer" was all she could reply to the hopeful Ethylene. Ethylene wanted to be near her family, so she didn't try to find any other place. She just sat on her savings and added to it as she could.

Two days later, after Able had gone, everyone had settled in for the night. The men decided to just sleep in, because nothing had happened on the land for the past two months or so.

The cabin with Henry and Grace Mae and the children was dark. The little house with Ben, Mema and a pregnant Bettern and her young field-hand husband was dark. The house was dark and even though Mor and Lifee had been talking as they lay in bed, Mor had fallen asleep. He was getting old and tired from the worry. He slept fretfully.

No one heard anything. Not even Lifee, whose mind was always on alert. Tonight she slept soundly because Mor was there beside her, safe. She thought. Mor was dreaming and heard little popping sounds, like bacon cracklings make. He turned over in his sleep, but didn't wake up. The sounds persisted.

Then Lifee heard someone yelling Mor's name, then Henry's name, then Ben's. She woke up to the smell of smoke. She jumped up as she smacked Mor on his shoulder. "Wake up, Papa! Wake up! I blive the house is on fire! Mor!"

Mor was instantly awake. Shaking from his need to get his

clothes on in the greatest hurry. "Don't grab nothin! Just get your-self outta here! Come on, Lifee!"

But Lifee had one thing she had to get. Her heritage. That little box, in a larger box now, was way back in the corner of her closet. She got it before she left that room. She hadn't even thought of the fact the money saved was in it. The bottom half of her house was almost entirely in flames. "Oh, my God! Sweet Jesus!" She started for her sewing room to get her machine, but Mor was right there, pulling her down the last of the stairs to the back door.

When he opened that door, flames shot from all parts of the house to the kitchen, singeing their backs as they squashed in the doorway til Mor pushed her out, then was pulled out by Lifee, even though he was coming out anyway. The cabin was not burn-ing, but Henry and Grace Mae had brought the children out and Henry was searching around the little cabin for signs of any fires starting.

Ben and Mema's house was just getting started burning, but all of them were busy hauling water from the well, putting it out, as it was still small and hadn't yet become a blaze. Ben told Mor, "Wasn't no sense in working on your house by the time we seen it, so I worked on mine."

"You did right. Mine gone too far. We lucky we got out in time. Was that you callin? All our stuff gonna all be burnt up. Gone! Oh! Man!" he cried. "My place is gone! Where is Lifee?" He yelled, "Lifee! Mama!"

Grace Mae called out, "She right chere!"

Pretti had come to stand by her parents in this terrible moment. One hand holding her now-large stomach. She was there hugging and crying with her parents.

Lifee was sitting on the ground in front of the cabin, tears run-ning down her face without a sound in her mouth. Staring, just staring at the house that had held so many dreams, plans and all the doings of her family.

Mor, shoulders slumped, almost beaten down to the bottom of

his will to prosper and survive, went over to Lifee, putting his arm around her and turning his face back to watch what it seemed were flames burning up his life. Lifee, then, came out of her trance, she screamed to the wind, "They ain't never going to let us have nothing! Then take it! Take it! Take the ashes! See what you can do with em, white man!"

Grace Mae spoke softly to Lifee and Mor, "Was a white man hollerin to wake us up! That Mr. Smith, next door. He the one calling out as he ran cross the field from his house in his night-clothes. They all torn from comin over that fence, I reckon. Don't be for him, we all be burned up. He helpin Ben and Mema now."

Mor turned slowly to see, "He told me. He told me to watch out."

"Maybe it was him who started the fire," snarled Lifee.

"No, mam, it wasn't, cause Henry heard em and woke up running out the cabin and seen him coming cross the field, hollerin. And he saw somebody, two of em, running off cross them fields over that'a way." She pointed to the rear of the farm.

Henry nodded, "Sho did. We knew it was them, Mor. You said it."

Lifee broke down again, picking up her heritage box. She held it to her breast and cried, cried, cried.

Mor sat down on the ground beside her, then scooped up a handful of dirt, staring at it as if it held life. "This my land. I paid for it. It blong to all of us. And they don't want us to have it. Not ne'er none."

He held on to the dirt in his hand as they all turned at a large cracking sound of the walls of the main house caving in. Then they all watched, firelight bright upon their faces, as the house burned down, all the way down, to the ground. Lifee crying all the way.

In the full morning, the others moving around to do whatever was necessary. They tried to get Mor and Lifee to get up off the ground and come in to one of the remaining houses.

"Not yet," said Mor. Lifee didn't say anything, just lay her head on her husband's shoulder. That shoulder she always leaned on.

While they were alone, Pretti was trying to fix them something to eat. Still sitting on the ground, Lifee raised her head and asked Mor, "Is this what we have from all the work, all the plans, all the sacrifice and pain we have gone through? Is this all we have? Nothing?"

Mor looked at the dirt still held in his hand, and then, back at the piles of charred, burnt wood of his home still breathing smoke into the wind. Mor didn't answer.

Pretti, expecting her child any day, would not go to her home. She stayed beside her parents. Bettern and her husband bedded down in the parlor room and Mor and Lifee were given the bedroom in spite of their protests. Only Pretti did not accept their protest. "Yes, give it to them. I want you all to rest, Mama!"

Bettern could have gone to her husband, Webster's family house, but Mema did not want her pregnant daughter gone from her sight. "Naw, she staying right where I can see her. Ain't but one left at home, now Babe teaching over in Savannah. She be home tonight, I reckon, I blive Able be in tonight. But we got room. We will make room! Ya'll gonna stay right chere with us! Now!"

Grace Mae spoke up, "She can take the children's room when she comes. And Able. The children can put in with me and Henry. Dingo, big as he is, can even sleep on the floor in the middle room."

When Able did come he was caught between sadness and happiness at the loss of the main house on the farm and the sadness and pain of his parents. "Now, they will move."

Able called a meeting of all the family and when they were all settled in Mema's parlor room, he spoke. "I didn't plan on this happening right at this time, but I do have a plan. Aman and I have bought some land in Virginia. About eight hundred acres. Mostly woodland. I have been building a house for my wife. Two months ago we started building a house for my parents."

Mor started, he didn't know what to think or feel. He looked at his son intently. Lifee gasped, but said nothing.

Able spoke on, "Now, eight hundred acres is a lot of land; there is room for everybody. You all will have all the wood and lumber you will need. I will get workmen to help you build the kind of buildings I want on my land, but you are all welcome to come there and live, but I am taking my parents with me. Now. Today. When I leave, with my wife."

Mor spoke first, "Your land."

Lifee turned to look at him and said, "He means . . ."

Mor waved her quiet, "Let him say what he means."

Able didn't know what was expected of him until Babe pushed him. "Well, I mean . . . You all know what belongs to one of us belongs to all of us. We are a family. Have been one all my life anyway."

Babe spoke up, "That's right! You got to go, too, Mama."

Henry hesitantly spoke, "Well . . . somebody got to stay here and look out for the land, so me and Grace can stay here. Ya'll won't have to worry bout this here place."

Able answered him, "We are not going to worry about this place. This won't be the first place we had to leave behind us. I am not going to leave anyone here to be under any white man's yoke and even be killed. They can't take it, it's in my parents' name. I will have it rented out to some decent farmers at a good rental they can afford so they will make a home here. But, us? We are going to make a new start with better equipment."

Everyone started speaking at once. Grace Mae just cried because she had never really believed she was part of their real family before. They hadn't done anything wrong to her, she had just never "belonged" anywhere before she came to them. Henry hugged her and felt tears coming to his eyes. He had always felt like he had broken into their family. He looked at Able, "the white man" he had always called him to himself. Now, he thought, "He ain no white man, he my relation."

Ben was ready! "We are ready whenever you say, Able!" It was understood Mema was going anywhere Ben and her family went. Her secret little thought was "I will be where my chile Babe is." Then another thought, "What bout Bettern?" Then she spoke out-loud, "What bout Bettern and Webster?"

"And we are taking Alma and Tooney. They are family also!"

Able took his hand off his wife and said, "Eight hundred acres is a lot of room. Like my family always said, 'If you are willing to work, you got a home.' We still say the same thing. We are my family. Now, listen you all, Aman hasn't heard of this yet, I will let him know so he can prepare things there. I am taking Babe back with me on the train. You all are not ready and I imagine you have a lot you want to bring. Papa's house is ready, our house is ready." He looked at Babe and smiled, then back to the others. "Now, I think we have a few wagons that were safe in the barn. You were smart, Pa, to build those wagons. We know they are strong. The rest of you come on in those wagons with your things. We can get train tickets for Bettern and Webster because she is having a baby."

Mema spoke up, "No you ain't! Bettern goin with me and her daddy. She be alright!"

Able laughed, "Whatever you say, Mema. You know you are my mama now, so what can I say?"

"I always been your mama, boy! You ate enough of my cooking to blong to me!"

Everyone laughed because they all knew how much Able loved to eat.

The fire was almost forgotten in the midst of the new plans. But not by Mor and Lifee. As preparation was made for their departure, they had chosen to travel on the wagons and make an adventure of the trip. They looked back at their home and land, remembering why they had come there and what they had gone through on it.

They walked the land early mornings and late evenings after they had eaten. Mor always scooping up a handful of his land and shaking his head slowly, brushing tears away. At those times, Lifee just watched, she understood. Once she asked him, "Mor? You are going to new land. We will have a new home. Why does this land still mean so much to you?"

"Cause I worked for this land. First of all . . . this was my land. Our land. We got it. Didn't nobody give it to us."

"But, Mor, darlin, we got Aman and Able. Them giving us something is like we gave it to ourselves. Isn't it?"

"I am not their son, they are my sons. They don't owe me nothin!"

"You never did anything for them because you owed them. You did it because you loved them. He is not giving us anything because he owes us. He is giving us this because he loves us." Then after a quiet moment, "But, they owe us, too! We worked hard for our sons and on our sons!"

Mor looked at her and laughed softly, "Well, Mother, I have never known you to let nobody owe you long, so let's get started and get on otta here, then!"

Lifee next went to her daughter. "Child, can not you make your husband see his place is where you are and your place is where I am?"

"Mama, I am a grown woman now, and my place is beside my husband. I remember all the things you taught me, I will do them. Your grandchild will be safe and strong. It has you and Papa's blood."

Lifee looked at her daughter a long moment, then said, "Pretti, I know you are a strong woman. Well, I am not so much strong anymore. I'm getting old. You bring yourself and my grandchild to me as soon as you can." She started walking away, then turned back and smiled, "You can bring your husband, too."

So Lifee began making her farewells to her friends. She knew she would see Tricia again and Laval. She simply told Ann Marie where she could be found if needed.

Finally the leaving day came and all was ready, wagons loaded, waiting. All Lifee had to carry was her heritage box. She hugged it to her because now, added to her own things, were the baby booties and blankets of her own children, a little dirt from every farm they had to leave behind. Now it was their heritage box and she was guarding it, protecting it for them. In between small duties, she showed Alma and Tooney how to knit tiny booties and sweaters for her coming grandchild. As her needles clicked, Life thought, "I know my daughter. I know she will not tarry long here." She thought of her daughter, the woman she knew was strong, whom she was leaving behind. "We got enough people in this family for her husband to bury. We'll build him his own funeral home, if that's what he wants. He is helping to give me something else to go in this box one day. And we got eight hundred acres of wood. He can make his own coffins, too!"

They loved their new home. Babe was already settled in hers and was pretty sure she was expecting the baby they wanted so much. She liked to think back to the time on the train when the conductor had urged Able to move to the white section of the train. Able had answered, "I am a Negro and I am traveling with my wife." He was setting his life. He told Babe, "If I don't have enough color in my skin, I have enough sense in my head, and am going to have enough money to live my life the way I want to. With you. God willing." With a smile, she thought to herself, "We have made this baby on that old farm of ours. Good. Now my baby is a part of the old place, too."

Babe had recently told Able she thought she was with child. He was ecstatic. "My God, my God, my child. My own. Our own."

Mor loved the land. It was beautiful in Virginia. Life loved their house. It was simple, as her son knew they would want, but plenty of space for Alma and Tooney. The parlor was full of the beautiful furniture her sons had taken her to choose. A lady's parlor it was.

Alma and Tooney could not believe their good fortune. They

cried, hugging each other. "A real honest-to-God home with a mama in it!" They hugged each other and their good fortune. "And learning to read, too!" Mor had his own favorite room filled with his special things, of which there were so few; Lifee was his favorite thing. He would make Lifee come to his room because it was kind of empty and, too, he did not like sitting in a lady's parlor. Their favorite place was still lying in bed, talking, but now they had huge windows from which Mor could see way off over the many trees. There were several small lakes on their property and he could see a good part of the one he fished in.

Henry and Grace Mae wore smiles all the time they were building their own small house with a bedroom for each child. Henry wanted a child of his and hers, but something Grace Mae had done to herself to keep from having another baby for "that white man," had blocked any new pregnancy, so far. But she was still young and Henry would be ready for a long time. Unless it was the result from the prison food and work.

"Now we got a home, but they ain't goin to farm much, so I'm got to get on out here and find me some work. I'm goin to take care my own family home."

Ben and Mema had built, with the help of Able's workmen, a nice home with bedrooms for her grandchildren when they visited. Mema demanded one thing, "I want a lady parlor like Lifee have." She got one, though a smaller one. She picked the furniture and it was a little gaudy, but it was pretty to her. So!

As they lay in bed one night, Ben told Mema, "I ain't too old yet, I'm goin to find me some jobs to do and pay our way for all this goodness we got. I can help watch over this here land for Aman and Able, and I can work, too."

Lifee had written Ethylene, "Now you can make your plans!" But Aman and Able had taken care of that also.

Aman told his mother, "There would not be enough students out here to make the school pay, so we have bought a good, big older house in Washington, D.C., and she can turn that into her school. Meda and her doctor husband are going to join her there so it can get a first-class rating as a school. We are giving her the house and land because we got it very cheaply; the rest she can do with her savings. Until she needs our help. And Alma can study there, too, unless she wants to be something else."

Lifee smiled at her son, she still watched him watching Alma around the house. "That's right, cause that girl loves learning. She asked him, "Son, why are you both giving such money away, even to the family? What are you going to do for yourself?" She hoped he would speak of marriage.

Aman laughed, "We do that first, Ma! I have a house of my own here, too! Ma, other than travel, or go back to school, I have no needs."

"You have needs. You need to get a wife. Have children."

"I'm young, Ma."

"No one is too young to die, son."

"I'm not afraid to die, Ma."

"Don't talk like that, son. It would near kill me to see one of my children die before I do. Without leaving a child either."

"Well, that reminds me, Ma. I want to show you something." He looked around the room for books. Lifee handed him the Bible because they often talked about what he had lately learned or found in it.

Alma came into the room at that time and Aman laughed happily and began turning pages as he spoke. "You know we talked about all the scriptures that say what the world is now will not last forever? That we are in God's sabbath day? And according to calendars of the world, we are in the six thousandth now. Four thousand before Jesus and this is 1893 after Christ Jesus."

"Of course. You showed it to me, didn't you?"

"And we talked about the meek inheriting the earth? At Psalms 37:9 to 11? And the meek are not weak people"—he smiled at Alma as he continued—"they are kind, considerate, patient, long-suffering and teachable and they love God's beautiful earth and try to care for it and the animals He put on it? Remember, Ma? And they come in all colors, for He created all peoples. It just depends on their hearts and their choosing Him and trying to live love. Remember, the road, at Matthew 7:13 and 14? That narrow road with few travelers on it? And that big wide road full of the other people going to destruction? And most churches lie saying everyone who dies goes to heaven?"

"Yes, son. That narrow road and a world without evil people would be beautiful indeed."

"And at Proverbs 2:22 it says the wicked will be cut off from the earth. And 1 John 4:20 and 21 says 'he who hates his brother on earth cannot love God.' Likely they will be on that wide road."

"I remember that one for sure."

"And at Revelation 11:18 it speaks of God ruining those who are ruining his earth. HIS earth, not theirs, as man seems to think and act."

"This a big earth, son, I don't know how anybody could ruin it."

Aman smiled at his mother, "If the Bible says they will be ruining it, they will be trying. We don't know, even now, all the things man may be doing that will ruin the earth. It says, also, the evil ones will be cut off of the earth at Proverbs 2:22 and the treacherous be torn away from it."

"Lord, I hope that's true, son."

"I've shown you enough things in this Bible to prove to you it can be trusted, Ma. Well, what I want to show you today, Ma and Alma, is about the new earth He will create."

"New earth! What is He going to do with this one?"

"It will be on this one. He will renew it. It says at Isaiah 45:18 it was created for man, to be inhabited. And He says it will never pass away, but will be to time indefinite. Ma, at Revelation 21 it talks about the new earth and how it will be. Oh, Ma, it is going to be beautiful and peaceful and full of love. I believe Him because that is what a God of love would do for the people who have proved they want to live and can live that way. Here, you read it. I'll leave you alone in peace. I have some other work to do. And, Ma, I think I have found someone who feels as I do about life. And love. A little while longer and I may be giving you a new daughter. Now, read!"

Alma, unconsciously, suddenly looked sad and forlorn.

Aman smiled at her, then down into his mother's eyes. "I have something special I want to tell you that I have found." Alma held her breath.

"What is it, son?"

"You know how when you say your prayers, 'Our Father, whom art in heaven. Hallowed be thy name?' "

Alma exhaled softly.

"Of course, yes, son."

"Well, God has a name."

"It's 'God,' isn't it?"

"No, Mama, God is what He is. He, also, has a name."

"What foolishness is this. I have been going to church for a hundred years practically, and I have never heard of such."

"Well, here is your Bible, your own Bible. Here at Psalms 83:18, it says, 'That people may know, that Thou alone, whose name is Jehovah, are the most high over the earth.' Read it for yourself."

Life's eyes were big with surprise and her heart was big with joy and love and she watched her son leave and go down the green, bird-filled trees lining the path to his own home. Then she turned to see Alma standing beside her, watching Aman walk away. She smiled at Alma and patted her hand. They understood each other.

Webster and Bettern were building a small cabin, but it had two bedrooms. It was close to Mema's, though Able had urged all of them to spread out, to make their own space. "You have no neighbors to look over a fence and see what you are doing now, but how close you want to see each other is your own business. There was a great deal of space around his and Babe's house, but paths was soon made going directly to Mema's and Lifee's.

Aman built a fine house for his own. "One day, soon now, I will be bringing a wife home, Ma. I hope she will like it as much as I do." He smiled at his mother and Alma, who were helping him decide about furniture. "But, for now, I want to travel a bit, out of this country, and learn more about this life."

"Son, don't go leaving the woman you love behind. If you want her, someone else will, too!"

"I thought about that, Ma. I'm . . . I'm trying to make up my mind. Fast."

"I know she is beautiful, son. Better marry and take her with you." She smiled as she asked, "Will you preach, son?"

"I will always talk about God. I don't know if that is preaching. But, you cannot know Him and not tell about Him. Able really does all the work after I do all the research on what we will invest in. I almost don't have anything to do. I intend to keep searching for His truth whether I do anything else or not, Mother dear. But, my body tells me I better get married. And, too, I need to be here to help Ethylene and Meda." They smiled together and Alma laughed a little in joy, before she could catch herself.

Lifee pushed, "Then get married and keep teaching me and your pa. And Alma."

They were all satisfied, but Alma wasn't sure how satisfied to be; she may not be the one he was thinking of. But she knew he liked her . . . some.

A year passed smooth and easy. Pretti had come with her new baby boy, Mordecai Amanable Rambo, and her husband. Mor and Life were beside themselves with joy. Mor strutted around talking about his two grandsons with his name.

The blood of Suwaibu and Kola was still strong and flowing, rushing on to the future.

One day, while mother and daughter with grandchild were talking, Lifee went to her closet and brought out her treasure box with two hand-stitched quilts atop it. All her heritage, and she was giving it over to Pretti. There were now the old photos, the handkerchief, baby booties of Aman, Able, Pretti and even the new babies; the blankets used to catch each of her children, a oilcloth packet of the dirt of their first farm and one of their second farm, a rock Lifee could not remember right off why she saved it. "It must be valuable though, so don't throw it away."

Pretti answered with much love on her face, "Mama, I would never throw anything away you gave me. I will share these things with all your grandchildren so they will know their heritage." Lifee's heart eased knowing their life memory would be cared for.

Babe had, also, had a son who she was hardly ever able to keep at home until his father was home. Mema always tried to keep him with her and could have just lain right down and died with her joy. "A grandmaw, child! Look'a here!"

They had named him Benjamin Mordecai Freeman. Babe no longer worked at anything except making a home for her growing family and her husband. They practically lived in the huge kitchen where she and Able tried cooking everything under the sun. He was happy and never far from his home. The blood of Kola was mixed with the blood of other African ancestors now, but was still flowing and rushing into the future. Soon Babe was pregnant again. More living blood for the future.

Often now, Mor looked back at what he had been, the things he had done striving to survive, the things he had had and lost, but with less and less sorrow. When he and Lifee sat out on their veranda late of an evening, swinging slowly in the porch swing, they talked about their life, laughing a little, holding hands.

On one of those evenings Lifee turned her head to look at her husband of many years. "Mor? You know how the Bible talks about striving after the wind? You reckon we got hold of the wind now?"

Mor patted her thigh, smiling, "Don't nobody get hold of the wind for long. That ole wind gon blow til time indefinite, as God say. But, it ain blowin on us as hard as it has done in the past. We worked for our children to be educated and now, they are. And, now, look what they done done for all of us. Our grands gonna have a better time of it on account'a that."

Lifee shook her head slowly, "That's what we planned. I was hoping . . . It's 1894 and I was hoping maybe the world would be doing better with Negroes. It isn't though; they still as hard on Negroes as they can be. No voting, segretion and all. But, anyway, we are doing fine here, now."

"We alright. But, ain nothin fine, baby. The wind of life is still blowing; rain still fallin in somebody's life. But,"—he turned to look at her—"you remember you ask me, some time ago, when our house burned down? You ask what all we had worked for, was it for nothin? Remember?"

Lifee nodded in the affirmative, slowly.

Mor pushed the swing with his feet and leaned back. "I thinks about that. I thinks about all the black bodies layin back of us on our path that led us here. They have died so we could get where we are; someday. They hoped for us, dreamed for us even. Hoped, if not them, maybe us. Well, we got us these children. And we strived hard, even with Tricia's help, and got them a education. So, now, it's all gonna be in their hands. But, it ain over. It's a plenty problems coming yet. And I blive my sons when they say it ain just black and white, it be poor and rich. It's some poor white people that rich white people call white trash, but won't let em get up either. They a people always tryin to get away from human life, but we all human anyway, no matter whatsomever them rich ones and hateful ones come up with."

They were quiet a moment, swinging, gently swinging.

Then Mor turned to Lifee again, "So, I'ma answer you now. All we done done ain been just done for nothin. We done the best we could and we got some good livin right now cause we got good sons, and a good daughter, grandbabies, too! And if they let me, I could plant up a many a acre and be workin it. But, the answer, I think, my wife, Lifee, is til God get ready for that new earth Aman done showed us about, the answer just fly in the wind. And the wind never will blow all life away, you just got to find a way to live in the wake of that wind. Cause it leaves a wake, full of trash flying round everywhere."

Lifee was trying to think if that was an answer, but made an observation, "White folks say after slavery, everything was gone with the wind."

But Mor continued, "Ain't nothin can get rid of us Negroes. We a strong people. We done seen em come and make do with nothin. Strive . . . and live." He turned to smile at her and patted her thigh again. "And you got to remember, I got you. Stilllllll got you. And you always will have me. Old and ugly as I am. I'm strong. The wind never can, never could and never will blow that away. We's together. All together. A family. You and me? We may not make it much further on down this road of life, but, our blood will. It's goin a long way. Even into the next century. That African blood is strong, ain't it, baby? That African blood has done survived. They couldn't kill it with a whip, nor a lie. The wind will die first before that stops. So, my wife, let's us just lay back and rest after our hardworkin days. We just be here, doin what we can, watchin over this family, in the wake of that wind what they say took everything away. It left us and we workin with it!"

Lifee smiled at her husband, "Yes, the wind left us and we worked in its wake. And our African blood is flowing on and spreading out. But that blood, one day, will run so far the people who carry it won't remember us; won't even think of us nor know what we went through for them to get here safe."

Mor laughed and patted his wife, "Well, it's some fools in every family, but there ain gonna be too many in ours. I bet. Lets me and you holler in the wind to our future blood, say, 'Don't ya'll forget us. We are how you got here!' "

So they hollered in the wind, "Don't you all forget us!" Laughing, but serious. And the wind carried the sounds off through the trees, toward the sun. Where did the words fly to? To me. To you?

Mor died three days later. Quietly, in his sleep. Lifee woke up beside him and knew her lover-husband was gone. She was inconsolable, needless to say. She suffered, she mourned deeply. Even her children around her did not lessen that grief, but made it stronger. Mabby, old now, came to grieve with her for a little time. Her other family needed her home.

Aman saw the woman he loved caring for his mother and he finally decided to speak up. It assuaged his mother's grief that her son was to marry Alma. Alma's joy was boundless. "A friend, a mother, a husband to help me raise my sister. A lover. A family. A home. Thank you, God."

Mor had been buried in a lovely spot where the grass was smooth green, surrounded by trees he loved, Lifee would walk to his grave every day. She would sit beside his tombstone, crying and thinking. Alma stayed by her side and came to the graveside with her when she didn't think she would intrude. One day she brought garden tools and dug furrows and planted seed; vegetable seeds and flowers.

That is where they found Lifee seven weeks later, dead, beside her husband. Among the growing vegetables and flowers.

Aman and Able had a coffin built for two, a beautiful oaken coffin. Mor was retrieved from his grave and buried with his wife, being careful not to disturb the plants. As they had been in life, so they were in death. Together. With the wind blowing gently through the trees and the growing vegetables and flowers. Something for the stomach and something for the soul.

But their blood rushed on and on and on and on. Into the future. African blood. African-American blood.

The voice that led me on this path never came back to tell me her name. But . . . it was the story that was the most important anyway, in the wake of the wind.

THE WAKE OF THE WIND